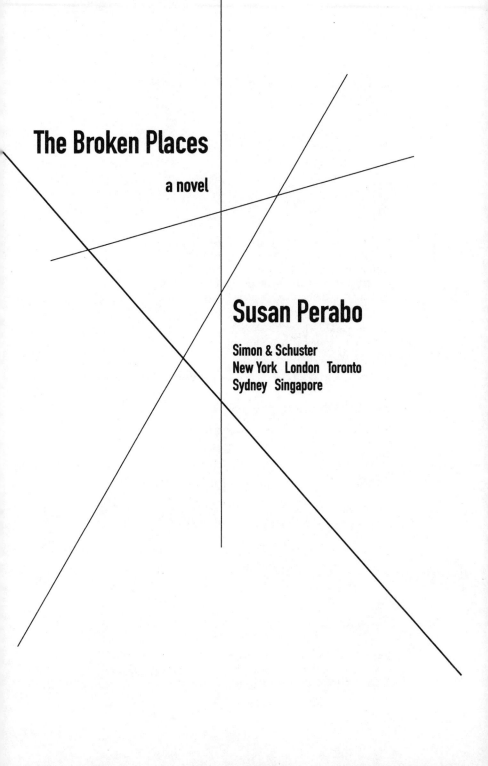

The Broken Places

a novel

Susan Perabo

Simon & Schuster
New York London Toronto
Sydney Singapore

For Sha'an

Copyright © 2001 by Susan Perabo
All rights reserved,
including the right of reproduction
in whole or in part in any form.

SIMON & SCHUSTER and colophon are registered trademarks
of Simon & Schuster, Inc.

Designed by DEIRDRE C. AMTHOR

Manufactured in the United States of America

10 9 8 7 6 5 4 3 2 1

Library of Congress Cataloging-in-Publication Data

Perabo, Susan, 1969–.
        The broken places : a novel / Susan Perabo.
            p.   cm.
        1. Fathers and sons—Fiction. 2. Fire fighters—Fiction. 3. Boys—
Fiction. I. Title.

    PS3566.E673 B7 2001
    813'.54—dc21   2001034151

ISBN 0-684-86234-4

For information regarding special discounts for bulk pur-
chases, please contact Simon & Schuster Special Sales at
1-800-456-6798 or business@simonandschuster.com

Acknowledgments

Thanks to firefighters too numerous to name, who helped me with the details. Thanks to Betsy Perabo, Brad Barkley, Sha'an Chilson, and my agent, Elyse Cheney, for their wisdom through several drafts. Thanks to my folks for their unwavering support. Thanks to David Rosenthal for his high expectations. Finally, most grateful thanks to my wonderful editor, and friend, Marysue Rucci.

The world breaks every one
and afterward
many are strong at the broken places.

—Ernest Hemingway, *A Farewell to Arms*

Chapter One

The wind was at his back. Heart pounding, Paul Tucker pedaled furiously through downtown Casey, soared past the firehouse, the barbershop, the drugstore, the post office. It was October, not cold, but plenty cool to chill his knuckles around the handlebars as he sped toward the Neidermeyer farm. An explosion! So far that was all he knew, but the word alone was enough to set his mind racing. Gas leak? Pesticides? Gunpowder? A gaping crater in the ground where the Neidermeyer home had stood for a hundred and thirty years? He hoped he wasn't too late. What if he'd missed all the good stuff? What if his father and the rest of the crew were already packing up their equipment, starting the engines, heading back to the station? He shifted gears, pedaled harder.

Paul had lied to his mother, claimed he was biking downtown to pick up a pack of gum at Dewey Drugs. He lied to his mother frequently these days, often for no other reason than to assert his independence from her, to prove to himself that he was his own man with his own life, a life full of rich adventures she had no cause to know about. He'd turned twelve at the end of August, and twelve had shifted something in him, something unnameable but unmistakable. Twelve was solid, just the sound of it. At ten you were still in elementary school, still prone to tantrums and tears. Then eleven, an unsettling and unsteady age, like you had one foot on the dock and one on the boat and you did everything you could just to keep your balance.

Then, at twelve, you got on the boat.

So here he was on his boat, a sturdy, well-made vessel that promised to sail him through adolescence with relative ease. He was well liked, athletic, bright enough for others to cheat off but not cerebral enough to be regarded as a nerd. His parents—especially his father—were respected and admired by everyone in town. And if they were a little tightly wound, if their brows furrowed even over matters of little consequence, it was nothing that could not be overcome, or at least dodged, with jokes and charm and innocent lies.

This particular lie—biking downtown for Bubble Yum—had been absolutely necessary; his mother did not believe in gawking, not at fights or car accidents or exploded houses or even funny looking dogs. Among the citizens of Casey she was pretty much alone in this distaste. Crossing from the final cluster of Main Street row house apartments and into the sprawling farmland, Paul ran smack into a traffic jam the magnitude of which the town usually saw only once a year—second week of August, for the county fair. Casey was a town of nine thousand; tucked in a valley between the Kittatinny and Tuscarora mountains, the town was surrounded by innumerable miles of swaying corn and the sweeping tails of dairy cows. Pittsburgh was two hours northwest on the Pennsylvania Turnpike, Harrisburg an hour east. Excitement was in short supply. And so it was that a quarter mile away from the Neidermeyer farm, cars and pickups were rumbling off the road and into the tall grass, entire families—many still clad in church clothes—piling out and heading west along the wide gravelly shoulder. Paul deftly wove his way through the pedestrians (some carried picnic baskets; most had cameras swinging from their necks) and stopped his bike at the foot of the long sloping dirt drive that led to the Neidermeyer house, which sat alone in the middle of six acres of unkempt brush. He had seen the house before, of course. It was hard to miss, a white clapboard two-story nineteenth-century farmhouse with a huge front porch, each weathered board of it a testament to simpler and sturdier days. Years before, Claude Neidermeyer and his wife had raised dairy cows—for chocolate made in nearby Hershey—in the vast pasture that was now nothing but uninhibited weeds. Three empty silos, their only silage the ashes of grain, towered over a ramshackle barn that had housed its last cow long before Paul was born. It was the kind of house people expected to see in the middle of Pennsylvania farm country, the kind of house that graced a thousand postcards, the kind of house tourists stopped to snap pictures of at sunset.

But what lay before Paul now was a photo opportunity of a different sort. An hour before, in the church courtyard after worship, word had spread of an explosion at the Neidermeyer farm and Paul had imagined the house would be totally destroyed, a massive pile of rubble that his father and the other firemen would pick through for clues to its demise. Instead, what he saw now was that the center of the Neidermeyer house had simply *vanished.* In its place, between the still-standing east and west walls, lay an enormous heap of debris—concrete, wood, furniture, pipes, wires . . .

"Shit," Paul muttered, steadying himself on his bike. A hot lump rose in his stomach and he swallowed hard, let his bike roll back a few inches. Well, okay then, he'd seen it. He'd taken a good long look at the thing and not broken into a cold sweat, so there was really no need to get any closer. Maybe his mother was right about the whole gawking thing, anyway. Maybe the cool thing to do was to go home. Maybe—

But no. He would not be a chicken. Not today.

Two years before, on a sticky August night, the tire factory on Route 11 had gone up in flames. He'd been ten that year—only ten!—practically still a baby if you thought about it. He'd been sleeping over at his friend Carson's house, camping out in the backyard, and moments after the second swell of sirens rose (and Paul had managed to still the shudder in his knees) Carson's dad had appeared out back in his bathrobe and sneakers, car keys in hand. In Mr. Diehl's stuffy Lincoln they'd followed the wail of sirens, then the swirling cloud of gray smoke, then the slow procession of other cars down the winding factory drive.

At first it had been impossible to distinguish among the firefighters; there were dozens of them rushing around the perimeter of the factory, laying long lines from the pumper and the hydrants. Flames rolled from the roof; windows exploded. Then Carson had shouted "There's your dad!" and Paul had followed Carson's pointing finger to a man (a man shorter than any of the others, a man who moved with skillful speed) fitting a SCBA mask over his face. Briefly, for a brilliant split second, Paul was thrilled; he'd never seen his father in action like this before. He'd seen only the aftermath of his father's work—scrapes, deep bruises, sometimes a broken finger—but never the work itself. Standing on the factory grounds, his cheeks warm and his eyes tearing from smoke, he felt what he thought was pride swell in his belly. But then suddenly, unexpectedly, the pride stung inside him, burned his gut like the flames that licked toward his father as he approached the factory doors. Paul stumbled behind the Diehls' car and threw up.

Had that been the end of it, it wouldn't have been so bad. He could have blamed it on the Dr Pepper and Doritos he'd consumed at Carson's earlier, maybe even convinced himself he'd been sickened by the flat, thick smell of melting tires. But following the fire he'd had night sweats for two weeks straight, woken up chilled to the bone, drenched in perspiration and one unforgettable night in his own pee. The night he wet his pajama pants he curled naked at the end of the bed, away from the spreading stain, crying quietly and aching from head to toe with shame. Here he was, the only son of the bravest man in town, who himself was the only son of the previous bravest man in town, and he'd peed himself like a baby. Imagine if word got out! Imagine if somehow his secret was revealed (it could happen . . . gossip in Casey swirled from lips to ears like funnel clouds) and everyone would know the best quarterback in Pony football, one of the coolest kids at school, was a chickenshit bed wetter. He'd played sick the next morning, then laundered his sheets while his mother was at the grocery store, flung them back on his bed, still damp, when he heard her car in the driveway.

He took a deep breath, gripped his handlebars with sweaty palms. Not today, he told himself. He'd toted around his shame long enough. Then his feet were on the dusty ground, his legs were moving, and he found himself walking slowly up the driveway pushing his bike. Surprisingly, there was something almost pleasurable about the sensation he was feeling, a kind of mad rush that came with the wooziness. It was a little like when his friend Joe Bower had shown him a grainy picture of the Elephant Man in a thick book from the study shelf in the science room. It had made him queasy, the giant, mangled head atop the twisted body, but in the days that followed he found himself returning to the dusty book again and again and opening to that page, willing himself to keep his eyes on the hideous man a little longer each time.

There were about three hundred people on the Neidermeyer property. Most of them were obviously townspeople, some of whom had portable video cameras (normally reserved for birthday parties and school plays) trained on the crumbling house. In addition to the town gawkers there were also several news vans, half a dozen fire trucks from neighboring communities, and more cop cruisers than Paul had ever seen in one place. Yellow police tape was wound around the ancient oaks bordering the lawn, so no one in the crowd could get closer than a hundred yards or so to the wrecked house. Men and women stood along the edge of the tape, talking chipperly with neighbors and snapping pictures. Beyond the lawn, in shin-high pasture weeds, a large group of boys and a few girls were playing Frisbee in the long shadows of the silos. Paul scanned the lawn for his father, then spotted Black Phil at the edge of the yellow tape, talking to a newswoman.

Black Phil had been Kittatinny County fire captain for six years, and was one of the few men remaining in the department who had worked alongside Paul's grandfather, the legendary Captain Sam. Phil had earned his nickname when another Phil—a white man—joined the department sometime in the mid-seventies, and Sam took to calling them Black Phil and White Phil to avoid confusion. White Phil was long gone, but Black Phil continued to go by his nickname even when identifying himself to strangers, half out of habit and half to get on the nerves of sensitive people—black and white—who thought the nickname was just a tiny bit in bad taste. He was a burly guy with a thick gray mustache and hands large enough to palm a basketball. He lived in the black section of Casey, four square blocks just east of downtown, with his wife and three teenage girls; sometimes in the summer Paul and his parents went to their place for barbecues and Black Phil would tell long and—after the third or fourth beer—extremely *loud* stories about Captain Sam's quarter of a century on the force. To hear Phil tell it—really, to hear most any of the firemen tell it—Sam fell somewhere between Jesus and Superman in the order of heroes.

A familiar hand clapped down firmly on his shoulder.

"Busted," Sonny said, when Paul turned.

Paul feigned confusion. "Busted for what?"

Sonny grinned. "You gonna try to tell me your mom knows you're out here? Next thing you'll be tellin' me she's out here herself."

"Don't rat, okay?" Paul recognized he needed to play up the team aspect of this particular lie, get his father to choose a side. In a family of three, alliances were weighty, crucial matters. "I'm just here for a minute."

Sonny raised his eyebrows. "Okay, but you owe me."

He was a small man, Sonny Tucker, only five feet eight inches tall, but a hundred and seventy pounds of just about pure muscle. In a suit and tie he looked unassuming, unthreatening, a man unaccustomed to danger. But in jeans and a T-shirt, or in his turnout gear, Paul thought his father looked like a first-rate ass kicker, the kind of guy other men would cross the street to avoid after dark. Sonny still pumped iron at the station four days a week and could make it up the eight-flight training staircase at the fire academy in Pittsburgh faster than any other man in the department, even the rookies who were now ten years younger than he. Sometimes he bench-pressed Paul in the middle of the living room, one hand set between the shoulders and the other at the small of the back. He did this, Paul had noticed, only when his mom was around, sitting on the couch pretending to be unimpressed as Paul counted off his father's reps—28, 29, 30, 31 . . .

Now Sonny gestured to the house. "It's something, huh?"

"What happened? Gas leak?"

Sonny shook his head. "Good guess, but no. Gas was shut off months ago, after the fire."

Six months before, eighty-six-year-old Claude Neidermeyer had fallen into a deep sleep in his recliner while heating tomato soup on his stovetop; by the time the firemen were able to drag him to safety and extinguish the blaze, the entire first floor of the house was gutted. Mr. Neidermeyer (an accident just waiting to happen, according to the town grapevine, left to teeter around that old house all by himself) had been sentenced to the local nursing home by his two grown sons. The house had been condemned by the fire department, but the Neidermeyer boys—perhaps lazy, perhaps nostalgic, most likely a little of both—had yet to clean out what items were salvageable, and so the house had sat there on the outskirts of town, empty—so everyone thought—of any life but carpenter ants and feral cats.

"So what was it?" Paul asked.

Sonny took off his sunglasses and wiped them with his T-shirt. "Water and fire damage, probably termites on top of that." He shrugged, ran his fingers through his hair. "Or maybe the old girl just decided she'd had enough, wanted to go out with a bang, give us all something to do on a Sunday afternoon."

"So what *do* you do?"

Sonny humphed. "Nothing but stand here. The whole place'll probably be down by nightfall . . . don't expect there's much holding it up anymore. So we're just gonna watch it crumble."

"You're not gonna try to save it?"

"Look at it," Sonny said. "What's there to save?"

"I don't know," Paul said. "I just thought—"

His father's buddy Ben Griffin appeared in his typical manner—out of nowhere—and smacked Paul sharply on the back of the head with an open palm. This was his usual greeting, one that occasionally brought tears to Paul's eyes that he'd quickly blink away. Ben was tall and broad-shouldered, had a square chin and a thick brown mustache that he was fond of combing. Unlike Sonny, Ben could wear just about anything and still look like a firefighter.

"That as hard as you can hit?" Paul taunted, squinting up at him.

Ben took a drag off his cigarette, raised his right eyebrow. "Want me to give it another try? Then we can add your head to that pile of crap over there." He flipped his cigarette to the ground; smoke wafted lazily through blades of dead grass. "Fire," Ben said, pointing. "Fire, fire . . . for Christ's sake somebody call a fireman."

Sonny stepped on the cigarette, ground it snugly into the dry earth with his boot. "Bored?" he asked.

"Nah. I've been having loads of fun letting kids try on my helmet." He set his helmet on Paul's head. "See there? A thrill a minute."

Ben had moved from Pittsburgh to join the Casey FD only a few years before and—following his divorce six months later—had become a regular guest at the Tucker house. At least once a week he came for dinner, then stayed and washed the dishes, tagged along for the nightly walking of the dogs, finally plopped down on the couch with the family for an evening of television. Sometimes Paul would find him curled up on the living room couch in the morning, an afghan bunched around his legs and a horseshoe of empty beer cans on the coffee table. Once, after a week of substance abuse education in the fifth grade, Paul had asked his mother if she thought Ben had a drinking problem. She'd considered for a moment, then shaken her head. More like a *lonely* problem, she'd said.

"Mama know you're out here?" Ben asked.

Sonny put a finger to his lips. "It's a secret."

Ben grinned. "A secret, huh? I can keep a secret—for the right price."

Paul took off the helmet and tossed it to Ben. "Your helmet smells like cigarettes."

Ben yawned. "Best ashtray I got, worm." He nodded toward the house. "Well, boys, we're gonna be in papers all over the state tomorrow. For about five minutes everybody in PA will be talking about Casey. Then somebody in Philly'll fart and we'll be forgotten again."

"Or somebody in Philly *won't* fart and we'll be forgotten," Sonny said. He gazed up at the broken house a little sadly, and Paul figured his father was sorry there was nothing to do, nothing and no one to save—yet again—and that all he'd be in newspaper photographs tomorrow was part of the scenery, another anonymous guy in T-shirt and shades, aimlessly hanging around. Except for the tire factory incident, there had been little drama, little genuine disaster, during his twelve years in the department. Every few months there was a pileup on the turnpike, an eighteen-wheeler in flames, a car to be cracked open with the Jaws of Life. Occasionally there were forgotten cigarettes, faulty wirings, leaf burnings gone awry, kids with lighter fluid and too much time on their hands. But mostly, Paul had learned, the life of a small-town career fireman was a never-ending series of false alarms, training exercises, fender benders, safety lectures, and fire drills.

"Think it'll be on TV?" Paul asked.

"Hell, yeah," Ben said. "Phil's been talking to cameras all morning, probably already called home to set the VCR."

"You should go now, quarterback," Sonny said. He touched the seat of Paul's bike. "Before your mom starts—"

Then the booming voice—

"Tucker! Griffin!"

—came from across the lawn. Black Phil was standing beside Casey Engine 14 with two grungy teenage boys. Paul recognized them from downtown, where they and their grungy friends—a handful of creepy teenagers who wore trench coats and heavy black boots—hung out in the abandoned lot behind the Hess gas station. They were the closest thing Casey had to a gang; mostly they just smoked cigarettes and leveled malevolent glares at passersby, but occasionally they'd knock a kid off his bike, shout lewdly at women, pick fights with jocks or black kids. One day, when Paul was six or seven, he and his mother were driving past the abandoned lot and his mother had shaken her head in disgust and said, "See those boys over there? They're goners, every one of them." From that point on Paul had always thought of them by that name: The Goners. It wasn't until a couple years later that he discovered the title was his mother's own, apparently drawn from a dozen years of teaching ninth-grade algebra at Casey High, and that not everyone referred to them that way. But the name had stuck in his mind.

"What rock they crawl out from under?" Ben asked.

Sonny shrugged. "Let's go find out."

They walked off without saying goodbye. Paul threw a leg over his bike and turned it around, started toward the driveway. He reached the crest and was about to begin his coast toward the road below when he heard voices behind him rise in expectation. He turned back and saw that the small group beside the fire truck had dispersed, that his father and Ben had put on their helmets and were walking across the lawn toward the house. They didn't look in any particular hurry, but even so all the gawkers were struggling for a better view, cameras at the ready. Paul considered—stay or go? His mother would be starting to wonder, perhaps even to suspect that he'd come out here to join in the unseemly gawking, would be all frowns and furrows when he arrived home. But so what? No, really . . . so what? He wasn't smoking dope, for Christsakes. He wasn't busting windows or stealing lawn ornaments or harassing girls.

He turned his bike around.

"What's up?" a newsman yelled at Sonny and Ben, as Paul squeezed in through the crowd to the line of reporters who were pressed against the tape. Sonny turned and waved, smiled the broad, toothy smile that Paul knew was usually saved for kindergarten classes who toured the station. Clearly, something was wrong. To the untrained eye his father's gait might have looked casual, but Paul noticed tension in the backs of the thighs, a stiffness in the upper back; this was the way his father walked when someone was in trouble, when one of the dogs had chewed up the mail, when a fire hose was stowed carelessly. Both Sonny and Ben had their chins tucked toward their chests; they were talking, intently, but they didn't want anyone to know this. Paul felt his heart quicken; the goners had told them something that had sparked renewed interest in the house.

"You getting all this?" a lady reporter beside Paul said to her cameraman. He was standing directly behind her, the lens of the camera bobbing above her shoulder like a giant horsefly. Paul recognized the woman—she was tiny, no bigger than the girls in his class—from the eleven o'clock news, one of the Harrisburg stations. "This might be something."

"Maybe there's gas after all," the cameraman said. "Maybe they're smellin'."

And they did look like they were smelling. At the edge of what had once been the front porch and was now the edge of the pile of debris, Sonny and Ben got down on their hands and knees. Paul could feel the heat of bodies pressing in behind him.

"What're they doing?"

"Looking for something, I guess."

"They're smellin'," the cameraman said knowingly. "They're smellin', all right."

Paul rolled his eyes: another know-it-all. That was about the last thing Casey needed, another guy with his head up his butt thinking he knew all about somebody else's business. Paul watched his father remove his helmet, then bend down and lay the side of his head against a slab of concrete at the foot of the rubble. Ben followed suit. Neither man moved a muscle, and the crowd fell suddenly still, hundreds of breaths held in, the only sound the whir of video rolling.

"They're listening," someone whispered.

"What for?"

"Maybe there's somebody down there."

"Under that?"

"No way. Be dead by now even if there was."

Then Sonny and Ben abruptly stood up. They exchanged a few words, stole a brief glance at the curious crowd, then started back down the lawn toward Black Phil, strolling casually, as if nothing but the weather occupied their minds.

"False alarm," someone said.

"They're bored," someone else added. "Just lookin' for something to look for, I bet."

Paul knew better. Before he could talk himself out of it, he laid his bike on the ground and ducked under the yellow tape, then crept around the back of Engine 14, out of sight from his father and Ben and Phil. He gently eased himself down on the wide silver bumper, his hands under his thighs to block the chill, and listened to the conversation.

". . . a loser," Ben was saying. "All the cops know him. Said he's some kind of Nazi or something."

Paul recognized his father's scoff. "Cops think every weird kid's a Nazi these days."

"Maybe," Ben said. "But not every weird kid has a swastika on his back."

"You kiddin' me?"

"I heard it too," Phil said. "Sixteen years old and he's got a damn swastika tattoo. All these little boys playin' at Nazi."

Nazi? The image in Paul's mind was from a video they'd seen at school the year before, black-and-white footage of tall men in steel helmets pulling dazed old women from sooty train cars, nudging them into long lines with the butts of machine guns, spitting into dirty snow.

"He's trouble," Ben said. "Building pipe bombs down there, I bet. Or mixing drugs. Like that guy, that comedian, blew himself up. You guys remember that?"

"His friends said they were just hanging out," Phil said. "Drinking beer, listening to music."

Paul peered around the corner of the truck to get a good look at the crowd, see if he could catch sight of those boys, the two goners, but they had vanished. They were always doing that, disappearing and then reappearing—like shadows or ghosts—in store aisles and school halls and darkened alleyways.

"You buying that?" Ben asked. "You think they're gonna tell you they got a friggin' bomb factory in the basement? I'll bet the wad that asshole brought the house down on himself."

"He'd be dead," Sonny said, "if a bomb blew in his face. He wouldn't be making all that racket. I'm telling you, Phil, he's banging like crazy on something down there. We're lookin' at a big dig."

"Backhoe?" Ben's voice had gone up half an octave. Paul smiled; he knew the truth about Ben, about his dad, about all the firemen in Casey, maybe all the firemen in the world: most of them sat around day in and day out just hoping something like this would happen.

"No way," Sonny said. "No bulldozer, no backhoe, no heavy equipment, unless we want the rest of the house coming down on our heads. We get a construction crew out here ASAP to shore the standing walls, then we go at it with our hands. Saws, axes, air chisels. We set up a cage over the dig spot to protect our guys in case anything comes loose upstairs."

"You did the training course," Phil said. "Last year?"

"Two years ago," Sonny said. "I know the drill. All we need is a passage big enough to fit one man through."

"I'm guessing that would be you," Ben said.

Paul leaned forward, peered at them around the corner of the truck. Ben and his father had their backs to him, and Phil wasn't taking any notice, his eyes narrowed with plans and expectation.

"I'm guessin' it would," Sonny answered humorlessly. "Since I took the course. Plus I'm the smallest. Listen, we know he's alive, and he's got enough strength to be making all that noise. No gas, no live wires, no water, probably plenty of air. We take our time and do it right, by the book, and then we go in and get him. Once we start digging we'll find some voids along the way, I guarantee it. The kid'll be out by nightfall."

Paul grinned. He remembered when his father had come to his fourth-grade class for a fire safety lecture, how he'd held all the kids spellbound, read them the riot act about lighter fluid, paint thinner, and aerosol cans so that even the most ill-mannered boys listened intently, mouths agape. These were the times he admired his father most—no hesitation, no doubt, and only a single viable option: his, the right one. At home, his mother always made the calls, overrode his father's decisions about sleepovers and vacations and meals and bedtime, often with no more than a word or a single well-placed expression. But out here, out in the real world, his father was boss.

"Sounds good, Sonny," Ben said. "I can only think of eight or nine hundred ways that plan could fuck up."

"You got a better idea?"

"Yeah—call in some guys who know what they're doing. No offense, but this ain't a job for the Kittatinny County boys."

"I took the course," Sonny said.

"In a conference room, right?" Ben asked, smirking. "Watched a slide show or something while you're drinking coffee and eating jelly doughnuts? I say we call the rescue response team in Pittsburgh, tell them—"

"They're two hours away!" Sonny interrupted. "And that's if they leave right now, which they won't. You want us to just sit around all afternoon waiting on 'em, looking like a bunch of assholes?"

Ben shook his head. "This isn't about how we *look,* Sonny. Those guys in Pittsburgh are experts. They do this stuff all the time." He turned to Phil. "Think about it," he said. Then he added, pointedly: "It's your call, Phil."

But it wasn't. Paul knew it wasn't, and he knew damn well the three of them knew it too, though they stood there in the dusty drive pretending otherwise. Phil may have been the chief on paper, but when something this momentous lay in the balance it was going to be Sonny—the blood of Captain Sam coursing through his veins, thirty years at the station imprinted on his face and hands—who'd have the final say.

Phil scratched his head and frowned thoughtfully. For a moment it looked to Paul like old Phil might actually make the decision on his own, might suck it up and pull rank. Then his eyes darted quickly to Sonny. "Wha'dya think?"

"You know what I think," Sonny said firmly. "I think we can do it ourselves. I *know* we can do it ourselves."

Phil nodded. "Then we do it ourselves. I'll call the construction guys. We can have a crew here in fifteen, twenty at—" A broad grin spread across his face; his eyes had locked with Paul's. Paul jerked his head back, but he knew he was too late.

"Just like your daddy," Phil shouted. "Come on out from there, pal."

Paul hopped down and sauntered around the corner of the truck, hands in his pockets. They were all staring at him. Phil and Ben were grinning, but his father looked mystified, as if Paul were a character in a movie he'd seen once, a long time ago, that had now inexplicably materialized in the real world.

"Time was," Phil said, "I'd be standing here talking to Captain Sam and your daddy'd be lurking around in the shadows just like you are now." He and Ben laughed lightly, and Paul laughed too.

"I thought I told you to go home," Sonny said. He wasn't laughing. He wasn't, Paul recognized, anywhere in the vicinity of a laugh.

"I'm not in the way."

"You are right now. 'Cause we're standing here talking to you, wasting valuable time."

"Let him be, Sonny," Phil said gently. " 'Bout time he starts learning a few things. He's just like you was at—"

"He's not like me," Sonny snapped, his face and shoulders stiffening at once. "He's got a mother at home."

Ben cleared his throat and looked away. Phil was silent for a moment, then shrugged. "No time for this talk," he said. "I gotta get on the phone, then go face the newshounds. They'll be shitting bricks when they hear about the Finch kid."

"Who's the Finch kid?" Paul asked.

"I'll fill in the others," Ben said, heading off to the congregation of firemen from neighboring towns.

"Home," Sonny told Paul when the other two were gone, a finger that might as well have belonged to the grim reaper pointing in the general direction of their house. "Right now."

Paul took a deep breath, didn't move. He knew he was on shaky ground, but what Phil had said stirred him. He *was* like his father, deep down—Phil had said it, had seen something in him that wasn't a coward. And right now, today, this very minute, with the sun high in the sky and the crisp fall air slipping up his shirtsleeves, he had his chance to prove it.

"Paul . . ."

"You really going down there, under the house?"

Sonny put his hands on his hips, the last gesture before real trouble. "It's gonna be a while before *anybody* goes down there. Right now you need to get your butt home. I don't wanna have to deal with your mother getting—"

"I wanna stay," Paul said. "Phil's right . . . it's time I start learning. I'll keep out of the way. I just want to see what you do."

"Paul, I *said*—" But then Sonny stopped, mid-demand. He was taken aback by the words; it was splashed all over his face, clear as bliss or sickness. Paul had never seen this particular expression before, and he wasn't sure what it meant. Perhaps his father had seen himself in him, just for a moment, and then, too, seen Captain Sam in himself, in an even briefer moment. A breeze kicked up and ruffled his father's blond hair, blew dust at their ankles. Still his father was silent.

"Dad . . ."

"All right already," Sonny said irritably. "You can stay. But you're not hanging around up here. I want you behind the tape with everybody else. I was gonna call your mom from the truck anyway; I'll tell her you met up with some kids and came out here and you guys are throwing the football around. Now you keep out of the way, I mean it."

"I will," Paul said, trying to muster a serious expression, trying desperately not to grin as he headed back toward the crowd. Thing was, when his mother said she meant it, he knew she meant it. But with his father it was different—everything was open to interpretation, open just wide enough to squeeze through. Somewhere beyond what his father *said* he wanted lay the things he really wanted. And those things, Paul knew, were out here, where the action was, among the cameras and the crowd and the crumbling house. So it was only right that he be here too.

❡

It took most of the afternoon to shore the standing walls to the rescue workers' satisfaction. Paul spent the majority of that time playing Frisbee golf with several dozen of his schoolmates in the Neidermeyer pasture. His best friends Carson Diehl and Joe Bower were there, and Paul was able to restrain himself for only a few minutes before dropping the first hint (*you guys ever seen a real rescue before?*) that the day was about to take an exciting turn. When Carson and Joe badgered him for details he clammed up. Confidential information, he told them, and he could see the envy in their faces. He'd always gotten a lot of mileage from his father; he knew, and didn't mind, that some of his popularity had to do with his heritage. Carson's dad was a loan officer; Joe's dad owned the shoe store. A lot of kids in his class had dads who worked in factories or on farms. Some of them didn't even have dads. He knew how lucky he was: not just a dad, but a dad who kicked ass.

His father replaced the cool that his mother depleted. She was a worry-mom of the highest order, and this was the primary reason he had to lie to her so often, to protect them both from embarrassing overreactions, especially in public. He lied to her more about football than anything else, because he knew the rules: let on he might be hurt, and he could kiss his football career (Casey High, Penn State, Pittsburgh Steelers) goodbye. His mother could spot a scratch from fifty feet, saw a limp in every misstep. From August to November he wore clothes that hid bruises, tended his wounds carefully in the privacy of the shower. Stiffness was the only acceptable injury. Sometimes when he was sacked and went down hard he'd see her rise to her feet in the bleachers; once or twice she'd even made it down a few rows toward the field before he hurriedly got up, signaling to the sidelines (to her, really) that he was fine. The possibility that someday she might actually make it onto the field before he staggered to his feet was too horrifying to even consider.

It was funny, though: for all her suffocating concern over the innumerable risks of Pony football, she had never shown a moment of trepidation at the thought of her husband charging into a burning building. "Sweetie, he'll be *fine*," she'd always told Paul when he was naive enough to actually share his fears with her. When other firemen's wives voiced their apprehensions, Laura would wave her hand dismissively. "They spend half the day playing cards," she'd say. Or: "What's so scary about telling kindergartners to stop, drop, and roll?"

What was her secret? Paul didn't know, but he admired it, harbored great envy for this remarkable talent. Even before the factory fire, the swell of sirens had the power to turn his knees to ice, to fill his mind, if only for a moment, with the certainty that his father was speeding toward a fiery death. Usually—usually—he could quell the panic in a moment or two with deep breaths and practiced reason. But his mother, it seemed, didn't even need a moment. "Kiss the kitty for me," she would often say when Sonny was called away on an emergency (the old joke—the cat up a tree) but this old joke never brought a smile to his father's lips. His sense of humor did not seem to extend to what he obviously saw as mockery; every time Laura shot one of her little arrows, made a lightly cutting remark about the lack of legitimate danger in the day-to-day affairs of a fireman, Paul noticed his father's eyes drop to the floor, his jaw stiffen. Out of embarrassment? Or anger? Paul wasn't sure—it was part of a language he didn't understand.

His father had once told him something he now could only imagine must have been a lie, a mistake, at least an exaggeration. The story was that after they were first married, Sonny would get reports from neighbors that Laura had been seen walking their dogs around town at all hours of the night and early morning while he was on duty. According to Sonny, it was the appearance of Paul in the world that had allowed Laura to finally sleep nights while he was at the station. Now Paul doubted this information. It was the neighbors who had said it, after all. Neighbors were always saying something.

In the Neidermeyer pasture, Frisbee golf turned to Frisbee football, then—with all the girls finally bullied out of the game—to kill-the-man-with-the-Frisbee. Every so often, when he wasn't being pursued by a pack of tacklers, Paul would steal a look at his father. While the other firemen paced the lawn impatiently, looking at their watches, frowning at the tedious work of the construction crew, Sonny stood alone off to the side of the house, his arms crossed loosely across his chest, his eyes closed as often as open, his breaths measured and calm. Paul thought he could even detect a faint smile on his father's lips—not exactly a happy smile, but a contented smile, the smile of a man who was finally standing on the very spot he'd been heading toward his whole life.

Following the death of Gramaw Tucker, from a cancer that spread and ravaged with mind-numbing speed, four-year-old Sonny had taken up permanent residence in Casey Station #1 with Captain Sam and the other firemen. He had his own cot in the sleeping quarters, ate and eventually cooked in the common kitchen, played Ping-Pong with the other firemen on the scarred and rickety table that still stood—barely—in the back room of the station house. In addition to Captain Sam, the county had employed seven other career firemen and Casey alone had a crew of nearly thirty volunteers. Before long Sonny had belonged to all of them and thus lost the name given to him by Gramaw Tucker—a name Paul had once seen on his father's driver's license and not recognized—and came to be known only as *Sonny*. Each man in the station played one part of the whole known as father: Black Phil taught him to make double-decker grilled cheese, Chris Elscot threw the football with him, Fred Randolph cut his hair, Jay Nichols helped him with his homework. And Captain Sam did what he had always done best: he oversaw.

It was usually Chris Elscot or Black Phil who roused young Sonny from sleep, hurried him from his squeaky cot as the alarm screamed bloody murder in the middle of the night. Sometimes weeks would go by without a night call, then there'd be a stretch of three or four in a row (*full moon*, the guys would say) when Sonny's dreams would be shattered first by the blast of sound ricocheting off the walls and then—before he was truly awake—thick fingers around his bicep, tugging him from under the covers.

"Up and at 'em, kid . . ."

On his feet, in his shoes, down the pole, blinking drowsy eyes in the glare of harsh light off chrome. As the men stepped into their turnout gear, he'd fumble his black jacket from its hook (*Sonny*, on a piece of duct tape, slapped to the wall beside the others' names) and climb on board. And then the best part, the part that always woke him more completely than any sunrise: engines roaring, sirens wailing, they'd sail out of the station and into the night.

But mostly, Paul knew, his father and the men who raised him had spent the majority of their time doing all the things normal families did. They ate big meals, played hearts and checkers, shot baskets in the drive, argued about whose turn it was to do the dishes. The TV was on twenty-four hours a day; Chris Elscot knew the twisted history of every character on *Days of Our Lives*, Black Phil was a *Wheel of Fortune* genius, and Fred Randolph howled at every episode of *Gomer Pyle*, no matter how many times he'd seen it before. Most of the time Captain Sam sat in his office filling out incident reports, a Marlboro burned to its quick pinched in the web between his index and middle finger. Sometimes Sonny would pull up a chair beside him, lay out his homework next to the incident reports, and set silently to his studies. Captain Sam would briefly look over, smile approvingly, and return to his work.

According to Black Phil, by the time Sonny was in his early teens he was living the life of a fireman. Though he had gone through no formal training, he was second only to his father as the most trusted man on the force. He never entered a burning building (Captain Sam's orders) but he did everything else expected of a seasoned volunteer—checked and cleaned equipment, laid lines from hydrant to pumper, sprayed debris from the scene of highway accidents. In his other world, away from the firehouse, he was an outsider. He lettered in football and track at Casey High, but had few close friends. His life, his home, his world, was the station.

His father didn't talk of these years much, but he didn't need to. Everyone else in town knew the story, and Paul had pieced together the history of his father detail by detail, one scene—sometimes one frame—at a time. Bits of the story came from the parents and grand-parents of his friends, but the bulk of it came from the firemen them-selves, men who liked nothing better on a rainy afternoon than to sit around the station house one-upping each other with their dueling memories. For a time Paul had been fascinated by the tale, had gath-ered all the information he could, had even written an essay in fourth grade about his father's unique upbringing that won honorable men-tion in a state contest. But in the last couple years he'd begun to lose interest in exploring the past, grown more concerned with the future—his own future, specifically—which seemed with each step toward manhood increasingly unrelated to his father's past.

By the time the shoring was complete, the Neidermeyer house resem-bled something a monkey would make if forced to take shop class, a motley mess of planks, steel bars, chains, and cables that lacked any aesthetic value but which, apparently, would keep the house from con-tinuing its collapse. A 10 x 10 chain-link dog kennel (brought to the site by Cole Colson, owner of the local pet and livestock supply) was placed over the spot where Sonny and Ben had first heard the banging from the basement. Then the initial dig team—Ben, Sonny, and two other Casey firemen—began their work.

Bored with Frisbee and antsy for a better view than his five feet af-forded him, Paul discovered what he thought was the ideal vantage point, a limb of one of the oak trees that the police tape was wound around. He could see the beginnings of the hole clearly from his perch. At first his father and the others dug—or flung, more accurately—with their hands; the first foot or two of rubble was relatively simple, consisted mostly of small pieces of plaster, planks of wood, bits of the roof, items from the upstairs rooms that could be pitched out the swinging kennel door. Once they got past the first layer, the task became more difficult. Each man took a saw or pick and began to grind and chip away at the debris. The plan was to make a shaft large enough to slip in a makeshift tunnel of wooden barrels, to secure a safe passage, guard against the tunnel caving in on itself once it was complete.

Darkness fell a little after five o'clock; floodlights borrowed from a nearby turnpike construction project were rigged up around the dog kennel. Powered by giant droning generators, the lights were powerful enough to cast the equivalent of sunlight over the dig spot plus a dim hint of dusk across the lawn and into the pasture. Sonny, straining to keep balance on the rubble despite the vibrations from the air chisel in his hands, called repeatedly for the Finch kid, but—from what Paul could see from the look on his father's face, ghostly in the glare—he seemed to be getting no answer. Paul recalled his confident words from earlier—*we'll have him out by nightfall*—and wondered if those words were ringing now in his father's ears as well, drowning out the buzz of the chisel and the shrill scrape of the saw. But surely, just a few more minutes, a few more inches . . .

"He's toast," the kid on the branch below Paul said. It was Alex Luckett, the son of one of the volunteer firemen. He was in eighth grade and stout as an ox; the branch dipped under his weight. "I'll bet ya anything."

"Maybe he's just passed out," Paul said. But looking at the house, he had to admit it was hard to imagine the Nazi as being anything but dead. He tried to get a picture of the goners in his mind, hoping to see the face that belonged to "the Finch kid," but he found he could only picture them as a group, lurking behind the Hess Station, as indistinguishable from one another as a pack of wolves. So he gave this Finch a face, a sketch of a convenience store thief he'd seen on the news a few nights before, a black-and-white line drawing of a man whose features were so ordinary he could have been just about anybody. He put the face in the basement, imagined the penciled face in agony, the penciled mouth shouting for help, the penciled eyes wild with fear. And then the penciled face dead, almost peaceful, his lines thickening and blurring until the face was only a scribble.

At six the second shift of diggers came on, and Sonny took a break, hobbled stiff-kneed to the water table and peeled apart an orange, stuffed it in his mouth. Paul scampered down from his perch on the tree and joined him.

"Everybody thinks he's dead," Paul said.

"He's not," Sonny said. He wet his hands under the watercooler and rubbed them gently together; even with his thick cowhide gloves, blisters puckered his palms—they were bright red and puffy, and Paul imagined late tonight, after all this was over, his mother would rub lotion into them and his father would smile through his wincing.

"You heard anything?"

"He's just takin' a rest," Sonny said. "That's all. You'd be taking a rest too if you'd been kickin' for eight hours."

"That's what I was thinking," Paul said.

His father nodded, wiped juice from his chin with the heel of his hand. "Then you're thinking like a fireman." He tossed his orange peel on the ground. "Once you start believin' a guy's dead you don't work quite so fast, lose a little bit of that urgency. That's when you get into trouble."

As his father had predicted, the second dig team hit a void at six feet, a space of about thirty inches in what had once been the Neidermeyer kitchen. Two men carried a large wooden barrel—the ends cut off to form a tube—into the cage and twisted it into the hole, and then the digging became the task of one man at a time, a tedious operation of small picks and saws, all of it done upside down, blood rushing to the temples, dust in the eyes and mouth. An hour passed, then another. Crickets chirped, kids hollered. Paul sat in the tree, his lower back cramping, his eyelids heavy; the unrelenting dusk made him sleepy.

"Tucker!"

Paul could hear Black Phil's voice even from his perch in the tree, and he slid clumsily down the trunk, ducked under the yellow tape and walked at a rapid clip toward the dog kennel, hoping to render himself more or less invisible by gliding across the lawn in the fluid and unself-conscious manner of a quarterback sneak. The crowd in the pasture had not dwindled; if anything, it had grown as expectation of a dramatic rescue—or the discovery of a mangled body—increased. A small group from the Baptist church had gathered in a circle and were reading Bible verses in grave tones, but most everyone else seemed more comfortable as onlookers than intercessors; instead of praying, they scrambled for a better view.

Ben and Phil were fitting Sonny into his nylon harness. Paul stood on his tiptoes, his nose poking through the kennel fencing, and peered down the black hole. His father, he knew, was accustomed to tight spaces. He had heard the drill many times: as a fireman, you had to be prepared for any size and variety of traps, because you never knew when you might find yourself in one; at any moment during a rescue a roof could collapse, a floor give way, leaving you blind and disoriented, wedged under, inside, between. And then, despite the darkness and the heat and the walls crushing you, you had to be calm. And calm, Paul knew, was his father's strong suit. It was not only his size that made him the best man for the job.

Ben and Phil hooked metal clips on the harness at both the chest and thighs. Sonny jerked on the clips, did a couple deep knee bends, rolled his neck around for a few good cracks. He took a long, deep breath, then stood perfectly still for about ten seconds under the blinding lights, as if he were waiting for someone to snap his picture. It was then that he noticed Paul.

"You're like a bad penny," he said.

Ben socked him on the shoulder. "Talk like that'll win you father-of-the-year for sure," he said. "Kid just wants to wish you well."

"Yeah, good luck," Paul said. Then, after brief consideration, he added the advice his father always added right before kickoff: "Don't forget to have fun."

Sonny grinned. "Go sit in the truck or something, willya?"

"I will," Paul said.

"Gotta pee before you go?" Ben asked. "It's a long ride."

"Shut up and let's do it," Sonny said.

Phil touched Sonny's sleeve. "Your daddy'd be proud of you. He'll be down there with you, you know."

"Hope not," Ben said. "Ain't room for both of 'em."

In the dark, in the wide and chilly cab of Engine 14, Paul thought of his grandfather. He'd heard the story of Captain Sam's death so many times that he felt he'd been there himself. A quiet February night in Casey. A foot of snow on the ground. His father and mother—though they weren't yet a father and mother, weren't even a husband and wife—two hundred miles away in the safety of a warm dorm room. Maybe they were studying when the call came in to the station, lying on his mother's bed with their elbows touching. Maybe, by the time Engine 14 arrived at the house on Dogwood Avenue, they had closed their books and put on some music—his mother's REM, or his father's Rolling Stones. Maybe they were making out as Sam stormed into the house to rescue a young boy whose parents believed was trapped upstairs, a boy who, as it happened, was already safe in a neighbor's kitchen down the street.

An hour later, after the blaze had been extinguished, Black Phil and Fred Randolph found their captain inside a closet in the master bedroom. He was sitting in a black puddle of his own skin, surrounded by dozens of melted shoes—their laces unlaced, their tongues pulled back. Apparently, Sam had been looking for the boy in the toes of his parents' shoes while sucking his last poisoned breaths.

Though he'd never known his grandfather, Paul had often imagined those final moments in the life of Captain Sam, this giant of a man prying apart shoe after shoe, disoriented in the thick black smoke, his tank of air depleted, half crazy, half dead, looking for a little boy he had to know, by that time, he was never going to find.

Chapter Two

Paul spat out the open window of the fire truck, kneaded the chill that crept over his kneecaps. His father had been in the hole for twenty minutes. Probably the leather straps of the harness were beginning to chafe the backs of his thighs, despite his heavy bunker pants. Probably his fingers were blistered, bent stiff in the shape of the narrow handle of the pry ax. Probably his feet were numb, his eyes beating from the blood settling in his head. Paul thought of Harry Houdini—same numb feet, same aching fingers, same clouded head—hanging bound ten stories above a crowd of skeptics, somehow having the wits and will to free himself from shackles designed to restrain the fiercest of men. Still, when you thought about it, Houdini had had it pretty easy; it was only himself he'd needed to free.

"Paul?"

He looked up, startled. His mother was standing outside the fire truck, a black sweater in her hand. She held it out to him sheepishly.

"I thought you might need this."

He might have been fooled had she not looked so completely guilt-ridden, so riddled with shame. She had cracked, he thought. She had sat at home all day, telling herself as the afternoon wore on that everything was fine, busied herself with mundane tasks as the dinner hour passed, maybe—around nine o'clock—even prepared for bed. But then (unnerved by the quiet house? the rising winds?) her iron defense system had finally overloaded—perhaps for the first time *ever*, he thought—and she'd come out here with some lame-ass justification, this black turtleneck sweater, to check on her husband.

"Thanks," he said. He hopped out of the truck and slipped on the sweater.

"Is that enough?" she asked. "I've got a coat in the car."

"This'll do," he said. "Kinda late to be out on a school night, isn't it?"

She adjusted his collar; rare was the day that she did not adjust some piece of clothing on him. "I was just going to say the same thing to you."

"I know," he said. "I was trying to beat you to it."

She smiled. She was the prettiest teacher at Casey High, Paul knew, pretty not in the way of moms but in the way of models and cheerleaders, long blond hair that she always wore in a tight braid, narrow nose and lips, pale blue eyes that sparkled when she laughed—not the teacher laugh (too high, too forced, too jolly to be genuine) but the real laugh she saved for his father, and sometimes for him. Later, in high school, Paul would learn that his mother—that hair and that chin and those blue blue eyes—was the first full-blown sex fantasy of nearly every boy in Casey. Who could say how many of them might have become brilliant mathematicians had they only been able to snap out of their daze long enough to master elementary algebra in the ninth grade?

"So where's your father?" she asked casually, although Paul figured she had to know, what with Ben and Phil up in the cage hovering over the hole, him here at the truck, and his father nowhere in sight.

"He's rescuing," Paul said. He looked for a flicker in her eyes, and when there was none, he added, "In the basement."

She looked up toward the decrepit house and he followed her gaze. It was then that he saw Ben sauntering down the lawn toward them, clearly struggling not to grin as he approached.

"Evenin', Laura," he said as he reached them. "Out for a walk, are you?"

"I brought Paul a sweater," she said. She hugged herself for dramatic effect. "It's getting chilly."

"Ah . . ." He nodded. "That's mighty thoughtful of you, coming all this way." He patted the hood of the engine. "This, by the way, is a fire truck. It's what Sonny drives when he's working. You may not be familiar with—"

"You're so funny," she said. "Isn't he a riot, Paul? Isn't he the funniest man you've ever known?"

"He's pretty funny," Paul admitted. He liked it when Ben chided his mother; he was about the only one who could get away with it on a regular basis.

"I come with a message from the chief," Ben said. "He told me to tell you he doesn't want any nervous wives hanging around. He wants all nervous wives to go home."

"You can tell the chief I'm not a nervous wife."

"Hey, I told him that. I said, 'You know our gal Laura, she never gets nervous. She's a rock.' But he said you'll need to get along even so. You and the nervous kid too."

"I'm not nervous," Paul protested.

"Do me a favor," Ben said to Laura. "You don't have to go home, just don't hang around the truck. You're a little too close here. Fact is, I think you're making *Phil* nervous."

"Fine," she said. "We'll stand with the rest of . . . them. Will that work?"

"Laura Tucker, common gawker," Ben said happily. "Yeah, that'll work."

The crowd parted for them as they ducked under the police tape. They were celebrities by association now, temporarily off-limits for polite conversation as long as Sonny remained underground, in potential danger; poignant glances of concern were as much as the onlookers were willing to chance. Laura shook her head in amazement as she looked at the house.

"How long has he been down there?"

"Not long. Half hour maybe."

"Half an hour?" Her forehead wrinkled. What was this? A hint of concern? Paul realized he would have to remember these moments carefully, report them to his father later. Surely he would get a kick out of it, maybe even rub it in a bit the next time she breezily made her little cat joke as he dashed out the front door.

"He had some digging left to do," Paul said. "To break through to where the kid is. Then he's gotta make sure he's okay and everything, then get a harness around him. Operation like that takes a while."

She eyed him suspiciously. "How do you know all this? I thought you were just playing with your friends."

"I did," he said. "I was. I—"

There was a sudden flurry of activity in the cage. Ben and Phil must have felt a tug from inside, the signal, because they started hauling in the cable. After a moment Sonny's heavy boots appeared above the top barrel, then his soiled knees, then his waist. Paul fully expected he'd be carrying the Finch kid, his strong arms wrapped around the goner's chest, but then he saw his father's arms were empty. Everyone in the crowd muttered, taking note of this unexpected development. Paul started forward, crouched to duck under the tape once more, but his mother put a firm grip on his shoulder. Sonny, squinting in the glare of the construction lights, had a few words with Phil and Ben while he was unharnessing himself, then left the cage and bolted for the drink table, where he slugged down a cup of water and poured another. Then he looked up, scanned the crowd; there were hundreds of bodies lined along the yellow tape, but his eyes moved directly to Laura and Paul as if they alone were real and everyone else were made of stone or smoke. Paul waved and Laura gave a slight nod. Sonny quickly walked over to where they stood.

"What're you doing here?" He didn't smile when he said it. His jacket was caked with dirt, his hair muddied and soaked with sweat.

"I brought Paul a sweater," she said. "It was getting cold and—"

He waved away the rest of her answer. "Forget it. Just go on home. I won't be long."

"Is he dead?" Paul asked.

Sonny shook his head. "Just a little . . . a little stuck. I gotta grab a few things and then I'm gonna go back in and bring him on up."

"You're going back?" Paul asked. He felt the first real flutterings of fear in his heart, and blamed them on his mother. Before, without her, he'd been fine. Her presence here had somehow shifted the balance, turned his clock back a couple years.

Laura took the cup of water from Sonny's hand, passed it to Paul. "Go get your father some water."

Paul looked in the cup. It was then that he saw the rain, for the first time. Not rain, no. Just a delicate mist, almost imperceptible, barely upsetting the surface of his father's water.

"It's full," he said.

"Paul," she said sternly. "Go get your father some water."

Still he hesitated. He felt he owed it to his father to stay. He knew that once they were alone she'd really let him have it. Never mind that it wasn't any of her business. Never mind she didn't know a hole in the ground from a hole in her head. She'd done the thing Paul had always feared, made it down those slippery bleachers and onto the field of play—but instead of doing it to her son she'd done it to her husband.

Then Ben was at his side, breathing heavy. He held a flat black pillow with a thick cord attached.

"Got the inflatable," he said, handing it to Sonny. "If you're gonna go you gotta go now. Starting to sprinkle. We don't—"

"Listen, Ben," Laura said. "Why doesn't somebody else go? He already did his turn. It can't be that difficult, right? Just tell him to let somebody else go."

"I tried . . ." Ben said, and Sonny shot him a killer look. "And besides," Ben added quickly, "the old boy's gonna be fine. Piece of cake, picking cherries, a regular walk in the park. Just in and out, lickety-splickety."

Laura shook her head. "Everybody wants to be a hero now that the cameras are on." She turned to Sonny. "That's it, isn't it? If you let someone else go, you might not get your picture in the paper?"

"Jesus," Sonny said. "Come on, honey . . ." He reached for her hand but she snatched it back, turned half away from him.

Sonny looked helplessly at Ben. Ben shrugged.

"Who is it?" Laura asked.

"Who's what?"

"Who's in there, in the basement? What's his name?"

"Finch," Sonny said. He spit a wad of gray mucus at his feet. "Ian Finch."

Laura's jaw dropped. "Ian Finch? You've got to be kidding me. You're going through all this for Ian Finch?"

"You know him?" Ben asked.

She snorted. "Oh, I know him all right. He terrorized the ninth grade two years ago, on the rare occasions he wasn't suspended. I can't believe this is all about Ian Finch."

"Maybe you're right, babe," Sonny snapped. "Maybe we should just leave him there, huh? Seeing as he's such a lowlife."

Paul clenched his toes inside his shoes. It was all downhill from here; his father didn't get angry often, but once he'd passed that point, once he'd taken the big step down to her level of discourse, the bickering could go on for hours. Another minute and they'd be fighting about stuff that had happened ten years ago.

"Okay, kids," Ben said, stepping between them. "Somebody's going down to get this creep, and somebody's going right now. You guys want to have a spat, why don't you save it for later?"

"Ian Finch," Laura said, apparently still unable to process this bit of news. "You're sure? Ian Finch? Tall? Weasel-faced?"

"Can't speak to his looks, sweetie," Ben said. "Seeing he's got half a house on top of him."

Paul laughed. It was the wrong move; everyone, even Ben, looked at him like he'd just run off a string of the most vile obscenities.

"Sorry," he said.

"Listen," Sonny said to Laura. "I'm going now, no matter what you say. But I'd be happier about it if you'd say something nice to me. Could you do that? Could you say just one nice thing?"

"I don't think so," she said, still not meeting his gaze. The rain—and it was real rain now, Paul realized, not just mist—splashed against her shoulders. "I think you'll just have to wait."

Ben took hold of her forearm. "Laura," he said flatly. "Say something nice to Sonny."

She looked hard at Ben for several seconds, stared him down until she could stand it no longer. It was rare for Ben to put more than three serious words together, and she knew the reason for it. Paul knew she must, because even he knew. Ben would do anything for Sonny, lie for him, lay down his life for him. He'd even ask his wife to say something nice if he thought it might be the last words Sonny would ever hear from her.

She turned to Sonny. "You have great feet," she said.

He smiled. "Thanks. You too." He reached for her hand and this time she let him have it. He gave it a quick squeeze, tossed her a little wink as if they were in on some secret together. Then he and Ben walked back toward the house.

The rain was heavy now, blown diagonally by the rising winds. The onlookers, fair-weather voyeurs, piled into their cars but didn't leave, and Paul had a spooky notion in the warm glare of the headlights that his father and Ben and the whole rescue effort were now a drive-in movie.

"He did it before," Paul said, more to reassure himself than anyone else. "I saw him. It was easy."

Back in his harness, the inflatable pillow and a small pry ax secured in his belt, Sonny got down on his belly and shimmied into the hole. Ben looked down at Laura and Paul and gave the thumbs-up, smiled. The rain fell harder; the wind spun oak leaves around the yard.

"He'll be fine," Laura murmured.

"Lickety-splickety," Paul said, with renewed certainty. His father was, after all, his father, a man who always got what he wanted, a man whom fortune had smiled upon again and again. Bread cast upon the waters and all that; Sonny Tucker put out goodness and goodness came rolling back to him in every imaginable way. Even when plans went seemingly awry—the death of Captain Sam, for instance—his father always wound up on top. He had wanted to be a fireman, hadn't he? And Captain Sam's death, as grim as it might have been, had removed the obstacle, had handed Sonny the life he wanted: the dream job, the dream girl, a town that worshiped him . . .

The sound Paul heard then was the sound of a creaky stair. A big stair, to be sure, but otherwise a familiar sound, a safe sound, the sound of his mother descending the basement stairs with a basket of laundry. But the sound didn't stop. It got louder, more emphatic, rose to a screech. Instinctively, Paul pressed an ear to his shoulder. Then a cable snapped with a wicked crack, slapped the sky like a giant bullwhip, and the east wall of the house buckled inward. Ben and Phil leapt out of the cage, stumbled across the pile of debris and onto the lawn just as the east wall came down and flattened the dog kennel as if it were made of paper clips.

"Wait," Laura said softly. "Wait . . ." She took one step forward, then stopped as the west wall crumpled in on itself, sending a huge plume of concrete and roof shingle dust billowing into the air. Then everything was very still, the only sound the splatter of rain on the cars behind them. The dust settled in the silence. The hole Sonny had just gone down had disappeared under the house.

❧

Stupid, what he thought of. Stupid, Paul told himself when that first long moment had passed. How stupid to think suddenly of last summer, the sparkle of Beaver Pond in the afternoon sun, the dogs paddling madly in pursuit of frantic ducks, he and his father and mother standing on the shore, all of them sharing fat red grapes from a baggie and skimming smooth stones across the surface of the water, the water shimmering like a blade, the suck of the mud under his shoes, the burst of sweet juice in his mouth, the day so clear his father said if you looked west and squinted that maybe, just maybe, you could see all the way to—

Car doors slammed. Flashbulbs popped. Radios crackled. Little kids squealed. Everyone was shouting at once. Firefighters descended onto the rubble like an army of ants.

Laura sat down on the ground with a dull squish, then reached up for Paul's hand, gently pulled him down on the wet grass beside her.

"Are you tired, honey?" she asked softly. It was a bizarre question, and he could think of no suitable answer. "You want to lie down?" she asked. "You want to put your head in my lap and close your eyes for a little while?"

"He's probably okay," Paul said. He didn't know where this came from, didn't remember even thinking the words before he heard them come from his lips. Looking at the scene that lay before him, he knew this simple word *okay* was probably the biggest lie he'd ever told, ever would tell. His mother said nothing. Her hand in his was cool and wet and limp. Rain dripped from the ends of his hair and under his collar and trickled down his bare back like tiny, cold bugs.

Mrs. Vegley, who taught eighth-grade English at Casey Junior, approached them cautiously and offered Laura an umbrella.

"Want to sit in our car?" She forced a tight-lipped smile.

"No," Laura said. "We'll stay here." She set the umbrella in her lap.

His father was dead. Paul licked the rain from his lips. Well, then: his father. His father. His father was dead. His father. Was dead. He couldn't quite wrap his mind around this, not enough to feel any of the things he suspected he should be feeling at such a moment. All he could see was this: hundreds of firemen in uniform standing along the sidewalk outside the Presbyterian church, standing like statues in two long solemn lines as his father's casket is carried between them. Six men carry the coffin. Six men, including Ben Griffin (he does not look sad, only furious) and Black Phil, whose face betrays the memory of another funeral, cruelly similar to this one, fourteen years before. And there he is himself, following the coffin, strangled by his poorly knotted tie. His mother is beside him, wearing a navy blue dress because she does not own a black one and she refuses to buy a new outfit to wear to her husband's funeral as if it were an occasion worth shopping for. Then they are in an impossibly long car with darkened windows. The trip to the cemetery seems to take forever, because his mother is a wall of terrible, impenetrable silence. She has shed no tears but speaks only in whispers if she speaks at all. At Pine Grove Cemetery, his father is lowered into the ground, beside Captain Sam and Gramaw Tucker. Someone behind him is weeping—the wife of another fireman? a friend from childhood?—but Paul will not turn to look, to acknowledge.

This was as far as he could get. After this, there was home, and he could not go there yet, not even in his mind.

He sensed movement and looked up. Ben was marching down the lawn. He was carrying his helmet and averting his eyes so as to focus at a spot over their shoulders, looked for all the world like a military officer sent to deliver the terrible but expected news. When he reached the spot where they sat he slowly crouched down in the grass in front of them, took Laura's hand in both of his.

"We're bringing in heavy equipment," he said. "Gonna start digging again. We're going to find him, Laura."

"Of course," she said, nodding.

"And he's gonna be fine."

"Ben," she said gently, as if he were the widow, "he's dead."

Ben shook his head vehemently. "Uh-uh. Don't do that. You think that's what he'd want right now? The two of you up here giving up on him? You think that's what he'd—"

"He doesn't want anything anymore," Laura said quietly.

Paul started shaking. Part of it was the cold and the wet, but part of it was that, no matter how he tried, he just couldn't be like his mother. He was not yet old enough to have developed such brilliant defense mechanisms. She could shut out the pain by being blunt, by tossing out news of his father's death with the clarity and certainty of a seasoned anchorwoman. But Paul was starting to feel it—*he doesn't want anything anymore . . . the long lines of firemen, like statues*—and he shuddered in the downpour.

Ben took off his black jacket and set it around Paul's shoulders. "I wanna get you two someplace dry," he said. "I'll take you up to sit in the ambulance. It's warm in the back there. I'll bring you some coffee and—"

"I'm going to stay here," Laura announced. She did, indeed, look rooted to the lawn, and Paul imagined she could sit in this very spot through a thousand sunsets, that he might have to travel in the long black car alone.

"Laura," Ben said carefully, as if he were talking to a child. "Think about Paul now. Paul's cold. Paul doesn't need to be sitting out in this rain. But you and Paul should be together, so I want the two of you to come with me and sit in the ambulance. It's warm there. And it's dry, at least."

He took Laura's arm firmly, pulled her to her feet. As Paul stood he turned back to the pasture behind them. It was a haunted place now, a graveyard, headstone cars and trucks with headlights burning, hundreds of silent and still figures with long coats and tall umbrellas, standing in the rain.

"Come on," Ben said.

They sloshed up the lawn toward the ambulance.

• • •

In years that followed, Paul would have dreams of that night that were more vivid than the reality. Beginning the moment the house shuddered and fell, the world seemed covered in a murky film. In part it was the strange combination of bad weather and artificial light; the glare from the headlights and construction lights and TV cameras gave a surreal sparkle to the rain; it was like glitter falling, some grotesque celebration. But more than that it was the sense of it being over without it being over. Surely his father was dead. Surely he had died instantly, been crushed, flattened, shattered. But what if he hadn't?

As soon as you start thinking a guy's dead . . .

He sat in the back of the ambulance with his mother, an empty stretcher between them. It was dry but chilly; they both wore heavy black Casey Fire Department jackets. She continued in her state of unnatural calm, tranquilly sipping from her Styrofoam cup of coffee as if she were sitting at the kitchen table perusing the Sunday paper, her face absent of even a single crease of worry. He wanted to say something to her but he didn't have any idea what it would be. He'd seen this in movies—the numb, vacant, retard look—when the baby stopped breathing or the boyfriend got shot or the body bobbed to the surface of the family pool. Indeed, in most people, Paul knew, this strange calm would be masking unbearable sadness. Behind that blank look would churn a river of tears, straining at the dam of numbness. But, in his mother's case, Paul suspected this composure masked something else entirely. It wasn't grief. And it wasn't despair.

She was pissed.

❡

It was widely assumed in Casey, during those many years he lived in the station, that Sonny Tucker would eventually take his rightful place as Kittatinny County fire captain. Captain Sam's shoes would clearly be impossible to fill by anyone else, anyone less, and it gave the people of the town comfort to know that they would at no time in the foreseeable future want for a leader or be without a hero. Sonny was the heir and he knew it. Everyone knew it. Everyone, that is, but Captain Sam.

"We already have a firefighter in the family," he said to Sonny the fall of his senior year of high school. "Cover another corner, why don't you? You got a brain. Be a doctor. Be a lawyer. Be anything you want to be."

"I want to be a fireman," Sonny said.

"You've already been a fireman," Captain Sam said. "It's time to try something else."

According to Black Phil, Sonny was furious, stomped around the station for months with his jaw clenched, speaking only when work demanded it. The other firefighters, at first amused by the drama and discord, eventually set about trying to patch things up. Phil, himself a new father, even mustered the courage to speak to Sam about the situation. Perhaps father and son could somehow meet in the middle? Perhaps Sonny could take classes at the junior college, see if anything struck a chord in him, and remain at the station as a volunteer? But Sam refused to budge. He was, after all, the chief, and this was as usual not a suggestion but an order, firm and nonnegotiable. And so Sonny tried to cover another corner. After graduation he went off to Penn State and set about a business major. What did one do with a business major? He hadn't a clue, but it sounded as good or better than anything else: broad, practical, respectable. He went about his studies with care and disinterest, certain his father would eventually recognize his mistake, call him back to the place he belonged.

And then his world, or what he thought was his world, came to a screeching halt. It was Sonny himself who had told Paul this next part, how, in the spring of his sophomore year, he met the girl who would become his wife. She was a year older than he, an education major, the secretary of the junior class. She sat in the row in front of him in astronomy and he bumped into her at the library a half-dozen times in the space of a month until he realized that it was too coincidental to be a coincidence. This realization completely threw him.

"How come?" Paul had asked. He and Sonny had been sitting in the yard, throwing a soggy tennis ball to the dogs.

"She was popular," Sonny said. He toed the grass at his feet and smiled, remembering. "She had about a million friends. I was a complete doofus. I never said a word. All I did in class was stare out the window."

It was Sam, Sonny said, who shifted the balance. "Listen, dummy," he told Sonny over the telephone. "You can sit on your ass wondering why she likes you, or you can take advantage of your good fortune. It's your choice."

And so Sonny chose. On a rainy night the following week he followed the pretty girl out of the library and saw her standing at the bottom of the stone steps struggling with a giant yellow umbrella. He splashed down the stairs to her, offered his assistance. She handed him the umbrella, which he tried to force open and promptly broke. Embarrassed, he quickly pulled off his black CFD Volunteer windbreaker and held it out to her. She took it, draped it over her head.

"What do you think?" she asked, striking a pose in the rain. "Is it me?"

"It's you," he said.

For the next nine months they were inseparable, and Sonny gradually came to the conclusion that he had been ridiculously naive for the first twenty years of his life. He actually felt sorry for the person he used to be. What had that guy been thinking? Of course there was more to life than fighting fires. There were pecan pancakes at the Eat 'n Park at three A.M. with a woman who looked across the table at you with sleepy blue eyes and said "let's go home."

"But home was a dorm room," Paul said, winging the ball across the yard.

"Didn't matter," Sonny said. "Coulda been a hole in the ground for all I cared. Home was wherever *she* was."

Plans were made. After Laura's graduation she would stay in State College for a year until Sonny finished his degree, then they would move to Philadelphia, buy a small house, two chocolate Labs, and a reliable used car—forest green, probably a Honda. She would take a job teaching junior high math in the city's public school system; he would find a small but growing business and get in on the ground floor. They were both planners, prudent beyond their years; life was a by-the-book venture. They were serious, even earnest, people (or were they children? not yet people, not really?) who rarely did anything on a whim. They believed in order, in logic, in permanence, even in forever.

But they forgot about the world, as can happen when you are earnest and twenty-one and in love and building your future as if with stepping stones across a muddy yard. On a chilly February night, while Sonny and Laura were busy laying their stones in State College, a call came in to the Casey station that a house on Dogwood Avenue was on fire, and that a little boy was as yet unaccounted for.

ᛆ

The whir of drills and gunfire of jackhammers filled the silence in the ambulance. Laura had a watch on, but Paul kept his eyes from straying to it. He played little games with himself, pretending that only five minutes had passed when he knew almost certainly it had been twenty or thirty. Every so often one of the firemen would pass by the back of the ambulance and glance in, then quickly turn away, not wanting to have to mutter any words of false comfort. Soon, Paul knew, one of them would turn over the stone under which his father lay. There would be an instant of expectation—could he be alive?—that quickly turned to sorrow when the chest did not rise, the pulse not pound. He remembered a hamster born in the Habitrail in his third-grade classroom, how the students had rushed to peer through the clear plastic the morning after the birth, stood in a silent circle waiting for one tiny pink ball—separated from the pile of tiny pink balls—to move, how after a few confused moments Mrs. Burns had shooed them out to the playground and when they returned that one tiny pink ball was gone.

The rescue plan had been altered. The crew was still wary of bringing in bulldozers; although the house was now completely collapsed, if Sonny was by some miracle alive, trapped in a void somewhere below the rubble, too much movement above could threaten the integrity of whatever fragile space held him. But they weren't going to dig with small tools anymore, not with the pile they faced now. They worked instead with larger drills and small jackhammers, tools powerful enough to make quick progress in what was now double the size of the original mound of rubble, but not so powerful that they could compromise the safety of whatever—whoever—remained inside.

Paul tucked his knees to his chin and wrapped himself entirely inside the fire jacket as if it were a sleeping bag. *Dead, but maybe not.* He wished for his bed, wished the day backwards, wished Ian Finch never born. Someone he didn't know, someone whose face he could not conjure, had murdered his father, just as surely as if he'd put a knife in his chest. He shook the thought away. With half-open eyes he watched his mother; she had pulled her hair from its tight braid and was now in the process of carefully rebraiding it. The efficiency with which she did this always amazed him, how fast her hands worked, how she could construct something so perfect without even being able to see it . . . swish, swish, swish, tug . . . swish, swish, swish, tug.

Sometime past midnight he left the ambulance and stumbled across the lawn toward one of the silos, looking for a private place to empty his bladder. He shivered in the cold rain and felt, for the first time, that he might cry—not from grief, but from exhaustion. Who could have imagined the simple act of waiting could be so taxing? Every time he had created a scenario of his father's death in the past, the awful news had come as quickly as a blow to the head. He had never expected to have to *wait* for it, to have it be only half true. He didn't know how to act, how to think. What would his father do in such a situation? He wouldn't cry, wouldn't complain, wouldn't get angry. He would just fix things. That's what his father was: a fixer. He fixed kinked hoses and twisted cars and smoldering rooftops, fixed bikes and guitars and wounded birds. And when he wasn't fixing, he was waiting for something to fix. That's what he did all day at the station, sat around waiting for something to fix, planning how he would fix it when it broke. His father was always three steps ahead. His father was always prepared. So if his father was dead, then he, Paul, had to prepare, because in the wake of Sonny Tucker's death there would be many things to fix. He would have to fix his mother. He would have to fix the town. He would have to fix himself, because he would become the new fixer, of all things broken.

He zipped up, came out from behind the silo. A few yards away he saw someone tall and broad standing in the darkness, staring at the house. The figure took something from his pocket and popped it in his mouth, then caught sight of Paul and turned, his face now half illuminated by the construction lights. It was Black Phil.

"How you doing there, kiddo?" Phil asked, straining to smile. "You holdin' up?"

"Sure," Paul said. "What're you doing?"

"Just standing back," Phil said, crossing his arms over his chest. "Standing back and trying to take this whole thing in. Your granddaddy taught me this. Sometimes, he said, when things seem most hopeless you just gotta stand back and look at the thing from the wide view. That's what he called it: the wide view. Said sometimes things are a lot clearer that way."

"Is it working?"

"I don't know," Phil said. He turned back to the house, sighed. "Don't think so."

There had been a string of fire chiefs since his grandfather's death, and Paul knew none of them had measured up in the eyes of the town, knew that most people—probably even Black Phil himself—were just waiting until Sonny had accumulated enough years on the force to be named chief. And now what? The heir apparent was probably dead, and in all likelihood Phil would be held at least partly responsible. Despite the fact that it was really Sonny who had made the decision to conduct the rescue without outside assistance, on paper this was Phil's operation, and it had failed. This night would be his legacy.

"You scared?" Paul asked.

"Scared? Nah." Then, after a moment, his face shrouded in darkness, Phil said, "Yeah, I'm scared. Down to my damn bones. Old Captain Sam, he was sure a lot better at being in charge than I am. Sometimes I don't think I got the stomach for it. Just took my last Tums."

"Maybe they got some in the ambulance," Paul said.

Phil grinned wearily and put out his hand. Paul didn't really want to take it; he was way too old for hand holding, under any circumstances, and especially if his father was dead. But he didn't want to hurt Phil's feelings, so he took it; the hand was warm, sturdy, familiar, a hand that had passed him a thousand footballs, cooked him a thousand burgers, a hand that had tugged his drowsy father from sleep a thousand times. They started back toward the house.

"Hey, you keep that to yourself, eh? That bit about being scared."

"Sure."

He squeezed Paul's fingers. "We're gonna get our Sonny out. Sure as I'm standing here. Don't you stop believing that."

Some while later, Ben brought Mrs. Finch and Ian's sister, Kally, to sit in the ambulance with Paul and Laura. Paul moved over to sit beside his mother and regarded Ian Finch's family across the stretcher with curiosity and distrust. Mrs. Finch was frumpy and disheveled, her permed hair askew and black lines of mascara smeared down her cheeks. Paul knew Kally Finch from school. Well, he didn't actually know her, but he sure knew *of* her. She was a grade ahead of him, but earlier in the year playground rumors were swirling that she let boys suck her boobs in the janitor's closet. Looking at her, shivering in the seat across from him skinny as a weed, her hair a wet mass of black curls, Paul tried to imagine her pressed up against the huge gray sink in that small, square room, her shirt hiked up to her throat, a boy's face pressed greedily to her bare chest, but he couldn't quite do it. She looked tiny and helpless, dwarfed by the black jacket that Ben had draped gently across her shoulders before going back out to the house.

"Well, I should have known it," Mrs. Finch announced, as if they were already in the midst of conversation. "I should have known something like this was going to happen."

"Don't blame yourself," Laura said evenly.

"Oh, I'm not blaming myself," Mrs. Finch said. "That'd be like blaming myself for this rain. Trouble follows that boy wherever he goes, and you won't see me taking any credit for it. Turn right, trouble. Turn left, trouble. Turn around, trouble. . . ."

Kally Finch looked at the floor, traced her braces slowly with her tongue. Paul could tell she wanted her mother to shut up, and he couldn't help but feel a little sorry for her, even if she was a slut.

"God knows I tried," Mrs. Finch went on, "but soon as he could walk he was wandering away from me, stepping into the street or turning on the stovetop or just plain disappearing. One mess after another. And now here's this thing."

She said it as if *this thing* were just one of a string of equally messy messes Ian had gotten himself into. Laura continued to smile politely, but Paul could tell she had stopped listening, was focusing again on her hair, pulling her taut braid apart once more. Her kinked hair fell across her shoulders and back. Kally was rubbing intently at a white streak on her rubber jacket.

"If they ever come out of there we've got your husband to thank," Mrs. Finch said. "Don't think I won't be reminding Ian of that every chance I get. You need a job done, you just call him up and tell him to come on over and I'll see that he does. Wash your car, mow your lawn, clean your—"

"That's really not necessary," Laura said blandly.

"You've got a good boy here, don't you?" Mrs. Finch said, smiling at Paul.

Paul shifted in his seat. He wished Mrs. Finch were dead. She was garbage, an ugly old hag, a goner grown up. It should have been her in the basement instead of his father.

"I'm going for a coffee," she said, rolling to her feet. "Anyone else?"

Laura shook her head. Swish, swisl , swish, tug, and the braid took form again.

"She talks all the time," Kally said quietly when her mother was gone. "Not just now. She just talks and talks and talks."

"It's all right," Laura said.

"It drives Ian half crazy," Kally said. "One time he told me we should see if we could get her de-barked, said he heard you could do that with dogs and maybe it worked with people too."

Paul imagined Mrs. Finch's mouth moving a mile a minute with no sound coming out. He started to grin, but stopped, remembering.

"You're in the eighth grade, aren't you?" his mother asked Kally.

She nodded, tried to flatten her wild curls with the palms of her hands.

"You might have me for math next year," Laura said.

"I hope so," Kally said. "I really like your hair."

"Paul's in the seventh grade," Laura said, nodding deliberately at him, obviously trying to encourage him into the conversation. "I bet he has some of the same teachers you had last year."

"You're in Pony football, right?" Kally asked him.

"Yeah."

"You any good?"

He shrugged. "I'm the quarterback."

"Do you do any extracurricular activities?" Laura asked, and Paul had to stop himself from smirking. Yeah, he thought, she's all about extracurricular. The whore club, membership one, meets in the janitor's closet.

"I'm in band," Kally said. "But I'm not very good. Fourth-chair clarinet."

"Fourth chair's not bad," Laura said.

Kally shrugged. "There are only five clarinets."

"But you're sticking with it—that's the important thing," Laura said, in what Paul recognized as one of her teacherly catchall phrases, designed to build up the brokenhearted.

"I guess I'll go find my mother," Kally said.

"You can stay here," Laura said. "If you'd like. Stay here with us and keep warm."

No, Paul thought. Please, no, let her leave. The whole thing was horrible enough, but to have to share the horror with a girl like Kally Finch, as if they had anything in common, was more than he could stand.

"I better go find her," she said.

After she had gone Laura turned to Paul. "Be nice," she said. "She's as scared as we are, you know."

"She's not that scared," he said. "It's just her loser brother. It's not like Dad."

She thought about this. "I don't know," she said. "I don't know if it is or not. But we can't blame her for having a loser brother. She seems nice enough."

He had half a mind to tell her about the things he had heard, but decided this wasn't really the appropriate time. Instead, suddenly dumb with fatigue, he leaned into her, allowed his head to rest against her arm, listened to her breathe. For a while, his eyes were closed. He didn't sleep, not exactly, but he came close enough to sleep that he could almost forget where he was, briefly convince himself that the whole night might be a dream, that the belly of the ambulance was really the belly of his bed, that any minute now his mother would nudge him awake and it would be another Monday like any other. But not like any other, not really, because he would remember this dream and when they sat down to cornflakes in the kitchen he might say something to his father—*hey, Dad, try to not get killed today, okay?*—to let him know it mattered, mattered a lot, to have him around.

It was a little after four A.M. when a chorus of shouts came from the rescue workers. Paul lunged to his feet, still half dreaming, took one step and tripped over the stretcher and toppled to his knees. His mother was climbing out of the ambulance without looking back; he heard her feet smack on the wet grass and he crawled frantically after her, certain in his stupor that his father's body was at this moment being dragged from the rubble, torn and lifeless, and goddammit if he was going to let his mother have this to herself, protect him from this moment that was as much his as it was hers.

The rain had slowed to a light drizzle. About two hundred people, apparently also roused by the shouting, were stretching the yellow tape taut, craning their necks, jostling their neighbors aside for a better view. All the rescue workers were running around to the west side of the house, away from the hole they'd been digging in the rubble.

"Over here!" a voice shouted. A fireman, his face obscured in darkness, was waving his arms wildly.

Paul stumbled after his mother, his heart thudding madly.

"Here! They're here!"

A floodlight trembled, swung, steadied. Then, slowly, a shadow unfurled across the wide lawn.

Chapter Three

Eighty-five trillion feet above Paul's thudding heart, a satellite spun slowly, gathering and unscrambling images and returning them to earth. Face waxen in the glare of the TV lights, arms and chest covered in blood and grime, the unscrambled Sonny Tucker appeared more dead than alive, more ghost than man, to the hundreds of thousands who sat transfixed in the glow of television screens. Thanks to the miracles of twenty-four-hour live news and a sleepless and bored nation, men and women in living rooms across the country had watched the dramatic rescue of young Ian Finch unfold through the night and into the early morning. Hearts across America wrenched at the sight of wrinkled photos from *The Casey Weekly* archives: Sonny as a young boy suiting up alongside Captain Sam at the station house, Sonny as a teenager sitting in the driver's seat of Engine 14. And who could blame them for watching, for wrenching, for briefly setting aside their own stories for another story, a fairer story, a braver story, decidedly a *better* story? There on that box in front of the couch, playing out before them, were all the elements of legend and distraction—a dire situation, a courageous man, a helpless victim, a frightened wife, a loyal friend, an innocent child—a story both familiar and affirming in days when so little else is, constructed from the very myths we most long to believe. Viewers listened, enchanted, as the mayor of Casey (who owned the sporting goods store as his real job, and loved nothing more than the chance to act like a mayor) relayed with heavy heart and heavy voice the saga of the brave Tucker men. Townspeople Sonny hardly knew had taken their turns before the cameras during those tense hours of waiting, some with tears streaming down their cheeks, the crumbled house over their shoulders a testament to certain tragedy. They spoke of Sonny as if he were already dead, already ascended to the right hand of his father. And yes, of course, there was the matter of Ian Finch, the poor boy trapped inside. But information on Ian was scant, vague; much to the frustration of the various media, his only mention in the Casey High yearbook was on the brief "not pictured" list following the sophomore class photos. When asked about him, citizens of Casey narrowed their eyes and shook their heads. So the focus, nearly all the attention, swerved toward this Sonny *(Sonny! a man named Sonny!)*, who by all accounts had the makings of a star. By the time Monday afternoon papers hit the stands, he was no longer merely Sonny Tucker the fireman; he was Sonny Tucker the hero.

Standing beside his mother's car outside the front entrance of Casey Hospital, Paul was dazed from lack of sleep, bewildered by the brief slip of time between devastation and relief. Once again fortune had smiled on his father; he had risen from the dead, emerged from the Neidermeyer tomb shrouded in a legend even Captain Sam had never known the likes of. Paul half expected his father to be actually *glowing* when he passed through the sliding doors of the hospital and into the throng of reporters and well-wishers that awaited him on the sidewalks outside. But instead—when the doors moved aside to reveal the hero—the hero tucked his chin to his chest and bolted for the open door of the Honda, ducked and dodged the chattering crowd as if he were a felon being transferred from one prison to another. He hardly spoke on the short ride home, stared out the rain-streaked window at the passing town as if he had never seen it before, absently fingering the fresh stitches that zigzagged above his left eye. He's tired, Paul thought. But couldn't he at least look a little satisfied? Every minute or two Laura would pat his thigh and say "You okay?" and Sonny would seem startled at the interruption of his thoughts, then gulp, blink, and nod. When they got to the house he staggered into the bedroom without a word.

"Is he all right?" Paul asked his mother.

"Pretty banged up," she said. "But nothing broken. I told—"

She stopped herself, but he could see it on her lips, see her nearly speak the words she knew by heart: *I told you everything was going to be fine.* She was a wonder, he thought, and in the vulnerability of his exhaustion he suddenly disliked her intensely. It was a shocking and unpleasant feeling, made all the more unpleasant by the fact that it didn't immediately disappear, but instead soured like an aftertaste on his tongue. It was as if the night had never happened, as if she had never pronounced him dead, sitting there in the rain with her arrogant certainty. Had she really forgotten?

She took a pitcher of iced tea from the refrigerator and poured a glass. "Take this to him," she said. "Talk with him for a few minutes before he sleeps. It'll make him feel better."

He took the glass without a word and started down the hall. He was exhausted; his knees wobbled as he walked. But he would say something great to his father, something tender but funny. Maybe they would talk for a while and then he would casually stretch out in his mother's spot and they would sleep through the day side by side so that when he woke with a start, thinking he was still in the belly of the ambulance, he would feel his father breathing beside him and know at once that everything was okay.

At the open door of their bedroom Paul stopped cold, his breath caught at the edge of his throat. His father was curled on top of the yellow bedspread, buck naked, his pale skin purpled with deep bruises.

"Dad?"

Paul took a few tentative steps toward the bed. His father's hands were swollen pink and balled into fists against his closed eyes. His elbows and his knees touched; his feet were linked at the ankles. His mother had once shown Paul a foggy ultrasound image of him in her womb; but for his hair, his father bore all the marks of a fetus, something newer and nakeder than Paul had ever seen. He quietly set the glass on the bedside table, then unfurled the afghan that lay at the end of the bed and draped it carefully over his father.

"Sleep good," he whispered.

Then he turned out the light and left.

❧

Lying in bed, the house quiet, the shades pulled to block the noonday sun, Paul waited to fall asleep. He'd been awake for over thirty hours; his eyes were dry and itchy, his hands so clumsy with exhaustion he'd barely been able to brush his teeth. His father was dead to the world, and now his mother too; she'd fed the dogs, taken the phone off the hook, then flopped on the couch and passed out with her shoes still on.

But every time Paul closed his eyes he was bombarded with flickering images of the day and night before—nothing he could actually fix on, just blurred pictures with backward colors (green sky, blue grass, black house) and morphing faces: his father, his mother, Ben, Phil, the penciled face of Ian Finch. It made him seasick, the constant movement, and again and again he was forced to open his eyes just to keep himself from throwing up.

Finally he gave in. He opened the shades, sat on the floor and picked quietly at his guitar. He had bought the guitar the summer before at the church rummage sale for six dollars. He'd clearly overpaid; the guitar's neck was broken, and thus the instrument had remained intact only by the good graces of three weathered strings. But his father had helped him superglue it back together, and they'd replaced all the strings, so it was fit enough for Paul since he couldn't really play anyway. He'd wanted the guitar because Black Phil had once told him that, every six months or so, Captain Sam would borrow somebody's guitar at a picnic or a party and just start playing. Nobody knew how he did it. Nobody ever heard him practice. He'd just pick the thing up and somebody would name a song and Captain Sam would play it. Didn't matter what it was, didn't matter if it was a year old or a hundred years old. It had sounded like a lie to Paul, a big fat firehouse lie, but his father had confirmed it. *Of course it's true,* his father had said with a shrug. *The old man could do it all.*

• • •

That night, the night they found Sam dead in the bedroom closet on Dogwood Avenue, the town went mad. Grown men wept and drank all night and into the next day; stores closed; people spoke in whispers. Sonny had rushed home from State College, having every intention of returning to school once his father's affairs were in order. But—as the story went—the moment Sonny walked into the station, felt simultaneously the stunning absence of his father and the breathtaking sensation of home, he knew that he would never again leave that place, not for a job, not for a woman, not for anything. The choice, it seemed, had been made for him, all other options slammed shut in an instant like wind-blown doors. With no captain to order him otherwise, he left Casey for the final time—to Pittsburgh, for twelve weeks of training at the fire academy. It's in his blood, people in Casey said. It's fate. It's meant to be.

Laura disagreed. For one month, they ran up an enormous phone bill with nothing but arguments. Paul imagined his father's words: *I have to do this. It's who I am.* And then his mother, enraged: *It's not "who you are" . . . no one single thing can be "who you are."*

Finally, resigned to their separate ways, they broke up. Following her graduation she got that job in Philadelphia, the one she had planned on, and went about saving the disadvantaged youth of America one algebra problem at a time. And then (it was she herself who'd told this part of the story, to a roomful of people on their tenth anniversary, after she'd had several glasses of champagne) on a sticky morning in mid-June, the school year over and an empty summer stretched out before her like a drained lake bed, she woke with the absolute certainty that perhaps comes only once in a lifetime, the utter, untarnished certainty that she had made a terrible mistake. In an hour her car was packed and she was on the road to Casey. She had not spoken to Sonny in over a year; for all she knew he was married, or dead. But she was young; life was ripe and beckoning and she was out of her mind, totally unlike herself. Paul liked to imagine her blasting down the Pennsylvania Turnpike, a beautiful young girl with the face of his mother, the radio blaring, her hair wild in the wind. When she reached town four hours later she stopped the first person she saw and demanded directions to the fire department. When she arrived Sonny was in the driveway of the station, standing on the roof of the engine, spraying it with a heavy stream of water. He looked down at her dubiously, thinking that—surely—there was a reasonable explanation for her presence, that—surely, surely—she was not here . . . for him?

"Hey," she said, squinting into the sun above him.

"Hey," he said, gazing down.

Tumbling to the pavement, he lost his grip on the hose; it spun and flipped and sprayed water over both of them, but they hardly noticed.

❡

"Lieutenant Tucker has definitely left the building," Ben whispered, returning to the kitchen after a quick peek into the master bedroom.

It had been almost twenty-four hours since they'd arrived home, and Sonny had yet to stir from his curl under the afghan. It was Tuesday, mid-morning; Ben had come to the house hoping for breakfast and found himself smack in the middle of the circus that was taking over Willow Lane. It had taken him fifteen minutes to get the thirty feet from his pickup truck to the front door of the house. News vans lined the block, and the front lawn was crawling with reporters desperate to get word from someone—anyone—with the current status of Sonny Tucker. They had already exhausted the neighbors' limited knowledge, and were anxious for firsthand information.

"This is getting ridiculous," Laura said. "I didn't think it was even *possible* to sleep so long." She had been scrambling eggs for almost an hour, nonstop. What Ben and Paul were unable to eat was heaped on a white china platter beside the stove, turning dark and rubbery. But she kept at it, as if Sonny's return to the world depended on how many plates of eggs awaited him.

Ben gulped from his coffee mug. "He was up for near two days, Laura. He's pooped."

She dismissed this with a wave of her spatula. "He's been up for two days before. He's never—"

"He's never spent six hours underground," Ben interrupted. "Never hacked off a kid's foot before, right?"

Paul shuddered at this thought, set down his fork. He hadn't seen Ian Finch as he was carried across the Neidermeyer lawn, surrounded as he was by the paramedics, but he'd caught a brief glimpse of the trail of dark blood left between the house and the ambulance. Word had spread in seconds—*foot was pinned . . . he had to amputate*—and although no one had yet gotten the full story from either Sonny or Ian the scenario seemed clear: Sonny had lost the inflatable in the collapse, Ian had been near death, Sonny had been forced to use his ax to remove Ian's foot so he could drag him to safety in time to save his life. Paul thought of his father's fingers wrapped around the ax handle, the blade against flesh and bone, what it must have felt like, for both of them.

"He was so weird yesterday morning," Laura said. "You should have seen the face he had on. It was like he didn't know who we were."

"Hell of an ordeal," Ben said. He shook some salt onto his eggs. "I'm thinking he's probably a little freaked out. Shit, I'm a little freaked out. Aren't you?"

"Sonny doesn't get freaked out," Laura said. "He'll be fine. By tomorrow he'll be back to his old self."

The clamor of voices from the front yard made it difficult for Paul to believe that *any* of them would be back to their old selves, not tomorrow and not ever, and sitting there at the kitchen table he found himself vaguely exhilarated by this thought. In fact, everything about that morning—the fact that he wasn't at school, the buzz on the lawn, the phone off the hook, Ben at the table, even the heap of cold eggs on the counter—was nearly thrilling in its novelty. *Today is the first day of the rest of your life,* the principal of Casey Elementary had declared to a stage full of students at Paul's fifth-grade graduation, and Paul had spotted his parents in the audience, rolling their eyes at this simplistic sentiment. But today, for the first time ever, it seemed to almost make sense.

"Were they really making bombs?" Paul asked. "In the basement?"

"They were too stupid to make bombs," Ben said sourly. "We found some small explosives, crap left over from the Fourth, bunch of M-80's all wired together in some half-assed way."

"Casey terrorists," Laura said with a smirk, cracking an egg expertly on the side of the skillet. "Their weapon of mass destruction . . . *firecrackers.*"

Ben shook his head. "Listen, they'd a done some damage at the high school with that shit. Just because they're stupid doesn't mean they're harmless. More power in half-assed than you might think."

"How'd they blow up?" Paul asked.

Ben shrugged. "Who knows? I'm thinking Finch or one of the other idiots left a cigarette smoldering, set it off, blew out one of the supports. House was pretty shaky anyway. Wouldn't of—"

Sonny shuffled into the kitchen. He was wearing boxer shorts and a ripped undershirt and his face looked like it had been crushed by a steamroller. He shuffled to the refrigerator and opened it, then stood there staring at its contents for several seconds, apparently oblivious to anyone else in the room.

"Good sleep?" Ben asked cheerfully.

Sonny looked at him blankly, then at Laura, then at Paul. Paul smiled, briefly considered introducing himself to break the ice, break his father's dead gaze into a grin.

"What day is it?" A low rumble, hardly a voice.

"Tuesday," Laura said. "You slept through Monday."

He took the plastic jug of orange juice from the refrigerator, slowly unscrewed the cap, took one sip, frowned, slowly rescrewed the cap, then replaced the jug on the shelf.

"Want some breakfast, honey? I've got eggs here, if you want them."

"Good eats," Ben said, slapping his stomach. "Bet you got some appetite, huh?"

Sonny shook his head slowly. "Not really. Not so much." His voice was flat and distant, as if he were mumbling in his sleep; he appeared slightly perplexed by his own words.

"You're famous," Paul said suddenly, hoping this would startle him back into himself. "There're a whole bunch of people outside who want to talk to you."

Sonny looked at him, cocked his head to the side. Had this been a comic strip, Paul thought, the phrase *does not compute* would surely have appeared in a bubble over his father's head. "Outside? Outside where?"

"In the yard," Laura said. She handed Sonny a plate of eggs which he looked at briefly and then set on the counter. "Don't worry about them. Just some reporters. You don't have to talk to them until you're ready."

But Sonny was already headed toward the front door. Apparently, Paul thought, his father had forgotten he was in his underwear. Or maybe he just didn't care. He swung open the door, looked puzzled, then intrigued, then slightly pleased. People were shouting. The popping of flashbulbs glimmered in his eyes.

"Mornin'," Sonny said, then yawned widely and scratched his bare stomach through the gaping hole in his undershirt.

"Clothes!" Laura shouted at Paul. "Go!"

But Ben had already taken hold of Sonny's shoulders and gently eased him back from the door. He kicked it closed and smiled at Sonny. "I'm thinking you're a little loopy there, old boy."

"Maybe so," Sonny answered airily. He considered something for a moment, then said: "What day is it?"

Ben laughed. "How's your head? You wanna sit? Wanna go back to bed?"

"You want some breakfast?" Laura asked.

"Wanna watch TV?" Paul asked, and now it was his own voice that was nearly unrecognizable, embarrassingly squeaky. "We could watch a movie or something."

Sonny touched the stitches on his forehead, swallowed with effort. "What're they doing out there? What do they want?"

"They want you," Ben said. He flipped a corner of the tear in Sonny's undershirt. "Not exactly dressed for the occasion."

"You're a hero," Paul said. "You're all over the news. Everybody knows what you did." Snap out of it, he wanted to add. Stop looking like you have the stomach flu. Stop looking like a retard. Stop looking like one-hundred-and-six-year-old Mr. O'Mally, who gets his picture in the paper every year on his birthday, every time with that same baffled expression on his face, gazing idiotically at his chocolate cake.

"What I did?" Sonny echoed, mystified. "What'd I do?"

Ben grinned, shook his head. "Just a little frontline surgery, buddy. Took off the kid's foot and dragged him outa the house. That's all. Coming back to you now?"

Sonny was silent. He rested his eyes momentarily, then opened them again with what looked to Paul like a hint of comprehension. "Where's Ian?"

"Hospital," Ben said. "In Hershey. But our little Nazi's doing just fine. You saved his life, Sonny. That's why all those folks want a piece of you."

"Oh, stop it," Laura said. She stepped forward and took hold of Sonny's fingers, and he looked down at her hand as if it were a foreign object that might cause him harm. "Nobody's getting a piece of you right now but me and Paul," she said gently. "We're going to have some quiet time, just the three of us, till you get yourself together. Then you can talk to them if you want."

Sonny bit his lower lip until it turned white. "I wanna see Ian."

"All right," she said. "After you feel a little stronger."

He shook his head angrily. "No. No. I want to see Ian *now*." And then, to Paul's utter disbelief, his father's eyes bubbled over with tears and just like that he was crying—bawling, really—standing there in his underwear in the middle of the living room. His lips trembled uncontrollably and his knees gave way and then he was sitting cross-legged on the carpet, his head in his hands, his shoulders shaking, sobbing in violent, ghastly spasms. Paul had seen his father cry only once, a couple years before when their dog Ginger was put to sleep, and then it was just sniffles and little tears in the corners of his eyes as they left the vet's office. It was nothing like this, and all he could do was stand there and stare at this *thing* on the floor, his mouth agape.

"Oh, Sonny . . ." Laura dropped to her knees, wrapped her arms around his head and held him tightly to her chest. "Everything's okay. We'll go see Ian right now, if that's what you want. Whatever you want, honey, that's what we'll do."

He didn't respond, and she looked up at Paul and Ben uneasily. Now she was shaking too, and starting to cry a tiny bit herself in a bewildered sort of way. Paul felt the lump of tears in his own throat; suddenly the day didn't seem so thrilling anymore.

"Honey, oh, honey . . ." his mother said softly, rocking his father back and forth as if he'd just tumbled off his tricycle. "Honey, it's okay. You're all right, you're okay . . ."

Paul felt Ben's thick fingers circle his bicep, a gentle tug and then a more urgent one. He allowed himself to be steered out of the living room and led down the hall to his bedroom. Ben quietly closed the door, then slumped back against it, let out a long sigh.

"I'm thinking they need some alone time," Ben said softly. "Why don't you and me just hang out here for a few?"

Paul sat down on his bed. His palms were pooled with sweat, and he rubbed them hard against the quilt beside his thighs. "What's wrong with him? Is he sick or something?"

Ben sat down on the floor in the middle of the room, picked up Paul's guitar and absently plucked a few strings. "He ain't sick," he said. "Your dad's been through a lot, sport. Had a big scare down there, and this happens to guys sometimes. Even to brave guys like Sonny. It's happened to me a time or two, I can tell you that."

"He's crying bad," Paul said. Like a baby, he wanted to add, but he decided it was too cruel to say. He picked at a hangnail on his pinkie, worrying and peeling until dots of blood appeared along the soft flesh of his fingertip. What did he know of what his father was feeling? Who was he to judge? "He's never been like that before," he finally added. "All . . . crazy and stuff."

Ben nodded thoughtfully. "Hard to see your old man shook up, huh? I tell you what . . . you'll never forget it." He set the guitar across his lap and stretched his long legs out in front of him. "I remember my dad— he was a cop, you know—he came home one day and went out to the backyard and sat down at our picnic table and started crying like a baby. My mom wasn't home and I didn't know what the hell to do, so I just kept going out there with stuff and giving it to him. I took him his Winstons and a can of pop and a box of crackers and some baseball cards and a couple toy trucks until finally there's this whole circle of stuff on the table meant to cheer him up and he's still sitting there bawling like the world's coming to an end."

"What was wrong with him?"

Ben shook his head. "Who knows? After a while I come out with my Duncan yo-yo and he's sitting there right as rain eating the Triscuits like nothing ever happened. It just happens to guys sometimes, a little crack in the old foundation."

Okay, Paul thought. It made sense, didn't it? Just a crack in the old foundation, like when he'd peed in his bed. He was pretty much fine after that, right? A little crack, but it wasn't like he was broken forever. He looked up at Ben. "So you think he'll be okay? Really?"

"Really," Ben said.

The Wickeds were up against the wall, again; in this month's installment, bounty hunter Roy Wicked had to transport the decapitated head of a vampire halfway across the country, to the Creek of Eternity in rural Kentucky, before the head woke up and realized what was happening. Paul's eyes scanned quickly from frame to frame; he always had to keep one hand covering the next page to prevent himself from skimming ahead. He could lose himself completely in *The Wickeds*, which was especially important on this afternoon. The adventures of Roy Wicked were more familiar, more comforting, than the state of his father.

Ben had taken him to Dewey's, bought him a couple Butterfingers and half a dozen comic books, which Paul devoured in his room while his father began the process of sealing the crack in the old foundation. From what Paul could tell, this process included a full hour to shower and another hour to dress. It was mid-afternoon before they were on the road to Hershey. The trees that lined the highway were dark orange and brown; the brilliant peak of reds and yellows had passed the week before, and only the remnants of color remained. Sonny, clean but quiet, carefully traced the scratches on his hands and wrists, as if following a line on a map from home to someplace he'd never been. Laura drove, filled the silence with small talk and innocuous questions that Sonny responded to with a shake or nod of the head. Finally, desperate for something that resembled actual conversation, she persuaded Paul to tell her the whole plot of *The Wickeds'* most recent issue, then spent the remainder of the trip explaining to him why none of it made any sense.

"Why doesn't he just put the head in a bag and take a plane?" she asked. "Why does he have to hitchhike?"

"It's a story, Mom," Paul groaned. "Just a *story.*"

Sonny's cuts and bruises had been treated at Casey Hospital, which really wasn't so much a hospital as a twenty-four-hour clinic. It was fine for a broken nose, a gash on the head, minor burns, a shoulder popped from the socket. But if you really needed a hospital—if you had a nameable disease, or needed heart surgery, or your foot had been hacked off with a pry ax—you made the hour drive (or in Ian's case, the twenty-minute airlift) to Hershey Medical Center.

The lobby at HMC was crowded with reporters, but Sonny plowed a path through the middle of the melee and the three of them silently rode the elevator up to ICU, which was closed to all media. Paul thought his father's skin looked yellow—not happy yellow like sunshine and bananas, but ugly yellow like piss or homemade applesauce—in the bright hall as he made his way to Ian's room, a full stride ahead of Paul and Laura. Without a word or look back to them he pushed open the door of the ICU unit and disappeared.

"Well, then," Laura said. "I guess that's that."

What had she expected? Paul thought. That they would all go in and say hello to Ian, stand around the bed cooing and tending like family? He hated Ian Finch, hated him as much as it was possible to hate someone who had no face and no voice, only a name and a bewildering effect on his father. Paul leaned against the wall and listened to the squeak of the wheels of the medication cart as it made its rounds from room to room. He had been here only once before, in second grade, to visit a classmate who'd been shot in the shoulder while deer hunting with his grandfather. The whole class had come by bus to visit. They sang "Waltzing Matilda" to the wounded boy, then took turns fooling with the bed controls.

His mother was sitting on the floor with her legs tucked under her, reading the hospital newsletter without a shred of interest. About every ninety seconds she looked at her watch. Once she even tapped it and held it to her ear. Finally, after more than a half hour had passed, she folded the newsletter and put it in her purse, stood up.

"You hungry?"

"Nah," he said.

"How about a Coke? You want a Coke? Let's have a Coke."

They left word with a nurse that they'd be in the snack bar. The snack bar was small and crowded, smelled of glazed doughnuts, strong coffee, and lemon Lysol. No sooner had they sat down with their drinks at the only available table when a half-dozen reporters circled them.

"Where's Sonny?"

It was a motley crew: familiar Ed Baines from *The Casey Weekly*, the tiny woman from the Harrisburg station, a fat man with dark ovals of sweat under his arms, three other eager faces, pens poised.

"He's with the Finch boy," Laura said.

"What're they talking about?" This from Ed Baines, the only truly local newsman. Thirty years putting out a paper that consisted mostly of wedding announcements, high school sports scores, and farm show results. Now, Paul thought, for the first time in ages he was getting a story people would actually read.

Laura set down her Coke. "I wouldn't know," she said deliberately. "Since I'm sitting here."

"Hey, Paul," the sweaty man said. It was strange that someone he didn't know knew his name, and he felt a surge of significance. "How's it feel to have a hero for a dad?"

Paul shrugged. "Feels good, I guess."

"Were you scared when he was trapped down there?"

Again he shrugged. He wished he could say something smart, something clever, but nothing leapt to mind. "Not really. I knew he'd be okay."

He looked at his mother and she smiled at him gently. "Give us some space," she said, not even looking up. "Okay?"

They wandered off, in search of Sonny, Paul supposed. Laura reached forward and rubbed something off his chin with her thumb.

"You did well," she said.

He shrugged, sucked down the last of his Coke, stifled a small burp. "Is Dad okay?"

"He will be," she said. "He's just a little frazzled right now. I think maybe talking to Ian will make him feel better."

Ian, Paul thought. Ian, Ian, Ian. Just *thinking* the name produced an unpleasant taste, jammed somewhere up in his sinuses. Why would talking to a loser like Ian Finch make his father feel better? Paul scratched grooves in his Styrofoam cup, fighting twinges of jealousy.

"Think Ian Finch is really a Nazi?" he asked.

Laura shook her head. "I don't know. Probably not."

"Think they were really gonna blow up the high school?"

"Paul," she said sternly. "No one is going to blow up the high school. Not Ian Finch, and not any of his goner friends. I don't want you worrying about things like that."

Paul glanced around the snack bar. The reporters had disappeared, but most of the tables were occupied. A stooped old man nibbled at some french fries. A nurse was writing on a paper napkin. Two young girls were coloring a place mat with bright crayons while their mother stared out the window, holding a coffee cup against her cheek as if she were cold, or had a toothache. Paul turned back to his mother.

"What do you think they're talking about up there?"

Laura set down her cup and pursed her lips. "You're as bad as those reporters," she said. "How would I know what they're talking about? It's between them, right?"

Paul fell silent again, watched the two little girls draw purple faces with jump-rope smiles and circle eyes. Were they waiting for their father too? Was he sick, injured, in surgery? Was he dead already?

"What's taking so—" Paul started.

"Let's go, then," Laura interrupted, snatching her purse. "We should be upstairs when he's ready to leave. We can warn him that the vultures are circling."

But they were too late. When they turned the corner to the elevators, Sonny was standing in the middle of the hallway surrounded by two dozen reporters and photographers. Paul experienced a moment of mortified panic, horrified by the thought that his father might start bawling again, this time in front of the whole world. But when he craned his neck to see over the reporters it was clear to him that his real father had returned, had replaced the frightened, dazed man who had woken up in their house just hours before. His shoulders were square, his chest full, his smile broad.

"I had a hell of a sleep, I'll tell you that," he was saying. "Probably best night's sleep I've had in my life."

"How's Ian doing?"

"Ian's all right," Sonny said. Then he lowered his voice. "He's lost a foot of course, and that's a trauma, a sad thing for anybody and certainly for a young man. But otherwise his health is good, and his spirits are high."

"How's it feel to be a hero, Sonny?" Ed Baines shouted gleefully.

Sonny considered. He brushed a wayward blond hair from his forehead, wiped a phantom spot of saliva from the corner of his mouth. "There are lots of heroes today," he finally said. "Ian's one of 'em—he never gave up, not for one minute. And there're about a hundred firemen and police officers who deserve your thanks as well. We were all doing our jobs; I just happened to be the guy little enough to squeeze through that hole."

Now he looked over their heads, caught sight of Laura and Paul. "And now I think it's time for me to go home with my family. I've got two days' worth of eating to do."

For the return trip, it was Sonny who drove. He rolled down the windows, turned up the radio, and pushed eighty on the turnpike. Paul sat in the backseat feeling his breathing return to normal, maybe, he realized, for the first time in forty-eight hours. He'd almost forgotten what it was to breathe, to really breathe, to have breath rise without thought or concern.

"Slow down, sweetie," Laura said as they zipped past an eighteen-wheeler, but she was smiling when she said it. She had let her hair down and it whipped in the wind. One hand rested on Sonny's knee; the other gripped the passenger-side door.

"No time, no time!" Sonny shouted against the howl of the wind. "Who wants to slow down? Paul? You wanna slow down?"

"No!" Paul shouted.

They went home—*home,* it really was, now, still, again—and took the phone off the hook, gobbled up a pot roast one of the neighbors had dropped off. After dark, in front of the TV, Paul looked up from his spot on the floor and saw his parents wrapped together on the couch, sleepy and comforted. Only then did he allow himself to close his eyes.

Sonny was scheduled to be interviewed on *Good Morning America* the following morning. The crew—two cameramen and a young reporter—arrived at the house at six A.M. to set up their makeshift studio in the living room. By seven, nearly every resident of Willow Lane was gathered on the Tucker lawn, some in their bathrobes and slippers, battling the shrubbery and each other to get a good peek through the front windows. They were making such a racket that one of the cameramen finally had to go out and tell them to settle down.

Paul was astonished by the difference a day had made in his father. It was as if after beginning the day before about three full notches *below* his normal self (the crying, the dead eyes, the twitchy lips) he had at some point rocketed blindly past this normal self and was now three full notches *above* it. He was practically dancing around the living room prior to the live telecast, so light on his feet as he flitted from person to person that Paul doubted he'd be able to sit still on the couch for four seconds, much less for the four minutes they'd allotted his segment.

"I look okay?" he asked Paul, reappearing from the bathroom for the third time in twenty minutes. "My tie straight?"

"You look fine," Paul said.

"You sure? Hair okay?" He thrust aside the offending bangs. "I shoulda got it cut yesterday, huh?"

"It's *fine*, Dad. Jeez."

"Sixty seconds!" one of the cameramen shouted, and Paul moved to the spot behind the camera, where his mother stood, a faint smile of bemusement on her lips.

"He's kinda hyper," Paul said.

She shook her head. "You'd think he was getting married."

The cameraman overheard and turned to them with a knowing grin. "With TV virgins, you got your pukers and you got your dancers. Take my word . . . you got the better of the two."

"I'll try to keep that in mind," Laura said.

"We're on in five . . . four . . . three . . . two . . ." The cameraman pointed at the reporter. The reporter was a young man, no older than Sonny, with the narrow sculpted face and the smooth intonation of obvious network material.

"How many real live heroes do we have?" he asked the camera, pausing a beat after the question just long enough for viewers to arrive at the correct answer. "How many of us would risk our lives to save another? Three nights ago, in the small town of Casey, Pennsylvania, veteran firefighter Sonny Tucker did just that. Many of you watched as Lieutenant Tucker crawled down a tiny hole and into the basement of a collapsed farmhouse to rescue Ian Finch, the high school student trapped inside. More than five hours later both men came out alive, thanks to quick thinking and unimaginable courage on the part of one hometown fireman. I'm here today with Sonny Tucker. Sonny, first, tell us how you're holding up."

"I'm great!" Sonny shouted. His hands were jumping all over his lap. "Fantastic! Never better!" For a second Paul thought he was going to try to give the guy a high five or something, and he felt briefly and intensely mortified. What had become of his father, the man who accepted compliments with a sheepish smile, the man who shied from adoration?

"What was it like down there under the house?" the reporter asked.

"Dark," Sonny said, and everyone in the room snickered. Paul had already heard his father use this line three times just this morning; each time the laugh was briefer. Sonny seemed to sense his joke was getting old, and he quickly went on. "Ian Finch was a trooper," he said. "He spent a lot more time in there than I did."

"You thought at first, once you reached him, that the rescue effort was going to move quickly."

"We did," Sonny said soberly. "But you learn to expect the unexpected. I'm just glad I was in there with him when the whole thing came down."

The reporter put on his most earnest expression. "This was a large rescue for such a small department. Had you ever faced anything of this magnitude before?"

"I've been a fireman my whole life," Sonny said. "We're trained to face any kind of situation that may arise."

The reporter nodded thoughtfully. "But had you ever faced something like this?"

"Not exactly like this, no," Sonny said. He shifted on the couch. "But I've been trained in extrication techniques. We knew what we were doing."

"You had to make a difficult decision down there, didn't you, the decision to amputate Ian Finch's left foot, which was pinned to the floor, making any escape attempt virtually impossible. It was a call that probably saved his life, but it still must have been—"

"Necessary," Sonny interrupted. "Sometimes you have to . . ." He searched for more words, came up empty. "Well, it was necessary."

"Why don't we bring your family over?" the reporter said, not wanting to burden morning TV viewers with any unnecessarily grisly detail. This had been planned, and Laura and Paul marched into the picture in their Sunday best, sat down on the couch on either side of Sonny. Paul kept staring at the red dot of light above the lens, thinking about all the people on the other side of that little light. It wasn't even the strangers who bothered him; all he could think about was all the kids in his class sitting out there eating cereal in front of their TVs, hoping he would say something stupid that they could give him crap about when he got to school. It was becoming increasingly apparent to him, judging from the hot lump in his stomach, that he was a puker and not a dancer.

"We're very proud of him," Laura said in answer to the reporter.

"We knew he would be fine, but of course we're very proud of what he did."

The reporter turned to Paul with a chummy wink. "And I guess young Paul Tucker knows the question on everyone's mind this morning, don't you, Paul?"

A question? How cruel was this? He'd been told he'd only have to smile and look proud, nod in agreement with whatever his parents said. And now: *the question on everyone's mind.* His brain went numb and he shook his head in slow motion, suddenly certain he had snot sliding out his left nostril.

The reporter smiled winningly. "Gonna be a firefighter like your dad?"

"Oh," Paul said, relieved. "That." He looked at his father for help, and Sonny smiled.

"We already got one fireman in the family," he said, patting Paul's knee. "This kid's gonna go off and cover another corner."

The following day Ian Finch was released from Hershey Medical Center. Before he even got the chance to go home, he was driven to the Tucker house in the back of the Channel 8 news van, rolled jerkily down the metal ramp in his wheelchair and right up to Sonny on the front stoop, while dozens of cameras rolled and clicked away for the first on-air reunion of hero and victim.

Laura and Paul were standing on the front steps with Sonny. This was the first time Paul had seen Ian in person. His left leg was propped up in the wheelchair, a roll of gauze jutting off the end of his shin where his ankle and foot should have been. Paul let his eyes fall on it for a moment and then politely looked away. Sonny made introductions all around and Paul shook Ian's bruised right hand. It was cool, like his mother's hands. Ian's face was narrow and light skinned, darkened by a smattering of coarse hair down his jawline and under his chin. He looked more eighteen than sixteen, his lips set in a lazy but permanent sneer. He was tall and gangly but his arms were tightly muscled; you could imagine that, if things had been different for him, he might be on the Casey High basketball team. He had a mess of black hair that appeared longer than it actually was, simply because it was so unkempt. It fell over his eyes and he was constantly tossing his head to the right so he could see.

"This way!" a reporter shouted. "Big smiles!" Sonny put his hand on Ian's shoulder and they all grinned on cue.

"Jesus," Ian muttered under his breath. He yawned.

"Why don't we go inside?" Laura said. "We'll have a glass of iced tea and then you can get home, Ian. I'm sure your family's anxious to see you."

"Yeah," Ian said. "I'm sure they got a big party planned."

"Grab the chair, Paul," Sonny said cheerfully. "Let's get him up this step."

Paul leaned forward to take the right side of the wheelchair and collided with the pungent smell of stale cigarettes and body odor that emanated from Ian's midsection. Instinctively he jerked his head away. What, he thought, there were no showers at Hershey Medical Center? No little soaps like they had even at the cheapest hotels? No deodorant deliveries from the gift shop? Ian glanced down at him.

"What?" Ian asked.

"What what?"

"I don't bite," Ian whispered. "Not boys, at least."

Paul took hold of the arm of the chair and he and Sonny lifted Ian into the house, then closed the door on the reporters. Ian wheeled himself into the middle of the living room and looked around with vague interest. Then he took a pack of cigarettes from his shirt pocket, tapped one out and lit it with a silver Zippo lighter. Paul waited for one of his parents to protest; usually they didn't let people smoke in the house—his mother was always making Ben stand in the backyard if he wanted a cigarette, even in the depths of winter. But now his father was silent. And his mother—though she shot a brief glare at the wafting smoke—didn't say anything either. Instead she went off for the tea.

"How you feeling?" Sonny asked. "You look better."

"You too," Ian said. He took a long drag off his cigarette. His hands, like Sonny's, were swollen purple and butchered with deep scratches.

Sonny poured the peppermints from the candy dish onto the coffee table and handed the dish to Ian. "Glad to be out of the hospital?"

Ian scoffed. "Tell you what—I'm never shittin' in a bedpan again."

Paul sat down on the edge of the couch with his hands between his knees, trying to think of something to say. Ian glanced at him perfunctorily, smoke drooling lazily from his lips.

"You know my sister? She goes to your school."

"She's a grade ahead of me," Paul said.

He smirked. "That mean you can't know her? 'Fraid of those eighth-grade pussies, huh?"

"Ian . . ." Sonny said uneasily, setting his hand on the arm of the wheelchair.

"Aw, I'm just messin' with the kid," Ian said. "Kid knows that." He winked at Paul. "You know that. Right?"

"Sure," Paul said. Asshole, he wanted to add. Shit-for-brains. Stink bomb. Footless freak.

Laura came back in the room with a tray full of sweaty glasses of tea. She handed one carefully to Ian, one to Sonny and Paul, and then stood there smiling expectantly.

"Here we are," she said.

"And here's to Sonny," Ian said abruptly and much louder than necessary, raising his glass, the cigarette dangling precariously from his lips. "Only guy crazy enough to save my sorry ass."

They laughed, the two of them, just a little at first. Then they looked at each other laughing and they laughed even harder, broadly, recklessly. Ian had a cackly kind of laugh that reminded Paul of the ancient checkout lady at the Eagle grocery who was always cracking up at her own stale jokes. He glanced at his mother; she looked like she was watching a small animal being dissected.

"So, Ian," Laura said tightly, when their hysterics had somewhat subsided. "Will you be going back to school soon?"

He raised his eyebrows. "Why? You miss me?" Again he laughed, just a single sharp cackle this time. An ash dropped off his cigarette and fell to the carpet, and Laura scowled at it intently, as if she could remove it by sheer will alone.

Ian turned to Sonny. "Hey, guess who called me this morning? Forget it, you won't guess. Some big-shot producer at Fox TV. They're all hot to make a movie about us. A movie, man, about you and me. They already got some guy working on the script. You believe that shit?"

Sonny frowned. "How come I haven't heard anything about it?"

Ian squashed out his cigarette in the candy dish. "This guy, Gordon something, said he's gonna call you later on today. I'm telling you they're hot to go, man. He says to me, 'Ian, you guys are hot right now.'"

"A movie?" Laura asked skeptically. "You're sure? An actual movie?"

"Wow . . ." Paul said. He couldn't help it. "Hey, Dad, maybe somebody cool'll play you. Like Harrison Ford or somebody."

"You dimmo," Ian said. "Harrison Ford's like sixty or something. You want some fat old geezer playing your dad?"

"Am I gonna be in it?" Paul asked, undeterred. "Did they say?"

Ian shrugged. "Me and Sonny are the stars, that's all I know. Most of it's about him and me, down in the dungeon. They said—"

"But they don't know anything," Sonny interrupted. "How are they supposed to write about stuff they don't even know?"

"That's why they need us, genius," Ian said. "We tell 'em." He shook another cigarette from his pack. "Just like we've told everybody else."

That night Ben Griffin arrived at the house with a six-pack of beer and the news that the mayor had decided to hold a parade on Main Street the following Saturday for everyone involved in the rescue. All the firefighters, all the police officers, the whole county was invited.

"Like for astronauts," he said, plucking a beer from the pack before handing it off to Sonny. "Except no astronauts. And probably no ticker tape."

"Makes sense," Sonny called on his way to the kitchen to put the beer away. "Since there's no building taller than two stories downtown."

Ben grinned at Paul, flopped down beside him on the couch. "That'd kinda defeat the purpose of it, huh? Everybody could just stand along the street and hand us ticker tape, I guess."

Laura rolled her eyes. "A parade," she said. She was sitting at the dining room table, marking student exams with a thick green pen. "Well now they've really thought of everything, haven't they?"

"Don't you think we deserve a parade?" Ben asked, taking a swallow from his bottle.

She smirked, nodded at the stack of papers before her. "Nobody's ever thrown me a parade for doing *my* job."

"Well you never rescued anybody, now did you?" Ben asked, winking at Paul, not understanding the trap he was setting for himself, not understanding that the conversation was about to take an ugly turn. Paul knew—didn't Ben too?—that his mother believed teaching was the most crucial responsibility anyone could undertake, that what she did was fifty times harder and a hundred times more important than pointing a hose at a flame.

"I rescue more kids in a week than you will in your whole life," she said flatly, setting down her pen, preparing for battle.

"Hey, no offense . . ." Ben held up his beer in a gesture of surrender. "Didn't mean—"

"I'd quit while you're ahead," Sonny said, returning to the room. He set his hands gently on Laura's shoulders, whether to comfort or restrain her Paul wasn't certain. She looked up at him, her grimace easing into a smile at his touch. It was practically magic, Paul thought, how sometimes they could drain the bad out of each other in the space of a breath.

"We're gonna be in a movie," Paul told Ben.

"Oh yeah?"

"Yeah, me and Dad and Mom and you and everybody. They're making a TV movie about all of us."

"Now hold on," Laura said. "It's not a sure thing yet. It's still in the planning stages."

"It's pretty sure, though," Sonny said. "I'm meeting some people tomorrow to talk it over. They're taking Ian and me out to lunch."

Ben snorted, propped his feet on the coffee table. "Where at? The truck stop?"

"They're flying in to talk to us," Sonny said. "Two of 'em. Remember that movie we watched with the guys a few months back, the one about the avalanche in Colorado? These are the guys who made that."

Ben took a gulp from his beer. "That the one where they all ate each other?"

"That was *Alive*," Paul said. "That wasn't even Americans. It was soccer players."

"Point is," Sonny said, "they know what they're doing."

"Well," Ben said. "I guess that's pretty cool. I'd just watch out for those Hollywood people if I was you. Bunch of scammers, you know. Don't go signin' your name to anything before—"

"What do you know about Hollywood people?" Sonny asked.

"Well shit," Ben said. "We've all heard stories, right? Some smooth-talkin' big shot fills everybody's heads with fame and fortune, then takes whatever they want and leaves the little guy in the dirt."

"Yeah, but I'm not the little guy here," Sonny said, tightening his grip on Laura's shoulders.

"He's right, though, honey," Laura said, wiggling loose from him. "You should probably talk to a lawyer, someone who knows about these kinds of things. You could give Vic Lucas a call. He wrote up a contract when—"

"What do you two take me for?" Sonny asked. He had a mild smile on his face when he said it, but Paul heard the bite behind the words. "You think I'm gonna sign away my soul to some smooth talker without checking it out first? You think I'm some kind of idiot 'cause I didn't grow up in the *big city* like the two of you?"

"Where did *that* come from?" Laura asked, craning her neck to look him full in the face.

Ben shook his head. "I didn't say you were an idiot, idiot. I just said be careful."

Paul thought this was pretty hilarious. Ben Griffin—of all people—telling Sonny Tucker—of all people—to be careful. His father wouldn't even pour a glass of milk until he'd taken a whiff to make sure it wasn't spoiled.

"Talk to somebody," Laura said, patting his hand before returning her attention to the stack of papers. "Will you?"

Sonny grinned wryly. "Aye, aye, Cap'n," he said.

Chapter Four

The parade was forming on Post Road, snaking erratically down three blocks from the intersection of Main and Post on the western edge of downtown. Sonny parked the car at the post office, near the head of the snake, so that they could all walk the length of the parade on the way to their place of honor at the end of it, see who had turned out for what was quickly beginning to feel to Paul like a full-fledged holiday. This was no Memorial Day Downtown Sidewalk Sale, no Labor Day Firehouse Pancake Breakfast. This was Christmas, Fourth of July, and a Casey Mustangs Conference Championship rolled into one delirious celebration of self-congratulation.

Leading the parade were the Casey High pom-pom squad and the Mustang marching band, third-place finishers in the Millennial Central PA high school spirit competition. Behind the band, a troop of earnest equestrian Girl Scouts were cautiously saddling their horses. Immediately following the horses, squealing every time one of the animals let loose a powerful stream of urine onto the pavement, was a mob of nursery school children dressed as firefighters in yellow raincoats and plastic red helmets. Next was the entire crew from Trusty Construction, then a half-dozen teenagers made up with varying success as clowns, then the Kittatinny County cycle club, a dozen or so middle-aged men who lovingly stroked their Harleys. Finally, near the end of the line, were the fire and rescue personnel. In addition to the two Casey stations—the handful of career firefighters, twenty-seven volunteers, two pumpers, one aerial, and one multipurpose EMS vehicle—the five neighboring towns that made up the whole of Kittatinny

County were represented, and they too had brought what appeared to be all volunteer personnel and apparatus. (Paul considered, briefly, the possibility of a great catastrophe, a chorus of alarms blaring in vacated stations across the valley.) Sonny waved cheerfully at his friends as they milled about their engines, securing hoses and ladders, steaming the chrome with breath and rubbing at phantom spots. The morning was cool, but the sun had burned through the clouds and bore hot as August on the back of Paul's neck.

Following Casey Engine 14, they came upon Ben and the mayor standing beside an enormous red convertible. Paul had never seen a car like it before: long as a stretch limousine and wide as a Winnebago, the car's backseat consisted of two couch-sized plush beige seats facing each other. On the side of the car in white script was written "Bernie's Classic Cars." A man, whom Paul assumed to be Bernie, was in the "driver's seat"—a giant recliner covered with fake white fur—guzzling a bottle of Mountain Dew. Bernie wore a wide red cowboy hat and a bright red blazer, had the broad, smile-lined face of a man who had clearly found his true calling parading down small-town Main Streets.

Sonny whistled under his breath. "Nice wheels."

"And check out that hat," Ben said, nodding at Bernie.

"The best for the best," the mayor said proudly, slapping Sonny between the shoulder blades. "We keep a little cash in the kitty for occasions like this."

"So where do I sit?" Sonny asked, rubbing his hands in anticipation, as if instead of riding in the car he was going to eat it.

The mayor cleared his throat in a long, drawn-out grumble, picked a ball of fuzz off his yellow wool sweater. Paul thought he looked a little uneasy; he was, after all, mayor only on weekends and when something needed fixing. He wasn't exactly respected, but he was likable and easily manipulated, which was plenty to get elected mayor in a town of nine thousand.

"Well, Sonny," the mayor began, "I was planning on having you in the car here, but Ben was just saying you'd prefer riding with the rest of the firemen, up ahead on the Casey truck."

Sonny glanced quickly at Ben, then at Engine 14, then back at the convertible. "Huh," he said, obviously puzzled. "So . . . who's gonna sit in the car then?"

"Well, I'll be up front with Bernie," the mayor said. "I thought Ian Finch could sit in the back. And of course your family is welcome to sit with Ian, if they'd like."

"Wha'dya think, worm?" Ben said, winking at Paul and patting the car door seductively. "Pretty sweet, ain't she? Why don't you hop in and try her on." He turned to Sonny. "Let's go, huh? We'll get you outa these church clothes and into the gear like everybody else."

Paul watched his father's fingers curl and uncurl. He lightly touched his narrow blue tie as if it were something precious. "It's just . . ." he started. "Well, see, I was thinking I might just ride in the car here. You know, with Ian . . . and Laura and Paul." He paused, carefully. "You think anybody'd mind?"

It was perfectly clear to Paul from the look on Ben's face that—even if nobody else gave a rat's ass—he himself minded. Minded pretty much, in fact. "The guys were thinking we'd all ride together," he said stiffly. "The whole team thing, you know?"

Paul stared intently at a crack on the sidewalk. The mayor looked at his watch. Up ahead, the Girl Scouts were mounting their horses. Ian Finch still hadn't appeared. No one spoke until Laura, mercifully, broke the cumbersome silence.

"Honey, it's okay," she said, touching Sonny's sleeve. "You go on and be with your team. This car, this whole thing . . . it's a little silly, really. Paul and I will just watch from the side."

Paul knew she was trying to give his father an easy out, trying to let him save face in front of everyone. It was a generous gift, but his father wouldn't accept it, no sir. This was his parade, dammit, and he wanted to be in the shiny red car.

"I . . ." he started. "Well, I just think . . . you know . . . the family should be together."

Paul blushed at the lie as if it were his own, glanced warily at Ben. He'd seen Ben Griffin mad before, and it wasn't pretty; he did a Jekyll and Hyde number, one moment a big stuffed teddy bear, the next a live gorilla who would happily pluck the beating heart from your chest. This talent was helpful in certain situations, allowed Ben and Sonny to play the fireman version of good cop/bad cop when trying to extract information about a suspicious fire. But this, really, was not the time nor the place for the gorilla to make an entrance, not with the whole town waiting for a parade. Before Ben could really lose it, Paul managed to catch his eye, just for a moment, managed to say *please* without actually saying a word.

"All right, then," Ben said gruffly. "I'll tell the guys."

He turned to leave and Paul breathed a quiet sigh of relief. His father had his hand on the door handle when Ben, nearly out of earshot, but not quite, muttered: "All for one and one for all . . ."

Sonny spun around. "You got a problem?"

Ben was still walking. "Forget it," he said, raising a dismissive wave.

"Come on," Sonny began. "I don't—"

Now Ben stopped, turned back. "I said forget it, Sonny. Do what you need to do. It's just you keep saying how we're all heroes, how we all worked together on this thing, and you sittin' back here might make some of the guys think you don't really mean all that."

"Which guys?" Sonny asked. "You and who else?"

Ben ignored the question. "A team rides together. You know that."

Sonny's jaw stiffened. "Yeah, well, the *team* wasn't underground for six hours."

At that moment Paul caught sight of Ian Finch. He was wheeling himself down the sidewalk toward them in wide, clumsy jolts.

"There's Ian!" Paul said, shouted actually, in an attempt to distract everyone from what had just come from his father's mouth.

"What's the holdup?" Ian asked, coming to a sudden and awkward halt with his wheels halfway over the curb. His pupils were obscured by a fog so dense even Paul knew he was stoned. His hair was damp and he wore ragged jeans and a long-sleeved black T-shirt with the words THE GRAVE written in white block letters.

Sonny turned to him, blinked at his outfit; by the time he turned back, Ben was twenty feet gone, already pulling himself swiftly aboard the rear of Engine 14. A ways up ahead, the marching band burst into a trumpet-heavy version of "Twist and Shout."

"You need some help there, kiddo?" the mayor asked Ian.

Ian scowled. If there was ever an anti-kiddo, Paul thought, it was Ian Finch. He gripped the arms of the chair and pushed himself up, out, and precariously against the car door. "Fold up the chair," he growled, "and slip it in here somewhere."

Once they were settled—the mayor in the front seat with red-hatted Bernie, Sonny and Ian facing Paul and Laura in back—Bernie whipped the keys from the pocket of his red blazer with a flourish and started the car.

"Let 'er rip!" the mayor shouted, slapping the side of the car as if it were a wily steed. The giant convertible rolled forward at three miles an hour, followed the Casey engine slowly up Post Road and made a wide turn onto Main Street. A huge cheer erupted, and Paul was stunned, struck dumb, at the sight. He'd never seen so many people in Casey before. The sidewalks were packed five deep as far as the eye could see. Streamers flapped from lampposts; bunting adorned the awning of every downtown business. People along the street waved Mustang pennants, handkerchiefs, and American flags. Most of the kids had blue and white helium balloons, and they bobbed and waved in the fall breeze.

"Wow," Sonny said breathlessly. "Will you look at that?"

"Smells like horse shit," Ian said, w ping his nose.

Sonny turned on him. "Cool it," he said. "What are you thinking anyway, showing up like this? You look like a damn bum."

Ian shrugged. "The maid forgot to wash my tuxedo." There was a plastic wastebasket of candy on the floor between the seats, and he took out three Tootsie Rolls, unwrapped them, and stuffed them into his mouth. Most of the scars on his hands had healed to faint lines the color of bubble gum.

"You're supposed to *throw* the candy," Sonny said.

"Missed breakfast," Ian said, chewing grotesquely, a gob of stringy chocolate sticking to his upper lip.

Paul smiled. Victory was imminent. Whatever brief bond Ian and his father had shared the week before was over, soaring away at this very moment like one of the colorful helium balloons, its string unwound from the wrist of a reckless child.

"Throw some candy, honey," his mother said, nudging the wastebasket in his direction with her foot.

Paul picked a few Jolly Ranchers from the basket and tossed them halfheartedly out into the crowd. Frankly, he found the whole thing a little embarrassing now that he was in the middle of it. He spotted Joe Bower and Carson Diehl perched on their bikes outside Pete's Pizza and Subs, angling droopy triangles of pepperoni pizza into their mouths, and he wished he were with them instead of with his parents. He felt like a fool. This car wasn't cool at all; it was a joke, a circus car. It was like having ponies at your birthday party.

"Where's your arm, quarterback?" Sonny asked. "Let's see you wing a couple."

"Isn't this a great day for a parade?" the mayor called back to them. "This old town is really something."

"It's something all right," Ian said, his words barely audible through the wad of candy in his mouth. "Something that stinks."

Sonny shook his head. "Just for a few minutes," he pleaded. "Just for this one time, act like a hero, why don't you?"

"You're the big hero, dimmo," Ian said. "Not me."

At least he's got that straight, Paul thought, lobbing a handful of jawbreakers over the outstretched fingers of young children and into the laps of Carson and Joe, who promptly picked them up and gleefully winged them back at the car.

"Ian," Laura said sternly, sounding exactly like an algebra teacher. "How about we all try to get along?"

Ian frowned. "Who's not getting along? I'm getting along fine."

"I'm just saying—"

"Shoot, a couple months and we'll all be on vacation together. Mom and Dad and Paul and Ian. California or bust." He picked some chocolate from his teeth with the nail of his pinkie finger, tossed the wing of black hair from his eyes. "Your mom got a bikini?" he asked Paul.

Paul stared at him. Their car had slowed to a stop. Up ahead, the cycle club was riding in figure-eight formations; the angry sputter of their engines drowned out all of the marching band but the steady throb of the bass drum.

"Practically the law out there," Ian shouted over the roar. "Not like the town pool, if you know what I'm saying."

"Vacation?" Laura asked, her eyes narrowed in doubt. "What are you talking about?"

Ian snorted. "S'up, Sonny? Didn't you tell them?"

Paul turned to his father. He had his back squarely to them and was waving enthusiastically at the crowd from the idling car, doing his best to pretend he couldn't hear a word anyone was saying.

"Tell us what?" Laura asked.

Ian shook his head, cupped his hand at his ear.

"Tell us *what?*" she shouted to him.

Ian leaned forward. "They're gonna fly us out to Hollywood while they shoot the movie. Sonny and me're gonna be technical advisors and Gordon said Sonny could bring you guys along if he wanted."

"Who's Gordon?" Paul asked.

"The producer," Ian yelled. Now he poked Sonny in the back. "Shit, ain't you told them anything?"

"I was waiting," Sonny said, finally turning to them, his cheeks flushed pink. "I wanted it to be a surprise. Plus," he added, covering his feeble primary lies with equally feeble secondary lies, "I wasn't even sure they'd want to go."

The car lurched forward again; the cycle club had completed their maneuvers. The marching band launched into the theme from *Superman*.

"Hey, I wanna go," Paul said. "Can I?"

"There's the news!" the mayor shouted over his shoulder, pointing ecstatically to a TV camera set up outside the St. Charles Diner. "Everybody wave!"

They all waved, even Laura, though her wave looked more like a swat. Her eyes were fixed on Sonny with a mixture of irritation and confusion. Paul was familiar with this look; he was treated to it himself occasionally, when he promised to take the dogs for a walk and then forgot, or promised to do the dishes and then was caught shoveling crusty plates into the dishwasher without doing a prerinse.

"Why didn't you tell us about this?" she asked.

"He was gonna," Paul said emphatically. "Can I go, Dad? Can I?"

"What about school?" Sonny asked. "You can't miss a whole month, right?" He looked imploringly at Laura, for support or forgiveness it wasn't clear. "Right? He can't just—"

"Shit," Ian interrupted. "It's just old Casey Junior. What're you studyin' now anyway?"

Paul ignored the question, looked back and forth between his parents; his father still looked embarrassed, his mother still bewildered. Neither of them spoke. A horse far ahead of them whinnied wildly, eliciting shrieks of excitement from children lined along the sidewalk in front of Larry's Barbershop.

"Constitution," he told Ian.

Ian shrugged. "We the people. Life, liberty, pursuit of happiness. Survival of the fittest. That's all you need to know."

Paul shook his head. "Amendments, too."

"Not important," Ian said, scratching the thin black stubble on his chin. "If they were important they'd a put 'em in to begin with, right?"

"Listen, we'll be working," Sonny said, smiling weakly at Laura. "Me and Ian, we've got real jobs on this thing. They want me to help with the rescue scenes. I'm gonna be working all day. I'm not gonna be having any fun."

"Keep trying," she said tightly. She snatched a blue jawbreaker from the wastebasket and winged it toward the crowd with a force that startled and impressed Paul. He'd always thought he'd gotten his arm from his father.

"Babe, I—" Sonny started.

"No, no . . ." she said. "Keep trying. You've almost got yourself convinced."

Sonny blanched, and Paul remembered something. A few years before he'd badgered his parents into taking him to Six Flags Great Adventure in New Jersey. They had a new roller coaster there, three full loops, and most of the other kids at school had already been. Paul talked about it the whole car trip there, stood in line in the blazing heat with his parents for an hour and a half. Then they finally got on the thing, pulled back the padded safety bar, and began what he would always remember as the four most harrowing minutes of his life. Who the hell ever thought of this? he'd wondered at the crest of that first impossibly steep drop. What lunatic ever imagined this would be *fun*? Sitting there in Bernie's classic car, he felt like he was on that awful roller coaster all over again, the one he couldn't wait to ride that turned out to be a no-holds-barred nightmare.

"He wants us to come," Paul said desperately. "Don't you, Dad?"

"Of course I do," Sonny said, frantically loosening his tie as if it were suddenly choking him. "Of course. Of course I do."

"Then it's settled," Paul said. "We're all going. Right, Mom?"

"We'll see," she said.

Ian barked a loud laugh. "That's a fat-ass *no* if I ever heard one."

Laura flattened herself against the seat, crossed her arms across her chest. It was clear that, despite the four Main Street blocks that remained to be traveled, her participation in the parade had come to an end.

"We love you, Sonny!" shouted someone from the crowd.

🎺

Three weeks passed. Trees resigned their leaves. Christmas lights and holly wreaths appeared on lampposts in downtown Casey. The Pony football season ended, and Paul began spending his afternoons playing video games with Carson and Joe in the Diehls' basement, or fumbling his way through his *E-Z Carols for Guitar* songbook in the otherwise silent house on Willow Lane. His mother was staying late at school almost every afternoon, coaching the geeks in math club in preparation for the math bee regionals in Harrisburg. And his father, for all intents and purposes, had disappeared.

The day following the parade, citing innumerable requests for interviews and appearances, Sonny had taken a temporary leave of absence from active duty. He met with reporters from *Esquire, People, Fire-house Magazine, The Mustang Monitor,* walked them around the rubble of the Neidermeyer house, telling and retelling his story. He appeared on talk radio in Harrisburg, Pittsburgh, and Washington, D.C., flew overnight to New York City for a spot on *Dateline's* "Survivor Stories," became official spokesman for Trusty Construction and half a dozen other local businesses, received invitations to speak at firefighters' conferences in Boston, Baltimore, and Chicago.

Paul was happy for him. He knew his father had spent most of his life butting up against the edges of Captain Sam's shadow, struggling to cast one of his own. So here, finally, was his opportunity. But it was weird . . . even when he wasn't giving an interview, even when Paul knew full well he was in town, Sonny rarely seemed to be around. He'd pop into the house and read his mail, have a snack, but he was never there long enough to even sit down. He slept there, of course, but usually didn't get home until after Paul was in bed (at which point, occasionally, unintelligibly whispered conversations could be heard from the living room) and was still in bed when Paul left for school in the morning. Twice a week, Paul knew, his father drove Ian to Hershey Medical Center for physical therapy. But there was nothing else, really, to explain his frequent absences. Adding up his hours with Ian and his hours as a celebrity (which Paul had done on more than one occasion), there were still several hours in his day unaccounted for, hours he could have been at home, with his family, enjoying his time off work. So where was he?

His mother didn't seem to be bothered by this, or—it seemed to Paul—even notice it. They ate their dinners alone, as they so often had before when Sonny was at the station, and never once did she offer any explanation or excuse for his absence, never once said "Where the hell is your father?" On the rare occasions Sonny was with them, they would talk about the same things they'd always talked about, focus all conversation on Paul: Paul and school, Paul and football, Paul and his friends. At those times everything seemed perfectly normal, and Paul would stifle the part of himself that worried over his father's whereabouts, chastise himself for acting like a baby. Why should he expect his father to hang around with him all afternoon, just because he wasn't working?

One Saturday morning in mid-November, desperate for a father-son game of horse or twenty-one, Paul gave in to his weakness and headed into town to look for his father. His first stop was the firehouse; it had taken him a while to think of it, but once he did he was sure he'd discovered his father's secret. Leave of absence or no, his father probably couldn't stand to be away from the familiar sounds and smells of Casey Station #1. He'd probably been sitting around there at every free moment, playing cards, drinking coffee, shooting the shit with the guys.

Inside he found Ben and Black Phil; they were testing the SCBA masks, inspecting for nicks and cracks in the plastic shields and tears in the rubber.

"Young Tucker . . ." Ben breathed through his thick mask, doing his best Darth Vader impersonation as Paul approached. "Young Tucker, give in to the dark side."

"Hey there," Phil said. He glanced curiously around the station, peered around the corner of the engine. "You here with your dad?"

"Nah," Paul said. "Just lookin' for him. You guys seen him today?"

Ben pulled the mask from his head, began rehooking it to its air-pack. "He don't work here anymore," he said. "Didn't he tell you?"

"I thought he might be hanging out," Paul said.

"Nope," Ben said. He lit a cigarette. "Last time I saw him was on TV."

Paul waited for the joke to follow. When it didn't, he toed at the floor with his sneaker, tried to think of something to say. The station felt strange, empty, without his father in it.

"Try the diner," Phil said. "Saw him headin' in there a couple times last week."

"The St. Charles?" Paul asked. He'd never actually been in the place, knew it only from the overpowering aroma of frying ham that emanated from it every time he walked by. It wasn't a place for families, for teenagers, even for the firemen. For as long as Paul could remember it had been a hangout for old men; just a block up from the nursing home, its customer base consisted almost entirely of those residents who were still semimobile.

He walked across the street, pushed open the door to the diner. It was a small, smoky, well-lit place. The mismatched tables were empty but for sugar jars and napkin dispensers. Only three customers sat at the counter, his father between two old men who wore nearly identical brown cardigan sweaters. The waitress, an elderly woman with arms skinny and bent as twigs, leaned lazily against the soda machine.

". . . didn't know there was dark like that," his father was saying. "It was different than smoke. In smoke sometimes you get snatches of light. But this was like—"

"France," said the man sitting to his left. He ground out a cigarette in a plastic ashtray. Paul noticed his hands: they shook and had a grayish hue to them, like spoiled meat. "Darkest dark I ever saw. France from a foxhole. No stars in France, not in those days. They don't tell you that now. They don't want you to know how dark it was."

"Like you could die and not know the difference," Sonny said.

"Exactly that," the gray-handed man said, tilting another cigarette from his pack.

They lapsed into silence. Sonny took a sip from his coffee mug. A plate piled with ham sat before him, untouched. In fact, Paul noticed, all three men had plates stacked with fatty ham, and all three stacks looked equally ignored. Was this really how his father had been spending his days? Sitting around with a bunch of mumbly old geezers? Where exactly was the fun in that? Paul backed slowly toward the door, bent on a quiet escape, when the waitress looked up.

"Hi, hon," she said.

Three stools swiveled around, giving off a horrible chorus of squawks.

"Hey," Sonny said. He smiled. "Whatcha doing here?"

"Just looking for you," Paul said with a shrug. "I thought you might want to play ball."

Sonny nodded to the men on either side of him. "This is Gus," he said of the gray-handed man. "And this is Earl. This is my son, Paul."

The two men scrutinized him. Earl wore thick glasses and had a Band-Aid on his earlobe. Gus had a bent, flattened nose. They didn't smile or say anything about how good-looking he was, not like the old people at church or his friends' grandparents. They just looked at him impassively, as if his presence were an interruption they would tolerate but not encourage.

"So . . . you wanna play?" Paul asked uneasily.

"Maybe later," Sonny said. He picked up his fork. "Still working on my breakfast here."

"Okay," Paul said. "See ya." He waited a moment more, waited to see if his father would ask him to join them. Then he turned to the door, heard the stools squeak back to the counter.

"Boy looks like his granddaddy," Earl said.

"You think?" Sonny asked.

"Spittin' image of Sam in high school," Gus added. "I recall one summer we all . . ."

❧

"Cheers," Sonny said. He raised his plastic tumbler of Coke and Paul followed suit. They were at Bonanza, squeezed into a vinyl booth. The restaurant was warm and noisy, and practically every kid in the place had a bright orange cheese mustache thanks to the nachos at the food bar. It was family night—kids under twelve paid their weight in pennies—and Paul was pleased that for the first time he would not have to step on the clown-faced scale at the checkout so his mother could fork over her handful of loose change.

"What are we toasting?" Laura asked.

Sonny shrugged. "Just seems like a long time since the three of us went out to dinner."

"All right," she said, raising her glass of tea. "I can toast to that."

Sonny struggled to cut into his thick steak. His hands were almost entirely healed, but the fingernails on the index and middle finger of his left hand, after appearing normal for nearly a month, had suddenly turned black halfway to the quick. He held them off to an angle as he anchored the steak with his fork.

"They gonna fall off?" Paul asked, nodding to the nails.

Sonny glanced down. "Probably. Must've smashed 'em pretty good, I guess."

"You don't remember?"

"Not how I got every bruise, no."

Paul hesitated. He wasn't quite sure what questions were off-limits. But his father had talked to those men about it, the men at the diner. So surely he wouldn't mind talking about it with his own son.

"Was it gross?" he asked.

Sonny chewed. "Smashing my fingers?"

"No, the whole thing." He shook some salt on his baked potato. "The . . . the foot and everything?"

"Paul," Laura said. "I don't think he wants to talk about it."

"It's okay," Sonny said. "I don't mind."

Laura scooted out of the booth. "I'm getting a refill on my soup," she said, though her bowl was three-quarters full. "Anybody else want anything?"

"Check out the desserts," Sonny said. When she was out of earshot he turned back to Paul. "It wasn't really gross. I couldn't see anything, you know, no blood or . . . or *anything*, really."

"So how'd you know where to cut?"

"I just had to feel it out. Put this hand"—he gripped the edge of the table with his left hand—"on his shin, a little up from where I wanted the blade to fall. I didn't figure one hand would cut the other, you know? Then I just went on faith. So it was more surreal than gross. You know what that means, surreal?"

"Like taking drugs?"

Sonny nodded, forked a piece of steak. "Right. Like drinking a cup of NyQuil and then waking up a couple hours later and having to find your way to the bathroom."

"Did he scream?"

"Did who scream?"

Paul rolled his eyes. Who did he think? The Elephant Man? "Ian. You know. When you did it."

"Oh." Sonny hesitated. "Yeah. Well, a little. I had to hold on to him real hard, keep him still. His adrenaline was pumping. I mean, mine too. But he was squirming all over the place."

"Did he cry?"

Now Sonny set down his fork, regarded Paul curiously. "Why?"

Paul shrugged. He'd gone too far; he could see it in his father's gaze. "I don't know. Just wondering." Truth was, he liked to think of Ian Finch crying. Sometimes, when he was a little bit intimidated by somebody, he'd imagine them finding out their dog had just been run over by a car. He'd found that picturing somebody bawling a mess of snot and tears was a way better confidence boost than thinking about them wearing only their underwear, which is what they'd been taught to do in speech class.

But it was more than that. What he really wanted was to know something nobody but his father knew, an intimate detail he could have all for himself. Ian and his father shared something he had no place in; if he could get the real story—the grisly one, the scary one, the one his father wouldn't tell the reporters—then maybe a little piece of it belonged to him.

"He cried a little bit," Sonny said. "At the end. He was hurt bad, you know, and he knew it. He'd had all day to think about it, how bad it was. He was pretty shook up by the time I got to him."

Paul tried to imagine Ian—the lazy smirk, the hard eyes—*shook up.* "How'd you get him to stop being scared?"

Sonny shrugged. "Mostly I just talked to him. Told him stories. Told him about growing up in the station, told him about you."

"You told him about *me?*" Paul asked. This was somewhat alarming. What if he'd told Ian something embarrassing? Something Ian could use against him?

Laura sat down with a new bowl of soup. "There's banana pudding up there," she said.

Sonny perked up. "Yellow or brown?"

She considered. "I'd say grayish gold."

"That's a hell of an endorsement, sweetie."

"Did he really pee his pants?" Paul asked. "That's what somebody at school said." In truth, pee was only half the story; word among the seventh graders was that down in the Neidermeyer basement Ian Finch had not only peed but also *shit* his pants. But Paul knew he'd get nailed if he said this in front of his mom, especially while she was eating.

"Are you still—" Laura began.

"How would somebody know that?" Sonny asked Paul. "You know better than to believe—"

"That's why I asked," Paul said. " 'Cause people are saying lots of things. I just wanted to get it straight. I won't tell anybody."

Laura put down her spoon. "Could we maybe not talk about this?" she asked.

"Sorry," Sonny said, waving his hand. "You're right. Lousy dinner conversation. What do you want to talk about?"

"I don't know." She shook her head. "Anything. Something. Something . . . else."

He smiled gently. "You have a good day today?"

"Not especially," she said. "The new basketball coach stormed into my classroom after school and accused me of grading one of his players unfairly. He apparently thinks I have it out for athletes."

"What player?" Paul asked.

She blew into her soup. "Brady Fischer."

"Wow," Paul said. "He's the best player on the team. He can dunk."

"That's nice," Laura said. "Unfortunately his talents do not extend to mathematics."

Sonny took a slug of his Coke. "Want me to talk to him?"

"Why would you talk to Brady Fischer? Do you know him?"

"No, I mean the coach," Sonny said. "I could have a little chat with the guy. You know, tell him to lay off you."

She set down her spoon. "Why would I want you to do that? You don't have anything to do with it."

He shrugged. "So what do you want me to do?"

"Nothing," she said. "I didn't ask you to fix it. You asked me how my day was and I was answering you. Maybe you could say, gosh, that's not very nice."

"Gosh," Sonny said. "That's not very nice."

The waitress approached with drink refills. She hovered around for a moment, looked nervously back toward the kitchen, then cleared her throat. "You're Sonny Tucker, aren't you?"

"Oh, Lord," Laura said. "Here we go."

The waitress ripped a page from her order tablet. "Would you sign this for me?"

"He'll be signing a credit card receipt later," Laura said.

The waitress smiled brightly, missing the joke entirely. "Oh, I don't think so. I think this dinner's on the house. For *all* of you."

"That's real nice," Sonny said. He took her slip of paper, scrawled his name.

"Well, we've officially arrived," Laura said, after the waitress had scurried away with an armful of plates and bowls and Sonny's autograph clenched between her teeth. "A free meal at Bonanza. Now if only there were a *good* restaurant in town . . . then we'd really get some mileage out of you."

Winter arrived the last day of November. No snow fell, but a brittle chill sank into the valley and the town turned silent, ghostly, eerily desolate. It happened every year. When it snowed, there were things to be done: driveways to clear, hills to sled. But the cold, just the bitter, unyielding cold, drove people inside their homes and inside they stayed until something snapped. This was Paul's favorite time of the year. He'd bundle up and take long walks through the hushed streets of downtown, pretending he was the only survivor of war or plague, that he had only his own wits and courage as means of survival. He liked playing sports in this weather too, liked the feeling of being hot in the cold, of working up a sweat until even in a sweater he was burning up. He'd inherited this from his father, and often on the coldest days of the year the two of them would play basketball in the driveway until their fingers turned numb. But this Saturday morning, again, his father wasn't at home. Who could say where he was? Maybe having breakfast at the St. Charles Diner, comparing darknesses with the old men who'd spent their youth with Captain Sam.

Paul had been outside shooting for about a half hour—using the garage door to feed himself passes in his father's absence—when he caught sight of Ian Finch gimping down the street toward their house. The street was deserted, motionless, and it was a surprise to see movement of any kind, much less movement in the dark, slouched form of Ian Finch. Paul stopped mid-shot, gripped the ball, blackened from the tarred driveway, tight in his hands, and watched Ian's gradual approach. He wasn't limping, not exactly. His left leg was just a bit slower on the step than his right, as if he had a pebble in his shoe or a blister on his heel. He wore a tattered black trench coat and a black wool hat that was pulled down to his eyebrows. When he reached the house, Ian stopped at the foot of the driveway and took a cigarette from his coat pocket. His hands were bare and bright pink.

"Hey," Paul said.

Ian shielded his silver Zippo against the wind and lit his cigarette. "Sonny around?"

"Nope," Paul said. He spat on the driveway. Who did Ian think he was anyway, coming to their house, even their neighborhood? It was one thing for him to hang out with his father somewhere else, another town, but this was their territory. Right now one of their neighbors was probably calling the police, reporting a criminal (the telltale trench coat and black wool cap) creeping down the lane.

"Where's he at?"

Paul twirled the ball in his hands. "Wha'dya want?"

"Little cold for shooting baskets, ain't it?" Ian asked, wiping his nose on his sleeve.

"I guess it depends on the person."

Ian smirked. "Never too cold for super jocks, huh?"

Paul dribbled the ball once and then rocketed his fiercest chest pass straight at Ian's throat. Ian caught it clean but nearly lost his balance, had to plant his good foot behind him to keep from tumbling backwards.

"Take a shot," Paul said, although—at the end of the driveway—Ian was thirty feet from the basket.

Ian took a drag, then flipped his cigarette into the street. "What do I look like? Michael Fucking Jordan?"

Paul fumbled for something cutting to say, but—in the heat of the moment—relied on the old standby. "You chicken?"

It didn't work, not by a stretch. Instead of looking offended Ian appeared only mildly amused. He smiled crookedly and rolled the ball lazily back to Paul. "You're a piece of work, jocko," he said. "Anyways, I thought you were a football player. Don't you know basketball's a nigger game these days?"

Paul swept up the ball and pivoted back to the basket, lofted an air ball five feet shy of the rim. He was shaking, although he wasn't cold. *Nigger.* Jesus Christ, there were words you just didn't say. You could say *shit* and *fuck* and even the occasional *cocksucker,* but you didn't say *nigger,* not even to your friends, not even as a joke. He wished his father were there in the driveway to hear this—surely he would have sent Ian sprawling to the pavement, dummy foot and all.

"Use your wrists," Ian said.

Paul spun around. "What?"

"You look like a girl, jocko, shooting with your elbows. Snap your wrists on a shot like that. Cuts down on the air balls."

The ball had rolled back to his feet and now Paul picked it up. How hard could he throw it? he wondered. Could you kill someone with a basketball if you hit them square in the face with it, sent all those little bones in the nose rocketing into the brain? "What do you want?" he demanded. "I told you my dad isn't home."

"Cool out," Ian said. "I'm just standing here. No crime to stand here."

"You're on my driveway," Paul said. "That's trespassing."

Ian lit another cigarette. "You gonna call the cops on me? You gonna tell them I'm harassing you, standing here giving you pointers on your shitty jump shot?"

The screen door banged. Paul turned and saw his mother standing on the porch in her bathrobe, hugging herself against the chill. It was nearly eleven o'clock but her face was creased with sleep. He knew she'd spent last Saturday in her pajamas, and it looked as if she were headed for a repeat performance. Her eyes passed over Ian, but she didn't acknowledge him.

"Paul? What's going on?"

He wished her back inside, wished it desperately. He thought about how, the winter before, she had interrupted an especially brutal iceball fight in their front yard and demanded that everyone involved go straight home. His friends had left laughing, hooting catcalls back at him as they made their way down the street. Paul had been humiliated. And now here she was again, protecting him when he needed no protection.

"Nothing," he muttered. "Nothing's going on."

"I can't hear you, honey."

"He's just looking for Dad!" he shouted angrily. *Honey!* Christ, why didn't she just put him in a stroller and give him a rattle? Out of the corner of his eye he saw Ian grinning.

"Your father's not home," she said.

"I know that. I told him that."

"Go home, Ian," Laura said sleepily. "Go on now . . ." It was the tone—irritation laced with pity—one would use with a skinny, unfamiliar dog lurking hopefully at the edge of the yard. *Go home, boy. Don't you have a home? Now scat, scat . . .*

Ian shrugged, tossed his cigarette on the lawn. Then he started back down the street in the direction from which he had come. Paul hurled the basketball angrily against the garage and brushed past his mother and into the house.

"What were you two talking about?"

He kicked off his shoes. "Nothing."

"Paul?"

"Nothing, okay? I was fine."

"Don't leave your shoes in the middle of the living room. Go put them away and I'll make you a cup of hot chocolate."

He wanted to turn it down, out of spite. But he looked at her and couldn't say no. She was shivering there at the door, a hopeful smile on her lips. You had to be nice to someone who stayed in a bathrobe all day, the same way you had to be nice to someone who had cancer, or someone whose cat had just died. "Okay," he said.

He snatched up his shoes and went to his room. A plan was what he needed. A strategy. A way away from shithead Ian Finch, from the ugly old men at the diner. A way to get his mother out of her robe on Saturday mornings. A way to stop the snipping that had become habit whenever his parents were together for more than a half hour. Christmas was in a few weeks, which meant they could all escape Casey, if only for a little while. They'd go to his grandparents in Philadelphia, like always, at least for a couple days. He'd sleep in the paneled bedroom in the attic, and it was almost like having a whole house to himself. He and his father and grandfather would play Chinese checkers in front of the fireplace while his mother and grandmother sat in the kitchen drinking tea. And the night after Christmas—this was how it always worked—he and his grandparents would order in pizza and his mother and father would go out to dinner alone, go to a fancy restaurant and come home holding hands, happy and tipsy. Yes, he thought, that was just what they needed—a vacation, a tradition.

He went into the kitchen where his mug of cocoa was waiting for him.

"I have an idea," he said.

She looked up sleepily. "Do you?"

"Why don't we go to Gramaw and Grandad's for a whole week?"

"I thought we'd just go for a few days," she said, sipping her tea. "Like usual."

"But Dad's not working," he said. "There's no reason we couldn't stay longer this year. We could do all sorts of stuff. You and Dad could go out to dinner a whole bunch of times. You could go dancing."

She laughed, surprised. "Dancing?"

"Or whatever. Maybe we could all go to a Sixers game. And hey, you could drive us around that neighborhood where you used to live."

This was a major sacrifice, an event that took up the better part of a day and was only surpassed on the dull-meter by the filmstrip on barrel making they had to watch every year at school. His mother had a story about every house along the long, winding block where she had grown up; every yard, every driveway, every porch had an elaborate tale attached. It was easily the most dreaded outing on any trip to Philadelphia, on any trip anywhere.

"You'd like that?" she asked, a glimmer of spirit in her eyes.

"Sure," he lied. "And then we could all go to that arcade and play Skee-Ball."

"We could," she said. "But it would just be the two of us. Your father's not coming."

Paul set down his mug. "What do you mean?"

"I mean he's not coming. To Philadelphia. He's staying here for Christmas."

"Why?"

She cleared her throat. "He has things to do," she said. "Things . . . things to take care of."

"What things?" Paul asked.

She sighed, fingered the handle of her coffee cup. "I don't know, honey. Just *things.*"

What the hell was that about? *Things.* He was sick of being left out, lied to. But then, reconsidering, it occurred to Paul that maybe his mother really didn't know what these *things* were, that this was something his father had simply announced—perhaps in one of those late-night whispered discussions—and that she had had little say in the matter.

"We—we can't go without him," he stammered.

"I don't see why not," she said. "Listen, honey, you're right. We could have a lot of fun, a real adventure. Just you and me and the open road, Philly or bust." She was bright now, upbeat for what seemed the first time in weeks. "We can stop at Roy Rogers and get hamburgers and onion rings. And then in the city we can do all sorts of things, just the two of us. We'll drive around the old neighborhood and then go to that arcade, just like you said. Wouldn't that be fun?"

He shrugged. "Wouldn't be much fun without Dad."

She gripped her mug tighter. "But we've done it before, honey. Remember? Remember that one time we went in the summer, just the two of us? Remember how much fun we had?" There was an edge of desperation to her voice that made Paul even less inclined to agree to this plan of hers. He knew how it would be. She would try so hard to make him have fun that he wouldn't have any fun at all. She would run him around from one thing to the next, and after each place she would say "wasn't that fun? wasn't it?" and he'd have to say yes, yes, it was fun, the funnest thing ever. But his father would be here. Doing what? Sitting by himself in front of the television? Sitting with the old men at the St. Charles Diner? Sitting somewhere—at this very table, *their* kitchen table—with Ian Finch?

"It's Christmas," he said. "I just think we should all be together."

"I'd like to go," she said wearily. "I'd really like to get out of town."

"Okay," he said. "Then you go and I'll stay here with Dad."

She looked at him curiously. "Would you?"

What was this? A choice? He had enough friends with divorced parents that he'd thought about it. Who hadn't? If you had to choose, who would you live with? He'd imagined himself in a courtroom, a sweet smiling old white-haired judge looking down on him from his enormous wooden throne, asking him where he wanted to live. There was little question. Maybe both his parents were a little too fussy for his liking, but with his father there was at least the possibility of fun.

"We should all stay," he said. "That's best."

She thought about this for a moment, then smiled sadly. "I guess you're right," she said.

He set off in search of his father. He wanted to tell him the news himself, wanted to tell him they'd all be together for Christmas. This time he didn't even bother going by the fire station. Outside the St. Charles Diner he stopped to look in the window. There were no old men around today; the chill, Paul figured, had kept them in. There were only two patrons at the counter, his father and Ian. Cigarette smoke curled between them. Their backs were hunched; their shoulders moved slightly as they spoke.

• • •

Laura turned thirty-five the fourteenth of December. As was tradition, Sonny and Paul worked together through the afternoon and into the early evening to prepare her birthday dinner. Sonny was no slouch of a cook. Skill in the kitchen was a matter of pride at Casey Station #1, a constant and intense competition for superiority; there was more trash talk in regard to casseroles than Ping-Pong or hearts or even basketball. So during these birthday preparations Sonny usually did most of the cooking while Paul sat on the kitchen counter, passing his father spices from the cabinet the way other sons passed their fathers wrenches as they toiled under the hood of a troublesome car.

"I won your mom over with my cooking," Sonny said, spinning a long wooden spoon in his hand. "I ever tell you that? On our third date I made her a four-course meal in my dorm room with only a hot pot and a toaster. I think that clinched it."

"A toaster?" Paul asked skeptically. "You can't cook in a toaster."

Sonny put his hands on his hips in mock disgust. "With patience, a little rewiring, and a good knife to scrape off the charred parts, you can cook *anything* in a toaster."

Paul smiled. "What about a turkey?"

"Anything that fits," Sonny said. "And with a little ingenuity, almost anything fits."

He was making veal parmigiana. He scooped a dollop of tomato sauce from the pot, extended the spoon to Paul.

"Careful," he said.

Paul touched the sauce with the tip of his tongue. He knew his father didn't really need him as a tester, but it was all part of the tradition, a tradition they had once gone along with for his sake that now he went along with for theirs. "It's good."

"As good as last year?"

"Better."

"I like having a yes-man," Sonny said. He flicked a final shake of paprika into the sauce, then tossed the bottle to Paul. "Everybody needs a yes-man."

"Look at what my boys have done," Laura said, when they emerged from the kitchen with dinner. This too was part of the custom, her fake surprise. She swooned over her plate, the steam from the sauce floating to her nostrils.

"I made the bread," Paul said. "I mean, cut and buttered it."

"It's perfect," Laura said, pulling a slice from the loaf.

Sonny opened a bottle of wine, poured a glass for Laura and one for himself, then sat down at the head of the table and cut into his veal.

"Tender . . ." he said, pleased with himself. "Tender as the night."

"It really is delicious," Laura said. "Once again, shown up in the kitchen by my husband."

"Every woman should be so lucky," Sonny said. He turned to Paul. "I'm telling you, you'll win the gals this way. But keep it quiet . . . too many guys learn the secret, we lose the advantage."

"Where are we staying in California?" Paul asked abruptly. He'd been plotting this surprise attack all week. From experience, he knew it was best to raise topics of parental controversy during some sort of celebration; the chances of him getting in trouble were cut in half on occasions when everyone was required to be cheerful.

"Beverly Hills Twin Crowns," Sonny announced with a smile. "Nice ring to it, huh? The royal treatment. A suite, a view of the city, a *Jacuzzi.*"

He raised his eyebrows across the table at Laura and Paul blushed.

"What do you think, babe? Doesn't a Jacuzzi sound pretty nice?"

Laura sipped delicately from her wine glass. "Not if Ian Finch is in it."

"Well Ian Finch won't be in it," Sonny said happily. "We'll reserve it, post a sign on the door. Jacuzzi for adults only."

"Sonny . . ." she said gently. She set down her glass. "You know what I—"

"It'll be great," Paul said. "We'll all—"

"Honey, I've told your father about ten times, I can't just leave," she said. "I would if I could . . . but the ninth graders take state exams in February. How would it look for me to just disappear? What kind of example does that set for—"

"So they'll get over it," Sonny said. "I wish you'd come. I really do."

She shook her head. "But why? You said yourself you wouldn't be having any fun. You're just going to be working. So Paul and I will stay at home."

"How come just 'cause you're staying means I have to stay?" Paul asked. He was pretty certain the whole state exam thing was a ruse, a convenient out, one he could use against her. "Seventh graders don't have state tests until March. What if I just went for a week? I could take my books and stuff."

Laura didn't even look at him; she answered his question to Sonny. "Frankly I don't relish the thought of him spending time with Ian Finch. I don't think he's a very good influence on—"

"You don't even know him," Sonny interrupted. "Besides, yeah, just a week. How much influence can—"

Laura bristled. "Okay, one"—she held up a finger—"I do know him. And because I know him I know that one week is plenty of influence."

Sonny was quiet for a moment. He wiped his face carefully, took a few sips of wine. This was the point, Paul thought, where his father would let go, back down. This was the point when he'd remember who was in charge on Willow Lane. And so this was the point he could kiss any hope of California goodbye.

"I don't see why you have to bad-mouth him at every turn," Sonny muttered into his wine glass.

Paul turned to him, surprised.

"Sonny," Laura said. "Let's not. Okay? Let's not."

He put down his glass. "Just because he wasn't one of your pets—"

"One of my pets?" Laura interrupted. "Sonny, he beat up kids in the boys' bathroom on a regular basis. He once threatened to *dismember* a student teacher."

Sonny burst into laughter. "For Christ's sake, he was fourteen years old! *Dismember?* Give me a break. Does that really scare you? He's all talk, can't you see that? Maybe if you and everybody'd spent a little less time punishing him and a little more—"

"Do *not* tell me how to do my job. I don't tell you how to do your job, do I?"

Paul closed his eyes.

"How could you possibly tell me how to do my job?" Sonny shouted. "Jesus Christ, you don't even acknowledge my—"

"Stop," Paul said.

They looked at him, dumbfounded and guilty as children caught fighting over a toy they were supposed to be sharing. Laura cleared her throat. Sonny smiled weakly. Paul took a breath; this was his opportunity, but he had to act fast, before the moment was gone. They had argued in front of him, so now he got something in return. A stroke of luck, one he hadn't anticipated: they owed him. Those were the rules, unwritten but known to all. When they argued they bought him an ice-cream cone or a new football or took him to a movie. But he didn't want any of those things now.

"I want to go to California," he said. "For a week, that's all. I'll probably never get to do anything like it again, never in my whole life, so I should get to do it now." He turned to his mother, went in for the kill. "You're always saying how everything here's so small. So don't you think I should get to go somewhere where things are big?"

A look passed between his parents over the flickering flames of the candles. Paul stifled the urge to say something else, to further his case. If he said another word it might start to sound like whining, and then he was sunk for sure. Best to let them come to it themselves.

"I can't wait until you're a parent," Laura said, smiling through a scowl, or scowling though a smile. "Don't you dare expect sympathy from me when your children use your own words against you."

"I think that's a yes," Sonny said, winking at Paul.

Laura sighed. She didn't look angry or sad. She just looked exhausted, spent, as if she'd been up for days on end. She picked up her fork with the effort of one picking up a brick.

"One week," she said.

Being an only child had certain advantages, the most significant of which became obvious every Christmas morning when the majority of the gigantic pile of presents under the tree bore tags with Paul's name. His parents might exchange a gift or two—a piece of jewelry for his mother, a sweater for his father—but the big haul was his and his alone. It was his father, he knew, who was primarily responsible for the volume of gifts. Years ago (in truth, it was only five) when he'd still believed in Santa Claus, his mother would shake her head every Christmas morning and look at his father and say "Santa's going to spoil this boy . . ." and now he understood that, of course, she'd been directing this warning to Sonny, who'd always smile innocently from his spot under the tree. But what had his father known of Christmas, ever? Sonny had once told Paul that Christmas when he was a child meant a long, quiet day at the station; wives of the other firemen would bring in Corning Ware dishes stacked with sliced turkey, maybe a pumpkin or a mincemeat pie, but rarely were there any toys. What did a fireman need with toys?

This year, most of Paul's presents centered around a theme: his upcoming trip to California. He scored a huge duffel bag, a pair of expensive, trendy sandals, a Game Boy Color, and a Nittany Lions beach towel that was taller than he was. The only gift he knew for certain was chosen by his mother was a bulky winter coat.

"You made out like a bandit, bandit," Ben said when he arrived for dinner. The only present he'd brought was himself—Paul had heard his mother on the phone with him the day before, practically pleading with him to come, to set things right with Sonny. Now his father wasn't even here. He'd gone out to walk the dogs, and Paul was in the process of attempting to put together his biggest present—a foosball table—by himself; the pieces of it were spread around him in disarray on the living room floor, the incomprehensible directions already wadded in a tight ball.

"You know what I got for Christmas when I was a kid?" Ben asked, shaking his head in astonishment at the sheets of wrapping paper strewn around the room. "Jacks. And maybe a pack of baseball cards. That was it."

"That's crap," Paul said.

"Okay, well, I never had a haul like this."

"You never had a father who never had toys," Laura said, handing him a glass of wine. "You know that's not staying in the living room, right Paul? It's going in the basement."

"You should start charging admission to your basement," Ben said. "What all you got down there now? Last year was that snazzy drum set, year before that the bumper pool table, year before that . . ."

"Can we keep it up here?" Paul asked Laura. "Just for vacation? Then me and Dad can move it downstairs."

"Dad and I."

"Where is old Dad anyways?" Ben asked, crouching on the floor beside Paul and uncrumpling the sheet of assembly directions. "Out gettin' his picture taken?"

"Ben," Laura said. "It's Christmas."

"Right," Ben said. "No pics on Christmas." He peered at the directions, tugging on the end of his mustache as he read, then looked at the parts on the floor. "Where's 'A'?" he asked. "Which one's that?"

By the time Sonny returned from his walk Ben had fully assembled the foosball table and Paul was well into getting his butt kicked. He'd played before, at the same arcade in Philadelphia where he'd played Skee-Ball with his parents, but Ben was ten times the foosballer he was, moving from one lever to the next with great prowess while Paul spun his rows of men around frantically, usually long after the ball had skidded under their collective feet.

"That was fast," his father said, shaking snowflakes off his coat before throwing it over Ben's on the back of the couch. He didn't say hello to Ben and Ben didn't say hello either. Paul took this as a good sign. You never have to say hello to your friends. You might as well say hello to yourself.

"I'm smokin' him," Ben said, stepping out of the way. "I can't help it. Step on in here so he's got somebody to beat."

"Uh-uh," Laura said, coming into the living room. "First we eat. Then the boys can play."

"So when you coming back to work?" Ben asked as they took their seats around the dinner table. Paul shrank a little in his chair. Couldn't they talk about the food first? Couldn't they talk about football or the weather?

"Pretty soon," Sonny said. He took a long swallow of his wine, smacked his lips. "We go to L.A. the middle of January, for four or five weeks. After that."

"After that you become a regular guy again, huh?"

Paul glanced at his father. Would he get angry? He plopped a spoonful of mashed potatoes on his overloaded plate and smiled. "That's right," he said pleasantly. "Just a regular guy."

"We'll all be back to normal," his mother said cheerfully.

They set to the business of eating. Wine glasses were emptied and promptly refilled. Laura and Sonny talked fondly about the holiday feast Paul had spent under his grandparents' dining room table, pretending he was the family dog. Ben told a story about an old woman in Pittsburgh who choked on a turkey bone while eating Christmas dinner by herself, then called 911 and—unable to report what the emergency was—gobbled into the phone until she died.

"You're a shameless liar," Laura said.

"Every time you tell that story I believe it *less,*" Sonny agreed.

Ben shrugged. "Believe it or not," he said. "It's all the same to me."

"Carson's uncle choked to death," Paul said. "On jujubes."

"I don't think so," Laura said.

"He did," Paul said. "Ask Mrs. Diehl. He was at a movie and—"

"Jesus . . ." Ben said. "If I choke to death on jujubes, somebody promise me right now you'll put a bullet through my head before the medical examiner arrives."

"You're on," Sonny said. He opened another bottle of wine. "As long as I get to finish the box."

"Then maybe they'll make another movie about you," Ben said. "Pitch 'em the story while you're out there. See if they like it."

"I'm going too," Paul chimed in. "I get to go to the studio and meet stars and stuff."

"Is that right?" Ben asked. He looked at Laura with surprise and—it seemed to Paul—maybe even a little disapproval. "Well how 'bout that?"

"For a week," Laura said.

"Hmm," Ben said. Then he winked at Paul. "Hey, listen, don't get mixed up with any of those Hollywood girls. They'll break your heart."

"He'd know," Sonny said. "Never seen one man go through so many hearts. What number you on now?"

Ben shrugged. "Stopped keeping track. Ran out of fingers."

Sonny turned to Paul. "Last time we went to Pittsburgh this guy had his heart broke in three days. It was like watching a movie on fast-forward. One day they meet, next day they're in love, third day she finds out he's a fireman and dumps him."

Ben smiled wryly. "Must be nice to be perfect," he said. "Not every guy scores the first time he touches the ball, Sonny."

"Thanks a lot," Laura said. "That makes me the ball, right?"

"But a *loved* ball," Ben said.

"She dumped you 'cause you're a fireman?" Paul asked. "What's wrong with firemen?"

"They die too much," Ben said, forking a piece of turkey. "For some gals that's a turnoff. Go figure."

"Maybe it has more to do with the way you live than the way you die," Laura said. "Did you ever ask them?"

"Ask 'em what?" Ben said.

Laura shook her head. "Oh, I don't know, Ben . . . anything?"

He sighed. "You don't understand. Most gals aren't like you, okay? Most gals won't—"

"And what am I like?"

Ben fingered his mustache. Sonny poured himself another glass of wine, swallowed half of it before he put it down. Paul said a silent prayer that a football would come crashing through the living room window.

"Let's forget it," Ben said.

"No, really," Laura said. "I'd like to know how you see me. Dutiful?"

Ben laughed. "That's not the word I was thinking of."

"Then what?" Laura asked. "What do—"

"Just make your little speech and get it over with," Sonny said abruptly.

Paul felt a tugging sensation at his feet, as if he and his parents and Ben and the tableful of turkey and potatoes and cranberry sauce were slowly being sucked into the floor. The sensation was so intense he braced himself against the undertow.

"My speech?"

"Yeah, you know, the one where me and him are idiots. Speech number four, I think. The selfish fireman speech. You know how it goes . . . pick it up from *can't you think of anything else to do with your lives?* Go on, we got nothing better to do than sit here and listen to it. I'm not sure Paul's heard it before." He turned to Paul. His bottom lip was heavy, pouty. This was the three-quarters-drunk look; Paul had seen it before, not a lot, but enough to know. "What do you say? You heard this one?"

"Bits and pieces," Paul muttered. He felt like strangling both of them. Why start this now? This was what bedrooms were for, what whispers were for.

"How 'bout the dessert speech instead?" Ben said. "Just pick it up from *how does a piece of pie sound?*"

"You're so pleased with yourself, aren't you?" Laura said to Sonny. "Sitting there like the cat who ate the canary, so puffed full of feathers you've had to let out your belt a few notches."

Good plan, Paul thought, his full stomach churning. The old stay-at-home plan, worked like a frigging charm. A nice family Christmas, just as he'd imagined.

Sonny turned to Ben. "She used to be crazy about me," he said. "You'd never know it, would you? Her eyes . . . oh yeah, they'd just light up. Now every year, every day, the light gets a little dimmer."

"Oh, stop it," Laura said. "You're embarrassing yourself. You're drunk. You've had about fifteen glasses of—"

"I'm drunk too," Ben said adamantly, though he clearly wasn't. "I'm drunk and I'm sorry. I got us all kinda carried away, didn't I?" He slammed his fist on the table; the wine glasses shuddered. "Who's up for foosball, dammit? I'll spot any one of you losers five points."

"You're on," Paul said. He rose quickly from his chair, thinking that this gift from Ben was worth a thousand whacks on the head; he couldn't remember ever being so grateful for anyone in his entire life.

• • •

The dream began familiarly—a test before him that he hadn't studied for, an unsharpened pencil, all the other students scribbling furiously while he stares at the sheet before him, a single page filled with incomprehensible words, absolute gibberish, followed by the only symbol on the entire sheet that he recognizes—a question mark. Usually at this point in the dream a long shadow would drape over him and he'd look up into the eyes of a disapproving teacher, one who sometimes wore the face of his mother. But now, tonight, a new turn: the other students are rising from their desks and rushing to the window. He turns to see what they're looking at and sees the Neidermeyer house, towering on a hill above the school, the middle caved in. The voices of the students are hushed but worried.

"Maybe there's somebody down there . . ." Carson Diehl says.

"Under that?" Jennie Weitzel asks. "Be dead now even if there was."

Paul started awake. He wasn't sure what had woken him, and he briefly treaded water on the surface of his dream, was slowly sinking back to the hushed voices of his classmates when he heard noises from the living room. It sounded like one of the dogs was scratching on the front door, had been left outside in the cold night. He looked at the clock. It was two-thirty. His heart, still pounding from the sight of the Neidermeyer house out the window of Casey Junior, would not still. He sat up, listened—definitely one of the dogs, he decided. Hugging himself against the chill, he left his room and trudged sleepily down the hallway.

"All right, already," he said. "Hold your—"

He stopped. His father, dressed in his bathrobe and sneakers, was sitting at the dining room table in the dark. He had a silver toaster clenched between his knees and was scrubbing it furiously with an orange scouring sponge. A bowl of soapy water sat on the table, and every few seconds Sonny plunged the sponge into the bowl, then yanked it out, flinging water everywhere, and set to scrubbing again. The innards of the toaster—screws, nuts, washers, four charred grills—were scattered on the table before him. Paul stood for a moment, watching in silence, before he mustered the courage to speak.

"Dad?"

Nothing. Not even a flinch. The scrubbing continued unabated. Had he even spoken? Or had he just thought the word *dad*? He'd try again, once more, and then he'd give up, go back to bed, chalk it up to dreaming. Who was to say otherwise?

"Dad?"

Sonny glanced up briefly, then returned his attention to the toaster. "Jelly," he said.

"What?"

"I think it's jelly. Hard as a rock."

Paul took a step closer. He wished it weren't so dark; in the light, he thought, this wouldn't seem so strange. In the light this would make sense.

"What are you doing?"

"It was buggin' me," Sonny said. He laid the sponge on the table and started picking at the spot with his thumbnail. "I couldn't think what coulda happened to it. Then just now I was lying in bed and it came to me. The closet in the laundry room, a box full of old shit, stuff from college."

Paul sat down at the table. "That's your toaster from college?"

Sonny looked up, smiled, but didn't stop picking. "I told you about it, remember? A while back? The magic toaster . . . it could cook anything. That got me thinking. I couldn't remember where it was. I couldn't remember throwing it out, giving it away, couldn't remember anything about it. But here it is, good as new."

"Why'd you take it apart?"

"It's broken," Sonny said. "I plugged it in in the kitchen and nothing happened. I thought maybe I could fix it, but now that I took everything out I don't remember where any of it goes. So I thought maybe I'd clean it up, so I could see it good, and then maybe I'd be able to see where to put everything."

Paul hesitated. Point out the obvious? Or let it go? He decided on the former. "We already have a toaster," he said.

"So?"

So who needs two toasters? So who gets up in the middle of the night to find a toaster that hasn't toasted in fifteen years? So who thinks cleaning it could possibly help to fix it? He wondered if his father was still drunk, if he'd kept at the wine after Ben had left and he and his mother had gone to sleep.

"Where's Mom?" Paul asked.

Sonny shrugged. "In bed, I guess."

Paul shifted in his chair. "Do you want me to go get her?"

Sonny looked up at him, flustered. "What for?" he asked.

"I don't know," Paul said. "I just—"

"What're you doing up anyway? What time is it? Why aren't you in bed?"

"I . . . I had a bad dream."

Now, finally, Sonny's face softened, his shoulders untensed. He set the toaster on the table. "You wanna tell me about it?"

"No."

"You sure?"

Paul shrugged. "It was dumb, that's all."

Sonny regarded the wreckage spread across the table. "Talk about dumb," he said, his face relaxing into a smile. "Huh? Talk about dumb. This probably looks pretty dumb, the old man sittin' here in the middle of the night."

"It's okay," Paul said. "It's just—"

"But it was buggin' me," Sonny said, his eyes darting to the toaster. "Buggin' me, trying to remember . . ."

"Sure," Paul said. "Little stuff like that, it can bug you bad."

Sonny picked up the toaster again, set it between his thighs, grabbed the scouring sponge. "I'm gonna give it one more try," he said. "It can't be stuck there forever. Right?"

"Right," Paul said meekly. No, he would not go wake his mother. And he wouldn't tell her either, not tomorrow and not ever. He wasn't sure exactly why, but he knew this was the kind of thing you just didn't tell. He would sit here, sleepy, while his father scrubbed. He would wait it out.

Chapter Five

The day Sonny was scheduled to leave for Los Angeles, Paul came into the kitchen for breakfast and spotted his father standing on the back steps, sipping a cup of coffee and watching the dogs bounding circles in the deep snow that blanketed the backyard. His mother was nowhere to be seen; he could hear the familiar steady hum of the shower coming from their bathroom. On impulse, Paul dropped his backpack, burst out the back door and down the wooden stairs past his father, then grabbed his football from the dry spot under the steps. They hadn't played in months; the pigskin was pliable, gave under the press of his fingers along the stitching. He spun to the yard and cocked his arm behind his shoulder.

"Go out!" he shouted.

Sonny laughed, blew steam from his mug into the cold morning. "Your mom'll kill me. You're all dressed for school."

"Twelve-ten-sixty-two . . . HIKE!"

Sonny set his mug at his feet and sprinted down the stairs and across the yard. The dogs abandoned their snow circles and stumbled after him. This was the way the game worked: he and his father on offense, the dogs on defense. Paul would call a play and his father would dash out into the yard with the dogs at his heels; he'd fake them left, right, then break long or short as Paul let the pass fly. If Sonny caught the ball (and he almost always did, even if the pass was wobbly or off target) he would dodge the dogs and make for the back steps, which served as the goal line. Paul's job was then to block—or, in extreme circumstances, distract—the dogs as they lunged for the ball in Sonny's arms. Sometimes they switched positions and Sonny played quarterback while

Paul went out for passes, but it was always Paul's task—part of his grid-iron education—to call the plays. It was a great game, in some ways even more fun than real football, though the dogs would only hold up their end of things for ten or fifteen minutes before getting worn out and collapsing happily by the stairs, tongues lolling.

The dogs were less hampered by the foot of snow than Sonny. June got a nose on the ball as Sonny staggered clumsily toward the steps, and this constituted a down.

"You really got to go?" Paul asked as Sonny handed him the ball. He hadn't meant to ask it but, out of breath and happy to have his father playing their game for the first time in months, he couldn't keep the question from his lips.

"Come on," Sonny said. "I'll see you in three weeks. Call your play."

"I'll receive. I'll fake left, go right, short. What time's your plane?"

"Eleven. I gotta pick up Ian at nine."

Ian. Stupid Ian. What did he have to go for anyway? What possible contribution could he have to make to the movie? It wasn't like he was an expert on anything—all he'd done was lie there like a retard, waiting to be rescued. He was no hero. So what did they need him for? What did they—

"HIKE!"

Paul slipped on his first step but quickly regained his footing, lost Hester by cutting left, then faked out June with a burst of speed as if going long and then stopping suddenly and turning just in time to catch the flawless pass thrown by his father. Hester was only a few yards away, but Sonny leapt forward and bumped her to the snow, leaving Paul a clear path to the steps.

"Guys six, Dogs zip," Sonny said.

Paul tossed him the ball. "You go long this time."

Sonny nodded, but didn't crouch for the hike. Instead, he spun the ball slowly in his hands. Paul always knew when his father wanted to say something serious; he always spun something—a fork, a pen, a book, a shoe—as if the momentum of an inert object would somehow dislodge the words that were stuck in his throat.

"What?" Paul said.

Sonny stopped spinning, grinned sheepishly. "Do me a favor, huh? Sounds kinda goofy, but . . . be a pal for your mom while I'm gone, okay?"

Paul scoffed. "A pal?"

"Yeah, you know . . ." Sonny looked at the house. "Just listen to her and stuff. I worry, you know, that she doesn't have anybody to—"

"She's fine," Paul said, kicking the snow, preparing a safe spot to plant his feet. "She's fine, Dad."

Sonny sighed. "Well, you'd think so, wouldn't you? I'm just saying . . ."

"Five-twenty-six-sixty-five . . . HIKE!"

Sonny hiked and went lurching across the yard, faking out Hester immediately and beating June by five full steps by the time he reached the doghouse. Paul reared back and let go with a perfect pass, watched it spiral a straight line toward the white sky, then begin its descent into his father's hands. In all ways it was an ordinary moment, but for an instant as the ball was falling a hole opened in Paul's chest and he felt suddenly sad and old, as if something he hadn't known he had were being taken from him.

It was basketball season now, although Casey basketball wasn't worshiped with nearly the same reverence as football. There were six junior high boys' teams that played at the Y—no uniforms, just red pinnies versus green pinnies—and Paul rarely scored unless he was fouled, in which case he almost always made his free throws. Between the driveway on Willow Lane and the drive at Casey Station #1, he figured he'd sunk about ten thousand free throws in his brief life, but he was one of the shorter kids in basketball and was usually dwarfed under the hoop, each layup attempt met with hands that reached six inches higher than his own.

That night when Paul got home from his game at the Y he heard a tremendous racket coming from the basement. Someone was whaling away on his drum set, which he himself hadn't touched in at least six months. He thought one of his friends must have come over, must be waiting for him, but when he descended the stairs to the basement he found his mother in what could only be construed as a trance: her eyes closed, her tongue poking through her teeth, her long braid whipping around as she hammered fiercely at the snare and the toms, sweat glistening her neck. She didn't even notice him standing there until, with a final and violent strike of the cymbal, she opened her eyes and blinked disconcertedly into the light of the basement, as if she'd forgotten where she was.

"Oh," she said. "Hi."

"Wow," Paul said. He couldn't find any other words. The whole scene made him uncomfortable, like he'd just caught his mother in the shower, or snorting cocaine off the coffee table, or torturing a cat.

"I didn't hear you come in," she said. She snatched a hand towel from beside the drums—a hand towel? like a rock and roll drummer?—and mopped her brow. "What time is it?"

"Almost six," he said. "Um . . . when'd you start playing the drums?"

"I don't know. A little while ago."

"How come?"

"Well, they were just sitting down here, gathering dust. I decided I needed a hobby." She crisscrossed the sticks onto the snare. "Are you embarrassed?"

She seemed to be asking if *she* should be embarrassed, that an outside opinion was necessary to fully assess the situation.

"No," he said quickly. "I just never knew a mom who played the drums." And she, he thought, would not have been the one he'd expect to make the plunge. There was something unnervingly imprecise about whaling away on the drums, something that seemed to contradict everything he thought he understood about his mother. Wouldn't needlework be more to her liking? Or crossword puzzles?

"Did you win?" she asked.

"Huh?"

"Weren't you playing basketball?"

"Oh yeah," he said. "No, we lost. Did you talk to Dad?"

"No," she said. "Why?"

He shrugged. "I just thought he might of called."

"It's still early out there. He's probably just getting settled. You ready to eat?"

"Sure," he said absently. His mind was stuck on *settled*, bouncing back over it again and again like one of those scratched record albums his parents unearthed from the depths of their closet every few months. There was something too permanent about that word, *settled*, something that implied a whole new life. Would his father unpack his two suitcases, fill a foreign chest of drawers with his clothes? Of course he would; he couldn't stand to live out of a suitcase, even for a couple days. He didn't even like putting on clothes straight out of the dryer. He had neatly full drawers at home and neatly full drawers at the station and now he'd have neatly full drawers in California. Another place to consider home. As if two weren't enough for any man.

Sonny called late that night, and again two nights later, and then four nights after that, but his conversations—with both Laura and Paul—were brief and noticeably low on details. The movie was going fine, Sonny said. The actors were fine. The director was fine. The weather, fine. The hotel, fine.

"How are you?" his father asked.

"I'm fine," Paul said.

And he guessed he was. Though he'd spent thousands of days and nights with his father absent, there was something about this excessive degree of absent—two thousand miles away, in a world Paul could not even imagine—that lent a strange serenity to the house and to his heart. For one, the possibility of his father in peril was nonexistent. Even during Sonny's recent months off active duty, there was always the chance an emergency would arise that would force his father back into his turnout gear. Now, when a siren wailed, Paul's heart did not skip, his knees not chill. Was this how other people felt all the time? he wondered. Was this how normal kids—kids like Carson and Joe—felt, going hours, days even, without fearing the worst?

And he found something else had changed too, something he couldn't have predicted. More and more each day without his father, he enjoyed spending time alone with his mother. He would have thought that in his father's absence her love and concern would have become more stifling, but just the opposite had occurred. One afternoon he came home from basketball practice with a fat knot on his forehead and all she'd said was "ouch," then gone to the freezer and gotten him a bag of frozen peas to slow the swelling. They ate takeout at odd hours, stayed up late watching movies rented from the video store, winged snowballs at the dogs in the backyard. They even started playing music together in the basement. He only knew a dozen or so songs on the guitar, but she would accompany him on the likes of "Michael, Row the Boat Ashore" and "I've Been Working on the Railroad," playing a soft 4/4 beat in the background with the snare and hi-hat cymbals while he stumbled through his chords, then coming in for a sloppy solo before the final verse.

"A couple years and we'll be ready to go on the road," she said one evening, tossing her towel at her feet.

"We need a lead singer," he said. "Maybe Dad'll do it."

Her expression soured. "Honey, you've heard your father sing. He'd ruin us."

"You're right," he said, recalling his father's and Ben's impromptu, half-drunken performance of the Doors at a department picnic a few years back, how someone's dog had sprinted away, barking hysterically, when his father—standing on the hood of Ben's pickup—had screamed: "Try to set the night on fiii-iiiire!"

"So it's just you and me," she said. "Cutting-edge instrumentals. We don't need anybody else."

He strummed absently on his guitar. They could make a video, he was thinking. They could make a video at the fire station. They could put the drum set on the roof of the engine and they could play from up there. No one had ever thought to do that before; it was surely as his mother had said: cutting-edge.

"Do you still want to go?"

"Huh?" he asked, jolted from his fantasy. "Go where?"

She thumped the bass twice. "To California."

He was set to leave the following weekend. He'd been talking about it at school nonstop, had already chosen the clothes he would take, picked up four rolls of film at Dewey's, paid for out of his allowance.

"What do you mean? Sure I still want to go."

"We're having pretty much fun here, aren't we? Just the two of us?"

He put down his guitar; if he'd kept it in his hands surely he would have hurled it at her, or snapped its neck over his knee. Had it all been a devious ploy, a master plan? Had his mother spent the last two weeks just *pretending* to be fun, just so she could talk him into staying home?

"You promised," he said sharply.

"Don't get angry," she said. "I'm thinking of you, honey. Your father's so busy. He might not—"

"You promised!" he shouted. "I've told everybody at school! I can't just tell them I'm not going now. It's not fair."

"I'm just saying—"

"You never let me do *anything*," he said. He felt tears swell in his eyes and quickly blinked them away. Jesus Christ . . . just *once* he wanted to be able to get mad at his mother without crying, wanted to be angry like a man and not like a baby. "It's embarrassing. People feel sorry for me. Everybody knows you'd probably keep me locked in the house if you could get away with it."

She recoiled, as if she'd been smacked across the face. "Honey, I didn't mean . . . I didn't know—"

"I'm going," he said, blinking madly against the tears. "You can't stop me."

Her eyes narrowed. "I could stop you," she warned.

"But you won't," he said, his heart pounding. "You won't." He was certain of himself in a panicked sort of way, as if he held a weapon on her, but a weapon he wasn't exactly sure how to fire.

It was Sunday the ninth of February, finally Paul's day of departure, and he was filling his bag with shorts and T-shirts in anticipation of the weather that awaited him in the West. He had never been so far from home before. The family had flown to Dallas once, for a firefighters' convention, and the summer before they'd taken a road trip to Michigan to see some of his mother's friends from college. But California was something else entirely, so far from central Pennsylvania that he couldn't even get there in one flight; he'd go from Harrisburg to Detroit, then from Detroit to Los Angeles. Hollywood! And a whole week off school! It seemed impossible, something that would happen only to the most fortunate boy in a made-up story, like Charlie Bucket getting the whole Wonka chocolate factory for himself. His mother had insisted that he take his textbooks, that he keep up with his class readings so he wouldn't be too far behind when he returned. But returning was a long way off—a world away, it seemed. He could read everything, he figured, on the long plane ride home.

"Can I help you pack?" his mother asked from his bedroom doorway.

"I guess," he said, glancing up. "I'm almost done, though."

She picked up his socks and began rolling them into baseballs and placing them around the edges of his duffel bag. Then she set to work on the pile of underwear that lay on the bed, folding each brief into a perfect square. Paul felt he was too old to have his underwear folded, and he told her so.

"Is it the underwear or the folding?" she asked, troubled.

"Both," he admitted. "I can pack on my own, you know."

"Of course I know. You can do all sorts of things on your own, but that doesn't mean I'm going to stop doing them."

"Ever?"

She sat down on the bed, resigned. "Listen, I kept my promise to you and now I want you to promise me something. I want you to promise me you'll be careful. Will you do that for me, honey? Will you promise me?"

She said it as if he were packing for a mission to the moon, as if his chances for safely breaching the atmosphere of Casey were slight at best. Paul wanted to ask her why, if she was so worried, she didn't just blow off school for a week and come along to California with him. Would she be happier here, alone?

"I'll be good," Paul said.

She shook her head. "I didn't say good, I said careful. You just pick up the phone and call me if you want to come home, if you don't like it out there."

"It's just a week."

"Nine days," she said. "And it's a whole different world out there, Paul. It's not like Casey. There are a million people there, honey. Literally, a million. You won't know anyone."

"I'll know Dad," he said, irritated.

"Of course."

"And Ian," he added, setting his new sandals on top of his underwear.

"Ian . . ." She sighed. "I'm not sure anyone knows Ian. Not even Ian. I don't want you following him around, you understand?"

"What would I want to follow him around for? I don't even like the guy."

"Well maybe you wouldn't," she said. "But your dad might. I just think you two need to look out for each other."

He smirked into the privacy of his closet, yanked another shirt off its hanger. So this was it; this was why she had given in so easily. It didn't have squat to do with keeping promises. She was letting him go to California so he could check up on his father. He was now the older sibling, the responsible one, the one who'd heed the warnings and spot danger—in the form of Ian Finch, or something else so wickedly foreign she couldn't name it—on the horizon.

"We'll be fine," he said, tossing in the last shirt and zipping up the duffel.

"Paul . . ." She reached out for his hand, and he took it loosely, sat down beside her. He felt awkward next to her, awkward in a way that made him want to put some distance, at least a foot of bedspread, between them. Long gone were the days when he could press his face into her shoulder for comfort; when would she finally realize this? When he was thirteen? Sixteen? Twenty-five?

"Your father . . ." she started.

"I *know*," he said impatiently, slipping his hand free from her grip. "I know he's been kinda weird. But you shouldn't give up on him."

Her eyes widened in surprise. "You think I'm giving up on him? Why would you think that?" Now her eyes narrowed. Her eyes, Paul thought, were her greatest weapon and her greatest weakness. Once you learned to read them you knew her words before she said them, maybe before she even knew them herself. "Did he tell you that?"

"He didn't tell me anything," Paul said. "I swear. It's just—"

"I haven't given up on him, honey," she said gloomily. "He's just been . . . unanchored, I guess. Drifting a little. And I think it's probably even worse when he's around Ian all the time. You know what I mean, don't you? He just might be . . . caught up in Ian things or something. I don't want you to go all the way across the country only to feel like a third wheel."

"I won't," Paul said, getting to his feet. "I'll be fine. *We'll* be fine."

She looked up at him hopefully. "Promise?"

❧

Stepping into the terminal at LAX, Paul was swallowed by the swirl of passengers and greeters, his heart fluttering with the vicarious joy of so many people genuinely happy to see each other. Hugging and rehugging, unabashed smiles, tender kisses, squealing children, rows of families holding hands as they departed the gate (*Red Rover, Red Rover . . . just try and break us*), years of disappointing baggage falling away around him—so briefly—at the moment of reunion.

But his father wasn't there. He turned circles in the melee, looking for a familiar face. Was that?—no. Oh, there he—no. Gradually the crowd dispersed, and he sat down, alone and deflated, cradling his duffel bag in his lap. There was some mix-up—his father had written down the wrong flight number, the wrong airline. Well heck, he wasn't a baby; he could take a taxi, could get there on his own . . . but what hotel were they staying at? He realized he didn't know, or if he knew he'd forgotten. He could call his mother and find out—but no, really, he couldn't. A call like that would only confirm her worst fears. She'd probably demand he get on the next plane back to Pennsylvania. And she would never forgive his father.

A heavyset man with a loosened tie sat down two chairs to his right and made a call on his cellular phone. At the gate across from his, three children were sitting on the floor playing cards. It had only been five minutes, Paul thought. Five minutes, ten at the outside. Dads were always late, right? When the boys took a Saturday trip to the mall for pizza and a movie, Mr. Diehl regularly screeched into the parking lot twenty minutes after the assigned pickup time. But that was Carson's dad. His own father was never late. Everything about his father was on time.

So okay, he reasoned, there'd been an accident on the way to the airport. His father was injured, but not severely, and right now he was lying in an ambulance telling the paramedics in no uncertain terms that someone needed to get to the airport *immediately* because his son was arriving and he didn't want to leave him there alone, sitting by himself in a strange city where he knew no one. Yes, an accident. He breathed a little easier. His father had not forgotten him. His father had merely been in an accident.

But then there he was, jogging down the terminal, dodging those who had the gall to walk at a relaxed pace. He wore black sweatpants, sneakers, and an old T-shirt. His usually clean-shaven face was covered by something just barely resembling a goatee. Clenched in his fist was what appeared to be a basketball jersey, which he held triumphantly in the air as he approached.

"Oh, man," he wheezed, reaching Paul and bending over, hands on his knees. "Oh man oh man oh man. . . . I been running all over this damn city half the day. Finally had to go to the stadium across town to get the right one." He unbent himself, shook out the jersey with a flourish, smiled broadly. "Official L.A. Lakers," he said. "Same one they wear on the court. You can show it off to everybody back home, hey?"

"Um, yeah," Paul said. He stood, steadied the bag on his shoulder, took the jersey. "I mean, the Lakers stink. But thanks."

"You're welcome." Sonny gave him a brief hug, the guy hug, sloppy and slappy. He smelled funny, his shirt and neck and arms. Paul couldn't identify the smell at first, but after a moment it came to him: on a rainy afternoon a few years before, he'd pried the slimy ball from a bottle of roll-on deodorant, curious to see how exactly it worked, then spilled the milky liquid all over the bathroom trying to jam the slippery ball back into place. His father smelled like a whole bottle of Right Guard.

"Are you all right?" Paul asked, curling his nose and backing away.

"Sure. Sure thing." Sonny coughed from deep in his chest, wiped a line of sweat from his upper lip. "I just ran about seventy gates, kiddo. Gotta be a mile at least. Been waiting long?"

"Only a few minutes," Paul said. "No big deal."

They began the long walk through the terminal. His father kept slapping him on the back or squeezing his shoulder, asking him questions about the flight, the food, his fellow travelers. Passing by an airport gift shop at the mouth of the terminal, Paul spotted a rack of L.A. Lakers jerseys he was pretty certain were identical to the one he held in his hand. If he'd been eight, even ten, the realization of "the airport gift" might have thrown him. But he was grown up, old enough to think his father's little lie was actually kind of sweet.

They stopped for dinner on the way back to the hotel. Over hamburgers, Sonny told Paul about the movie. It was amazing, he said, the way things worked out here. They were building the entire exterior of the Neidermeyer house just so they could knock it down. The movie was cool—no Shakespeare or anything, Sonny was quick to point out—but better than most anything else you'd see on TV these days. Paul was so excited he could hardly eat. He felt like he was on an adventure with his father, felt finally like it was just the two of them. He knew, of course, that Ian was at the hotel, but in the weeks that had passed since he'd last seen Ian, Paul had been able to once again assign him the penciled face of the convenience store thief, a face so void of character that it could pose no real threat to what he and his father had.

Square-footage-wise, the Tucker suite at the Beverly Hills Twin Crowns Hotel was twice the size of the Tucker home in Casey, Pennsylvania. They each had their own bedroom and the living room was massive: a wet bar, three couches, a glass coffee table big enough to sleep on, a big-screen television, a desk with a phone, computer, fax machine, and portable copier. On the other side of two sliding glass doors, a wide balcony with a glass-top table and four wrought iron chairs looked down onto the shops and restaurants below.

Upon arriving in the suite Sonny had immediately departed for the shower. Paul sat on a padded stool at the wet bar in the corner of the living room, munching on some nuts from a gigantic fruit basket that had already been picked over thoroughly. He was digging the last cashew from the bottom of the basket when he heard coughing from Ian's bedroom. The door was open a bit and he peered in. The bed was unmade and vacant. Beside it, on the floor, lay Ian's leg. The upper part—the shin—was rubbery and flesh colored; the middle—the ankle—was simply a rod of steel about the width of a tire iron; the foot wore a black shoe and a thick sock. Paul crept toward it, intrigued. Did the shin feel like skin? Was the steel rod solid or hollow? What did the foot look like, under the shoe? Did it have toes?

Another cough. Paul turned toward the sound and saw Ian in the bathroom. He was lounging in a giant sunken Jacuzzi, his eyes closed, a cigarette in one hand and a bottle of beer in the other. Paul approached the door, his eyes widening. The bathroom was nearly as big as his room at home.

Ian opened his eyes, took a languid drag from his cigarette. "Look what the cat drug all the way from Pennsylvania," he said.

Paul didn't respond. He was looking at Ian's bare back. This was the first time he'd seen the infamous tattoo; as wide as his palm, the swastika seemed to glow in the fluorescent lights of the bathroom. The lines intersected at Ian's shoulder blade, so as Ian reached to stub out his cigarette the swastika shuddered and rolled.

"Something, isn't it?"

Paul turned. His father was standing in the doorway in a white bathrobe. He had trimmed his "goatee" so it didn't look quite so much like roadkill. He smiled as he nodded toward the tub. "Beats a hot bath at home, I'll tell you that."

"How come he got the room with the Jacuzzi?" Paul asked.

Sonny shrugged. "I dunno. I—"

"I'm the one bringin' in all the babes," Ian said. "What's your old man need with a Jacuzzi anyways?"

Sonny sat down on the edge of the tub, dangled his feet in the water. "Give it a go," he said.

Paul kicked off his shoes. For a moment he considered taking off his pants, but he wasn't sure he wanted Ian to see him in his underwear, so he simply rolled the cuffs up to his knees and stepped into the tub, sat down beside his father.

"Tell me more about the movie," he said. His toes tingled from the hot water, and he clenched them against the tile. "Are the actors cool?"

"Guy who plays me is a fag," Ian said.

Sonny kicked a splash in his direction. "I told you to cut that out."

"Why? 'Cause half the guys in town are fags? What're they gonna do? Slap me?"

"What about the guy who plays me?" Paul asked. He was looking directly at his father when he asked, but it was Ian who answered.

"Oh, he's a big star. Name's Luke Milo. You see *Titanic?*"

"Sure," Paul said. "He's in that?"

"You better believe it. Know that part when the boat tips over and there're like a thousand people sliding into the ocean? He's one of the sliders. I think if you play the movie real slow—go frame by frame, you know?—you can see the back of his head when he falls in the water."

"The Academy overlooked his performance," Sonny said with a straight face.

"A crime," Ian added.

"Is *anybody* good?" Paul asked.

"The whole thing sucks, jocko," Ian said, plucking a cigarette from his pack. "I'm telling you, it's the biggest piece of shit you've ever seen."

"He likes it," Paul said, gesturing toward his father. "He said it was cool."

"Lousy taste," Ian said. "You ever hear the music he listens to?"

• • •

Maybe the kid who played Ian was a fag, but Paul wasn't sure. You couldn't tell just by looking, not always. A kid in his class, Joel Lebo, had a big brother who had turned out to be a fag, but Dave Lebo still held the Casey High record for the most total yards in one season. So who knew anymore what was what? And since Roger Rhodes, the young actor, was dressed as Ian—jeans, heavy boots, long-sleeved black shirt—he looked mostly like a regular guy. He was standing with the director, Lilly Douglass, a broomstick-thin black woman with huge round glasses.

"Hey, boss," Ian said, sliding up next to her and tossing his hair from his face.

Roger Rhodes looked Ian up and down. "You're back," he said dolefully, as if Ian were a recurring bout of bronchitis.

The set was smaller than Paul had imagined it would be, no bigger than the narrow gymnasium at Casey Junior High. Wires crisscrossed the floor, taped down with gray duct tape. Three huge cameras were pointed toward a blue couch on which sat a boy of about Paul's age—it must have been Luke Milo, of *Titanic* fame—flipping through a magazine. Beside the cameras were half a dozen tan directors' chairs. On the back of one was the name "Douglass"—Lilly's chair. On another was the name "Markham," the actor who played Sonny.

"What's the schedule today?" Sonny asked Lilly eagerly, popping up behind her shoulder and peering at the piece of paper in her hand. Paul felt vaguely embarrassed by his father. He wondered what these people thought of him. Were they really listening to anything he had to say? Or did they make fun of him when he was out of earshot, roll their eyes and make snide comments about the small-town fireman? Could you take the man out of Casey but not Casey out of the man?

"Nothing, right now," Lilly said, glancing at her watch. "We're waiting on rewrites. We've got to ax four minutes off the script."

"You're gonna end up on the cutting room floor," Ian said to Paul. He nodded toward the set. "You and the slider over there."

Lilly smiled at Paul. "Contrary to his belief," she said, "Ian is actually *not* in charge of the movie."

Eventually they cleared the set for a scene between Dale Markham and Olivia Chase, the actress who was playing Laura. It was supposed to be the morning of the house collapse, and Sonny was saying goodbye to his wife. Paul sat in Dale Markham's chair and Sonny and Ian sat in unmarked chairs that they had apparently claimed as their own.

"Hey, Dad," Paul said. "You weren't home that morning."

"Shhh," Sonny said, putting a finger to his lips.

"Welcome to Hollywood," Ian said cheerfully. "If they say he was home, then he was home. That's the way it works, jocko: they got their story and they're stickin' to it."

"But it's wrong," Paul said, and Ian cackled.

"ACTION," Lilly Douglass shouted.

Olivia Chase didn't talk anything like his mother; her voice was high, just on the edge of chipper, a far cry from his mother's measured tones. And Dale Markham had at least three inches on Sonny. They stood in the middle of the "living room" and touched each other on the cheeks as they spoke, which Paul recognized as an outright fraud; sometimes his parents touched each other's hands as they talked, lightly and intimately, but never on the face like some moronic soap opera.

Laura

I don't know what it is. I've just got a bad feeling
about today. I can't shake the feeling that—

Sonny

(smiling gently) You worry too much, sweetie.
Today's gonna be no different from any other day
in the last thirteen years.

"That's what they call 'dramatic foreshadowing,'" Ian whispered to Paul. "Subtle, huh?"

Sonny shot them a stern look from his chair; he was watching the scene intently, seemed to be hanging on every word. Paul marveled at the distortion that was unfolding in front of him; sure, the lines stunk, but what really amazed him was how wrong they'd gotten his mother. A bad feeling she couldn't shake? What had happened to "kiss the kitty for me"?

"They don't know *anything*," he whispered to Ian.

Ian winked. "Now you're catching on."

"What're we doing tonight?" Paul asked Sonny when they arrived back at the hotel. "Can we go out somewhere?"

"Sounds like a plan," Sonny said. He went to the bar and grabbed a beer from the refrigerator. "Where you wanna go?"

"Can we go to the Hard Rock Cafe? I wanna get a T-shirt."

"You sucker," Ian said. He plopped down on the recliner and cranked it back, stretched his arms above his head and yawned. "Those Hard Rock guys've made a billion dollars off dimmos like you. And anyway," he added, "I don't wanna go out. I been out all day."

"Then you stay here," Paul said happily. "And we'll go. Right, Dad?"

Sonny was silent, stared into the mouth of the beer bottle as if a Magic 8 Ball triangle might reveal the answer at any moment. "I don't know," he finally said. "I'm kinda pooped too. But hey, did I tell you? They got great room service here. We could order up some food, whatever you want. They got an ice-cream sundae with seven scoops. How's that for a killer dinner?"

"So we're just gonna sit around here all night?" Paul asked. There was a little whine to his voice, a whine he hadn't intended and didn't approve of, a whine he hoped no one had noticed.

"Wah, wah, wah, baby wanna go out," Ian said, flipping the wing of black hair from his eyes. "Baby sad and he no like it here."

Paul sat down on the couch. It was a hideous thing, slick green leather and so overly inflated it sighed with every movement. Paul felt like he was perched on a raft. "I like it here fine," he said.

"You sure?" Sonny asked. "I mean I—"

"Sure," Paul said casually. He couldn't very well complain now, once he'd already sunk himself with his stupid whining. "Whatever you want. I'm cool."

"We just split around," Sonny explained to Paul after placing the order, plopping down on the couch beside him. "We're trying to sample everything."

"We're halfway through seafood," Ian said. "You missed squid."

"But we can do squid again," Sonny said, nodding enthusiastically at Paul. "If you want. We can do squid tomorrow."

He picked up the televeision remote—it had enough buttons, Paul thought, to control an aircraft carrier—and displayed it from several different angles, as if he were a model at a car show.

"Guess how many channels," he said.

Paul shrugged.

"C'mon, guess. Be a sport."

"A hundred?"

Sonny scoffed. "Three hundred. Three-zero-zero. Ian and me did the math—you could watch TV nonstop for nineteen months and never see the same show twice."

"Cool," Paul said. So this, he thought, was how his father and Ian had been entertaining themselves every evening, holed up like a couple of fugitives in their royal suite, with their precious TV and their precious hot tub and their precious room service.

"The kid's with me," Ian said, jerking his thumb toward Paul. "He thinks the movie sucks."

"I didn't say it sucked," Paul said, wanting—more than just about anything, really—to not side with Ian, on matters large or small. "It's just . . . weird. Like, they're making most of it up."

Sonny rubbed the uneven stubble on his chin. Paul still couldn't get used to the hair on his father's face. Was he trying to look cool? Was he trying to look like Ian? Could he not see, in the mirror, that he looked like a homeless person?

"That's what they do out here," Sonny said. "With everything. Real life doesn't fit into a movie."

"When do they shoot the part of you guys in the basement?"

"Soon," Sonny said. He reached absently for Ian's pack of cigarettes on the coffee table. For a moment it looked to Paul like he was going to take one, but then he just turned the pack over a couple of times in his hand and set it down again. "End of the week, I think."

"You should hear some of the crap they got us sayin'," Ian said. "It's like a fucking Hallmark card."

"They gotta write something," Sonny said. "People don't want to see two guys just lying around, right? I slept through half of it. Who's gonna want to watch me sleep?"

Ian smirked at Paul. "Yeah, this guy's snoozin'," he said. "I mean sawing logs, drool, the whole deal. Meanwhile my foot's so flat under that fridge they coulda served it at IHOP. So much for search and rescue. More like search and *nap.*"

Asshole, Paul thought. Why did his father put up with it, Ian ragging on him, mocking him? It was as if Ian had taken over the role once reserved exclusively for his mother. Didn't anybody take his father seriously?

"Were you scared?" Paul asked. He remembered what his father had told him that night at Bonanza, had taken pleasure on several occasions imagining Ian with muddy tears streaming down his cheeks, his hands trembling, his teeth chattering. If his father wasn't going to stand up for himself, then Paul would do the payback for him.

"Me?" Ian asked. "Me, scared?"

Paul shrugged. "Just wondering." He nodded to his father. " 'Cause he said you were kinda scared."

Ian scoffed, raised his eyebrows at Sonny. "Oh he did, did he?"

"I didn't say that," Sonny snapped, glaring at Paul. "I didn't say anything like that. All I said was—"

"I'll tell you what he said," Ian hissed, his eyes locked with Sonny's. "He said he was sure glad his pussy son wasn't trapped in that basement, 'cause he'd be bawling like a baby, calling for his mommy, wettin' his—"

"I didn't say that either," Sonny said. He stood up, looked around for something to do, then sat down again. "Joke's over, okay?" He forced a smile, squeezed Paul's shoulder. "Seven scoops," he said. "Every one a different flavor."

"That's great, Dad," Paul said, shrugging his shoulder free. "Great."

• • •

The following day they shot the final scenes on the set of the Tucker house, and Paul got his first opportunity to watch the boy, Luke Milo, who played him. Watching strangers play his parents had been laughable, but watching someone play him was downright creepy. The things Luke Milo said to Dale Markham were things he never would have said to his father in real life, but they were things he'd thought in real life, bits of sentimental garbage that he'd never have let slip, no matter how scared he was.

That night they went to the hotel pub for dinner. After they finished eating, Sonny gave Paul twenty dollars and told him he could do whatever he wanted. Since everything but the video games—bumper pool, air hockey, tabletop shuffleboard—required more than one person, and both his father and Ian appeared to be rooted to the booth, Paul ended up playing Vigilante, a video game that honed the player's skills for the not unlikely possibility of winding up in postapocalyptic Los Angeles with an arsenal of postapocalyptic weapons to put to use against postapocalyptic gangs that were threatening to take over the city. After an hour or so of decapitating and disemboweling animated thugs (some of whom, Paul noted happily, bore a striking resemblance to Ian) he returned to the booth. Sonny and Ian were in the middle of a conversation that ended abruptly when Paul slid in beside his father.

"Out of quarters already?" Sonny asked, reaching for his pocket.

"Nah," Paul said. "I just got bored."

"You can only blow a guy's head off so many times," Ian agreed. "I used to play those games till I saw 'em in my sleep. Finally broke the habit."

"And turned your talents onto the real world," Sonny added.

"Funny, Sonny. You're killin' me, man."

"What're you guys talking about?" Paul asked.

"Nothin'," Sonny said, signaling the waitress for another round.

"Your dad here was telling me more tales about the great Captain Sam," Ian said, rolling a cold french fry in a puddle of ketchup. "Faster than a speeding bullet, more powerful than a locomotive . . ."

"I've heard those stories a million times," Paul said. "You tell him the one about the truck driver, Dad? His rig caught fire and practically his whole face fell off. When Sam pulled him out of the cab, the guy's cheeks started dripping all over the road."

Ian glanced down at the ketchup on his plate. "Nice," he said. He pushed the plate away. "You know the hooker story?"

Paul glanced at Sonny, then back at Ian. "What hooker story?"

Ian smirked. "Captain Sam and the hooker. The thing with the hose?"

"Hey, why don't you shoot some darts?" Sonny said, punching Paul lightly in the shoulder. "You like darts, right? Go see how long it takes you to hit the bull's-eye ten times."

"I wanna hear the hooker story," Paul said, trying to construct a picture in his mind of what *the thing with the hose* might look like. "C'mon, Dad. I won't tell anybody."

"Later," Sonny said.

"Yeah, like five years later, eh, Son?" Ian said.

Son? Paul thought. Who called his father *Son?* Not his mom, not Ben, not any of the guys at the station. The waitress appeared with two foamy beers, and Paul wondered if she had bothered to ask Ian for identification. He didn't look sixteen, maybe, but he sure didn't look twenty-one either. Maybe she was scared of him, he reasoned. Maybe he, Paul, should mention to her that Ian was underage.

"You want anything, honey?" she asked Paul.

"What're they having?" he asked.

The waitress chuckled. "Aren't you a cutie," she said.

"Get the cutie a milk shake," Ian said.

"There you go, quarterback," Sonny said. "Drink a chocolate milk shake and throw some darts. That'll be fun."

"You wanna play?"

"No, I don't wanna play. I thought *you* might wanna play."

Paul clenched his fists. "I already said I didn't." He felt the bite of his nails against his palms. "Weren't you listening?"

"Jee-sus," Ian said. "I ever talk to my dad that way he'd smack me around good."

"You don't even have a dad," Paul said. For a split second he was sorry he'd said it, was startled by his capacity for such meanness. But come on . . . Ian was all about meanness. What other way could you talk to him?

"Hey . . ." Sonny said.

"That's right, moron," Ian said. "I'm a fucking miracle baby. Immasculate conception. God jerked off on my mom in some—"

"Immaculate," Paul said. "Not immas—"

"Stop," Sonny said. He snatched a cigarette from Ian's pack and lit it. "You guys're givin' me a headache."

Paul stared at him. "When'd you start smoking?"

Sonny looked at the cigarette, took a quick puff and then stubbed it out. "I have one every now and again."

"You just wasted a perfectly good cigarette," Ian said. "You steal 'em, you smoke 'em. Got it?"

"I'm gonna go back to the room," Paul said.

"No . . . hey," Sonny said. "You want to play darts? I'll play darts with you."

Paul sighed. "May I have the key, *please?*"

"Okay. Sure," Sonny said, digging it out of his pocket. "Probably something good on TV, huh?"

"Whatever," Paul said, snatching the key from his father's hand. He strode out of the pub and took the elevator upstairs. So this was how it was going to be. Six months ago, his father would have passed by Ian Finch without giving him a second look. He would not have called him a *goner*, no, only dismissively accepted him as just another face that was part of the grand family portrait of Casey, Pennsylvania. But now Ian *was* the picture. And he, Paul, was just another face.

In the darkness of the suite he saw the red light on the telephone flashing, so he picked up the message. It was his mother. She was trying to sound nonchalant, disinterested, but the tone of her voice made it clear she was angry, at the very least irritated, that Paul had neglected to call her for two days. He dialed their number and after three rings she picked up. She sounded sleepy.

"Hi, Mom."

"Paul? What time is it?"

He looked at the clock on the fax machine. "Ten."

"Honey, that's one o'clock here. I was asleep."

"Oh, sorry," he said. "I'll call you tomorrow."

"No, no, no," she said frantically. He imagined her thrashing about the covers, fumbling for the light. "Don't hang up! It's okay, honey. I was just asleep and you took me by surprise. What are you doing up so late?"

"I just got in," he said. "We were in the bar."

"The bar?"

"Playing games," he added.

"Oh," she said, relieved in her delusion. "That sounds like fun. Is your father there?"

"He's still downstairs. With Ian."

"How's the movie going, honey?"

"It's fine."

"How's your father?"

"He's fine," he said. "He's having a good time."

"Well, that's nice, I guess. Is that nice?"

"You can go to sleep now," he said. "I'm okay. Everything's okay."

"All right, honey. You call me soon. Tomorrow if you can. And call me when your father's there so I can say hello to him."

"I will," he said.

After he hung up he undressed and sat in the hot tub, naked. He wished he were older, as old as Ian, so that he could drink a beer with his father, smoke cigarettes in the bar and listen to R-rated (maybe even X-rated?) stories about the fire station. Ian was only four years older than he was; it wasn't fair that four measly years could make such a difference.

The next thing he knew Ian was splashing in beside him, dressed only in his boxer shorts.

"Sleeping naked in the tub," Ian sang joyfully. Then he quickly sobered up. "Didn't pee in here, did you?"

"Time is it?" Paul asked groggily, reaching for his shorts and slipping them on underwater.

"Time for you to go to bed," his father said, coming into the bathroom and kicking off his loafers.

"I talked to Mom," Paul said. "She wants you to call her tomorrow."

Ian laughed. "Hear that, Sonny? Mom wants you to call tomorrow. Better be a good boy and do what Mom says."

"Fine," Sonny said. He stepped into the tub without bothering to take off his pants or shirt. His blue oxford filled with water and rode up to his chest, bobbed in the bubbles. Paul could smell the beer on him all the way across the tub.

"You look like a blowfish," Ian said. "You bring me a beer, blowfish?"

"Get your own beer."

"Wha'dya want me to do, crawl there? I'm a cripple, man, remember?"

Paul's eyes darted to Ian's left foot. It wasn't there, and he quickly looked away. "Mom said—" he started.

"Paul," his father said evenly. "I said I'd call her tomorrow. I'm not going to call her right now. It's the middle of the night."

"I know," Paul said. "I know it's—"

"Go get Ian a beer," Sonny interrupted.

"Can I stay up?"

"Sure. If you get Ian a beer, you can stay up for another half hour."

"Can I have a beer?"

His father seemed to consider this for an instant, then caught himself. "No you can't have a beer. Of course you can't have a beer."

"Just one? Half a one?"

Sonny shook his head, bewildered. "No. And you know what? I don't want a beer either. Here . . ." He handed his bottle over to Ian. "I'm going to bed." Without another word he climbed out of the tub and trudged out of the bathroom, bathwater raining from his pants, puddled footprints on the silver tile in his wake.

"Way to go," Ian said, when they heard the door to Sonny's bedroom slam shut. "He was havin' a good time 'fore you got here." He lit another cigarette and inhaled deeply, bounced his stump in the water, fluttering little swirls in the middle of the tub. Paul found himself studying the place where the leg stopped, midway down the shin; it looked like the end of a wooden baseball bat. He imagined the surgeons sewing it shut, how the skin must have been ripped and tattered from the ax, how they must have had to even out the edges before they stitched it, the way you had to snip along the edges of a construction paper Valentine, evening it so the front and back fit together neatly.

"You wanna give it a feel?" Ian asked, nodding toward his leg. "Or you just wanna stare at it?"

"I wasn't staring," Paul said.

"Give you the willies, jocko?"

"No. I just don't like touching guys is all."

Ian smirked. "Whatever," he said.

Paul did want to touch it, but only if Ian was asleep or otherwise too occupied to watch his reaction. What if he made a face? What if he recoiled, yanked his hand away the way you'd do if you reached for a football in the yard and instead found your fingers buried in dog shit?

Ian splashed him. "Ain't it past your bedtime, little boy?"

Paul scowled. "Why are you here?"

"Bar's closed, dimmo. Where else am I gonna be?"

Paul shook his head. "I mean *here* here, with my father. You're not even helping with the movie. All you do is sit around and—"

"Why the fuck would I want to help with the movie? This is my vacation, man."

"I don't understand why the people at the studio would pay for you to be on vacation."

"They hafta." Ian burped. "Part of the deal."

Paul frowned. "What deal?"

"Deal Sonny signed." Ian took a swig of beer. "They want his side of the story, they gotta get his permission, right? Nobody else knows the story like he knows it. So old Sonny says no permission unless they pay for us, him and me, to come out here and watch."

Paul recalled the conversation from months earlier, the day his mother had made his father promise he'd talk to a lawyer before he signed anything from the producers. This didn't sound like any deal a lawyer would come up with. Even a stupid Casey lawyer.

Ian singed out his cigarette in the water and tossed it beside the tub. "Pretty smart, huh?"

"Yeah," Paul said, his head swimming. "Yeah, I guess."

Paul awoke Wednesday morning to an empty suite. He knew they were scheduled to be at the studio at nine, and the clock above the wet bar (although it had no numbers, only thin black hands) said it was almost nine-thirty. Maybe his father and Ian had gone downstairs for a quick breakfast. Maybe they had even gone for a swim. It would be like them—like Ian, at least—to be late, especially since they were probably hungover. He dressed quickly and took the elevator down to the second-floor restaurant, a dimly lit place with plush green carpet, tinkling chandeliers, and burgundy napkins folded into perfect cones around each table. The waiters eyed him with suspicion—did he look like a beggar or something? he wondered—as he walked shyly from table to table in search of his father. No dice. He followed the signs in the lobby and found his way to the pool exit, forgot his purpose for a moment as he took in the pool, the glistening water shooting sun in a thousand directions. There were some pale kids knocking a beach ball around in the shallow end and about a hundred glowing bronze women stretched out on lounge chairs in the sun, Walkmans closed over their ears. Still no dice. Frustrated, he returned to the room. It was then that he found the note, sitting under the remote control on the glass coffee table.

Paul

You were so asleep I didn't want to wake you. We went on to the studio. We'll be back later.

Dad

Paul crumpled the note in his hand. What a load of crap! He was furious with himself. He had blown it. Why'd he have to mention his

mother in the Jacuzzi? Why'd he have to be a baby? Ian was right . . .
he had sucked all the fun out of his father's adventure. So now he was
going to be left out of all the good parts, just so he wouldn't spoil them.

Fine, then. He wasn't going to waste the day moping about it. He
changed into his swim trunks and went out to the pool. There were
some other kids there, three freckled siblings (*from Leesiana,* they told
him), and he spent the morning goofing off with them, playing Marco
Polo and cannonballing off the diving board—competing for the
biggest splash—until the lifeguard told them to quit because they were
drenching everyone within fifteen feet of the pool. Weary and wrinkled
from water, Paul spent the afternoon in the empty pub, sucking down
sodas and throwing darts. When he returned to the room there was a
message from his father. The crew was behind schedule, Sonny said,
and he didn't know when they would make it back to the hotel, so Paul
should go on and have dinner on his own. Paul bit his lip as he set down
the phone. Again: fine, then. He ordered a steak from room service and
watched two R-rated movies, drank from a bottle of beer until his
stomach churned and then poured the rest of it down the sink. When,
by eleven o'clock, his father and Ian had still not appeared, he went
to bed.

When he was a little boy, only four or five, there was no greater thrill
for Paul than that of his father carrying him over his shoulder, fireman
style, to bed. Sonny would surprise him with this move; one moment
Paul would be standing at the kitchen sink in his footie pajamas or sitting on the couch watching television and then—in a swooping flash of
light and color—he would be upside down and squealing with laughter,
his nose pressed to the small of his father's back, a powerful left arm
strapped across the backs of his thighs. Sonny would sprint wildly to
the bedroom, dodging imaginary obstacles along the hallway, then flip
Paul flat on his back onto the bed. *Just in time,* Sonny would say, wiping
imaginary sweat from his forehead. *Gotcha just in the nick of time. . . .*

Paul dreamed of this that night and woke with a start. His father was
lying beside him in his bed, propped up on one elbow, regarding him
curiously.

"What?" Paul asked.

Sonny smiled. "What what?"

Paul looked at the clock over his father's shoulder; it was two forty-five. "You just get home?"

"Been here awhile," Sonny said. "But sorry about bein' gone all day. Things were crazy over on the set. You dreaming just now?"

"Why?"

"You were laughing," Sonny said, shifting his elbow. "I came in here thinking I was missing a party and there you were, sound asleep, giggling like a maniac. So I thought I'd lie here next to you for a while and watch. Didn't mean to wake you up. What were you dreamin' about?"

Paul was embarrassed. He didn't like to think of his father—of anybody—watching him while he slept. But he supposed it could have been worse—he could have been crying, or slobbering. Or pissing himself.

"Remember when you used to carry me to bed?"

"Sure. That's what you were dreaming about?"

"Yeah." Paul shrugged. "That was fun."

"Seems like that was last night. You know what I mean? Either last night or a thousand years ago." He sighed. "Funny, I was just lying here looking at you thinking, when'd this kid get to be so old? When'd this kid start being a person? A real guy, with his own dreams and monsters."

"What monsters?" Paul asked.

Sonny ignored the question. "It's like you're mine, but you're not mine either. When I carried you to bed, you were mostly mine. But now you mostly belong to yourself. You know what I mean?"

Was he drunk? Paul wondered. He didn't smell drunk. And his words weren't slurred—they were only distant, dreamy. His eyes shimmered with thought, as if he were trying to recall the face of someone he hadn't seen in years.

"Dad?" Paul asked cautiously. "Do you like it out here?"

"It's all right," Sonny said with a shrug. "Why? Do you?"

"Do you like it better than being at home?"

For a long moment he didn't answer. He scratched his stubbly chin, pursed his lips. "Home seems a long way away," he said finally. "You know what I mean? It's like with you. You belong to me, but you don't.

And I belong to home, but out here home doesn't mean anything. You know, like I could say it over and over again, 'home . . . home . . . home . . .' and after a while it's just gibberish. I can do the same thing with you. I can go 'Paul . . . Paul . . . Paul . . .' until your name's just a sound my throat makes. Like when you've sung along with a song a thousand times but you know it so well that the words don't even mean anything anymore. They're just bits of air coming out of your mouth. You know what I mean?"

"Not really," Paul said.

Sonny leaned back onto the pillow, closed his eyes. "That makes two of us," he said. He sighed, was silent for a moment. Then he opened his eyes and gazed at the ceiling. "Sometimes these days I think things and I don't even know where they're coming from. It's like I'm thinking somebody else's thoughts. Like I'm . . . I'm empty. And somebody else is fillin' in the blanks."

He'd never heard his father say anything like this before. His father was about precision, about clarity, about things you could hear and smell, things you could get a firm grip on. He thought of the word his mother had used—*unanchored.* He imagined his father on a boat, drifting from shore, pulled by some current toward . . . toward what?

"And sometimes . . ." Sonny went on. "Sometimes I'm not sure I even know what I'm doing." He opened his eyes, glanced over. "Think I'm losing it?"

"No," Paul said. "I just think you're tired."

Sonny yawned. "I am," he said. "Sometimes I think I'm so tired I might just be sleepwalking and not even know it. Like maybe I'm dreaming everything. Like maybe this conversation is a dream. Like maybe I'm twenty years old asleep in my dorm room and my dad's still alive and tomorrow I'll wake up and see your mother in Astronomy at nine-thirty. Know what I mean?"

"Sure," Paul lied. He wanted to touch his father's hand. He wanted to still his brain. He wanted to say *I know what you mean* and have it be true, about everything. Instead he said, "Dad, let's go to sleep."

• • •

There wasn't much chance of him being ditched the next day, what with his father curled beside him in bed. On the set, they'd finally reached the scenes of Sonny and Ian in the basement. Ian watched from his usual spot, muttering a running commentary of insults and mockery, but Sonny paced the studio floor incessantly, twice walking in front of shooting cameras and once tripping over the leg of a tripod. The crew, it was clear, had had about enough of him. *Just be still!* Lilly Douglass had finally snapped, and Sonny sat down abruptly in his chair, though it wasn't long before he was up again. Paul thought about the day at Neidermeyers', how his father had been the calm one during the long afternoon of waiting, how everybody else had been pacing like he was now. By the end of the day, Paul was a little sorry he hadn't been ditched; he couldn't help but see his father through the eyes of the crew, this foolish man, so entirely out of his element. He closed his eyes and pictured his father in his turnout gear. Nobody laughed at him then.

Later, after dinner in the room, Sonny announced he was going out for cigarettes and an hour later had still not returned. Ian was napping on the leather couch, drooling onto the cushions. Paul took a room key and set off in search of his father.

It was past eight o'clock; darkness had long fallen in the city. Well-dressed couples on their way to dinner strolled the sidewalks. An old lady wearing a bright pink cape walked a tiny black dog that was no bigger than a squirrel. Two men held hands as they waited for a taxi. Paul peered into the windows of every restaurant that lined the boulevard, hoping he might catch sight of his father. Maybe he'd run into somebody from the movie, had stopped for a drink. But no . . . Paul knew this was wishful thinking. His father had simply vanished into the city, had set his feet away from the hotel and kept walking. But why?

He turned a corner, walked two blocks, turned another corner. Probably his father was just out wandering around, smoking cigarettes, thinking more of those crazy thoughts about belonging and not belonging and whatever all that had been about. Probably Paul would bump into him around the next corner and Sonny would look at his watch and be genuinely startled by the time, apologize for being gone so long. Probably he'd just wanted a little while to himself. There was nothing wrong with that, was there?

The block Paul now found himself on was deserted. There were no streetlights, and he'd lost his bearings a bit. How many times had he turned? An expensive car with darkened windows slowed as it passed him, crept along beside him as he walked. He stared at the sidewalk, quickened his pace. Did gangs travel in cars? The gangs on MTV didn't, not cars like this at least. Well, this would show his father, wouldn't it? He imagined his father and Ian in a dim morgue, a stony-faced orderly pulling out a long metal slab on which lay his horribly beaten body.

"Why'd he go out?" his father would ask in a trembling voice. "Why? Why? Why?"

Ian would shrug. "Guess he went lookin' for you, Son."

The car pulled away from him, turned left at the next corner. Paul turned right, saw lights up ahead: the boulevard. He wasn't lost after all, and he wouldn't be murdered either. Strangely, this realization didn't make him feel much better. The fear had subsided, but in its wake was fury. Where the hell was his father? What was his problem anyway? There was only one possible cause: Ian. His mother had been right (*he just might be . . . caught up in Ian things or something*) and Paul was too little and too late to stop it. Ian had corrupted his father. For surely his father had not become this—this what?—all on his own.

Ian was smoking a joint and staring vacantly at the television when Paul slammed the door of the suite.

"My dad back?"

"Uh-uh," Ian said. A cloud of smoke hung over his head. He was shirtless and wore baggy gray sweatpants. His eyes looked like a polluted river. "Hey, *Die Hard's* coming on. You seen it?"

"What'd you do to him?"

He took a hit off the joint. "What'd I do to who?" he croaked.

"To my dad. He's never been like this before. He—"

"Listen, jocko," Ian said, expelling his smoke. "That fucker's been going crazy on me since the day we got here. I got nothin' to do with it."

Outside, on the street below, sirens rose and fell. An ambulance, heading west. Paul had spent his life learning to follow the sounds of danger. These sounds, his senses . . . that was all he could trust. Were there any other reliable sources?

"Hey, throw me those chips on the bar, willya?"

"I'm not gonna be your friend," Paul said.

Ian raised his eyebrows. "What's your problem, man? Grab the chips and sit down and watch the movie, why don't you?"

"I'm not gonna be your friend," Paul said again. "Not ever."

Ian tossed the remote onto the coffee table. "Who says I want you to be my friend? You're twelve years old. I got plenty of friends."

"You don't have *any* friends," Paul said. "You don't even know what it's like to have friends."

Ian stared at him. He didn't look angry. He looked curious.

"You're a loser," Paul said. "Everybody knows it. Everybody in the whole town. If it weren't for my dad you'd be back in Casey with your stupid mother and your slutty sister sitting in your trailer park eating Hamburger Helper."

Ian carefully squashed out his joint, cleared his throat. "You know I could break your neck, right?" he said evenly. "I mean, if I wanted to. I could break your neck in about half a second."

"You won't break my neck," Paul said. "You won't break my neck because then my father wouldn't like you anymore, and he's the only person in the world who likes you. He saved your ass and now he feels like he has to look out for you. He feels sorry for you. But sooner or later he's gonna figure out what everybody else knows, that you're a goner."

"A goner?"

"That's what my mother calls you. A goner."

Ian uncoiled from the couch. He rose like a snake, bare-chested, narrow and menacing, a perfect deadly line of muscle and fury. "What's that supposed to mean?"

Paul stood his ground. He was in the pocket with the ball, defenders hurtling toward him. He would not cower, not falter, not now. "It means you'll never amount to anything," he said coldly. "It means you might as well be dead already. It means it doesn't make any difference that my dad saved your life, 'cause your life wasn't even worth saving."

Ian raised his eyebrows. "And what about Daddy's life? Was that worth saving?"

"He saved his own life," Paul said through clenched teeth. "And yours."

"He saved *nothing*," Ian spat.

Paul opened his mouth to respond, but no words materialized for his voice to take hold of. He blinked his eyes away from Ian's for a moment and when he looked back Ian was staring intently at his own bare feet, his lips pressed tightly together, his face flushed with . . . with what? With shame?

"What're you talking about?" Paul asked.

Ian shook his head. "Forget it, jocko. Get outa here, willya? Go to bed or something."

"You're jealous," Paul said. "That's it, right? You're jealous because you never did anything. You never did anything worth anything."

Ian looked up. "I saved your father," he said quietly, his eyes locked on Paul's. "First his life and then his precious reputation. Is that anything?"

Paul giggled. He hadn't meant to giggle; he had meant to laugh, laugh a full, hearty Santa Claus belly laugh that would be heard by people across the hall, heard on the street below, heard all the way in Casey. But his throat was tight and his diaphragm wasn't cooperating either. He felt like he'd just swallowed a golf ball. Little wheezes of laughter were sputtering from his lips and he was at once humiliated and furious. He clenched his fists, pulled himself together.

"You . . . liar," he stammered. "You . . . piece of shit."

"That's right, little boy," Ian said, his eyes narrowing. "I'm a piece of shit. And everybody can sleep well tonight knowing that Ian Finch is a piece of shit." He went out onto the balcony, made tight fists around the iron railing, looked out into the night. For one numb moment Paul was certain he was going to hoist himself over the rail and plummet nine stories to the sidewalk. But of course not, he reasoned. Not Ian. But what if? People were full of surprises. You never knew what could happen. So what made a life worth saving? He stared at the swastika on Ian's back, dimly lit from the streetlights below. Maybe something was worth saving just because it was there in front of you and you were the only one around, because something—or someone—could flicker out in the blink of an eye while you stood there watching, doing nothing, admitting nothing. Paul slid open the glass door and Ian turned. His eyes were red. Was he crying? No, Paul remembered. He was stoned. But his cheekbones were tensed, his lips quivering.

"I'm not a goner," Ian said, his voice thin and strained. "That's a wicked thing to say about somebody. Do you know how wicked it is?"

"You saved him," Paul whispered. He meant it as a question, but it came out certain as a statement. The sun will rise. Dogs chase squirrels. Three comes after two. And Ian Finch had saved his father's life.

Ian shook his head, waved his hand in an effort to dismiss the entire night, perhaps the entire year. "Go to bed," he said. "I'm wasted, man. I'm babblin'."

"You saved him," Paul said again.

"Fuck it," Ian said. He sank down on the floor of the balcony, wiped his nose on his sleeve. For all these months Paul had thought of Ian as an adult—his beer and his smokes and his sneering, filthy mouth—but now, sitting on the floor in the dark with snot running out of his nose, he finally looked like the kid he was. Sixteen, Paul thought. It had seemed so old to him, but it didn't seem so old anymore. Ian lit a cigarette. The flame from his Zippo quivered in the light breeze. "Probably the one fucking thing I ever did worth talking about . . ."

"What happened down there?"

He wished the words back then, for a moment, wished himself back ten minutes, ten days, ten years, wished himself over his father's shoulder, barreling down the hallway to bed. But then Ian looked at him square, suddenly and briefly hopeful, and he knew there was no going back.

"You can't tell anyone," Ian whispered. "Not your mom, not anyone. You got to swear to me, Paul. You'll never tell."

Paul nodded. "I swear."

Chapter Six

Could the dark kill you?

No, Ian told himself. No. Just breathe. There's air here. Breathe.

Where the hell was he? He wasn't anywhere. Darkness was nothing and nothing was nowhere and so he was nowhere. Or anywhere. He could be anywhere, and anything could be here with him. Snakes. Spiders. Scorpions. Things with razor claws. Things with leathery tongues. Things without names. They could be slithering squirming stealing across the floor toward him at this very moment and he would never know it until they were on his arms and legs and face and in his mouth . . .

He felt a bubble rise in the back of his throat, choked out a sob.

Breathe, idiot. Just breathe.

He put his hand on his chest to try to calm himself. He rubbed up and down firmly, imagining other hands, his mother's even, on him, comforting him. He pretended he was a baby, asleep in some dark safe place. Darkness didn't always have to be scary, did it? There were some nice dark places. Movie theaters. Cars at night. Forts under front porches. All was well. All was well. Easy now. Then a jolt (a mahogany dresser from the master bedroom, though he had no way of knowing this) and he cried out, wet his pants with a burst of hot urine, shielded his face with his arms. He wished himself dead, willed it to be his last moment. Anything but this. Terror and dark. Not just dark. Black. Blacker black than the deepest sleep, blacker black than he ever would have believed black could be. Breathe, idiot. Breathe. Then:

Sirens.

He didn't dare believe it, not at first. He lay completely still, listened intently. But now the sound was gone, had vanished as quickly as it rose. Had he imagined it? Had he made the sound himself? His breath was coming in ragged bits, as if he had swallowed glass. Was he choking? He was choking. Choking on dark, on black, on spiders. No, you idiot, just dust, something, in the deep of his throat. He lifted his head and shoulders, sat up as much as he was able, spit up onto himself, gagged out something thick and lumpy that dribbled down his chin like oatmeal.

Why the fuck am I still alive?

Okay. A mystery. A riddle. A dilemma. Something to focus on (and breathe, yes, breathe): he couldn't for the world figure out why he wasn't dead. The rat lying beside him clearly was; he became aware of it now for the first time, its thick fur against his bare elbow, matted with blood and some kind of gummy puss he was grateful he couldn't see (there you go, darkness wasn't so bad . . . some advantages). He pretended the rat was a kitten, petted what was left of it with his right hand and it soothed him, this easy motion. Perhaps the worst was over. Perhaps everything that was going to come down had come down.

He began to feel out the space he was in. Above him, at the fingertips of his outstretched arms, something jagged but solid. The ceiling? Possibly, but it couldn't have been more than three feet from the floor. He stretched out both arms to the sides: darkness, space, something cool and rounded—a pipe?—to his right; a corner of grimy, tattered fabric to his left. The couch? He'd been asleep on the couch, hadn't he? Charlie and Kevin had left as the sun was coming up, crawled through the busted window, and he had stayed behind, too tired, too lazy, too stoned, to wander home. Five minutes or five hours ago? Five days?

He kicked out his right foot and connected with something metal that made a dull clanging noise: it was the kitchen stove, though he didn't know it. He tried to kick his left foot, but it wouldn't budge. It was pinned under something, and he attempted to jerk it free. If he could just move, roll over onto his stomach, start crawling to someplace . . . where? He sat up and leaned down as far as he could, got a grip on his jeans below the knee, and tugged on his leg until sweat popped on his temples. Nothing. No movement, no hint of movement, no scrape no shift no give. His foot was trapped. He was trapped.

"Help," he said. "Help me."

He said it so quietly he could hardly hear himself. He lay back down flat, spit up a little more, wiped his mouth with the heel of his hand. Who the hell would know he was here? Charlie and Kevin . . . they'd been so fucked up they probably wouldn't even remember that he'd stayed behind. Christ, he'd be a goner by the time they even rolled out of bed. They'd been up all night, the three of them, smoking weed and listening to music, screwing around with those goddamn M-80's.

The M-80's. There'd been a dozen of them, wired together with stripped pipe cleaners. They were going to rig up something like a bomb, then blow it out back, in the pasture, just to see how much damage it could do, just to see what you could make out of nothing. He giggled. The giggle sounded like something that would come out of his sister's mouth, and this made him giggle even more. Oh yeah, he had heard stories about shit like this, guys in avalanches or guys in Vietnam who got trapped in tunnels or whatever and started freaking out, giggling like girls, shitting their pants and playing with themselves and whatever. If only there were a little light, just a tiny bit, a pinprick of light, maybe he could see his way clear to something. He promised himself that if he ever got out of this he would never again take light for granted. Not any kind of light, not for one moment. He started listing all the kinds of light he could think of: sunlight, moonlight, nightlight, lamplight, headlight, starlight, firelight, penlight.

"Light," he yelled, kicking the stove in time with his shouting. "Light! Light! Light! Light! Light! Light! Light! Light!"

He stopped, exhausted from this brief effort. He was a pussy, a pansy, a lame-ass stupid son-of-a-bitch weakling. Well, his sister could have his CDs now, the whole fucking lot of them. He had stolen most of them from the Kmart over in Chambersburg anyway, and his crappy CD player was so screwed up she wouldn't even be able to listen to them without that thunking in the bass. He had a decent jacket he'd been looking forward to wearing when the weather got colder; it would probably fit Charlie, not that he deserved it, but it was either that or the trash. What else was there? He had fifty-some T-shirts that someone could donate to the car wash, a couple busted watches and a big ugly gold ring his grandfather had given him, some Rollerblades and base-balls in the garage from when he was a kid. He had nothing, really, nothing worth anything to anybody, not even to him. This was the worst part. He wanted to have to think hard about it, to consider carefully where each of his belongings would go, what he would bequeath to whom. But he didn't have shit.

"Shit!" He kicked again with his right foot, ferociously, and broke his big toe. He heard it snap in his sock and a rush of cool pain shot up his leg all the way into his temples. "Shit!"

His father would make the trip from Cleveland for the funeral, bring the wife. They would stand in the weedy front yard of his mother's house smoking cigarettes, not even wanting to set foot inside. Kally would cry, he knew this. She would sit on his bed and cry, wipe her face on his tiger blanket, and nobody would do anything about it. It hurt his chest to think of her crying, even if she was a pain in his ass. His mother would be yakking a mile a minute and his father would say something like: well, you had to expect a thing like this was going to happen sooner or later, didn't you? His father would say something like this to his mother, and his mother would stop talking and just stare at him through a few heartbeats, remembering why she hated his fucking guts. Do you have one decent bone in your body? she would say to him, her eyes burning, while all the while the new wife looked off in another direction, wishing for Cleveland. He was your son, for God's sake. He was your only son.

Ian was crying. What the fuck? They'd never find him anyway, and by the time they did his eyes wouldn't be red from crying anymore, so no one would know he went out bawling like a baby. They wouldn't even be eyes, probably: they'd be holes. Bugs would eat his eyes. *Bugs would eat his eyes.* This made him cry harder. God, he didn't want his eyes to be eaten by bugs, even if he'd be dead and never know it. He imagined his own face, the face his saw in the bathroom mirror every day, chewed up by bugs. Jesus Christ.

He started kicking again.

• • •

Sometime later he woke with a start. How long had he been out? His right leg was limp from kicking, his toes throbbing, his head swimming, his eyes burning, his throat parched, his jeans damp from when he'd peed himself. Black. More black. His hands were moist and trembling.

Breathe, idiot.

He couldn't feel his left foot. His knee he could feel, and part of his calf; the cold from the concrete floor chilled his legs even through the thick denim of his jeans. But it was like that left foot wasn't even there anymore, not even a part of his body. It didn't even hurt. It just *wasn't*. He thought about a movie he'd seen once, some guy in a car wreck laid up in the hospital, the doctor pricking the guy's toes with a little pin. Feel this? the doctor would say. Feel this? And the guy just lies there looking down at his foot, half pissed and half heartbroken, and you know the doctor could shove that little pin all the way through the toe and the guy would never feel a damn thing.

But you couldn't be paralyzed in just one foot, right? Sure, he was no doctor, but even he knew that either your spine was busted or it wasn't. And his left foot couldn't really be gone, cut off or anything, because if it was he'd be lying in a lake of blood and probably dead by now anyway. It's there, he told himself. Broken, sure. Maybe broken real bad. But there, somewhere down there, in the black. The black. Who knew it could be this black? Who knew?

He heard something.

Really? No. Yes. Really? Yes. Sounds from up above. Voices? Maybe. Probably not. Grinding. Chipping. A drill? What if he was at the dentist, stoned on gas, getting a root canal? What if this whole thing was some fucked-up dental trip? A flake of dirt landed on his lip and he licked it off to prove to himself it was real. Yes. Someone was up there. Maybe. A glimmer of hope, fleeting but intense. He might get out. He might actually get out.

He sat up, stretched his arms until the skin in his pits felt like it was tearing, and grasped ahold of the ceiling. He got his hands around a plank of wood and started shaking with all his might.

"Hey!" he yelled. "Somebody's down here! Hey!"

Splinters of wood sliced into his fingers and bits of the ceiling (or the floor? or the walls?) began falling around him.

"Hey! Somebody's here!"

He'd get himself out, that was it. Hell, he wasn't totally useless, was he? He could weasel himself out of this on his own, goddammit. A chunk of plaster from the ceiling struck him hard on the shoulder but he kept tugging. It was his fault he was here, so he'd be the one to get himself out. He didn't need any help. If he could just get this one piece loose, this one plank of wood, maybe there would be light above it, maybe there'd be some guy on the other side with a fucking glass of water, maybe there'd be—

The plank of wood pulled free and slammed him across the forehead, knocking him out cold.

And then there was a dream, or he thought it was a dream. It must have been a dream because there was light, a dim circle of it, falling on his stomach from somewhere high above. But no, not a dream. He was dead, that was it. And here was God Almighty, right on time, getting ready to slurp him up into the light. Heaven! Who would have believed it? Apparently the requirements for paradise weren't so strict after all. Apparently old God wasn't the tight-ass everyone would have you believe. Well, he'd never killed anyone, right? He'd never done anything *that* bad. And God knew things no one else knew. God knew he took turtles out from the middle of the road. God knew he always gave Kally the bigger order of fries. God knew sometimes he turned on the coffeemaker when he got home at three or four A.M. so his mother would have hot coffee when she woke up.

But no. Scratch that. It wasn't God here in this tomb at all. It was a guy. Sonny, the guy said his name was. But Sonny was speaking some crazy language, some Chinese thing, all the words mashed up together. I'm American, Ian tried to tell Sonny. I don't know Chinese. Were they in China? He'd fallen down a hole in the basement, all the way through the middle of the earth, and now he was in some Chinaman's basement. But this Sonny guy, his eyes weren't all slanty, and the yellow writing on the back of his coat was in English: Casey Fire Department. Sonny was a fireman. Was there a fire? Was that what the light was? But if he was a fireman, where was his hose? Sonny the fireman was crawling all over him. Sonny was at his feet. Sonny was touching him everywhere now: his legs, his chest, his throat, his face. Sonny's lips were moving but now no words in any language were coming out. Now Sonny was flying. Now Sonny's feet were gone and now Sonny's knees were gone and now it was just Sonny's head getting further and further away. Wait, he said to Sonny. Wait, don't go.

"Ian!"

He jolted into consciousness. Him? Ian? Was that him?

"Ian!"

"What?" he called. Fucking moron . . . how stupid to yell *what?* His voice was thin. He sounded like his grandmother. But there was the beam of light on his stomach—it was a hole!—and a voice, a real voice: "Hold on! I'm comin'!"

And then Ian breathed what was perhaps his first truly deep breath of the day. So it hadn't been a dream after all: he wasn't dead, wasn't at the dentist, wasn't in China. He was in the basement of old man Neidermeyer's house lying in his own piss, and Sonny the fireman was coming for him. Sonny the fireman was going to free his trapped leg and carry him to the light. Sonny the fireman was going to save his life.

And then he heard the sad, deep groan, like weary thunder. It wasn't coming from him. And it wasn't coming from Sonny. It was the house. The house was groaning.

"Shit," he said. "Shit mother fucker goddamn son of a—"

He closed his eyes tight, tucked his chin to his chest, held his breath. Quick, he was thinking. Just make it quick.

He'd never felt an earthquake before, but he was pretty damn sure this was what one would feel like. The shudder (was this possible?) was *inside* him, in his bones, his organs, his tissue, his teeth, his tongue, his blood. And the circle of light, instead of closing, seemed to be sucked upward as the hole above his stomach collapsed. He waited to feel the weight of the house crush him, waited for his lungs to flatten, but instead he felt the fireman, who dropped from the sudden darkness like a sack of dirt and landed on top of him, diagonally, an elbow so sharp into his gut it took the breath right out of him. Blood spattered onto Ian's face, blood from the fireman's head, which cracked against the floor beside his left shoulder, knocking the fireman out cold.

Then everything was still. And Jesus Christ if he wasn't still alive. He felt himself smiling—smiling! what was he thinking anyway?—and his heart was beating a mile a minute at the miracle of it all. Alive! Jesus H. Christ—it was enough to make him think someone might be looking out for him. The same couldn't be said for the fireman, who lay motionless across Ian's stomach and chest and who felt like dead weight. Literally.

"Fireman," he said. "Hey, fireman. You dead?"

No, the fireman wasn't dead. He could feel the rise and fall of breath—peaceful, unaware—feel the thump of the fireman's heart against his own rib cage. He'd had a few girls lie on top of him like this, liked to feel the breath and the beat, to pretend he was asleep so they wouldn't roll off. But this guy weighed more than any girl, and stunk to boot. He heaved him off to the side.

"Huh?" the fireman asked, slamming into consciousness and thrashing wildly around, striking Ian squarely in the chin, kicking him in the thigh. "Huh? What?"

"Cool out!" Ian shouted, shielding himself against the blows. Just his luck, right, survives the house falling down on him—twice!—only to be beaten to death by the guy who's supposed to rescue him. "Cool out, man! Just cool it."

A brief stillness in the darkness. Silence, but for breathing. Then, suddenly, more frantic shuffling, another elbow in the ribs.

"Jesus, quit it! You're beating the crap outa me."

"Shit. . . . Shit!"

"Shit what?"

A long sigh, nearly a wail. "Half my gear's gone. Flashlight. Air bag. Must of got torn off on the way down."

"It was bad," Ian said.

"How bad?"

"Bad bad. Earthquake bad. No way we should still be alive bad."

Silence. Then: "This my blood or yours?"

"Where's it at?"

"All over the floor here."

Ian tried to turn his head toward the voice. It was difficult. With his foot pinned, the only position that resembled anything close to comfort was flat on his back, arms at his sides, staring straight up. "Sounded like you cracked your head when you landed. You were out for a minute."

Raspy breathing. More shifting. Weird, Ian thought, to feel the guy and hear the guy but not be able to see him, not one bit, not even an outline in the dark. It was like he wasn't real.

"Is this part of the plan?" Ian asked, returning his gaze to the ceiling he couldn't see, letting his neck relax.

"Huh? What plan?"

"The rescue plan."

The fireman lay back, sighed, was finally still. "I think the whole house caved in," he said. "Musta been the wind. Either that or Trusty Construction isn't so trusty after all. They're gonna have to start diggin' all over again. If all the walls are down they can come at us with jackhammers, speed things up. We're just gonna have to lie here until they find us. That's all we can do. So that's the plan."

Ian marveled at the guy. Here he was in his own dusty black grave, and his voice was steady as a stone, full of practiced confidence, arrogant in its sureness. It was the voice, Ian thought, of a guy who usually got what he wanted, a guy who didn't have reason to doubt much. Asshole.

"I think the plan is we die," Ian said.

"Today's not my day to die," the fireman said. "I don't think it's yours either. They got through once, they'll get through again."

"Took 'em long enough," Ian said. "What were you guys doing up there? Having a picnic?"

"You're a real piece of work, Finch," the fireman said angrily. "Guys up there've been busting their asses all day to get you outa here. You might think to thank 'em sometime, if it's not too much trouble."

Great, Ian thought. Perfect. Of all the firemen who could have dropped down the rabbit hole, he gets Mr. Holier Than Thou Smart-Ass.

"What happened down here anyway?" the fireman asked.

"How should I know?"

"You got no idea?" The voice was laced with suspicion. It was a tone Ian was profoundly familiar with. From the time he was a kid, whenever anything went wrong, all heads swerved his way. Half the times he'd been suspended from school it was for shit he hadn't even done.

"I was asleep," Ian said. "On the couch. When I woke up I was lying here, just like this."

"I was down here earlier. You remember?"

"Kinda. Sonny, right?"

"That's right." A pause. "What were you guys doing down here? You know, before."

Ian didn't say anything. Who knew what had knocked the place down? It was barely standing to begin with. One time a bunch of them had gone upstairs to poke around and Charlie'd put his foot right through the kitchen floor. So maybe the M-80's hadn't gone off. Maybe the house just decided to fall down, the way old people sometimes just decide to die.

"You and your buddies messin' around with explosives maybe?"

"No way," Ian said quickly, much too quickly. Christ, what was wrong with him? He was lying like a five-year-old, his lips smeared with powdered sugar, an empty box of doughnuts on the counter.

"Pipe bomb?"

Pipe bomb. That was how the whole thing started. *Let's make a pipe bomb,* he'd said to Charlie. *For what?* Charlie'd asked. *Shit, I dunno. Just to see if we can.* Charlie had looked at him doubtfully. Charlie was dumb as a cow. *You know how to do that?* No, he didn't know how. But everybody was making pipe bombs these days. How hard could it be?

"It was nothing, man," Ian said. "Nothing like that. We were just screwing around." He squirmed; the backs of his thighs were aching and numb from the cold, hard floor. *I got some M-80's,* Charlie had said. *Left over from summer.* Yeah, Ian had thought, they'd done some damage with those babies, hadn't they? One of them could blow your average mailbox into a million silver splinters; they'd butchered at least a dozen the week of the Fourth. So what if you wired a bunch together? What could you do with that?

"We were just passin' the time," he said. "We weren't gonna do anything."

A snort of a laugh from the fireman. "What? Like blow up the high school?"

"Shit," Ian said. "See, there you go. That's what I knew you'd say. That's what everybody's gonna think now, right, that we were some psychos or something, getting ready for a rampage? It was nothing like that. We were just screwing around, man, having a good time."

"You having a good time now, Ian?"

Okay. He deserved that. He was an idiot. And now him and the fireman were going to die because he was an idiot. The high school. Good old Casey Fuck You High. That wasn't part of the plan. And if it was, if it had ever crossed his mind for even an instant, it wasn't because he wanted to kill anybody. If he was going to do it, if he'd ever thought about it, it was just so he could scare them. All he'd wanted—if he wanted it—was for those pricks to not be so sure of themselves. He didn't want to kill them. He just wanted them to know that, if he wanted to kill them, he could.

"How's your head, fireman? Not gonna conk out on me again, are you?"

Silence.

"Sonny?"

"I'm just lying here thinking about what kind of asshole would set off a bomb *inside* a house."

"All right," Ian said. "I'm an asshole, all right? You feel better now? I was asking you a question, man, out of genuine concern for your well-being, so if you want to stop raggin' on me for one fucking minute maybe you could answer."

"I'll be okay as long as I stay awake," Sonny said. "I think I've got a concussion."

"I'll belt you if you fall asleep. They won't arrest me for that, will they?"

"Not for that," Sonny said. "They'll be too busy arresting you for other stuff."

"I'm surprised the cops wanted to rescue me at all. Some of 'em probably happy to leave me down here."

"You're in luck," Sonny said. "Now they gotta rescue you 'cause they gotta rescue me."

Well, there was probably some truth to that. They'd probably work a little faster now, pick up the pace, now that their own boy was down here. *No more cigarette breaks, guys,* the chief would say. *Now we got something really worth saving. . . .*

"Anything like this ever happened to you before?" Ian asked.

"Oh, sure. Two or three times a week I get crushed by a house. I'm getting bored with it."

"A comedian and a fireman. You should take your show on the road, man."

"You could go on the road yourself, Ian. America's favorite Nazi comedian. Bet you'd get a nice audience . . . skinheads, Klansmen, all the good folk."

Ian felt his stomach knot. "Who told you I was a Nazi?"

"A couple reliable sources."

Ian scoffed. "You believe everything you hear?"

"You got a swastika on your back, don't you?"

That fucking swastika. Like that made him a Nazi or something? Why did people always assume the worst? He'd been drunk, plastered. They'd been in Lancaster, at a club. Tattoos! It had sounded like a great idea. Who'd have thought you could really get a tattoo at two in the morning anyway? He'd stood there in that nasty basement on Prince Street—it stunk of beer and sweat and piss, wasn't even a legal operation, just some old biker guy with the tools in his basement—looking over the three walls of choices. He'd wanted the meanest baddest thing they had. There were guns and knives and skulls and chicks with blood coming out of their ears and everything you could think of. And then that fat black swastika. This one, he'd said, laying his finger at the point where the lines intersected. I want this one.

"Who told you that?" he asked. "My idiot friends?"

"Christ, Ian. You don't tattoo a swastika on your back if you don't want people to know about it, right? Isn't that part of the point?"

"You a shrink too? You don't know shit about me."

"Maybe I don't want to either."

"You're hurting my feelings, fireman. Here I was feelin' sorry for myself for being trapped underground all day and now, on top of everything, you don't even like me. This has to be the saddest moment of my life."

"Mine too. Trapped with a Nazi who stinks."

"I stink? *I* stink? You smell yourself lately?"

Sonny laughed. Not a crazy laugh, not the laugh of a guy half cocked or half dead. It was easy and real and full and it made Ian smile. It felt like it had been a million years since he'd heard anyone laugh.

"At least you're gonna die laughing, fireman."

"I'm not dying. Nobody's dying. They're coming for us."

"You hear anything?" Ian asked doubtfully. "I don't hear anything."

"They're up there."

"They're thinking we're dead for sure. Probably all went home. They'll come back tomorrow with bulldozers and start looking for our bodies."

"They haven't left, Ian. They won't leave until they find us."

"I guess those are your buddies up there, huh?"

"Yeah. My wife too. You think she'll let them leave? And I don't think your mom'll be heading home any time soon."

Ian's heart did a double beat. It was Sunday; his mother should be at home, cackling at some stupid video, munching on microwave popcorn. "My mom? She's here? You sure?"

"Well she said she was your mom. I don't know why anybody'd make *that* up."

"What'd she look like?"

"Christ, Ian, she's there."

"Did she talk your ear off? That's her then, if she did. She'll talk to anybody about anything, for a thousand hours. I've had friends offer her money to shut up, I swear it. But she never gets the clue. She just laughs and keeps yakking."

"What about your dad? What's he do?"

"She talked him off to Cleveland a long time ago."

Had his mother even called him? Called to say, well, Ian's buried under a house. And by the way you owe me about nine years' worth of child support. He tried to imagine a house he'd never been in, a kitchen he'd never seen, his father holding the phone, probably rolling his eyes. Nah, he thought, she wouldn't of called him. She wouldn't call until she was sure their son was dead.

"What about you?" he asked. "What family you got?"

"Wife and son."

"What's she do? Your wife. Raise the kid?"

"She teaches math at the high school."

"Yeah? What's her name?"

"Laura Tucker."

Jesus . . . had he failed that class? A dim memory, the back row, the desk next to the window, his head cool against the glass, his eyes half open, watching Mrs. Tucker's blond braid flap against her back as she wrote, the squeaky chalk, the shuffle of pencils on notebook paper.

"Mrs. Tucker? That's your old lady?"

"Not so old," Sonny murmured.

"I'll say. Whoo." Ian shook his head. "I'm feeling a whole lot better about you, Sonny. Every guy in town wants to bag that babe. How's it feel to be the guy who gets to do it every night?"

"You got some mouth on you, I'll give you that."

"I figure we'll be dead before you can kick my ass."

"We're not dying," Sonny said roughly. "Shut up about dying, all right? I don't want to hear any more about it."

"I've been down here a long damn time, man. I got my whole funeral planned."

"The town's first Nazi funeral. . . ."

"Hey, fuck you." Ian tried to shift his weight, tried to turn away from Sonny, as if they were a couple lying in bed, arguing the same argument they'd slogged through a thousand times before. He felt something wrench in his ankle and grimaced.

"My foot's flat," he said. "You know that, Sonny? Flat as a fucking pancake, I can tell."

"Maybe not."

"You gonna get it out of there?"

"Can't," Sonny said. "Not until they come for us."

"How come?"

" 'Cause the thing I was gonna jack up the fridge with, the air bag, the inflatable, it's buried about five feet above us. Snapped off my belt, I guess, along with the flashlight."

"Great," Ian said. He licked his teeth. He was thirsty. The last liquid he'd had was a Busch beer, probably around three in the morning, however long ago that was. You could go without food for days, he remembered, but drink was different. At some point, your body started drinking itself, or something crazy like that. Then your organs got all shriveled and—

"Hey," Sonny said softly. "I might drift off here for a minute."

"I get to hit you then, right?"

"Not for a while. I'm tired. I've been up forty-eight hours."

"My heart's breakin' for you. All I been doing is lying in the dirt all day. Wake up and talk to me, man. We need a plan. You're the man with the plan, right?"

Silence. Then: "If I had a little light maybe we could cut our way out of here."

"With what? Our fingernails?"

"I got an ax," Sonny said. "At least I did."

Ian scoffed. "Probably up there with everything else."

"No. No, I had it in my hand when I fell. I was diggin' with it. Must be around here somewhere."

Ian felt a jolt of hope. "So you can bust through maybe? Dig up while those guys're digging down, meet 'em in the middle."

"No way. If I just start swinging in the dark I might knock out the only thing that's keeping this space a space. If I had some light, maybe . . . maybe. But I'm not just gonna start swinging."

"So we just lie here and wait? That's it?"

Silence. Ian listened to Sonny breathe. He didn't want to be a baby about it, but he didn't want Sonny falling asleep on him either. What if he died? That wound on his head was pretty bad. What if the guy died and he had to lie here in the dark with a dead body? How long before it'd start to rot, to stink? He'd have to close the eyes, that was for sure. He wouldn't be able to see them, but he'd know just how they looked, glazed over and staring glassy at the beginning of dead.

"Hey, Sonny."

Nothing.

"Sonny."

"What?"

"Just making sure you're not checking out on me."

"I'm not going to die," Sonny said. "I'm not allowed; Laura'd never forgive me. She'd come to my grave every day and spit on it."

"That's sweet. Hey, I know what'll wake you up. Singing."

"Singing?"

"You know, camp songs or something. This is kinda like camp, right?"

"What kind of camp your mother send you to?"

"You know what I mean. All dark and quiet, like spooky woods or something."

"Let's just be still for a while," Sonny said. "Can we do that?"

"Not if you're gonna pass out on me."

"I'm not going to pass out. I just want to be quiet."

Quiet. Of all things Ian did not want to be, it was quiet. There'd be plenty of time for quiet when they were dead. He remembered when his grandfather finally kicked a few years back, his mom's dad, how the old guy had gone out talking a blue streak from his hospital bed because he knew the end was near and who knew what the end meant—maybe no more talking forever, not another word spoken in that voice you've gotten so used to. Plenty of time for quiet when you're lying in your coffin, your lips sewn shut.

"This what you thought would happen when you became a fireman?"

Sonny sighed. "I didn't ever *become* a fireman. I started out a fireman."

"In your blood, huh?"

Sonny didn't say anything.

"You with me, man? Still awake?"

"I keep trying to think what my dad would do in this situation. I keep thinking he'd know what to do."

"Yeah? So what would he do?"

He felt Sonny's whole body tighten, squeeze up on itself like a fat ball of rubber bands. "I don't know. That's the friggin' point. If I knew I'd have done it by now. But he wouldn't have waited, I know that much. He would have acted."

"He a good guy, your dad? You like him?"

"Sure I liked him. What wasn't to like? Jesus, it was like growing up with a movie star. It was like having Clint Eastwood as your dad."

"You got big shoes to fill, I guess. Me, I never had much of a problem with that. You know you always see those people on talk shows saying shit like, 'My daddy always expected too much of me' or 'My father never thought I was good enough.' My old man, he never expected shit from me. I think he musta took one look at me and said, this kid's never gonna amount to nothing. I'm not gonna expect anything from this kid. I'll be happy if this moron learns to fucking *walk*."

Sonny was quiet.

"Sonny?"

Nothing.

"Hey, Sonny?"

Nothing again. He was out. But breathing. Out but breathing. When Ian was little, six or seven, when Kally was still a baby and his dad had just bailed out, he used to go into her room at night and watch her sleep. He had this thing, this fear, that she was going to die. He'd heard about it on TV, on a show his mother liked to watch. Crib death, they called it. Little babies, healthy little babies, babies who didn't have a thing wrong with them, they'd just stop breathing in the middle of the night and when you woke up in the morning they were dead. So two or three times a night he'd go into Kally's room and make sure she was still breathing. He'd stand there in his pajamas and watch her sleep, listen to those tiny breaths. As long as she was breathing, she was still alive. And if he heard her stop breathing, if he shook her awake real fast, she would be okay again. That's what they said on TV. So this would work with Sonny too. If he just kept listening, he could make sure Sonny wouldn't die. 'Cause if Sonny didn't die then he might not die. And— although twice in the last year he'd eyed a bottle of Drano and imagined how it must burn going down the throat—he found he'd never wanted to *not* die more than he did right now. Yes indeed, if God was a bargainer (and he'd be a fool if he wasn't) Ian was going to start bargaining his way out of this coffin right now.

Okay. One. He was going to stop being an asshole to his mother. His mother had had a crappy life, and there was no doubt he had only been making it crappier for the last sixteen years. Maybe she was a nag, and maybe she ran her mouth until everybody wanted to shoot themselves in the goddamn temple, but she had raised him and Kally all on her own and he was going to show her a little bit of respect for that, if for nothing else. It was too late to be the son she—or anyone—wanted, but maybe sometimes he could stay around and eat dinner at the house, and maybe he'd mow the lawn if it wasn't too damn hot, and maybe he'd even get a job—okay, maybe—and pitch in some money so she didn't have to work weekends anymore.

Okay. Two. He wasn't going to let anybody talk him into doing something that would get his ass thrown in jail. He was almost seventeen now, his carefree juvy delinquent days nearly over. No more social workers, no more anger management, no more lame-ass community service. If he kept beating the shit out of people he was going to get thrown in jail, real jail, and right now he'd had about enough of small spaces, thank you very much. He was going to start thinking ahead a little. Maybe when Charlie wanted to jump some nigger who was strutting his cocky ass home from basketball practice, maybe he'd say

"Forget it, man. He ain't worth our energy." He could say that and still be cool. He could say it if it meant staying out of jail.

Okay. Three. No more talk about blowing shit up. No more half-serious plans. The way things went these days, all the crazies out there tasting blood everywhere they looked, they could lock you up just for talking about it. And now there were all these pussy kids just waiting for a chance to squeal, wanting to get a little attention, wanting to act like heroes. It wouldn't matter if he didn't even really want to blow anything up. They could make it seem like he could. They could make like thinking about it was as bad as doing it.

He closed his eyes. If God was a bargainer. Well, maybe he wasn't. Maybe you could say anything and it didn't make any difference. Maybe all the promising in the world didn't mean squat to God. Probably it just cracked him up. Listen to this guy, he was probably saying to Jesus right now. Just listen to this asshole, willya?

"Ian?"

Again, he started awake. How long? Then he heard a whimper. Like a dog, a puppy, closed up out in the cold.

"Sonny? You okay?"

Another whimper. "Ian? Where are you?"

What the hell kind of question was that? Where exactly would he be besides right here, flush up against Sonny?

"S'all right. I'm right here. Feel me? I'm right next to you."

A clammy hand seized his fingers. "I woke up and it was dark. It was dark, but in my sleep it was light. Bright light. It's like everything's backwards, you know? It's like you could forget who you are. Do you know who you are?"

Oh man, Ian thought. Oh man oh man oh man oh man . . . this was fucking perfect. How long had they been out? It seemed like a long time, but there was no way to tell. "How's your head, Sonny?"

"My head?"

Like he had to ask. Like Sonny wasn't babbling like an idiot. He probably had a concussion. Maybe he even had brain damage. Maybe he'd fallen asleep and woken up a retard. That's just what he needed, a retard fireman.

"What day is it?" Sonny asked.

"It doesn't matter," Ian said. "Don't worry about it."

Sonny gripped his arm frantically. "What if it's Wednesday?"

"It ain't Wednesday," Ian said. "You know why? 'Cause if it was Wednesday we'd be dead. We're gonna be dead or eatin' each other by Wednesday, Sonny."

"I'm not eating you," Sonny said matter-of-factly. "No matter what happens."

Ian laughed, though he didn't think Sonny knew what it meant to tell a joke anymore. "That's fine, old boy. Don't eat me if you don't want. But if you die first you can be damn sure I'm eating you. I'll find that little ax of yours and go at it. Filet o' Sonny. Sonny McNuggets."

A girlish giggle. "You want fries with that?"

"Supersize," Ian said.

"You know what?" Sonny asked.

"What?"

"This goddamn house might fall on us in five seconds no matter what we do."

A chill rippled down Ian's spine. "Hey, idiot. Hey, stupid. Hey, moron. You're supposed to be the cheerleader, okay? I'm the one supposed to be freaking out. Don't you go all loco on me."

"My father," Sonny said. "He sent me away to school, to college. Did I tell you that? Sent me away to the good old Pennsylvania State University. Happy Valley, home of the Nittany Lions. I tell you that?"

"Nope."

"Well he did. Didn't matter that I didn't want to go. You think that'd matter to him? Last couple years I started thinking, what if he didn't think I had it in me to be a fireman? What if he didn't think I had the balls for it? What if that's why he sent me away?"

Ian shook his head. "That's crap. More'n likely he did it 'cause he didn't want you spending your days like this."

"What do you know?" Sonny asked. "You didn't know him."

"No I didn't."

"They fucking *worshiped* him. Sometimes he looked at me and I could see he was thinking I didn't have it."

"I think you're making that up," Ian said. "I think you're making that up on the spot, 'cause you're freaked out. You're making up all sorts of lies about your life 'cause you're scared and it's dark and you're fucked in the head. Been there, done that, old boy. I told myself lots of shit about my father this morning, I was thinkin' he left because of me, 'cause I was such a hopeless case. But you know what? He was just an asshole. He left. So what? You gotta not dwell on that stuff, man. That's why we gotta sing. Singing's good for us."

"I can't sing," Sonny said. "Dogs run away when I sing."

"No dogs here," Ian said. "Just my little rat, and he ain't listening. Let's sing songs about light, okay? 'Light My Fire.' 'This Little Light of Mine.' 'You Light Up My Life.' "

Above them, something creaked ominously. Ian pretended he didn't hear it. " 'The Night the Lights Went Out in Georgia.' 'Glow Little Glow Worm.' "

"We're dead," Sonny said flatly. "You hear that shit upstairs? We're dead."

"Shut up!" Ian shouted. "Listen, man. Here's what you're gonna do. You're gonna get your ass on the move. Right now. You're gonna find a way out of here. There's a window, somewhere in this place. I don't know where, but it's how we got in all the time. Can't be more than twenty feet away, off to your left if I got my bearings straight. You're just gonna slide on your belly, man, all the way over to that wall. You use that ax if you need it, hack your way through whatever's in the way. You get out and then you send somebody to come back in for me. I'm good for a little while, Sonny. But you gotta get started, you hear me?"

Silence.

"You hear me?"

"I can't do it," Sonny whispered.

"Wha'dya mean you can't do it?"

"My back's broken. I can't move. It's dark, Ian. I think I'm paralyzed. I can't even lift up my head."

"That's horseshit," Ian said. "What kind of fireman are you? Your back ain't busted. You're just freaking yourself out. You wanna prove something to your father, then—"

Something above them shuddered and then gave way; a piece of the ceiling crashed to the floor beside Ian's right shoulder. This was it now, the end, he was sure of it. Once one thing went the whole thing would fall. But it didn't. Everything was silent. And then, from Sonny, a new sound. Spit and phlegm and little squeaks. Christ Almighty, he was crying. The fireman, the brave guy, was crying.

"Get your shit together," Ian said. "Come on, man, pull yourself together."

"It's all comin' down."

"It's not."

"I'm so dizzy."

The fireman was cracking up. Jesus Christ. A whack on the head and hour upon hour of dark and now he's a babbling dimwit chickenshit baby. If he'd only just *go,* just take that goddamn ax and go. This house had had it with them; it had given them every opportunity, given them a fighting chance, left them this safe space for all these hours, and it was sick of waiting. If Sonny didn't drop dead from the wound on his head, surely the house would collapse anyway. Either way he was stuck, either way dead.

"Go," Ian said. "Take the ax and go."

"I can't."

And then, in the quiet, in the silence and the darkness and the chill of bad luck and bad decisions, the truth dawned on Ian slowly. It must have always been there, though, in the back of his mind, its whispering lost in the din of everything else. He'd been saving it for this moment, for the moment when all hope seemed lost. There was only one way he was getting out of here, only one way Sonny was getting out of here.

"Sonny, listen to me," he said. "You listening?"

"What?"

"We can't wait here any longer. You're right, man. The house is coming down. So you're gonna have to cut off my foot."

Silence.

"You hear me?"

"You're crazy."

"I'm not. It's the only way."

"The air bag," Sonny mumbled.

"The air bag's gone. You said so yourself."

"Oh, you wouldn't believe it," Sonny moaned. "This thing, it looks like a balloon. Or a little pillow, really, like those pillows they give you on airplanes. But this thing, this tiny little thing, can lift half a ton. Half a ton! All you do, you just slide it under—"

"That's great!" Ian interrupted. "I'm really happy to hear about all the great fucking equipment we don't have. Let's see, we don't have an air bag, we don't have a flashlight, we don't have a goddamn drop of water. So what do we have, Sonny? Huh? What we got left?"

"Nothing," Sonny said.

"No, no. We got one thing. Right? We got an ax."

"An ax," Sonny echoed.

Would he die? How long could you live with your foot cut off, with the blood pouring out? Would he have enough time to find the window? Where the hell were those guys, those stupid firemen? Why couldn't he hear anybody digging? How big a pile could a house make if it all fell down? Twenty feet? Forty feet?

"You're gonna cut off my foot," Ian said evenly. "You're gonna go down there, and you're just gonna hack it off, wham bam thank you ma'am. Shit, it's probably half cut off already, right? Then you tie it up with your shirt or something, squeeze off the bleeding. And then we're getting out of here together, you hear me? We're going together."

"He didn't want me in the fire department," Sonny murmured.

"Jesus, shut up!" Ian shouted, pounding his fists on the floor. "I don't wanna hear any more about your goddamn father!" With great effort he turned, flipped himself onto his side and nearly onto his stomach, felt the thigh muscles in his left leg strain, pull taut. He felt around Sonny blindly, recklessly. It had to be around here somewhere, probably within his grasp, if Sonny had really had it in his hand when he fell. He reached above where Sonny lay, felt his way along the ragged boards, his already torn hands catching on shards and splinters as he

grappled with the wood. Would he even know it if he felt it? He would
. . . he did. His fingers closed around the foam rubber handle. Foam
rubber—sure, it made sense. Sweaty hands, nervous hands, needed to
keep a firm grip. The handle was thin, no bigger than the handle of a
broom. The blade was snagged in a board above them. He shimmied it
a few times until it squeaked free, then thrust it in the direction of
Sonny's hands.

"Take it. Come on, man. Get down there and cut my fucking foot off
and then we're going to find that window."

He felt Sonny start to sit up.

"That's right," Ian said. "There you go."

Sonny fell over on top of him, his face against his chest. He could
feel Sonny's lips moving. What was he babbling about now?

"Come on," Ian said, pulling him up by his hair. "You're not passing
out on me, asshole. Not now."

The way out? The window. But where? He tried to focus. The couch
was to his left. The wall where the window was was behind that. Eight
feet? Ten feet? And what between here and there? What if Sonny cut
off his foot and they crawled forward six inches and ran into solid
stone?

"Get up, Sonny."

"Can't," Sonny mumbled. "Can't do it."

Ian fumbled in the dark, found Sonny's hand, set the ax in it, bent his
stiff fingers around the handle. "It's your job," he said. "It's your job to
do it, you chickenshit." He pushed the heap that was Sonny down toward his leg.

"I can't do it. I can't."

"Do it!" Ian shouted. He sat up and seized the hand with the ax in it,
set it against his left shin, felt the press of it through his jeans. "I can't
even feel it, Sonny, I swear, I can't feel a damn thing. Just one stroke,
man."

"It's against the rules."

Ian laughed out loud, part from the words themselves but mostly
from the way the words were spoken. It was the first composed sen-

tence to come out of Sonny's mouth since he'd woken up, spoken with measured calm as if Ian had asked for two milks in the cafeteria line.

"Are you kidding me, you maniac? Against the rules? What rules are those? The rules that say you and me are supposed to sit here and wait until we're dead?"

"You don't understand. I'm not a surgeon. You need a surgeon. I don't have the—I can't just—"

"Give it here!"

Ian wrenched the ax from Sonny's fingers, shoved him away, bent forward as far as he was able. His palm was slick with sweat, the beat of his pulse straining against the skin of his neck. He felt Sonny crawling around blindly, bumping into things, bawling again. He wiped his palm on his jeans and took a firm grip on the handle, set it on his shin directly above the ankle, an inch or two away from where the foot disappeared under the refrigerator. One quick stroke, he thought. One quick stroke and we're on our way. No pain. No pain. Just dark. Dark, some advantages. Some advantages.

It was not the burst of agony that would remain with him, not the sensation of his leg falling free from the foot (distinctly opposed to the foot falling free from his leg) nor the warm splash of blood on his right wrist nor the first moment of shocking coldness and absence mid-shin. Instead, it would be years before he would execute that simple motion, raise his right arm in that particular way, and not recall vividly that fleeting instant when the ax reached its highest point and then, in less than a heartbeat, began its descent. He would never swat a mosquito or swing a hammer or toss a ball without thinking of that moment when the motion back suddenly ceased and reversed into motion forward, the brief instant when—too late to reconsider, yet his body still whole—the deed was both done and not done.

Ian gagged and vomited the last contents of his stomach onto his lap. The ax fell free from his trembling fingers and he fumbled to retrieve it. He pulled off his shirt, felt for the raw bone, tied the shirt tight around it. His temples and forehead throbbed, a hissing filled his ears, and as hard as he tried he couldn't seem to close his mouth, couldn't seem to work his jaw. Sonny was on the floor in a ball and Ian grabbed him by the collar of his jacket, flopped over on his belly and started lurching forward in the dark, dragging Sonny behind him. Lights were popping in his head like flashbulbs. He tore out at things blindly with the hand that held the ax. It was all madness for a few minutes, his stump oozing blood through the shirt and slithering behind him like some wet dying animal. Sonny was dead weight, worse than dead weight as he squirmed in Ian's grip. There was no way he could do this himself, blind and in a maze of plaster and wood, no way he could get across the floor dragging Sonny. He stopped.

"Help me, Sonny," he gasped. "For Christsakes!"

"I can't." He was sobbing.

Ian's leg was beating like a heart. He wondered what it looked like, imagined flesh flapping from the bone, stringy tendons curling like spider's legs, his black T-shirt soaked and sticky. No, he told himself. Don't wonder. Don't wonder anything. The time for wondering is past.

"Tell me about your kid," he said.

"Who?"

"Your kid. Your boy. What's he like?"

Silence.

"Sonny?"

A sound, half sob, half laugh. "You should see that little bastard throw a football."

"Yeah? He's good?"

"He threw a football over our house last summer. Over the house. Eleven years old and he threw a football over the goddamn house."

"Tell me," Ian said. "Come on with me and tell me."

And then Sonny was beside him, clawing too, burrowing with his hands, butting with his head, clearing a path.

"I was standing in the backyard," Sonny whispered. "Listen, Ian. Listen . . ."

"I'm listening, man."

"Standing in the backyard. He made me stand back there. He says to me, Dad, go stand in the backyard and catch it when I throw it over the house. You know what I'm thinking? I'm thinking there's no goddamn way. But I go back there. I go back there and you know why? Because if it were my dad he woulda gotten one of the other guys to go stand behind the house. So I go back there and I'm standing in the backyard thinking it's about time for the lawn to be mowed and he yells You ready? and I yell Ready and I hear this *thunk* and I know he's thrown it against the house, probably didn't even come near the roof. And he yells that his hand slipped. His hand slipped! And Laura, she comes to the back door. And she's like what are you guys doing? Why is Paul throwing a football at the house? And I say Hush. Let him have his fun. And he yells Ready? and I say Ready and I look up and there it is—goddamn, there it is!—wobbling against the blue sky, perfect as some perfect bird, clearing the roof and coming down at me."

Ian smiled. What, was he crazy, smiling? How far had they gone? Two feet? Four feet? "You catch it?"

"Hell no, I didn't catch it."

"I know there's a window," Ian said. "A few more feet and we'll be at the window."

"There's no window," Sonny said. "No window." But he kept clawing.

It was like a dream. He lost all track of time. He lost all track of himself, forgot who he was, forgot everything but what lay in front of him, what he had to break through. He clawed at wood until his hands were numb and bloody, his fingernails ripped to the quick. He dug from instinct. He dug knowing that if he stopped digging he would die, and Sonny would die too. They would both die down here and it would be his fault.

He scooted forward another inch. Something gouged his bare chest and he cried out. Christ, how could he still feel pain? How was it possible? This was just a small thing, a prick; he rolled onto his side and touched the place on his chest that was pierced. What was it? A nail? He twisted it from his skin, plucked it free, turned it in his fingers. It was a shard of glass. Glass from the window? Maybe. Maybe.

"Hey, Sonny," he whispered. "You still with me?"

Chapter Seven

In his spacious room at the Beverly Hills Twin Crowns, Paul Tucker slept the sleep of the dead, a numb and dreamless sleep that knew nothing of the world that had created and now awaited him. *Sleep.* Thousands of years of man-made escape and diversion—drink and drug, the dark theater, the open road—none have managed to equal this gift that comes more naturally than any other. There is no deed nor lot that sleep cannot erase, and in their slumber all sleepers are joined together in one vast harbor of blissful ignorance. The bereaved sleep as the lovers sleep. The dying sleep as the infant sleeps. The raped sleeps as the rapist sleeps. Whatever waits for them waits in another world that is as far removed as dreams are from the waking.

When Paul finally opened his eyes, rolled over and looked at the clock beside his bed, he was relieved to see it was past ten. A blessing: his father would be gone, he and Ian both, so the suite was his for the rest of the day. He could lie on the puffy couch and watch reruns or talk shows or *SportsCenter.* He could sit on the balcony, his feet propped on the rail, and watch the river of strangers flow by beneath him. He could psych himself up the way he'd done on his ride out to the Neidermeyer house those months ago, picturing the scene in his mind so it wouldn't take him by surprise, wouldn't make him sick to his stomach. Yes, he would have time to prepare, to brace himself for the inevitable moment when his father came through the door late in the day and he'd have to look at him as if nothing had changed, as if today and tomorrow and the day after that could be the same as yesterday. But everything had changed. Paul's joints ached from change, ached more than the morning-after of any football game he'd ever played, as if throughout the night he'd been sacked a thousand times.

He rolled out of bed and shuffled to the door. Emerging from his room he saw his father—shirtless, his hair wet from the shower—sitting on one of the stools at the bar, eating a bagel and sipping a cup of coffee. The film script was opened in front of him. He looked up, his forehead wrinkled with concern.

"It's late. You sick or something?"

Paul looked at the floor, his heart thumping wildly. "How come you're not at the studio?"

"They're out working on the house. No shooting today. Remember?"

He hadn't. He was lucky, at this point, to remember his own name. He'd never felt so disconnected from the world before; everything was foreign, suspect. He looked down at his feet; even they were unfamiliar—huge, his toes undefinably malformed—as if they belonged to some stranger.

"I'm going out there this afternoon," Sonny said, lathering his bagel with cream cheese. "On-site. To work out some of the details."

The details, Paul thought wryly. And which details would those be? The ones he'd concocted in his head, the ones he and Ian had cooked up that afternoon in the hospital? He pictured them there in that cold white room in ICU, conspiring in hushed tones, weaving the tangled web while he and his mother waited just on the other side of the door, ignorant, unsuspecting. Did his father even know what was real anymore? Or had he gotten his story so straight, so cleverly concealed all the evidence in his own mind, that he'd come to believe the lies that came from his lips? He remembered a fairy tale his mother had read to him (a million years ago?) in which a spell had been cast on a cruel and dishonest man so that whenever he spoke toads spilled from his mouth.

"You can come if you want," his father said. "Bet it'll be pretty cool."

And hop hop hop went the slimy toads across the bar. They tumbled onto the floor and looked around the room, bewildered.

"I don't—" Paul started.

"What're you standing over there for?" Hop hop. "You want some breakfast?"

"Nah," Paul said. "Not hungry." Still he looked at his bare feet, feeling a mixture of shame and anger and pity so intense that he knew his father would see it immediately were he to fix even a casual gaze upon him.

"You are sick, aren't you? You got a bug or something?"

"No," Paul said sharply. Now he met his father's eyes. Still blue gray, still slightly pinched at the corners with the beginnings of crow's feet. But now they were coward's eyes, liar's eyes. It would have been better, he thought, if his father had robbed a bank, stolen a car, even murdered someone. At least those things took some balls. At least those things weren't so goddamn pathetic. He watched his father munch on his bagel in what now seemed an appalling display of gluttony, although it was the same way he'd always eaten a bagel—around and around in a circle, spiraling toward the hole—and nothing had seemed wrong with it *before*. But before was over.

"You look like you lost your best friend," Sonny said. "Something happen last night?"

"What time'd you get home?"

A dismissive shrug. "I don't know. One-something. Why?"

"I didn't go to bed till two-thirty. You weren't here."

Now Sonny set down his bagel and slid off the stool, raised his hands in a gesture of surrender. "All right, quarterback, you got a bug up your butt," he said. "That's fine. You're getting to be a big kid now and some days you're just gonna wake up with that bug up your butt. It's part of life. But now you gotta learn the most important bug-up-your-butt lesson. Just because you've got one doesn't mean everybody does. So you keep it to yourself. You know what I'm saying?"

Paul scowled. "If you weren't planning on spending any time with me why didn't you just call last week and tell me not to come?"

His father's cheeks reddened momentarily. He looked small, tiny even, behind the bar, looked like he might just disappear from view at any moment, ash back to the earth. The months off work—combined with a thousand bottles of beer and three greasy meals a day—had taken a toll; his biceps were no longer rock solid, his shoulders not so square. Even his face seemed heavier, bloated somehow. Before, in his smallness, he had been a bulldog; now, Paul thought, he was just another short man who had to wiggle into his jeans.

"Look, I'm sorry," Sonny said. "Things are nuts out here. I didn't know I was going to be so busy. But listen . . . on Sunday we got a whole free day. Why don't we do something then, just the two of us? You wanna go somewhere? You haven't gotten to Hard Rock yet. We could do that."

"Hard Rock's for suckers."

Sonny frowned, then rebounded. "All right, then. How about Disneyland? Half hour away, tops."

Paul shook his head. "I'm too old for Disney. It's stupid."

"Man . . ." Sonny said, exasperated. "You're not gonna give me a break, are you?"

"I'm going to the pool," Paul said, though water was not what he was after. He wanted only to be alone, away from his tiny father, alone with the suffocating heat and the shouts of children and the voices of strangers.

"Want some company?" Sonny asked hopefully.

"I just feel like bein' by myself for a while," Paul said.

The day was hot but overcast, so the pool area behind the hotel wasn't very crowded. The diehard tanners, those eking out the last of their vacations, slicked lotion across their already charred bodies. A few shivering kids—no sun to warm them—took turns leaping off the diving board. The bronze lifeguard sat atop his tower, swinging a whistle on its lanyard. Paul spread his blue Nittany Lions towel on a lounge chair and lay back, closed his eyes. In the row of chairs behind his, two women were discussing a mutual friend who was going blind for reasons no doctor could determine. *It's hysterical,* one of the women said in a low, knowing voice. *She's never been able to pull herself together.* The other one sighed, and they both lapsed into a thoughtful silence. Paul drowsed, imagining this woman who could not pull herself together

(from what? after what?) clumsily feeling her way through a once familiar house, lunging from one piece of furniture to the next. In his
half-sleep the house was his own and the blind woman had the face of
his mother. She was helpless, blind and alone. Why had he left her?

"What'd you say to him?"

He started awake. Ian was standing over him, dressed in his tattered
jeans and a brown button-down shirt that wasn't buttoned. His Penn-
sylvania-pale chest looked sickly amidst the California tans that surrounded him.

"Wha'dya mean? Who?"

Ian jerked his thumb at the hotel. "I asked him where you were at
and he just about bit my head off. You didn't tell him about last night,
did ya?"

"No," Paul said. "I didn't tell him."

Ian moved to sit on the lounge beside Paul's, then snagged his
dummy foot in the Penn State beach towel and toppled onto the chair
awkwardly, face first, causing it to scrape a few inches on the concrete
toward the row behind them. The friends of the blind woman blinked
and frowned.

"Son of a bitch," Ian said, his cheeks flushing. "Try to keep your shit
out of my way, okay?"

"Sorry."

"Now listen," Ian said. He adjusted himself quickly in the chair,
turned to Paul. "We made a pact, me and him. So do me a favor and
fake you don't know."

"I can't just pretend I—"

"Just leave him be for a while, jocko, don't think about it. Play along.
Then in a couple days you might forget about it, if you don't keep reminding yourself every minute." He coughed hoarsely, slapped himself in the chest, smacked his lips. "You got something to drink down
here? Got a Coke or something?"

"No." Paul nibbled on his thumbnail. "Is that what you do?"

"What?"

"You know, play along. Pretend."

Ian shrugged. "I guess so. Whatever, you know. Play along long enough, you start wondering yourself. Like, when it's only you who knows, maybe it don't even count. Like it might as well have happened the way everybody thinks. Majority rules or something, you know?"

"It counts," Paul said. "It can't not count." He looked toward the pool. On the diving board a tanned muscular boy about his age sprung from the lip of the blue board, turned a tight somersault in the air, then knifed into the water.

"You do that?" Ian asked, nodding toward the boy as he emerged, breathless and smiling, at the edge of the pool.

"That? No way."

"I used to think it would be cool," Ian said. "Watched it on TV sometimes, Olympics or whatever, watched those guys go off that high board. How cool would that be? Doing all that shit while you're *fallin'*."

"You should try it," Paul said.

"Right, jocko. What am I gonna do? Hop to the end of the board?"

It was easy enough to forget. Except for in the hot tub, Ian looked whole. He still walked as if he had a stone in his shoe, but you got used to it, stopped noticing. Paul had had a teacher once with a wandering eye; it was like that, or like ET, like how halfway through the movie you forgot how ugly he really was.

"When I get back I get my real one," Ian said. "My real fake one, you know, the one that'll do more stuff. This one's temporary, a piece of crap. But they can't make you the real one until the leg heals up all the way."

"Does it hurt?"

"Nah. Sweats like a bitch, though."

The boy was on the board again, his brown back to the pool, his heels edging off the metal tip. He breathed deeply, his lips in the shape of a whistle.

"Didja think about it?" Paul asked.

"What?"

"About what you were doing. When you did it."

Ian sighed. "You think it'd cross your mind, right? Like hey, dimmo, you're chopping off your foot. You need this foot, idiot. Like, you're gonna have to walk with it and shit. But I didn't think anything like that. Not until after."

Paul chewed the inside of his lip. "What'd you think after?"

"What are you now, Perry Fucking Mason?"

Ian drew a crumpled cigarette from his shirt pocket and lit it. The gate to the pool area squawked open and clanked closed and Paul glanced up. It was his father in his navy blue swim trunks, a hotel towel slung around his neck. He looked around helplessly for a moment and then caught Paul's eye, smiled, started toward them.

"Dickhead," Paul muttered under his breath.

"Cool out," Ian said. "He's still your dad."

"What're you guys up to?" Sonny asked cheerfully, approaching with a phony bounce in his step. He tossed his towel on the ground between the two lounge chairs.

"Tanning," Ian said. "No more white titties for me."

"That's a relief," Sonny said. He slapped Paul's foot. "Wanna go for a swim? Wanna race or something? I'll give you three strokes."

Paul shook his head. "Ian can't go in the water," he said.

"So Ian'll be the judge. He'll be the starter pistol."

"Bang," Ian said, ashing on Sonny's towel.

"We're talking," Paul said, settling himself further into his chair. "We're having a conversation."

Sonny looked back and forth between them, an uncomfortable smile twitching on his lips. That's right, Paul thought, now you're the odd man, the third wheel, the runt of the litter, the cheese standing alone. I've had my turn, and Ian's whole life has been his turn. So now it's your turn.

"Okay," Sonny said. "We'll race later."

Paul watched his father dive into the pool, then smoothly take the length of it with a practiced, flawless crawl stroke; his flutter kicks were powerful and even, barely gave up a splash.

"Hey, jocko . . . wanna go to Disney?"

Paul grinned, certain it was a joke; he imagined Ian would rather trek across the Sahara than set foot in Disney. "Yeah, right."

"I'm serious," Ian said. "We leave now we get there in time for lunch."

"What do you want to go to Disney for?"

"Wha'dya think? Rides, man. Space Mountain."

Paul grimaced, recalling vividly his last roller-coaster experience at Six Flags in New Jersey, the certainty of his own death he'd felt at the crest of that first hill. "Rides are stupid," he said.

Ian smiled, tossed some hair from his eyes. "Chicken, huh? Gobble gobble."

"That's turkeys."

"So? You in or aren't you?"

Paul watched his father's feet slap against the gleaming blue surface of the pool, his toes, his ten toes, spiraling the water in his wake. He closed his eyes.

"All right," he said. "I'm in."

"This way!" Ian shouted, already quickening his stutter step as they passed through the entrance gate. But Paul needed a moment. He was, despite the events of the past days, still twelve years old and thus stunned into stillness upon entering the Magic Kingdom. Shoot, he decided in an instant, it probably wasn't the *stuff* that made heaven so great; it was that everyone there was so damn *happy*. And so it was at Disneyland. Looking at the crowds swarming around him, it was hard to imagine that there was any sadness left in the world. Even the adults—faces that had surely been pinched and creased from traffic and parking and the $48.50 to get in—looked now as if unweighed by any burden.

"Come on!" Ian had stopped several yards in front of him, was beckoning him forward. "You gonna stand there all day lookin' like a retard?"

Paul skipped to catch up, then followed Ian into a store called The Mad Hatter.

"What're we doing? Ian, what—"

"First stop," Ian said soberly. "Mouse ears."

There might have been a thousand of them, arranged neatly on a long table that stretched nearly the width of the store, perfectly identical but for size, black felt beanies with two plastic circles sticking up on top. Ian grabbed one and fixed it delicately on his head.

"No *way,*" Paul said.

"Listen, dimmo. We're at Disney. This is what you do at Disney."

Ian looked beyond ridiculous: ragged jeans, black boots that could stomp the shit out of Donald Duck, a faded gray T-shirt, and a Mouseketeer hat flattening clumps of dirty black hair against his forehead.

"Are you stoned?"

"Screw you," Ian shot back. "You think I'd have to be wasted to wear these? It's *Disney.* It's part of the package."

"We'll look stupid."

"You're such a pussy. See, it's cool if we make it cool." Ian snatched a hat from the table and set it atop Paul's head, stepped back. "Oh yeah. You're the man now."

"Where's a mirror?"

"No mirrors. You go on faith. Didn't you see *The Lion King?*"

He had this way about him, Paul thought, especially when he was smiling the sloppy smile, the one absent of any trace of snarl or sneer. You could see how he'd come this far in life without getting killed, how he must have talked himself—maybe grinned himself—out of a thousand deaths. But maybe it was more than that. Maybe, as his father's face had changed, shifted shape, so too had Ian's.

By the middle of the afternoon they had ridden most of the rides. Space Mountain they braved twice in a row, and Paul was pleased to see that Ian seemed even more petrified than he was, white-knuckled the safety bar on the steep descents instead of flinging his arms in the air as tradition dictated. In Fantasyland they rode Mr. Toad's Wild Ride, It's a Small World, and Peter Pan's Flight. ("Peter Pan's a fag," Ian informed Paul. "You know that, right?") Then they stopped and ate lunch on a bench outside Sleeping Beauty's Castle. Ian scarfed down a hamburger and two hot dogs and was in the middle of his second Goofy Ice Cream Pop when an overweight girl dressed as Sleeping Beauty wandered by.

"Hey, babe," Ian yelled. "Need some kissin'?"

"Gee, I've never heard that one before," the girl said snottily, though she slowed her pace a bit. "Nice ears."

"You like 'em?" Ian stood up and stroked the plastic ears seductively.

He had a bubble of vanilla ice cream on his chin. "Know what they say about big ears, don't you?"

They decided to try the Mad Tea Party next. It sounded innocent enough—how bad could a pink teacup be, really?—although the sign at the front of the line warned passengers against boarding if they were pregnant, wore a pacemaker, or had ever experienced motion sickness. It neglected to mention Goofy Pops. Paul had a ball, screamed his head off with everybody else as the dizzying speed made everything around him disappear into wild streams of color. But by the time they were done spinning, Ian stumbled off the ride a unique color of his own.

"I'm dying," he said, staggering in wide circles, one hand on his belly and the other flailing for Paul's arm. "Help me, man. I'm dying."

People were staring at them with a mixture of concern and amusement. A little boy tugged on his mother's sleeve and said *look at that funny man* and Paul had to stop himself from laughing. If Ian's friends could see him now, he thought, the toughest guy in Casey TKO'd by the Mad Tea Party.

"Let's do the boats," Paul said, steadying him, praying Ian wouldn't throw up on him. "They go slow. You just look at stuff."

There was no line for the Storybook Land Canal Boats; it wasn't exactly a thrill ride. Passengers swooshed slowly down a makeshift river in little wooden boats, passing animatronic Disney characters along the way. Ian plopped down on his wooden seat, hunched over cradling his stomach. His mouse ears fell at his feet.

"Never eating again," he moaned. "Remind me . . ."

"You already got a beer gut."

"Thanks, jocko. That's real nice." He raised his head and took a deep breath, let it out slow. "Hey, blame the old man for that anyway. He's the boozehound keeps restocking the bar."

Paul shifted uncomfortably on the hard seat, then gave up and sat on his hands for some padding. "He didn't used to be like that. Drinking so much. I mean sometimes, every once in a while, but not every night."

Ian considered, rubbed his stomach. "I'm thinking it's the movie," he said eventually. "It's gettin' to him. And he doesn't even know it. He still thinks he's having a good time."

"Wha'dya mean?"

"Well, you know . . ." He shrugged, shook a cigarette from his pack and lit it.

"You can't smoke here," Paul said.

"You rather me puke?"

They were quiet for a moment. Paul trailed his fingers in the lake; it was warm and silky, felt as much like oil as water.

"What about the movie?" he asked.

Ian took a drag from his cigarette. "Seems like every day he watches he gets a little crazier. You know how it is, right? You tell a lie, a big fat one, and for a while you spend so much time covering it up you don't have time to even think about it. You're too busy, you know, tying up all the loose ends, gettin' your story straight."

"Talking about it to anyone who'll listen," Paul said. He thought of all the interviews, his father on radio and TV, his father in print, the lie winding its way out into the world. And then—worse—that night at Bonanza, his father sitting there in that booth talking about Ian screaming, Ian crying, Ian being afraid.

"Right," Ian said. "So then everybody knows the story. You pulled it off. You're a fucking wonderboy. But now that everybody's bought into your bullshit you don't having nothing to do anymore but wade around in it twenty-four seven. And then you start to notice how bad it stinks."

"He tell you that?"

"Shit, no." He ashed in the water, onto the claws of Sebastian the crab. "All I know's the stink's gettin' to him."

Paul rested his elbows on his knees. To his left, on a small AstroTurf Island, loomed the cursed castle from *Beauty and the Beast;* every few seconds a wooden door on the top floor would creak open and the plastic Beast would stick his head out, look around warily, then duck back inside.

"So what happens?" Paul asked.

Ian shrugged. "Nothin'," he said. "He goes home, boinks your mom, starts working again, end of story. Movie stuff's over, people start forgetting, he starts forgetting. He lives with the stink."

You keep the windows open, Paul thought. You keep the air moving.

You fill the house with other smells: dinner, perfume, Mop & Glo. You blame the smell on the dogs, the radiator, sweaty socks. When it's really bad you hold your breath and make for the door.

"What about you?" Paul asked.

"What about me what?"

"What do you do? When we go home?"

Ian tossed his cigarette into the water. "I dunno. Weird thing is, I keep forgettin' I gotta go back at all."

Paul thought about what waited for Ian in Casey: his yammering mom, the goners by the Hess Station, his real fake foot. No wonder he kept forgetting about it; it wasn't like he had much to be homesick for.

"You still feel like puking?" he asked.

"Nah." Ian grabbed his mouse ears from the bottom of the boat, fitted them again on his head. "I'm ready for the Mountain. One more time, no hands, and then we head home, yeah?"

"Sure," Paul said.

They returned to Tomorrowland. It was late in the afternoon, and the line for Space Mountain was twice the length it had been earlier, snaking back on itself twenty times over. To entertain themselves they guessed at the lives of the people immediately preceding and following them in line. Ahead of them were two young couples ("Newlyweds?" Paul suggested, to which Ian scoffed, "They're still pawin' each other . . . no way they're married") and behind them a middle-aged father with a pretty preteen redhead. Definitely a weekend visit, they decided, based on the way the father was talking to the girl nonstop, asking her what she was studying in school and how many gerbils she had and what position she was going to play in softball when the season started.

"I hope my parents don't get divorced," Paul said.

"You and me both," Ian said. " 'Cause don't think I won't be taking the blame for it."

Paul thought of that judge again, the kindly one with the white hair, looking down at him, waiting patiently for an answer. But surely his father would be out of the running as far as the law was concerned. Surely his father's character would be used as evidence against him. He'd probably show up in the courtroom drunk, stumble in unshaven and poorly dressed. *He's mine,* his father would say. *He belongs with me.* And his mother would be sitting behind a long wooden table, tight-lipped, would be shaking her head grimly, all ready to take her precious boy home and lock him up in the house until he turned thirty. *Ian,* he'd have to tell the kindly judge. *I choose Ian.*

"Hey, watch it!" Ian shouted.

Paul was knocked off balance by someone—someones—pushing past him in line. It was a couple of black kids; they continued forward, squeezing themselves against the yellow iron bars to shimmy past the two young couples.

"Hey," Paul said. "No butting!"

The kids didn't pause, didn't turn around, paid him no attention.

"Hey, asshole . . ." Ian took a few quick steps forward and grabbed the wrist of one of the kids, the younger one, and jerked him backwards a few feet. The kid was maybe ten, a year or two shorter and skinnier than Paul. He looked up fiercely at Ian.

"Lemme go!"

"How 'bout starting at the back of the line?"

"We're meetin' somebody," the kid said, trying in vain to shake free from Ian's firm grasp. "We're meeting my brother's friends."

"I don't think so," Ian said cheerfully. "I think you're getting your little black ass to the end of the line."

The older kid had stopped now, a few yards ahead of them, and turned back irately. "C'mon, Gary. Quit your—" Then he noticed Ian's fingers wrapped tightly around his brother's wrist. "What's up with that?" he asked, genuinely surprised.

"No butting," Paul said confidently. "Start at the back of the line." He was impressed with himself, liked the confidence that being beside Ian gave him. Ian didn't treat him like a baby. Ian was his friend.

"Let go of him," the older kid said to Ian. He looked to be about seventeen. He wore a Chicago Bulls jersey and a thin gold chain around his neck.

"We been standing here a half hour," Ian said. "You can't just—"

"We're meeting somebody," the older brother said. "Up ahead in line."

"Yeah, so I heard. That's a pile of shit, man, and you know it."

The weekend father stepped forward, touched Ian's back. "Let 'em go on," he said, smiling gently. "It's no big deal."

Ian's jaw clenched. "You afraid of these guys?"

"It's not worth it," the father said. "Just let 'em have their way."

It was the wrong thing to say. Ian turned to the older brother with a sneer. He still had his fingers clenched around the younger boy's— Gary's—wrist.

"You think everybody's just gonna let you pass 'cause you got on your bad-ass Michael Jordan shirt and your Mr. T gold chains? Is that it?"

Paul suddenly felt sick to his stomach. "Ian—" he started.

"Shut up, Paul." His eyes didn't leave the older brother. "That what you're thinking, boy? That we're just gonna move aside?"

The big guy swaggered back toward them, slowly. He was in no rush now; Space Mountain could wait. Paul looked at Gary. His bottom lip was trembling. This was not their affair. Sure, they could talk big, give each other a little junior high dose of crap, but why not end it there? He wanted to say to this Gary, hey, you want to head over to Frontierland? They got another coaster over there, you wanna give that one a whirl?

"Let him go," big brother said, coming to a halt about six inches from Ian, squaring his feet.

Ian smirked. "Or what?"

"Come on, man. No more games." He was right up in Ian's face now. The couples in front of them bunched forward; they were looking around for assistance, for help. Where was that goddamn big-headed mouse now, when they needed him most?

"I'm not playing games," Ian said. "You playin' games, Mr. T?"

"I said *let him go.*"

"And I said *or what?*" Ian's felt beanie had shifted so that the plastic mouse ears were off center, tilted slightly left as if the mouse were drunk or dizzy. Why notice this? Paul asked himself. Why, of all the things to notice—

"Think you can take me, nigger?"

The big guy swung. Ian was obviously waiting for it; he easily ducked the punch and let loose a swift right uppercut to the gut. The older brother doubled over and Ian kneed him between the eyes, knocking him to the ground. The little brother, now free, wrapped his arms around Ian's waist and tried to wrestle him to the cement. Paul backed away, into the chest of the weekend father.

"Hey!" the man was shouting. "Hey! Hey!"

Ian twisted around and flung the little brother off him; the kid—Gary—stumbled into the iron railing and toppled to the ground. Ian stood over him for an instant, his fists clenched, giving big brother enough time to recover himself. He grabbed the back of Ian's T-shirt, whirled him around and smacked his face against a concrete pillar. Blood exploded from Ian's mouth and the redheaded girl screamed. Tottering backwards from the pillar, Ian took another punch—this one in his right eye—and Paul thought *now, now, now,* willed himself to move forward into the brawl, to make himself useful, to . . . to *what?*

"Fuckin' nigger!" Ian shouted, blood bubbling over his lips. And then went berserk. He downed the big brother with one furious jab to the throat, and then—once the guy was on the ground—started kicking him savagely in the stomach. Big brother covered up, one arm over his face and one over his belly, but Ian kept kicking. It was his fake foot he was kicking with, keeping balance with his real foot, and Paul knew there was no give in those steel toes as they connected with ribs.

"Stupid nigger . . . stupid motherfucker . . ."

The little brother lay on the ground, holding his own stomach and sobbing tears of surprise. Finally the weekend father stopped shouting "Hey" and made a flailing grab at Ian's shoulders, yanked him backwards; they both tumbled onto the ground at Paul's feet. The redhead was sobbing. Paul couldn't move; his feet were tingling and frozen to the spot on which he stood.

Ian broke free from the father's tenuous grip, regained his footing for a moment and then pounced on the little brother, who was now up on his hands and knees beside the railing and frantically trying to scuttle away. Ian took a fistful of Gary's hair in his right hand, then lifted the

boy's head an inch or two off the pavement and slammed it into the
iron railing. It was a sound Paul would never forget, a resonant *twong*,
part cymbal (the railing) and part bass (the head). Ian yanked the head
back in preparation for another shot against the railing. He was going
to kill this boy, Paul thought. He was—

"Ian!" Paul yelled, finally finding his voice. "Ian, stop!"

Ian stopped. He looked up at Paul, bug-eyed and bright red with
fury. Paul wasn't even sure he knew who he was. There was blood
streaming from his mouth, and he let go of Gary's hair, staggered to his
feet, then pulled off his T-shirt and pressed it to his face.

"Jesus!" the father said, staring at Ian's back.

It was the swastika he saw, carved deep and dark into Ian's left shoulder blade. The man scooted backwards on his butt to his daughter, his
arms outstretched to protect her. Everyone behind him cowered, literally *cowered*. They all crouched down and covered their heads, as if Ian
were waving a pistol.

"Police!" someone was yelling. "Police!"

"Come on," Ian said, roughly grabbing Paul's arm. "Let's get outa
here."

They didn't speak the whole ride back to the hotel. Ian sat in the cab
with his shirt to his face. He was shaking violently, twitching from his
lips to his feet. Paul was trembling too, and trying not to cry, trying to
get the *twong* of the boy's head against metal out of his ears. What if
they died? What if Ian had killed them? But no, they were moving
when Ian had taken off his shirt, still moving, still crying. But the older
brother . . . his lung could be punctured. And Gary's head—*twong*.

"Asshole," Ian was muttering under his breath. "Asshole asshole ass-
hole asshole asshole asshole asshole asshole . . ."

The cab driver glanced warily at them in his rearview mirror, sped up.

When they got to their suite Ian made a beeline for his room,
slammed the door so hard the windows rattled. Sonny was sitting on
the balcony smoking a cigarette and Paul went straight to him. He'd

forgotten, in this terrifying moment, that his father was no longer fixer of all things.

"Ian beat up some black kids," he wailed.

"What?" Sonny exploded, leaping to his feet. "Where is he?"

"In his room."

Sonny pushed past him, stormed across the room to Ian's door, turned the knob. It didn't budge.

"Get out here," Sonny yelled, shaking the door violently.

"Fuck you, Sonny!"

"Get your ass out here right now!"

The door swung open. Ian stood there bare-chested, scowling defiantly. His lips were gruesomely bloated, his right eye swollen nearly shut. His chest was streaked with blood.

"Jesus," Sonny said, stepping back instinctively. "Guess they put up a fight, huh?"

"They *started* the fight, Sonny. I finished it."

"He kicked them when they were down," Paul said. "He was gonna kill 'em."

"Shut up, you chickenshit!" Ian shouted. "Where were you when I was getting my ass kicked? There were two of 'em on me, Sonny. Two of 'em. Stupid niggers, thinking they could—"

Sonny thrust his cigarette into Ian's face. It was hard to tell if he meant to punch him or burn him or just shut him up; the butt glanced off Ian's cheek and dropped to the carpet. "You know what you are?" Sonny said coldly. "You're a mean, stupid country dog, pissing and growling and biting everything that scares you. And someday somebody's gonna come along and run you down in the road and you're not even gonna know what hit you. And nobody's gonna give a shit you're gone, nobody's gonna shed one tear. You're just gonna be one more thing to scrape off the road. Is that how you want it? 'Cause it's right around the corner, Ian."

"Don't you lecture me," Ian said, his swollen lips quivering. "You're not my dad and you're not my fucking hero, Sonny. I'll do what I want."

"And what is that?" Sonny asked. "Do you have any fucking clue what—"

Ian slammed the door. Sonny spun to Paul, his eyes as wild with fury as Ian's had been right before the final flurry of blows in Tomorrowland.

"I can't let you out of my sight for one goddamn day, can I?"

"Me?" Paul asked, stunned. "I didn't do anything."

"Did you try to stop him? Or did you just stand there doing nothing?"

"I—" Paul started. Had he tried? But he couldn't have stopped him, could he? Not with Ian like he was, crazy, fists flying. "I didn't know what to do," he said. "I didn't—"

"You *act*," Sonny said, slapping his fist in his palm. "You see something go wrong, you act. You don't stand there doing nothing. You don't stand there waiting for it to be over. You take charge of the situation. You fix it. You save lives. Do you understand what I'm saying?"

Paul's jaw went rigid. He lungs expanded, his eyes narrowed, and he stood a little taller in his shoes. In his chest hardened something unfamiliar, something that he thought must have been courage or strength, when in fact it was only walls dropping around his heart.

"Yes *sir*," he said coldly. "Yes sir, I understand."

Sonny scrutinized him furiously. "Do you?"

❧

Could the dark kill you?

No, Sonny told himself. No. Just breathe. There's air here. Breathe.

At the end, his father had been without light and breath. Disoriented, his air tank depleted, the thick black smoke in the master bedroom had sealed shut around Captain Sam Tucker like a body bag. From outside, the house was a wall of light. Inside, Sam turned circles in the pitch-black, finally stumbled backwards into a closet. And there, among strangers' clothes, he lived his last moments. A shoe . . . a child? A shoe . . . a child?

Stop, Sonny told himself. Stop. Don't. Not now. Beside him, Ian slept. Ian was counting on him. (. . . *call in some guys who know what they're doing . . .*) He had to remain focused, keep himself together.

(. . . *rescue response team in Pittsburgh* . . .) He had to think of some way to get them out of here. Ian's life was in his hands, his hands alone, his hand . . .

The smack of a screen door behind him. His hand moist around the handle of a small suitcase. They would never again return to that house. Why should they? It had been *her* house, not his. The squeaky cot in the station, the alarm in the middle of the night, the rush of voices, Phil tugging his arm. On his feet, in his shoes, down the pole, the glare of chrome, the roar of the engine, his father's voice shouting instructions, the rise of the siren. And then . . . sailing into the night . . .

"Ian . . ." he whispered. He didn't want to be alone. Not now. Not here. Not for this. His father had been alone at the end, the contents of the closet his only company. Empty shoes and shirts and dresses, abandoned shells all of them, blackened by smoke and curling in the heat, dancing as they melted, while his father sat dying, thinking—

Stop, Sonny told himself. Sleep. Sleep and all is forgotten. Sleep and slip away, die quietly. Die first, die before Ian. Both dead, no blame. And if he dies, and Ian lives, still no blame. His father knew this. His father had to stay in that house. If the little boy dies he has to die too. He cannot come from that house empty-handed. Better to play it safe and die than presume the child is not there and come out alone. For, if the boy dies and the fireman lives, what waits for him outside, in the light?

I do . . .

"Paul," he whispered.

Paul . . . Paul . . . this boy beside him? The boy in the shoe? The boy on the squeaky cot? No—no—*Paul*, his son, the boy somewhere above him, the boy who sat on the branch of a tree all day, the boy who said *I just want to see what you do* and now all these boys were melting in the dark, all the boys, in the dark, the body bag sealing around them as they gasped and clawed for light.

Light. Yes. In his sleep it was light. So light he squinted, shielded his eyes against the flames shooting from the house where his father sat dying, so light the eyes of the melting boys shimmered as if they burned from within, their faces so washed in light they were indistinguishable from one another, indistinguishable from himself. Which

one was he? He was this one, the one thinking, but they were all thinking the same thing, all thinking of light and light and light and dark and
dark and dark and—

"S'all right, man. I'm right here. Feel me? I'm right next to you, man."
Words spilled from Sonny's lips as he felt frantically for Ian's hand.
". . . do you know who you are?"

༈

>   Sonny
>   We're gonna have to get out of here, kid. And
>   we're gonna have to get out *now*. This house isn't
>   gonna hold itself together much longer.

>   Ian
>   *(sniffling)* Go without me, Sonny. You find the way.
>   After that, if there's still time, you can come back
>   for me. *(laughs ruefully)* I'm not going anywhere.

>   Sonny
>   *(forcefully)* Listen to me, Ian. Either we go
>   together or we don't go at all.

>   Ian
>   But I can't *move*, Sonny.

>   *Sonny reaches above him, wrenches the pry ax
>   from where it is lodged in the ceiling.*

>   Ian
>   What're you doin'?

>   Sonny
>   I want you to think good thoughts, Ian. I want
>   you to think about the sun shining on your face.

Close your eyes and go there, Ian. Go to where
the sun is . . .

Ian
Tell me what you're doing, Sonny.

Sonny
(*gently*) I'll tell you what I'm doing. I'm gettin'
us the hell out of here.

"Cut!" Lilly Douglass shouted. "Blood!"

Two young men trotted onto the set. Dale Markham stood up slowly, shook his head, wiped some authentic sweat from his brow. He looked over at the row of directors' chairs at the edge of the set, nodded at Sonny soberly, respectfully.

"You got balls of steel," he said.

Paul turned deliberately to his father. Sonny pulled a cigarette from his shirt pocket and turned it over and over in his hand. He was as pale as someone midway through a faint. Paul had found him asleep on the balcony at nine A.M., already sweating in the morning sun. If he'd been strong enough, he would have carried his father to bed, let him sleep through this day. But he couldn't carry his father, and so here they were, witnessing the climactic scene, the climactic lie.

"Can I get some water over here?" Roger Rhodes yelled from his spot on the floor. "I'm burning up."

"Poor baby," Ian said, nudging Paul. Paul didn't acknowledge him. He didn't want to have anything to do with Ian. His right eye was purple and open only a slit, his lips and chin bruised blue. He'd gotten a thousand looks on the set that day but no one had asked him what had happened. Why bother to ask? It was Ian . . . enough said.

Dale Markham came over, crouched in front of Sonny, weighing the pry ax in his hands. "How'd you do it? Fast? No hesitation?"

"No hesitation," Sonny echoed, blinking sweat from his eyes.

"Hey, buddy," Markham said, swatting him playfully on the knee. "This bothering you? No need for sweat now. Your job's over."

"Yeah," Sonny mumbled. He looked across Paul at Ian.

"You keep your eyes open?" Markham asked.

"Yeah," Sonny said, looking back to him. "I mean . . ." He shrugged, half smiled. The cigarette broke between his fingers and shreds of tobacco fell at his feet. "It's hard to remember everything. Kind of a blur. Just . . . it was real fast. That's how I remember it."

Paul looked at the floor. He hated his father. He hated Ian. It was a sensation that made him feel strong, old, unafraid. This was the secret, the thing that had exceeded his grasp for so long. Finally he had the upper hand. He was better than either one of them. He was better than any of these idiots, better than tight-ass Lilly and Roger the fag and has-been Dale Markham. He didn't need to be afraid anymore, of anyone, because none of them could hurt him. His jaw taut, he watched the techies rig the blood bag inside Roger's jeans. There was a hole cut through the denim that his ankle and foot went through and disappeared safely under the floor. The blood bag fit snugly into the ankle of the jeans; it would explode on impact.

"Further up," Ian said softly.

"What?" Lilly asked, turning to him.

"The cut . . ." Sonny added meekly. "It was a little further up."

Ian knocked on his jeans where the temporary prosthesis began and Lilly frowned thoughtfully. "Why don't you two take a look up close before we shoot? We really want to get this right."

Paul shook his head, stifled the laugh that rose like bile in his throat. So now it had come to this, he thought, liars directing liars. Call in the expert witnesses to oversee their expert fantasy.

Sonny and Ian rose uneasily from their chairs and took a few baby steps into the shot. Neither of them seemed especially anxious to get too close to the spot where Roger lay. They took a perfunctory glance at the scene—the baggie fat with blood, the awkward angle of the leg— then both looked away.

"It's cool, eh, Sonny?" Ian asked, touching Sonny's elbow, tugging him back toward the chairs. "Looks about right, yeah? Looks good to me."

Sonny nodded dumbly. He might have been sleepwalking.

"All right, then," Lilly said. "Let's do it."

Ian
Sonny, what—

Sonny
Forgive me . . .

He raises the ax in the air. Ian screams.

"No!" Sonny shouted, stumbling forward into the scene.

"Cut!" Lilly yelled. She turned to Sonny, annoyed. "What is it?"

"It's wrong."

"No, it's cool, Sonny," Ian said gently. Again he reached for Sonny's elbow, pulled him back a few steps. "It's all right. It's fine."

"He didn't scream like that," Sonny said to Lilly. "He didn't scream at all."

"I have to scream," Roger protested from his spot on the floor. "Somebody cuts off your foot, you scream."

"I'm telling you right now," Sonny said, turning on him furiously. "He did not fucking scream."

Lilly raised her eyebrows and glanced at the cameraman, who was grinning sheepishly. Paul's stomach clenched. *Stop,* he wanted to say to his father. *Please, just stop.* Ian was apparently thinking the same thing. "Don't worry about it, man," he said calmly to Sonny. "Let me scream. What difference does it make?"

Sonny looked at Ian with pleading eyes, frantic words forming on his lips.

"No," Ian said, shaking his head to the unspoken words. "No, Sonny. It doesn't matter. It doesn't. Let 'em do it however they want."

Lilly Douglass cleared her throat. "Take two!" she called.

Ian nudged Sonny into his chair, looked down briefly at Paul and smiled weakly. Paul turned to the scene, to the basement, watched the ax rise in Dale Markham's unwavering hand. It was a real ax, and the glint from the edge of the blade in the set lights blinded him momentarily as the ax reached its highest point. Then the ax was falling and Paul looked back at Ian. His eyes were shut.

• • •

"Can it, asshole!"

Paul started awake. His sleep had been fitful, full of whispers and darkened faces. Had he dreamed *Can it asshole?* No . . . it was Ian's voice that had shouted, startled him from his half-sleep. He tumbled out of bed, drowsy and disoriented, and wandered into the living room. His father was sitting on the balcony with a bottle clenched between his thighs. Ian was standing at the iron railing, shouting at somebody.

"Go home, you stinkin' drunk!"

"What's up?" Paul asked, stepping outside.

"Kathy!" a voice bellowed from below. "Please! Kathy!"

Ian turned to Paul with a smirk. "Some idiot's lookin' for his girlfriend. Thinks she's in the hotel somewhere."

"Kathy!"

Ian turned back to the street. "Kathy's up here givin' me a blow job!" he shouted. "She says she don't want to see you!"

Paul turned to his father, expecting some kind of reaction. You couldn't just yell *blow job* from your balcony, right? But Sonny's expression didn't change. His mouth was hanging open at an odd angle, as if he were asleep. He was shirtless; his belly hung over the tight band of his sweatpants and pressed against the wet lip of the liquor bottle. Fucking pathetic, Paul thought. Fucking—

"C'mere," Ian said, gesturing to Paul. "Take a look at this guy."

Paul scooted past his father and joined Ian at the edge of the railing. Nine stories below, half lit by streetlights, a man about his father's age stood with his arms outstretched and his head tilted up.

"Kathy!" he wailed.

Paul smiled. "She's givin' us blow jobs!" he shouted euphorically. He spun around to look at his father; still no reaction. He'd never felt so free in his life! He could do anything, say anything, and no one could stop him. And the guy, way down there, he couldn't hit back.

Ian laughed and elbowed him in the ribs. "Check out those sweet titties, Paulie!"

"Those are some sweet tits!" Paul shouted.

"Cut it out," Sonny said softly from behind him.

"She's doing all of us!" Paul shouted. "All of us at once!"

The voice, still soft, but a hint of authority behind it: "I said cut it out."

Paul turned to his father. "No," he said.

Sonny sat back. His eyes were two dark holes. "Alrighty," he said. "I'll just sit here quietly. Nobody has to pay me any attention. You two go on about your business. If anybody wants anything from me I'll just be sitting here quietly."

Ian turned to him. "Why don't you go to bed?"

"It's early," Sonny said. "I'm just gettin' started." He took a drink from the bottle, offered it to Ian.

"I'm done," Ian said, waving it away.

Sonny shrugged, then held the bottle out to Paul. "Wha'dya say, tough guy? Have a drink with the old man?"

Paul stared at him, bewildered, his brain turning flips in his head. A small sound came from his mouth, a pointless release of air with no word attached.

"Jesus, Sonny . . ." Ian reached out and snatched the bottle from Sonny's grip, dropped it over the balcony railing. A few seconds later Paul heard it shatter on the sidewalk.

"What the fuck!" the voice shouted from below.

"Have another drink—you'll feel better," Ian yelled. Then he turned to Sonny. "What're you thinking, man? Kid's twelve years old."

"You think I don't know how old my own kid is?"

"I think you're having a really shitty day," Ian said wearily. He rubbed the corner of his mouth, winced. "I think you need a break. And I think you need to give *Paul* a break."

"Forget it," Paul said. "I—"

Sonny stood up slowly. It wasn't like Ian standing slowly, wasn't anywhere near uncoiling; it was like an old man lifting himself from a soft, low chair that he'd been sitting in for six hours. "You trying to tell me how to raise my own son, you moron?"

Ian didn't move an inch. He shook his head. "Go to bed, man. You'll feel better tomorrow."

"No I won't," Sonny said. "And stop telling me what to do. You think you own me? Think you can hold it over me forever?"

Ian scowled. "You're talking crazy. Why don't you just shut up and go to bed?"

"Kathy!"

"Let's *all* go to bed," Paul said hopefully. He didn't feel so free anymore, felt in fact that the balcony was a cage they'd all been dropped into by some mad scientist, that—if the scientist's hypothesis was correct—someone would be eaten before morning.

Sonny looked at him briefly, blinked twice, then turned back to Ian. "You think you can say whatever you want to me, don't you?" he asked. He smirked and wavered a bit on his feet, an idiot drunk at last call, picking a fight he'd have no chance of winning. "You think I'll let you roll right over me. You got all the cards, don't you Nazi boy?"

"Don't push it, Sonny."

"Why? What're you gonna do? Gonna kick my ass? Gonna kick me when I'm down like you did those nigger boys?"

"Don't do this, man," Ian pleaded. "You've had a bad day. We all know that. Just sleep it off, okay? You—"

"Just get it over with!" Sonny shouted. He teetered on his feet and grabbed hold of Paul's shoulder for balance. "I know you want to. I know you're just dying to spill the whole—"

"C'mon man, I—"

Sonny dug his fingernails into Paul's bare shoulder. "Just tell *him,* why don't you? He's just sittin' here waiting for you to tell him. Can't you see that? You think I fucking care anymore? He's just—"

"Dad . . ." Paul squirmed in pain. "Dad, that hurts."

Ian grabbed Sonny's forearm with one hand; with the other, he pried the trembling fingers loose one by one, freeing Paul from his father's grip.

"Please," Sonny said. "I *want* you to tell him. Don't tell him. Please? Please?"

"Sonny . . ." Ian said gently. "He already knows."

Chapter Eight

A cloud of cigarette smoke loomed just beyond the foot of Paul's bed. Below it, on his knees with his back to his son, Sonny was picking rumpled clothes from the floor; he shook out, folded, then set each article of clothing carefully into the duffel bag beside the dresser. Paul lay motionless, his eyes open to slits, watching his father go about this odd business. He did not want to ask him what he was doing. He thought perhaps if he remained silent long enough his father would have time to reconsider, return the clothes to their heaps on the floor, go back to bed. From the way the sun slanted through the room, Paul knew it was early, probably just the other side of night. Maybe his father was still drunk. Dressed in only blue pajama bottoms and bath slippers, Sonny packed slowly, thoughtfully, almost cautiously. Sometimes before he folded a shirt he held it out in front of him and looked at it for several moments, as if it might contain some secret truth.

"Paul," he said sharply, without turning.

Paul quickly closed his eyes, tried to breathe evenly. The zipper scratched around the bag; the small silver latch clicked into place.

"Get up, Paul."

Now he opened his eyes. Still his father had not turned or risen, remained on his knees at the foot of the bed as if praying or vomiting.

"Dad? What're you doing? What's goin' on?"

Perhaps feigned confusion would stall his father, would make him pause just long enough to ask, yeah, hey, what the hell *was* going on? But it didn't work. Sonny stood slowly, turned.

"Time to go."

Paul sat up. "Go where?"

"Home." Sonny dropped his cigarette on the carpet and stepped on it with his slipper. "I changed your ticket, called your mom. She's gonna pick you up in Harrisburg this afternoon."

"Are you comin'?"

He already knew the answer, but he asked anyway, out of some tender hope that maybe his father had decided they had both had enough, that now that all skeletons were loosed from their enormous closet those same skeletons could just keep on dancing right on down the road and the world as it had been before could be promptly and magically reconstructed. Yesterday he'd wanted to leave his father behind, maybe forever. But today, this morning, he just wanted things to go back to the way they had been. But there was nothing in Sonny's face that indicated this might be even a remote possibility. His eyes were weary, his lips bloodless.

"No," Sonny said. "Just you."

"I'm leaving in a couple days anyway. Can't I stay till then?"

Sonny cleared his throat belaboredly, searching for words in the scrape of cigarettes. "I don't think it's right for you to be here anymore," he finally said. "I don't want you hanging around Ian, don't want a repeat of the other day. Next time you might get caught in the middle. I can't have that."

The lie was so outrageous it propelled Paul out of bed. "I wanna go home anyway," he said bluntly, hoping it would hurt his father, scare him, even humiliate him. He possessed so few weapons; he had to utilize the ones he had. "I was thinking about it yesterday. I'm glad to go."

He pulled off his T-shirt and threw it onto the duffel, then stared at his father, daring him to meet his eyes. At that moment Ian hopped into the room, steadying himself with one hand against the door frame.

"What's up?" he asked, yawning. "It's like six o'clock, you guys."

"Paul's leaving," Sonny said. "He's going home."

"Wow," Ian said. "How come?"

Sonny scratched the back of his neck, vigorously, as if he'd been struck with poison ivy. "Because I say so. Because I'm his father."

"Hmmm," Ian said. He looked back and forth between Paul and Sonny sleepily, processing this new information. Paul caught his eye;

though still bruised from the fight at Disney, it had turned almost sky blue in its healing. Ian gave a brief smile and Paul looked away.

"I'll go too," Ian said.

Sonny blinked. "What?"

Ian shrugged. "If Paul's going then I'm going. I'm sick of this place anyhow."

Sonny shook his head. "You should stay. They need you."

Ian cackled. "They don't need me. They hate my guts, every one of 'em. And you know what? They don't need you much either. Why don't you come with us? Why don't we *all* get out of here?"

Paul's head was spinning. Another new Ian: an Ian who would manipulate his father into leaving, who would take his side, who would back Sonny into a corner. A safe corner. Home.

"But we wrap in a couple weeks," Sonny said, just on the cusp of desperate. "You stay here with me. Let Paul get back to school."

Ian took two hops across the room and sat down heavily on the foot of Paul's bed. He rubbed his face, groaned, then looked up at Sonny. "Haven't you had enough, man? Really, haven't you? Yet?"

Sonny clenched his jaw. "I'm staying," he said firmly.

"Fine," Ian said, shrugging. "I'm going."

He got up and left the room without so much as another glance at Sonny, who pressed his eyes with the heels of his hands, rocked a little on his unsteady legs. Paul felt sorry for him. He couldn't hate him now, looking like he did, no matter how many lies he told. He would be here alone. It was like dropping an infant in the middle of the ocean.

"Dad . . ." he started.

"Get the rest of your shit together," Sonny said.

Their plane sat at the gate at LAX for nearly an hour—mechanical problem, a valve that needed replacing. Fate, Paul thought hopefully. His father would have an extra slice of time, enough silent moments alone in the suite to realize he was a fool for staying behind. Any minute now, he would sprint breathlessly on board, flop down in the open seat in the row in front of them, look over his shoulder and give Paul a smile, a knowing, easy smile that said *you had to know I couldn't let you go.*

"Think those guys know what they're doing?" Ian asked, nodding out the window. His chin was three different shades of blue.

Paul followed Ian's gaze. There were two men in yellow jumpsuits and giant headphones standing under the wing of the plane, signaling to each other with their hands.

"Probably out partying last night," Ian said. "Probably trying to remember what plane they're working on."

"My mom'll kill me if I die," Paul said, imagining the 747, a twisted ball of silver and fire, dropping from the sky somewhere in the broad Midwest, while his mother waited impatiently at the Harrisburg airport.

Ian laughed. "That's kinda funny. That's what your dad said when we were in the basement. You know what, though? If we crash?"

"What?"

"Bet they'd make a movie out of it."

Paul smiled despite himself. A hint of movement at the front of the cabin caused him to swivel his head in anticipation. But no. Only a flight attendant with an armful of pillows. Fine, he thought. Let his father stay here if that was what he wanted. The intercom crackled and the pilot announced that the mechanical problem had been fixed, the broken part replaced, that they'd be pulling back from the gate shortly.

"He's a bastard," Paul decided, as the wheels folded up under them and the city disappeared in the morning below. "A crazy, stupid bastard."

"Settle down, jocko," Ian said. He was leaned back in his seat, his eyes closed. "You're just pissed."

"You thought he'd come, didn't you?"

Now Ian opened his eyes, smiled wearily. "Kinda."

Paul twisted uncomfortably in his seat. He was burning up. His hair stuck to the back of his neck and the seat belt was wearing a line of sweat across his middle. "What's he want to stay there for anyway?

They probably all think he's a freak, the way he was acting yesterday. Isn't he embarrassed?"

"Not as embarrassed as he would be at home."

"But nobody knows. Nobody but you and me."

Ian shook his head. "Don't matter anymore. He's blown a gasket, man. He wouldn't even be able to look at your mom, much less you."

"But I don't care," Paul said. "I don't care what happened."

Ian looked at him for a long time. It seemed to Paul that Ian was looking right through his face and into his head, at all those thoughts squirming around in the muck that he himself couldn't make any sense of.

"Yeah you do," Ian said.

Paul turned to the window. Did he? Below them, the business of the world continued. They had reached an altitude where the only things he could be certain of were freeways, swimming pools, and baseball diamonds. From this height, who really cared what his father had done? Down there were dads and moms and sons and daughters spinning their own private webs of lies that he knew nothing of and never would. So what did it matter, really? His father's lie was one more victimless crime, perpetrated on a world that expected stories to unfold in certain ways. His father had told the story that everyone wanted to hear. And Ian had told it too, had gone along. If there was any victim, wasn't it him?

Ian was asleep, his cheek against his shoulder, his swollen lips parted. Paul looked at him, tried to figure out what it was that drove him to do the things he did. His father he could understand; his goal was to save face, to remain the hero everyone thought he was. But Ian's motivation was a mystery. Why lie? Why cover for his father, a man he didn't know until the day he wound up beside him in a cold, dark basement? Ian was too full of contradictions, unreconcilable. How could you save a stranger and then turn around and bash a kid's head into an iron railing? How could you be a hero and a monster at the same time?

"Hey," Paul said.

Ian didn't stir.

"Hey . . ." Paul nudged him in the side and he opened his eyes.

"We crashing?"

"Why'd you do it?" Paul asked. "Why'd you lie for him? Why'd you let him take all the credit?"

It was the question he'd wanted to ask all along, but he didn't know how. *What* and *who* and *where,* those were pretty simple. But *why* was a bitch, always the last question on the lips of the devastated. *Why* was the thing that kept you up nights, the thing that made you cry when you'd sworn to yourself there'd be no more crying, the thing that took root in your gut and stayed there, maybe until the end of you.

Ian shrugged sleepily. "I dunno."

"Did he give you money or something?"

Ian stared blankly at him for several moments, then shook his head in amazement. "Fuck you," he said.

"What? I—"

"Fuck you, Paul. "

"I just don't understand why—"

"Maybe I did it 'cause it was a better story this way," Ian said bitterly. "You ever think of that? Maybe I was sitting down there hacking off my foot and thinking, shit, I bet this'd make a hell of a movie if Sonny and me pretend he did the deed. Maybe I thought it was my only way out of town. It worked, didn't it?"

Paul was quiet for a moment. "Is that really why?" he finally asked.

Ian closed his eyes. "Why else?"

Laura was smiling as bright and false as neon when Paul stepped into the sterile terminal at Harrisburg International Airport. She hugged him tightly, didn't even notice that he wasn't traveling alone until he wriggled free from her embrace and she caught sight of Ian hovering a safe distance away, his brown duffel bag thrown over his shoulder, an unlit cigarette in his hand.

"I'm surprised to see you here," she said curtly.

Ian shrugged. "I was homesick."

She put her arm protectively around Paul's shoulders, eyed Ian as if he were a bowl of month-old leftovers just discovered in the back of the refrigerator. There was no fear in her eyes, only distaste, disgust. "I guess you need a ride home," she said after a moment.

"Nah," Ian said. "Just seventy miles. I can hoof it."

She considered this in silence for so long that Paul finally felt compelled to step in.

"We'll take you," he said. "We practically go right by your place. Right, Mom?"

Ian chain-smoked in the backseat as they sped west along the turnpike toward Casey. Paul suspected this blatant lack of consideration was actually a relief to his mother—it gave her reason to open all four windows of the Honda, filling the car with a blast of wind so deafening that anything resembling conversation was impossible. An hour later— ears ringing, faces chilled by the February air—Laura swung to the curb along D Street at Ian's direction, idled in front of a squat yellow house with an unmowed lawn. She tapped her fingers on the steering wheel impatiently as Ian wrestled his duffel bag out of the backseat. Then he leaned back into the car.

"See you around, jocko," he said, winking his bruised eye.

"Yeah," Paul said. "See ya."

The door swung closed and Paul felt a pang of grief.

"If he thinks he'll see you around he's crazy," Laura said, peeling away from the curb so quickly that the tires screeched.

"He's all right," Paul said, looking over his shoulder out the back window to where Ian stood on the edge of the lawn, watching them speed away.

"Honey," she said, aghast. "He's *not* all right. He's not all right at all. Your father told me what happened. You can't think there's anything all right about that."

Paul looked at his lap. "I know. It's just . . . he's not always that way."

She scowled, shook her head. "Honey, I know all about kids like Ian. I know that once they reach a certain point they don't change, they can't change. It's not their fault always. But it's the way it is."

"It's just . . ." Paul said. But what could he say? Just what? Just, he chopped off his own foot, then dragged Dad across the basement?

Just, he lied about the whole thing for four months, piled lie on top of lie on top of lie, just so Dad could be a hero?

"Listen, I don't want to talk about Ian," his mother said cheerfully, depositing her scowl back into its standby position. "I want to talk about you. Tell me everything. Start with the day you got there and tell me all the exciting things that happened."

Paul looked sadly out the window. He'd been gone only a week, but Casey looked bleaker than he'd remembered. The day was gray and muddy slush covered the streets. Solitary figures bundled in heavy coats traipsed heavily along the sidewalks. Mourning doves scuttled along the curbs, picking stupidly at bits of gravel, too dumb to recognize their own sustenance.

"I pretty much told you everything," he muttered.

"Indulge me," she said. "I've missed you, you know." She paused. They were at the center of town, idling at the sole stoplight. She rubbed her thumbs on the steering wheel. "Did you miss me, honey? A little?"

"Maybe a little," he whispered.

Paul returned to school the next morning and was for several exhausting and bewildering hours the most revered soul ever to grace the halls of Casey Junior High. The first question on every pair of lips: *who did you meet?* For a brief period Paul maintained relative honesty, but this tactic was clearly a disappointment to all. They didn't want the truth, he realized—they wanted the fantasy. And who, he reasoned, would ever know the difference anyway? It was as Ian had said: majority rules. The lies began as exaggerations: first he told Brad Hogentogler that the boy who played him in the movie had a small role in *Titanic.* Then at lunch he let it slip to Jennie Weitzel that Luke Milo was actually best friends with Leonardo DiCaprio, which made several girls touch the sleeves of his shirt, mouths agape. Carson and Joe thought this was the greatest thing going; they became his handlers, clearing a path for him in the crowded hallways, stars in their own right as long as they were attached to him. As the afternoon wore on Paul's lies grew larger; he had been swimming at Winona Ryder's house, had shot hoops with Tom Cruise's kids, had walked Brad Pitt's German shepherd around the studio lot. He was amazed at how easily the lies—meticulously detailed, full-blown fabrications—came from his lips. Was this, he wondered briefly (only as long as he'd allow himself to wonder anything) how it had been for his father? Once the toads started spilling from your mouth, was there any way to stop them?

That evening Ben came over for dinner. He went directly to the fridge and grabbed a bottle of beer, patted Laura familiarly on the small of the back as she stood at the stove stirring mashed potatoes, gave Paul the customary smack in the head. Laura had made pork chops, and they dined leisurely around the table while Paul told Ben a new version of his Hollywood story, a version somewhere in between the vague truth he'd told his mother and the outright lies he'd told the kids at school. Ben wasn't nearly as impressed as Paul's classmates had been. "DiCaprio?" he'd say. "That guy can't act to save his life." Or: "Winona Ryder? I'll never understand what people see in *her.*"

"You're just jealous," Laura teased him.

"Oh no," he said seriously. "If it's one thing I'm not, it's jealous. It's all phony baloney out there. Ain't that right, worm?"

Paul sawed into his pork chop. "Not *everything.*"

"Everything but Samuel L. Jackson," Ben said, his mouth full. "That's the one guy I can stand."

"He's kind of a jerk," Paul said.

"You're full of crap," Ben said. But he said it cheerfully, like a compliment, and Paul grinned.

"How's your dad holdin' up?"

Paul looked at his plate, tried to think of a quick and reasonable answer that wasn't more than half a lie. His mother hadn't even asked about his father, not once, as if by not mentioning him the fact of his absence in the house was somehow less unsettling. Paul found this slightly alarming, but he also greatly appreciated it.

"He's all right," Paul said. "Pretty busy with the movie."

"I guess so . . . lettin' you run around with that—"

"Ben," Laura said softly. "Let's not go there."

"No, let's do go there," Ben said sourly. He turned to Paul. "How many times did he leave you alone with Finch? Just the once?"

Paul looked at him curiously. Ben had changed; the expression on his face was uncharacteristically sober. He looked worried, serious. He looked like a father.

"Let him be, Ben," Laura said. "Let him eat his food. He doesn't need to—"

"You never should have let him go in the first place," Ben said. "I don't want to say I told you so, but goddammit I told you so. If it was just Sonny out there, maybe . . . maybe. But not the Nazi."

"Ian's not a Nazi," Paul said quietly.

"What do you mean he's not a Nazi? Did he tell you that?"

"I mean—" Paul started.

"You see?" Ben said, turning on Laura. "You see what's happened to him? Brainwashed. Kids like Finch, they creep into other kids' minds. Before long they—"

"Don't you *dare* lecture me about kids," she said severely, her fork clattering to her plate. "You think I don't know about the Ian Finches of the world? Let me tell you something: every year I have an Ian Finch, and every year I have to remind myself that the kids I have to concentrate on are the ones who aren't Ian Finch, not yet, that the Ian Finches are always going to be there and we're never going to be able to do anything about them but make sure they don't ruin the good kids. So don't you sit there and—"

The telephone rang and they all jolted as if someone had fired a shotgun. On the second ring Laura threw her napkin on the table and went into the kitchen. Ben looked at Paul somberly. "We're gonna have a talk," he said.

Paul glared at him. Who did he think he was anyway, sitting there as if he were the man of the house, acting like he could tell everyone what to do?

"Honey," Laura said, leaning into the dining room. "Your father's on the phone."

"Surprised he remembered you were here," Ben murmured.

Paul got up from the table and went into the kitchen, picked up the phone. His mother hovered in the doorway for a moment and he looked at her, silently, until she went away.

"Hi," he said into the phone.

"Hey." A pause. To light a cigarette? Pour a drink? To wipe away tears or stifle a laugh or scratch his head or roll his eyes or turn down the TV or put a gun to his temple or take off his shoes or blow a kiss?

"You okay, quarterback?"

"Yeah. I'm okay."

Silence. Was that all he wanted to know? Paul tried to picture his father, sitting on the puffy leather couch with his feet on the coffee table and the phone in his lap, the glass doors opened behind him, the city sprawling and spiraling westward. He felt like he'd been gone from that place two years instead of two days, the images fluttering through his mind like a dimly recollected dream.

"You're better off with your mother," Sonny said. "You know that, right?"

Paul didn't answer. He didn't know anything. Why pretend otherwise?

"Paul?"

"What."

"You know that, right? Don't be thinking bad thoughts about the old man, okay?"

Paul felt the threat of tears in his throat. How could he explain to his father that it wasn't anything bad that was the problem? That it was instead some good thing *gone* that made everything in his life blurry and unfamiliar? He could hear the hiss of Ben and his mother whispering heatedly in the dining room.

"Come home," Paul said quietly. "It's okay to come home, you know."

He heard him drag off a cigarette. "Soon."

"You wanna talk to Mom again?"

"No," he said. "We're done."

Done. Now there was a loaded word for you, full as a bloated whale. Done: when the doing is over, the business completed, the matter closed. It was a word that drove his mother crazy when used incorrectly. "I'm done," Paul would say upon finishing his meal or his homework or cleaning his room, to which his mother would always reply: "What are you, a pot roast?" People, she insisted, could not be done. Things were done: people were *finished.*

"Hey," Sonny said. "You seen Ian at all?"

Paul frowned into the receiver. Sonny and Laura: finished. Sonny and Ian: unfinished. "Why would I?" he asked.

"I don't know. You're right. Forget it. I'll talk to you later."

Now the line went dead. Paul stood there holding the phone for a minute, then replaced it. He went back into the dining room and sat down, looked at his half-eaten pork chop. He had lost his appetite.

"How is he?" Laura asked.

"You talked to him," Paul snapped. "Didn't you ask?"

"Don't be that way, honey. Don't be so angry."

"I'm not angry."

Ben set his crumpled napkin on the table. "We're a little worried about your father," he said. "But mostly we're worried about you. Now, I don't know what exactly went on out there, but—"

"I'm fine," Paul said. "Nothing went on. And if you're so worried about Dad why don't you talk to him yourself?"

Ben let a big breath out, exhaled dramatically for at least ten seconds. He was getting angry; his cheekbones were twitching. "You look different," he finally said, pointing at Paul with his fork. "And you sound different. Everything about you is different. This attitude . . ." He paused. "Your mother and I—"

"Stop talking like you're my dad."

Ben blanched, lowered the fork.

"Honey," Laura said. "He's just concerned. I'm concerned too.

Frankly I'm glad Ian came home with you. Now your father can concentrate on the movie without having to deal with Ian."

"Ian's not the problem," Paul said.

"That's crap, mister," Ben said, apparently unable to keep his mouth shut for more than five seconds at a stretch. He turned to Laura. "See what I mean? He's—"

"Wait," Laura said. "Let him talk, will you? What *is* the problem, Paul? Is he drinking? Is that it? It's okay for you to tell me."

"He's fine," Paul said. "I'm fine and he's fine. Why don't you just call him and tell him to come home?"

"He'll be home in two weeks," she said. "When the movie's done."

"No, now," Paul said. "Tell him to come home now."

"Who wants him home like this?" Ben asked. "Acting like a freakin' maniac."

"That's enough," Laura said. "Please, just . . ."

Paul got up from the table.

"Sit down, mister," Ben demanded. "We're not done here."

Paul scowled. "It's *finished,* dimmo," he said.

Life, as it will, rapidly became a drag. The first few days at school were okay, but once Paul's celebrity waned he became unbearably restless, perpetually distracted. Classes were insufferable: what did he need with fractions anyway? who gave a crap about the Emancipation Proclamation? so what if his book report didn't have an introduction? Even his friends bored him, with their endless chatter about the upcoming soccer season, who was going with whom, who could kick whose ass. Sitting in class, he'd chew on the gritty pink eraser of his #2 pencil and look out the window at the drifting snow, wondering about his father. What was he doing? Was he at the set every day? Had he calmed down? Or was he still acting like a lunatic (*I'm telling you, he did not fucking scream!*)? Or had he perhaps given up on the movie altogether? What if he was just sitting in the hotel room, boozing it up and feeling sorry for himself? After that first night back they'd heard noth-

ing from him, but still Paul opened the door to the house every afternoon with a faint glimmer of hope. And he was thinking about Ian, too.
He'd look for him around town when he walked to and from school, or
when he and his mother went shopping. He saw some of the goners
huddled and smoking behind the Hess Station, but Ian wasn't with
them. He thought of calling, but he didn't know what he would say.

A week after his return, he was standing at his locker with Joe and
Carson between second and third periods when Kally Finch walked by.
She was alone, held her notebooks pressed to her chest, passed swiftly
through the crowd of mingling students without averting her eyes from
the hallway ahead.

"She's in a hurry," Joe said, raising his eyebrows at Paul.

"Must be on her way to the janitor's closet," Carson said, grinning.
"Wonder who she's got lined up for today."

Paul felt his cheeks flush. He was sick of Carson and Joe. When had
they gotten so stupid? He slammed his locker shut. "Let's go," he said,
starting toward their classroom.

"Know what I heard?" Joe asked, stumbling to catch up. "Brad
Hogentogler told me that his sister's boyfriend heard from somebody
that Kally Finch became a whore 'cause her brother *sold* her to his
friends—like as a hooker or whatever—so he could get money to buy
drugs."

Paul stopped, his head spinning. "What?" he asked tightly.

"That's what I heard."

He turned on Joe. "How stupid are you? You believe everything you
hear?"

"He didn't say he believed it," Carson said. "He just said he heard it."

"But it's bullshit," Paul said. "Why would you say something if—"

"Chill out," Joe said irately. "What's your problem anyway? What do
you care what people're saying about Finch? Guy like that . . . shit, he
brings it on himself."

"You gotta admit, Paul," Carson said gently, "he's kinda psycho."

He didn't remember dropping his books, didn't remember the two
steps it took him to reach Carson, didn't remember barreling into his
chest and sending them both sprawling to the floor. The next thing he

remembered, after Carson's words *(kinda psycho)* was the look on Carson's face—no fear, only surprise—as Paul reared back to hit him.

"Fight!" a voice shouted.

But he never swung. His clenched fist still in the air, frozen at the point before the motion reversed itself, he was yanked backwards off Carson and spun into the wall. His face collided with the metal edge of a bulletin board and he felt his lip burst open. Silence fell in the hallway. The circle of openmouthed students that surrounded him—at first only eager for a fight—now simply stared. Paul put his hand to his face, then looked down at the blood. Bright blood. The blood of the boys at Disney. Fake blood, spurting out of a baggie attached inside Roger Rhodes' blue jeans. Blood on the blade of the ax as it slipped from Ian's hand. It all ran an ocean together in the grooves of his palms.

"Hey . . ." Joe said, stepping forward.

Carson got slowly to his feet. "Paul—" he started.

And then he was running. He pushed his way through the circle of kids and broke into a sprint, burst out the front doors of the school and raced across the lawn. He was finished with school. He was finished with all of it. Lurching across the snowy parking lot, he heard his name called from behind him and quickened his pace. He reached the street and turned instinctively toward home, but gradually slowed to a wobbly jog as he closed the distance between himself and Willow Lane. His lip was throbbing and his eyes were moist with tears. God, he was sick of his own tears, disgusted by his inability to keep them from spilling. He'd never been a crier before; he'd always felt sorry for the boys who teared up when they banged a knee on the blacktop or got a bad grade on a test, the boys who needed a Kleenex and a kind glance slipped to them from the teacher. What had happened to him? He'd become a baby again, a weakling, a coward. He'd become his father's son.

He stopped at the corner of Willow Lane. He had no coat; his fingers and thighs were chilled numb. Streaks of sunlight filtered through the bare trees. A small brown rabbit padded softly across a nearby yard. Someone close by had a fire in the fireplace; he could smell the rich wood burn and his tears thickened. A bright red cardinal descended and perched on the street sign, its feathers flicking.

He did not want to go home.

He turned right. His chilly tears dried. His knees stopped wobbling. By the time he reached the other side of town a peculiar sense of elation had taken hold of him. He was skipping school. He'd fought in the hallway. It was twenty degrees out but he wore no coat. He had blood on his face. His father was two thousand miles away, his mother concerned with other people's children. This, he decided, must be how bad boys felt. This was how they swaggered—free and alone—when no one was waiting for them.

By the time he got to D Street, twenty minutes later, his feet felt stifled by his shoes. He knocked on the Finches' door with numb hands; nobody answered, but he could hear the TV blaring. He wiped his nose, knocked again, louder, and was about to give up when the door opened.

"Hey," Ian said. He yawned. He was wearing jeans and a black sweater, but from the lines on his face Paul could see he'd just woken up. "Who kicked your ass?"

"Bulletin board," Paul muttered, wiping his runny nose on his shoulder.

"Oughta watch where you're walking," Ian said. He stepped back and let Paul in, didn't even question why he was there, why he would show up out of the blue in the middle of the morning with his lip busted and his eyes still red from crying.

The living room of the Finch house was covered with light blue shag carpeting with about ten cats' worth of hair entwined in the thick shag. Other than that the room was tidy. An ashtray and a can of root beer sat on the narrow coffee table beside a huge orange tabby. *The Price Is Right* was on the TV. Paul sank down on the couch and Ian hobbled off, disappeared. He came back a moment later with a wet paper towel.

"Wipe up," he said, tossing it to Paul.

Paul gingerly touched his lip with the soggy towel, winced.

"Ain't bad," Ian said. "Lips bleed like crazy, even when it's just a little thing."

He flopped down next to Paul, put his feet up on the coffee table and looked at the TV. "Relax," he said after a minute. "I ain't going anywhere."

"Did I wake you up?"

"Sort of," Ian admitted. "Drifted off here for a minute." He pointed to the television. Bob Barker was talking merrily into his skinny microphone. "We should have gone when we were out there, to this show. I swear I coulda won a car. I'm way better than any of the dimmos they ever pick."

Paul set the bloody paper towel on the coffee table. The orange tabby sniffed it and looked at him curiously, then hopped down onto the floor and wandered off.

"How many cats you got?"

"Shit, I dunno. My mom brings home strays when it's cold. Probably six or seven. We'll throw 'em all back outside come spring."

Paul looked at the TV for a moment, then turned to Ian.

"You talk to my dad?"

"Nah. You?"

"He called a few nights ago. Asked if I had seen you."

"Where'd he think you'd see me? On the news? Robbin' a bank or something?"

Paul grinned. "Maybe."

"How's Mom? Happy to have you back in the nest?"

"I guess."

"S'pose she hates my guts, huh? Pretty obvious in the car the other day, taking off before I even had the damn door closed."

"My dad told her about what happened at Disney," Paul said. "He told her that was why he sent me home."

Ian nodded. "Figured it was something like that. Well, it wasn't like she was my biggest fan anyway, right? No harm done."

Paul scowled. "My dad's friend Ben thinks you brainwashed me. He thinks I'm gonna be a Nazi or something."

"That guy's kind of a dick," Ian said. He lit a cigarette. "Stupid too. Reminds me of my old man. Gets something in his mind and you couldn't get it out with a friggin' hacksaw."

"He's all right," Paul said quickly, and suddenly he felt incredibly weary. It seemed he was defending everyone to everyone. It was exhausting being on more than one team at once; he felt like he was intercepting his own passes and then tackling himself.

"See, look at this lady," Ian said, pointing to the TV with his cigarette. "Thinks a bag of candy costs more than vitamins. Do people ever watch the show before they go on? Vitamins always cost the most."

"What have you been doing?" Paul asked. "Just sitting around watching TV?"

"Hell, no. I've been doing a lot of stuff."

"Like what?"

"Like stuff."

"Are you even in school anymore?"

Ian shrugged. "How should I know? Probably took me off the list by now. I don't think I been in about five months. But hey, you know what? I saw this thing on TV the other day, this deal where you can get your degree in a whole bunch of things and do it all at home. There's all this repair crap, you know, stuff for dummies, but you can get it to be a vet assistant. I'm thinking that might be kinda cool, saving dogs and stuff. Wha'dya think? You think I could do that?"

"You have to have a diploma to do that," Paul said. "You gotta finish high school at least."

"But I could do that GED," Ian said, leaning forward. On his face was an expression Paul had never seen on him before. Hope? No . . . not that extreme. But maybe expectation, a hope of hope. "That's what a bunch of guys I knew in juvy did. You take this bonehead test and it's just like you finished high school. You get your diploma without having to go to any classes or see anybody."

"Wow," Paul said. "That's pretty cool."

"Yeah, well," Ian said, the new expression vanishing as quickly as it had risen, "I don't know. I was just kind of thinking about it. I'm pretty good with dogs, you know. They'll follow me just about anywhere. And I'm fixing up these cats here all the time, the ones my mom finds. Just little stuff, you know, scratches and shit, but I'm pretty good at it."

"I'll take my dogs to you," Paul said. "When I have dogs of my own."

"Yeah?"

"Sure," he said. "I bet you'd be pretty good at being a vet."

"Vet assistant," Ian said.

Paul kicked off his shoes and put his feet on the coffee table beside Ian's. "I wish I could drop out of school. I hate school."

"Twelve's a little young for dropping out, jocko," Ian said. "I mean unless you're a retard, or you got a terminal disease or something." He grinned, then shook his head. "You know, when I was a kid, like your age, I used to wish I'd get brain cancer or something so I'd get to stay in the hospital and not go to school and everybody would bring me presents and all the kids in my class would send me stupid pictures to hang up in my hospital room and some stranger would pay for me to go to Disney. How nuts is that?"

"You got to go to Disney," Paul said. "And you're not even dying."

"Yeah. Funny, huh?" He paused, touched a tiny spot at the corner of his eye that was still slightly discolored, the only remaining evidence of Disney. "Hey, I been thinking," he said. "You know those guys pushed me that day, right? It wasn't like I just started swinging at them, right? That one big guy got right up in my face. And they were buttin' in line, right? You said so yourself."

"Yeah," Paul said. "They were buttin'."

"Pisses me off when people do that," he said. He looked at Paul sideways. "Buttin', you know? That's not so weird, right?"

"I guess," Paul said.

"Grandfather clock," Ian said, looking at the TV and shaking his head. "I'd be pissed off if I went through all that to get on and ended up winning a damn clock. I don't care if they say it's worth four grand. I got a clock cost me three bucks. Who needs a four-thousand-dollar clock? Only thing worse is a piano. What if you don't play the piano? What're you gonna do with it?"

"Maybe you learn," Paul said. "Or sell it or something."

Ian was quiet for a moment. Then he said: "Would you tell me if you thought it was weird?"

"What?"

"Gettin' so mad at those guys. At Disney."

Paul considered. "It was a little weird," he said. "Not the gettin' mad. Just all the hittin'."

Ian crushed out his cigarette. "The nigger swung first. Right? You saw that."

"Yeah," Paul said sadly. "I saw it." *See it,* he thought to add. See it at least once a day, when I close my eyes. But he knew Ian would not understand this.

They watched TV well into the afternoon. Ian made turkey and cheese sandwiches and they ate two each and split a bag of Cheetos. Paul's lip was hardly hurting at all anymore, just throbbing a little. He lay on the floor and played with a couple of the cats, swung around his shoelace while they batted it. Ian just sat there the whole time, his feet propped up in front of him, a cigarette going as often as not, alternately watching Paul and the television.

Around two o'clock there was a knock on the front door.

"I'm popular today," Ian said, heaving himself up off the couch.

It was Laura. She looked over Ian's shoulder, caught sight of Paul lazing on the floor, and came charging into the house. "Oh my god," she said. "Oh my god oh my god you are in so much trouble."

Paul thought she was mad because he was at Ian's, and he sat up, started to say something, to defend Ian, to defend himself. Then she started to cry. Not baby crying, not wailing or anything, just the only cry she knew: a few perfect round drops rolling slowly down her cheeks.

"I didn't know where you were," she said, brushing the tears away, practically swatting at them, as if they were mosquitoes. "They told me you were hurt in a fight and I went home and you weren't there and I drove around town and couldn't find you *anywhere.*"

"Hey, he's okay," Ian said lightly. "He's okay, Mrs. Tucker, really. He just busted up his lip is all."

"How was I supposed to know he was okay?" Laura shouted. "I thought he might have a concussion, I thought he might be lying along the street somewhere, bleeding. Three hours I've been looking for you, Paul. Did you think to call me?"

"I thought you were at work," Paul said. This was the truth, but it sounded pretty lame right then, even to him, what with the teardrop that wobbled on her chin.

"They came and got me in class," she said. "They told me you ran off. Carson said you . . ."

She trailed off and sank down in a chair, barely missing an enormous black cat which scurried away with a wicked glance back.

"Honey," she said. "You can't do this to me. I can't take this on top of everything else."

"I'm sorry," Paul said. "I didn't think they'd come get you. Really, I didn't."

She looked around then, suddenly seemed to register where she was.

"What are you doing here?"

"I . . ." he started, but could think of nowhere to go with the sentence.

"I fixed him up," Ian said quickly. "He just stopped over so I could fix up his lip."

"Are you a doctor?" she asked. "Do you have a medical degree?"

"Mom . . ." Paul groaned.

"Could you have at least called me, Ian?" she asked. "Or am I expecting too much?"

Ian shrugged. "Sorry. I guess I didn't think of it."

"What did you think of?" she snapped. "Did you think of anything, ever?"

"Mom . . ." Paul said.

"Are you stoned, Ian, is that it? Did you give him drugs?"

"No way," Ian said angrily. "I wouldn't do that. Paul's my buddy."

"Oh no no no," Laura said, leaning forward in her chair, looking like she might tilt herself right out of it. "If Sonny's your buddy, Ian, I can't do anything about it. But Paul is my son and he's twelve years old and he's not going to have anything to do with you."

"But he fixed up my lip," Paul said, giving as much weight to a wet paper towel as was possible, hoping his mother would see Ian in anything but the blackest of lights.

"That's fine," she said. "That was very nice of him. But we're going home now. Ian, please, I'm doing my best to speak to you as an adult. If he comes here again, will you please call me?"

Ian looked at Paul, shrugged an apology.

"Okay," he said. "I'll call."

Paul was sent directly to his room when they arrived home. He didn't really mind; punishment in his house usually took the form of an earnest lecture, so being grounded was something of a novelty, far better than having to avert his gaze from a set or two of disappointed eyes. Lying on his bed, he listened to the clamor of drums coming from the basement. Each stroke came with its own distinct sensation: the bed rattled when his mother rolled the snare, trembled when she struck the cymbal, jerked when she pummeled the bass. He couldn't help but notice that she had improved. How many hours had she spent down there while he'd been gone? She sounded almost like an actual drummer now, not just some idiot whaling away. He tried to imagine what his father would think of this. If only his father could hear her, could have his own bed tremble two thousand miles away, he would know it was time to come home. Because either his mother's new hobby was the most beautiful thing in the world or a sure sign of her own unraveling. Or both.

After about twenty minutes the drumming came to an abrupt halt. A moment later she swung open his bedroom door, announced they were going out for pizza at the Casey Mall.

"I thought I was grounded," he said.

Laura braced herself in the doorway, one hand on each doorjamb, as if she were the only thing keeping the house from collapsing. "You want pizza or don't you?"

The Casey Mall didn't really deserve to be called a mall. It was filled with mostly grimy dollar stores, no-name restaurants, and chains nobody'd ever heard of outside central Pennsylvania. But kids from school hung out there even so, especially in the winter, their small and territorial packs congregating at certain predetermined circles of benches along the mallway. Beside the music store—The Wall—was the place where Ian's friends hung around when it was too cold to be outside, hovering like wasps, scratching obscenities in the wood benches, scowling at everyone who passed.

"Aren't you hungry?" Laura asked.

He'd managed to finish only one slice of pizza, slid a second one from the platter but then only nibbled at it. Now he gazed down at his plate, his stomach churning.

"Not really," he said. Truth was, he'd eaten so many Cheetos at Ian's he felt like barfing. But he was wary of admitting this—not the barfing part, but the Ian part.

"Don't you have to get in shape for something?" she asked. "I saw a flyer for Junior baseball. Sign-up's next week."

He picked a nugget of sausage from his pizza, put it under his tongue like a pill, sucked the salt from it to delay a response. Junior baseball? Where was this coming from? The only sign-ups she'd ever mentioned before were for crap like chorus and speech club.

"I can't hit," he said.

She clicked her tongue. "That's not true. You used to hit a Wiffle ball clear across the yard."

"Mom," he said. "You know how fast some guys pitch in Juniors? Like sixty miles an hour."

"Wow," she said. "That is fast."

"Right," Paul said. "So I'm not playing Junior baseball. Unless you want me to look like a total asshole."

"Honey," she said softly, pushing her plate away. "Two things. First, please don't feel you can casually say *asshole* in front of me. I don't think I'm quite prepared for that stage yet."

He sighed impatiently. "What's the second thing?"

She smiled. "I've never once seen you look like an asshole. Not once. And I'm not just saying that because I'm your mother."

He didn't want to grin, but he couldn't help it. "Okay," he said.

After paying the bill Laura said she wanted to stop in at Deep Discount Shoes to look for a pair of good winter boots. She had been wearing Sonny's old boots all winter, she told Paul, and needed to buy a pair that actually fit her. Paul was surprised she'd managed to mention his father at all, even if it was in reference to footwear.

"I'm gonna look at CDs," he said. "I'll come over when I'm done."

She eyed him warily, as if he might make a run for it (but for where? for what?) the moment he was out of her sight.

"Five minutes," she said.

There were two goners loafing on the bench outside The Wall. Paul strolled casually over and lingered near them, picking pepperoni from his teeth with a minty toothpick, hoping they would notice him. They didn't pay any attention. They were talking about a band called the Boat People that was going to be playing at a club in Lancaster the next week, trying to figure out how they were going to scrounge up enough cash to pay the cover. Finally one of them stopped talking mid-sentence and eyed Paul contemptuously.

"What're you lookin' at?" he growled. He was a cartoon of himself, Paul thought, everything about him an exaggeration of the expected. Six and a half feet tall, thick forearms, a nose that had clearly suffered. His head was covered by a thin coat of black hair; a silver hoop was snagged at the top of his left ear; on his shirt was a grotesque scarecrow, crucified on a cross, blood dripping from its straw hands.

"Nothin'," Paul said, flicking his toothpick into the ashtray. "I'm Paul."

"You want to suck my dick or something, Paul?"

"Um, no."

"So what're you staring at me for, fucko?"

Paul tried a little sneer, a smirk. He wished he'd planned ahead, practiced it first in front of a mirror, so he could see how it looked. "I'm a friend of Ian's," he said.

"Finch? You know Finch?" the other one said. Paul recognized him from the day at Neidermeyers'; this was Charlie, or Kevin, one of the boys who had been in the basement with Ian the night before the house collapsed. He wasn't quite the cartoon the scarecrow guy was; he was short and a little pudgy in the gut, had hair like Ian's, floppy over the forehead, but blond instead of black.

"We just got back from California," Paul said. "Me and Ian."

"Hey, you're the fireman's kid," Pudgy said. "Yeah?"

"Yeah."

"You sure Ian's back?" Scarecrow asked. "Where's he at?"

"I dunno. Around."

Pudgy butted him in the shoulder with the heel of his hand. "Hey, you see him, you tell him Kevin's lookin' for him. Asshole owes me ten bucks."

Scarecrow eyed Paul. "*You* got any money?"

Paul shook his head.

"Not even a buck? My little brother needs an operation, see. He's got dick cancer and if he don't get the operation they're gonna have to cut off his dick."

"There's no dick cancer," Kevin said.

"You wanna bet?" Scarecrow said, turning to him. "You wanna fuckin' bet? I'll bet you five thousand dollars there's dick cancer, fucko."

Paul left them to their dispute, went into the music store and picked out a CD. After a few minutes his mother wandered in. She was still bootless. Holding his thumb over the orange "parental advisory" label, he asked her for an advance on his allowance to buy the CD. She peered at it dubiously.

"The Boat People?" she said. "Who are they?"

"They're like . . . folk rock," Paul said.

"Is that back in?"

"Yeah. It's like . . . new folk rock."

Her eyes narrowed. "Is this a California thing?"

"Kinda," he said.

A few days later, on a Sunday afternoon, he found himself at the Finches' again. He had intended only to pass by and see if Ian was by chance outside, maybe shoveling the driveway, he told himself, though this was something he knew Ian would never do unless a gun were held to his head, and probably not even then. Paul figured if Ian was outside it wasn't really like going to see him; it was like bumping into him. But when he found the yard and the drive empty, he went up and knocked on the door. Ian's mother answered. He hadn't seen her since the night of the rescue and he almost didn't recognize her. Without mascara running down her face she didn't look half bad. Of course she hadn't opened her mouth yet.

"Hi, sweetie," she said. "Ian's in his room. I don't know what he's doing in there. Doing what he always does, I suppose, although what that is is anybody's guess."

"Thanks," Paul said, scooting past her.

Kally Finch was lying on the floor of the living room reading *Seventeen* magazine. There was a black cat sitting on her back, methodically grooming itself.

"Hey," she said, throwing Paul a fleeting glance.

"Hi," he said. He stopped, not wanting to be impolite.

She looked up. "What?"

"Nothin'. Just hi."

She wiggled her shoulders and the cat hopped off her back. "I heard about your fight," she said.

His heart shuddered. She couldn't know, could she, what had been said about her? That it had been her, first, before Ian, that he had been moved to defend?

"What about it?" he asked casually.

"Nothin'. Just about it." Now she eyed him suspiciously. "Was there really a whirl tub in you guys' hotel room?"

He smiled, relieved. "Yeah."

"Did it whirl?"

"Not really," he said. "More bubbled than whirled, I guess."

"Ian said it whirled," she said. She snorted, looked back to her magazine. "I *knew* he was lying."

"Well, it kinda whirled," Paul said.

"What*ever*," she said.

Paul walked toward the back of the Finch house, in the direction where he assumed Ian's room would be. He hadn't been anywhere but the living room before, but Ian's door—despite the fact all the doors were closed—was easy enough to find.

GO AWAY, read a hand-printed sign on the door.

Paul grinned, then knocked.

"Read the sign!" shouted a voice from inside.

"It's Paul."

There was a complex series of locks being unlocked, then Ian opened the door.

"You're a very, very bad boy," he said, although Paul thought he didn't seem especially surprised to see him. "Does Mommy know you're here?"

Paul unzipped his backpack and took out the Boat People CD. "I got this for you," he said, holding it out. "You like 'em, right?"

Ian looked at it, nodded appreciatively. "Yeah, they're cool. You steal it or buy it?"

"Stole it," Paul said. "From The Wall."

"Bullshit," Ian said. "They got like twenty alarms there."

"Musta been broken," Paul said. He took a step into Ian's room. On the walls were posters of bands he'd never heard of—Furious George, The Grubs, Three Blind Mimes—plus a tattered map of the world and a giant photo of the mushroom cloud billowing over Hiroshima. The room was much neater than he would have imagined. There were a few magazines piled on the floor beside the bed and an overflowing ashtray in the middle of the floor. On the desk was a banged-up CD player and several stacks of CDs.

Ian went and flopped down on his bed, which was covered by a fleece leopard-skin blanket. There was a book open on the pillow and he shoved it to the floor.

"Whatcha reading?" Paul asked.

"*Treasure Island.* For about the twentieth time."

"I didn't know you read."

"Just that one," Ian said. "And a couple others, maybe."

"I bet you're smart," Paul said. "You might be really smart and not even know it."

"What're you, my mother?"

"I just—"

There was a knock on the door. Ian raised his eyebrows as he rolled off his bed. "Your mommy?"

"I don't think so," Paul stuttered, suddenly horrified by the possibility that his mother had actually developed some kind of crisis radar system, had already tracked him here, would never let him out of the house again.

Ian opened the door. Mrs. Finch was standing there with a bright smile. "You boys want some snacks?"

"No, Mom, we don't want *snacks*," Ian said. "Stop bothering us, okay?" He closed the door in her face and flopped down on the bed again.

"You're a dick to your mom," Paul said.

"Shut up," Ian said. "Or leave."

Paul stood. "I just wanted to bring that CD by anyway. Those guys're playing in Lancaster next week."

"What do you know about that? Got some secret life?"

"Your friends told me," Paul said. "I talked to 'em at the mall the other night. They said—"

"Hold on." Ian held up his hand. "You talked to them? What, like a conversation?"

Paul shrugged. "Kinda. Kevin said to tell you he was lookin' for you. He said you owed him ten bucks."

"Aw Jesus, man. What were you doing talking to them? You crazy?"

Paul sat down backwards on Ian's desk chair, rested his elbows on the back of it. "I just kinda bumped into them. Outside The Wall."

"Kevin," he said. "Fucking Kevin. That guy's had his head up his butt since first grade. Don't talk to him, okay?"

"Now who's acting like a mom?"

Ian blushed. "I'm just saying—"

"The other guy asked me if I wanted to suck his dick."

Ian shook his head. "Shit . . . that's Leo. Big bastard, right? Yeah, that's how he says hello. Jesus, those idiots."

"I thought those guys were your friends."

Ian lit a cigarette, expelled an exasperated cloud. "My friends, yeah.

You wanna know something? I was in that goddamn basement with
your dad for six hours and by the time we came up I was tighter with
him than I'd ever been with Kevin or Leo or any of those assholes.
Wha'dya think of that?"

"You miss him?"

"Nah," Ian said quickly. "You?"

"Nah," Paul said, matching lie for lie in an unspoken agreement of
necessary denial. He nodded at Ian's foot, which lay at an unnatural
angle on the bedspread. "You get the real one yet?"

"Couple weeks," Ian said. "And hey, you know what this one nurse
told me? She said in a few years they're gonna have legs you can just
think into moving, almost like it was your real leg. Like if you just think
about wiggling your toe, the fake toe'll know to wiggle. You believe that
shit?"

"Like Luke Skywalker's hand," Paul said.

"Right," Ian said. "But was that computers or the Force?"

"I don't remember," Paul said. "Maybe both."

They lapsed into silence. Ian smoked; Paul picked at some dried
paint on the back of the desk chair. He wanted to talk to Ian but he
couldn't really think of anything to talk about. He remembered what it
had felt like to hang out with Carson and Joe, before he'd gone to L.A.,
how they'd all lounge around in Carson's basement talking about
classes and teachers and other kids in their class, about football and
comics and Nintendo and the shows they watched on TV. There was a
shared history, an unending supply of topics they had in common, most
trivial, a few of consequence. With Ian, chatting about dumb stuff felt
awkward. With Ian, the only thing they really had in common was too
big for small talk.

Ian lit a fresh cigarette off the butt of the one he'd just finished. "I
been thinking about my tattoo," he said.

Paul perked up. "Yeah? Thinking about it how?"

He shrugged. "I think I want something cooler than what I got. I'm
thinking I might do some work on it."

"Wha'dya mean?"

"I don't know, play around with it or something, get some cool picture outa what's already there. I made some drawings."

He leaned over and snatched a thick notebook from the other side of his bed. "First I thought of this." He held up the page for Paul to see.

"It's just boxes," Paul said.

"Yeah, but it could be like a window. And maybe there could be stuff inside it, you know, weird faces or something."

"I guess," Paul said, unconvinced.

Ian turned the page. "I like this one better anyway," he said, holding it up.

"Huh," Paul said, noncommittally.

"Snakes," he said. "They're cool, yeah?"

"They're okay," Paul said. "But it kinda still looks like . . . like it did before, just made out of snakes. What else you got?"

"Stupid stuff." He flipped over to the next page, held it up.

"What is that?"

"A horse." Ian grinned, embarrassed. "I know. Shit, I don't even like horses. I was runnin' out of ideas. It's a bitch making something into something else, you know, once it's already there? Your options are kinda limited."

"Can't you just get it erased? Can't you get it burned off or something?"

"Sure, if I want a butt-ugly scar for the rest of my life." He flipped back to the snakes, cocked his head to look at them from different angles. "Maybe if we make 'em loopier," he said. "I wanna try it out on the real thing, see what it'd really look like, but I can't do it myself. You give me a hand?"

"I don't know how to do tattoos," Paul said. "It's dangerous, right?"

Ian rolled his eyes. "I don't want you to give me a *real* tattoo, dimmo. I just want you to draw on it, see what you can do, see if you can do something cool with these snakes. You can draw, right? You can do everything. Then if you do something I like I can go someplace and get it done up for real."

He grabbed a black Magic Marker from the floor, tossed it to Paul, then peeled off his T-shirt. Paul stood behind him, uncapped the marker and set it carefully on the lines on Ian's back. That's what they were, just lines, and Paul was suddenly struck by their simplicity, remembering how all those people had cowered at Disney, just because of some intersecting lines, some arbitrary shape. Weird, he thought, how something so simple could be so wicked.

"Do the snakes," Ian said, lighting a cigarette. "Try that."

"I don't like the snakes so much," Paul said, scrunching his nose to ward off the smoke that drifted from Ian's lips and directly into his face. "I'm thinking."

"Do the snakes, man. The snakes are cool. Make 'em loopy."

Paul started drawing. He set his left hand on Ian's shoulder to keep him still and drew with his right. Ian's back was smooth and the marker shiny. It wasn't like drawing on paper at all; it was soft, there was some give to it, like making lines in the sand: SOS; HELP; THERE ARE PEOPLE DOWN HERE.

"Whatcha doin'? You're doing something retarded, aren't you?"

"You'll see."

Paul finished, lifted the marker from Ian's back. What he'd come up with was pretty rough, but he liked it better than anything Ian had done. They went into the bathroom and Ian looked over his shoulder into the mirror at this:

"Hey," he said. "That ain't half bad."

"Somebody else could do it better probably," Paul said. "A real tattoo guy. It's just an idea."

"I like it," Ian said. " 'Cept it's got that line sticking off to nowhere. Doesn't make any sense. Gotta do something with that."

Paul put the marker to his back again, added this:

"Yeah," Ian said. "There you go."

"You got your snake."

Ian turned, nodded. "Well," he said. "It's an improvement anyways." He tossed his cigarette into the toilet. "Hey, you should go home. Your mom, right, she'll kick my ass if she finds out you're here."

"I don't wanna go home," Paul said quickly. He hadn't exactly been aware of thinking it, but now it seemed truer than anything anyone had said in a long time. So what if he and Ian didn't have much to talk about? So what if they sat in Ian's room, for hours even, without saying a word? Did that mean they didn't belong together? Did that mean they couldn't really be friends?

"What's wrong with home? You got a nice place over there."

Paul shrugged. "I just . . . just kinda like hangin' with you."

Ian was silent. He turned the marker over and over in his hand. Like Sonny, Paul thought. Turning and turning and turning, hoping the words would come.

"Well, yeah," Ian finally said, scratching his stubble. "Yeah, I can see that. But you shouldn't hang with me. You shouldn't come back here anymore. I'm a bad influence, right?" He paused. "Go on home, jocko. I got shit to do anyway."

"You do not," Paul said. "You're full of crap."

"Paul," Ian said. "Go home."

Chapter Nine

A week passed. The weather turned. It happens in Pennsylvania; you can always count on a few glorious days late in February to fool you, to hint at spring before winter comes roaring back for its final blast. But fool you it does, every year, no matter how many times you've promised yourself you won't be taken in by it again. *Winter is through,* your body tells you, despite the calendar. *You have prevailed.* The sun blazes against the snow, the temperature reaches into the low sixties, and the town sheds its winter coats like skins. High school kids, their nakedness stifled for months, immediately don shorts and tank tops. Paul and his classmates wear sweatshirts, jeans, and soggy sneakers, splash giddily through slush puddles, nostalgic for weather like this as if it and their very happiness have been absent for years. Shopkeepers open their doors. Schools open their windows. Firemen sit in front of the fire station on lawn chairs. Mothers and sons unroll hoses in driveways and wash cars, dirty from salt and snow.

"No spraying," Laura said, handing Paul the nozzle. "I've seen how you and your father wash the car. We'll have none of that, mister."

He grinned. "We'll see."

They'd heard nothing from Sonny since the brief phone call the night after Paul's return. For ten days his absence had filled the house on Willow Lane like the proverbial elephant in the middle of the living room, but with each day the elephant was becoming increasingly manageable, even cooperative. He made little noise, required no tending, did not attempt to shuffle into their path when they made the wide berth around him.

"When I first moved here," Laura said as she scoured the wheels, "they still used sand on the streets, instead of salt. I couldn't believe it. I thought I'd traveled back in time."

Paul fixed his thumb over the nozzle, sprayed the hood of the car; streams of gray rained onto the driveway. "Did it work?"

"Better than salt," she said. She flung her braid behind her shoulder. "But the glop on the streets, all spring . . . it was pretty bad."

"How'd they get rid of it?"

She looked up at him, squinted against the sun, an answer on her lips. He saw something pass over her face then, a strange expression of recognition and grief, as if she'd heard the distinctive bark of a childhood dog, long dead.

He turned the hose toward the ground, alarmed. "What?" he asked.

She smiled, shook her head. "You looked like your father there for a minute. Standing there with that hose."

He rolled his eyes. "It's a *garden* hose, Mom."

"I know," she said, blushing slightly. "Just, for a second there I—"

"Is that a good thing?" he asked. "Lookin' like Dad?"

She hesitated, turned back to the filthy hubcap, raised her sponge. "It's not a bad thing," she finally said.

It was Friday and Paul was taking the long way home from school, planning a stop by Dewey's for a fat bag of sunflower seeds in preparation for a mild weekend that promised to be filled with hours of muddy football. He had made his apologies to Carson and Joe and they had accepted them without question, wanting—Paul imagined—no complicated explanations but only for things to be like they had been before. And that was what he wanted too. The change in weather—a familiar event—had reminded him of all things familiar, all things that were part of his old life, an easier life, a life he desperately wanted to return to.

Nearing Dewey Drugs he passed across the street from the fire station and glanced over purely out of habit. There, on a beat-up lawn chair in the driveway, sat his father. He was talking to Black Phil. Paul ducked down behind a parked pickup truck, for what reason he wasn't entirely certain, and peered through the smudged windows of the truck across the street at them. His father wore jeans and a black Casey FD sweatshirt. He was smoking a cigarette. He had cut his hair and was clean-shaven. He and Phil were talking casually.

Paul slunk into Dewey's and wandered around aimlessly for a half hour—flipping through comic books, comparing the trigger action on cap guns—passing stealthily by the front window every few minutes to see if his father was still there. Perhaps he'd come home just today, Paul told himself. Perhaps his things were already in the house, his bags already unpacked. Perhaps he had just stopped by the fire station for a visit, knowing Paul and Laura wouldn't be home until late afternoon. But why wouldn't he have called to tell them he was coming? If he was home, truly home, he surely would have let them know. He passed by the front window once again and his father was gone; Black Phil sat alone, paging through *The Casey Weekly*. Paul paid old Mr. Dewey for the sunflower seeds and meandered across the street. Phil saw him coming and closed the paper, laid it in his lap. Paul sat down beside him, in the chair that was still warm from his father's weight.

"Fancy meeting you here," Phil said. "School out already?"

"Yep. I was over at Dewey's." Paul held up the bag of seeds. "Want some?"

"Sure. I'll have a handful."

Paul poured a small pile into Phil's open hand and Phil picked and cracked one seed at a time, the sure sign of a novice.

"Long time no see," he said. "How was your trip?"

"It was okay."

"Meet any movie stars?"

"Depends what you call movie stars," Paul said.

Phil spat a splintered seed at his feet. "How's your mom doin'?"

"She's okay."

"We'll have to have a barbecue one of these days," he said. "Once the weather gets nice and holds. Be just like old times. Your mom can make that potato salad everybody loves so much."

"Sure," Paul said.

"She's ruined all other potato salad for me, you know that? That stuff they sell at the Eagle, I can't even take a bite of it."

He fell silent. Paul spat out a mouthful of shells.

"Is my dad here?" he asked.

Phil didn't say anything for a minute, just sucked on his seed. Then he said: "I 'spect you saw him, huh? 'Spect that's why you're sittin' here now."

"Maybe," Paul said, siphoning another handful of seeds into his mouth. "Or maybe I'm just sittin' here to be sittin' here."

Phil smiled. "He's been here a couple days. Been sleeping upstairs."

"How come?"

Phil raised his thick eyebrows. "Maybe you should ask him that, eh?"

"I don't guess he wants to talk to me," Paul said. "Otherwise I guess he would've come home. Is he hiding or something?"

Phil considered. "Came here a couple nights ago," he finally said. "Showed up out of the blue and crashed on a cot. I just thought he didn't want to wake you all in the middle of the night, but he's been here two days now, sleeping mostly, piddlin' around the station a little."

"Does Ben know he's here?"

"He's been off last few days," Phil said. "So I don't guess he does."

"What've you guys been talking about?"

Phil was quiet. He rubbed his chin and crossed and recrossed his legs.

"Phil?"

"I've known your father a long damn time," he said. "Long as just about anybody in this town, I guess. I met him my first day at the station here. He was seven years old, came to about here on me, stomped around in boots two sizes too big. He was the one who showed me around the place, showed me where to put my stuff, showed me where my gear was, opened up the fridge and told me what food was off-limits. Captain Sam had his things, see, stuff nobody but him got to eat. He made Jell-O with those little sour oranges in it, ate that stuff morning, noon, and night. He saw anybody else take a dip into it and that guy'd be scrubbing the toilet for a week."

He paused, remembering.

"Phil," Paul said. "What about my dad?"

"Known him longer than anybody," he began again. "Saw him grow up, go away, come back, get married, have a boy of his own. I've seen him through a lot of things."

He took the bag of sunflower seeds from Paul's lap and dumped what was left of his back in, wiped his hands on his pants. "Guess I don't like those too much. No offense."

Paul shrugged. "None taken."

"He told me what happened," Phil said, gazing across the street. "Told me about what the boy did, cutting off his own foot, gettin' them both out of the house."

"He told you?"

"He told me." He paused, turned to Paul. "Now I'm gonna tell you something, something you might not know. What happened to Sonny . . . something like that happens to every one of us, every guy who wears the gear. Different circumstances, different outcome every time, but the same type of thing. Losing your nerve the moment you need it most. Blowin' the save. Just usually it don't happen when the whole world's watching. Usually you screw up and you learn to live with it, and nobody much knows or cares but you. You don't have it in your face all the time."

"I don't even care that he freaked out down there," Paul said. "I just don't know why he lied about it to everybody."

"Don't you?" Phil asked, surprised. He thought for a moment. "Let me ask you something. You ever feel like you got something to live up to? You ever feel like you gotta prove yourself to somebody?"

"Sure. My dad. At least I used to."

"Okay, then. You know who your dad has to prove himself to?"

"His dad?"

"That's right. And you know who else?"

Paul thought. "The other guys?"

"That's right. And you know who else?"

"No."

"Your mom. And you."

"He doesn't have to prove himself to me," Paul protested. "I don't think—"

"This doesn't have squat to do with what you think. Right now it's all about what he thinks. Who else?"

"I don't know."

Phil pointed. "See that guy across the street there? Him. And that lady in the truck. And Harold Dewey at the drugstore. And the counter girl at the DQ. And that squirrelly kid who sells papers at the corner. And maybe all the cats in town."

Paul smiled. "Okay," he said. "I get it."

"No," Phil said. "Not yet. You know who else, most of all?"

Well, who else was there? God? Nah . . . too distant, too slippery. Gramaw Tucker? He had barely known her. Then Paul thought of the day at Neidermeyers', how he'd been tempted to turn around once he reached the house, but how he'd pushed his bike up that dusty drive, drawn forward. Why? Not for his friends. Not even for his father.

"Himself," Paul said.

Phil nodded. "You got it. Spent his whole life trying to prove himself to himself. Spent his whole life dreaming of being a hero. Then along comes his chance and he blows it. Thirty years waiting for the big day and he loses his nerve. Maybe *'cause* he waited so long. I don't know."

"But why'd he come here?"

" 'Cause this is his home."

"No," Paul said. "His home's at home. With my mom. And me."

"Not anymore," Phil said. "When you get scared, you wind up at your real home. You wind up at the place where you feel like no more bad will happen to you. That's what he's doing. He's just holing up."

"For how long?"

"Why don't you go on up and ask him that yourself? I'm bettin' he'd like to see you."

"Really?" Paul doubted this. He wanted to believe it, but he couldn't, not quite. After everything that had happened, all bets were off.

"Worth a try, ain't it?"

Paul went into the station, climbed the steep stairs to the sleeping quarters, opened the door softly. There was no one inside but his father, and he was asleep. He lay on the cot on his side. Paul sat down on the floor, at eye level with him. If his father really loved him, he told himself, he'd wake up. If everything was really okay, he would know that this was the moment to open his eyes. But instead of opening, his father's eyes fluttered with dreams. Dreams of what? Paul wondered. Of being a hero? Of beginning again, that morning, but this time with the knowledge of what was to come? Of the ax, steady in his hand? Of Ian, steady in his grip?

"Dad?" Paul whispered.

Sonny didn't stir. And Paul did not have the heart to wake him, to steal him from those dreams.

Earlier that day he'd been at the Casey Public Library with his English class. They were doing research papers on the maneuvers of Confederate troops in the area prior to the battle of Gettysburg. Amongst the research section, Paul had stumbled across a test prep book for the GED. The librarian had eyed him suspiciously when he'd checked it out and tucked it away in his backpack. Now, his father asleep at the station and he in no hurry to face his mother, to keep yet another secret, he decided to go to Ian's to drop off the book. He'd been busy with school, with friends, hadn't seen Ian since the Sunday before when he'd worked on his tattoo.

The Finches' yard was muddy from the melting snow. The lowest branches of the lone tree in the front yard drooped nearly to the ground. Paul reached the porch and wiped his feet on the mat, pulled the book from his backpack and rapped on the door. It was Kally who opened it.

"Hey," she said.

"Hey. Ian around?"

She didn't answer. Instead, she peered curiously at the thick book under Paul's arm. "What's that?"

"A book."

"Ha-ha. *What* book?"

"It's for Ian." He held it out for her to see and she took it from him, then gazed at the cover, the beginnings of a smile on her lips.

"GED?"

"Yeah," Paul said. "I found it at the library. I thought he could use it to study."

Her eyebrows made a V. "Study what?"

"For his test. He's gonna do the GED, get his diploma. He's probably gonna go to vet school. This book has all the stuff that's on the test."

She handed the book back to him. "He told you that? About vet school?"

"He said he was thinking about it."

"He says a lot of things," she said. "Two years ago he said he was going to fix my Rollerblades and they're still broken." She leaned against the door frame, rubbed her tongue along the top row of her braces.

"Listen," Paul said. "Just go get him, okay?"

"Ain't here."

"Where is he?"

"How should I know? He's hardly been around the last week or so."

"He's probably out studying," Paul said. "Probably been at the library or something."

She smirked. In smirking she looked vaguely like Ian, although on a girl, and a girl of thirteen, the smirk wasn't a bit scary, not any more scary than if she'd been wearing a Halloween mask.

"You don't know him very well, do you?" she asked.

"I know him better than you."

"If that were true you wouldn't be looking for him here," Kally said. "And you wouldn't've bothered getting that book. You really think he's gonna take that test? Be a veterinarian? How old *are* you?"

Paul felt his cheeks redden. What did she know of Ian? Stupid slut, thirteen years old and already fucking a blue streak through town. She thought she was so smart. It had never occurred to her that her brother might be a hero.

"He's probably with his friends," she said. "Kevin and Charlie and whoever. Probably hanging out with them somewhere."

"He's not friends with those guys anymore," Paul said. "He doesn't even like 'em. He told me that himself, just last week."

"So?" she said. "Last week was last week. And anyways, just because he doesn't like 'em doesn't mean they aren't his friends."

He shook his head. "You're crazy."

"I feel kinda sorry for you," she said, but he was already walking away.

Late that night he was awakened by the jingling of leashes. He looked at his clock—3:15—and stumbled sleepily to the living room. In the dark he saw his mother by the front hall closet clipping leashes on the dogs. June was stretched out, sound asleep, at her feet; Hester was sitting but yawning widely.

"Mom?"

She gasped, put her hand over her heart.

"Sorry," he said. "Whatcha doing?"

There wasn't a hint of sleep in her face; but for the bathrobe under her heavy coat and her long hair loose around her shoulders, it may as well have been three-fifteen in the afternoon. She nodded to the dogs. "They were antsy," she said. "I thought I'd walk them around the block." She tugged on one of the leashes and June rose with a lengthy sigh, thumping her tail in aggravation.

"Kinda late, isn't it? Or early?"

She smiled, guilty. "Come with me?"

He put on his coat and boots and took Hester's leash from her hand. The night was windy but cool instead of cold; he could only see wisps of his breath as they crossed the front yard and turned right for the trek down Willow Lane.

"It's funny bein' out so late," he said, looking at the dark houses that lined the street, indistinguishable in the moonless night.

"I like it," she said. "It's peaceful, isn't it?"

"Or creepy," he said, and she laughed.

"I used to do this all the time before you were born. I'd get up almost every night your father was at work and walk the dogs all over town. Did I ever tell you that?"

"No," Paul said. "Dad did, but I didn't believe him."

She sighed. "I was such a wreck those first months. Up all night and then having to teach in the morning. I don't think I did anybody much good that year."

"Up all night how come?" he asked. "Were you scared?"

"Foolish was more like it," she said wryly. "I'd spend all night making up all sorts of things in my head, awful things, things that might happen to him. Isn't that silly?"

"I do that," Paul said. "All the time."

She stopped walking. "You do?" She seemed genuinely surprised, as if she thought fear and worry were traits to be found only in people she didn't like. And now, here was her own flesh and blood, admitting to this greatest of all weaknesses.

"My knees get cold," he said. "When I hear sirens. Sometimes I feel like I might throw up."

They were at the foot of the Bakers' lawn. June trotted to a drooping snowman and sniffed around its base, then peed on it. Both dogs were wide awake now; invigorated by the night air, they strained at their leashes toward the next scent.

"But it doesn't make sense," Laura said, moving forward again. "To feel that way, I mean. This little town . . . what could happen? If we lived in a city, if he were going out on a hundred calls a week, if he—"

"I don't think sense has a whole lot to do with it," Paul said. His eyes had grown accustomed to the dark and he saw her frown, dissatisfied, in response to his words. The wind whistled low in the bare trees.

"Some nights I thought I'd go right out of my mind," she said. "I wondered why he couldn't just be something else, anything else."

"How'd you get used to it?"

She smiled self-consciously. "Really want to know?"

"Sure," he said.

"I just went ahead and made him something else. I decided—pretended—that he worked at the tollbooth on the turnpike exit, sat out there with a transistor radio and a long book and made change for people. I got it all set in my mind. If someone got on in Philadelphia the charge would be $6.40; I imagined most people would give him a ten and he'd peel off three ones, then slide two quarters and a dime out of the tray. I'd make myself picture it as I walked along this street, shiny quarters glinting in the light, a dull dime. And he'd smile and say 'have a nice night' and they'd be on their way."

"Did it work?"

"Well enough," she said. "To get through the night. And then, before long, there was you to worry about."

"You worry about me too much," he said.

"I know," she said, and he was surprised. Who would have thought she knew? His mother, the open book of furrows and frowns. A funny thought occurred to him: maybe she didn't want to come stumbling down those bleachers any more than he wanted her to.

Hester halted suddenly, nosed at the wing of a dead bird that lay in the street. The bird wasn't mangled or gnawed, just still, as if sleeping. It reminded him of his father, how still he'd been at the station that afternoon, lifeless but for the flutter of his eyes, dead but for his dreams.

"Poor bird," Laura said, nudging Hester away from it.

"Dad's always going to be a fireman," Paul said. "It's who he is."

She clicked her tongue. "People keep telling me that," she sighed. "Since the day I moved to this town, people have said those exact words: oh, it's who he is, you know, it's who he is. But you know what, Paul? It's not really *who he is*. At least it doesn't have to be. When I met him, he didn't have a thing to do with the fire department. He was going to be a businessman. Sounds funny now, doesn't it, thinking of your father in a suit and tie? But that's what I thought. What *we* thought, both of us. And then your grandfather died, and it was like the part of your father that could be something else died too. It's who he is, everyone says, but I know better. Maybe I'm the only one who does, because I know he was something without that too, Paul, something just as strong and just as bright and just as brave. He could be all those things without . . . without scaring the life out of his own son . . . and everybody else."

"After a while," Paul said, looking at her, "you get kinda used to being scared. Never all the way used to it. But kinda."

"That may be," she said. "But I've gotten kinda used to him in his little booth at Exit 15, warm and safe. That's my story and I'm sticking to it."

"But—"

"We do what we have to," she said. "Someday you'll understand that, honey. You make trade-offs. You do what you need to do so you can sleep nights, so you can have a life, so you can be safe."

Safe. His mother was safe. But his father would never be safe again. There were too many things on his tail now, nipping madly at his heels. His parents had pretended for so many years that to look at the truth of who they were must have seemed impossible. But his father had done it, had seen the truth in the basement, had come face to face with the fact that he wasn't the man he wanted to be, wasn't the man everyone thought he was. And it had made him nuts, a raving lunatic. So who could blame him—anyone, really?—for not wanting to see the facts of a life, of a marriage, of a career, of anything? What fool would want to see the truth? What good was there in that? Better to stick with the toll-booth, two shiny quarters and a dull dime.

"I'm sorry about last week," he said. "About runnin' off. Is that why you can't sleep now?"

"Oh, there are so many reasons why I can't sleep. I'm not going to let you take all the credit for it. Just promise me you'll come to me next time. When something scary happens."

"I wasn't scared," Paul said.

"What were you then?"

"Lonely," he said, before he had a chance to check his words.

"For Ian?" she asked, bewildered. "You were lonely for Ian?"

"Ian's all right," he said. "Ian . . ."

She stopped, looked at him curiously. "Ian's what?"

"He's . . . he's all right. That's all."

"Next time," she said, "will you come to me? Whatever it is you are, scared or lonely or sad. Will you come to me? Will you promise? I need a few things in life, honey, that I can count on. Can you understand that?"

"Dad's home," he said. He hadn't thought to say it, but there it was, swirling in the steam from his mouth, hovering in the night. He was tired of keeping secrets. He just didn't have the stomach for it any-more. And he, too, needed a few things in life that he could count on. His father was out. So, apparently, was Ian. What did he have left but his mother and full disclosure?

"Honey?"

"I saw him at the station this afternoon. He was sleeping. Phil said he's been there a couple days."

She gripped the leash tighter, as if steadying herself for a blow. "Is it me?" she asked. "Does he not want to see me?"

"He doesn't want to see anybody."

"Why?" she asked helplessly. "Do you know?"

They had reached the end of the block, made the turn to head back down Willow Lane. "It's kinda a long story," he said.

She nodded. "That much I guessed."

Early the next morning Laura called the station and left a message for Sonny to join them that night for dinner at the house. Paul wasn't at all sure his father would come; he had learned he could no longer predict anything about anyone with any respectable degree of accuracy, and this realization made his hands and feet tingle almost constantly, a symptom he expected might indicate adulthood and thus one that would, unfortunately, continue for the remainder of his life. His mother—typically mute regarding doubt, her midnight confession about the turnpike tollbooth notwithstanding—set three places at the dinner table and cooked up a wokful of chicken fried rice that was ready to serve at six-thirty. Then they sat in the living room, watching television and waiting.

At seven o'clock Sonny still hadn't shown. At seven-thirty Laura scooped the rice into a Corning Ware bowl and put it in the refrigerator. At eight o'clock the doorbell rang. Paul hopped up and opened the door.

"Hey, quarterback."

His father was carrying a loaf of French bread. He had on khakis and a blue wool sweater. His hair was brushed. He didn't smell of cigarettes or beer. Paul took all these things as positive signs.

"Hey," he said.

His father didn't move to come in, as if he were selling religion or vacuum cleaners and didn't want to spoil the sale by making inappropriate presumptions too soon.

"Am I too late?"

"No," Laura said from over Paul's shoulder. "You're just in time. It'll be ready in a few minutes."

"I got held up," he said, stepping over the threshold. "I . . . there were some things going on at the station I had to deal with. Then I went by the Eagle for some bread and they didn't have the right kind so—"

"It's fine," Laura said. She squeezed past Paul and they hugged there in the doorway quickly and carefully, like strangers. Maybe they were strangers, Paul thought. His father had been gone for six weeks— for four months, really, if you counted the time between the rescue and the trip to California, when his father had been absent in all but body.

Laura took the loaf of bread and went into the kitchen. Paul and Sonny sat down at the dinner table. A moment later the silence was broken by the whir of the microwave.

"I know I'm really late," Sonny whispered to Paul, not meeting his eyes. "I don't know what I . . ." Now he looked up and forced a smile. "You must be pretty hungry."

"Not really," Paul said. "I had a big lunch."

"Yeah? What'd you have?"

"Hot dogs. Two hot dogs. And potato chips. And milk."

"Hmmmm," Sonny said, nodding thoughtfully, as if this were fascinating information. He glanced around the house nervously. What was he looking for? Paul wondered. Some sign that he didn't belong? Or some sign that he did? He wanted to tell his father something, but it was something he didn't have the words for. He wished he were older and smarter, wished he knew how to say the thing that was stuck in his chest.

"They done shootin' the movie?" he asked instead.

"No," Sonny said. "I left before they . . . I was, you know . . ." He gave up, went in another direction. "How's school goin'?"

Paul shrugged. "All right, I guess. We're reading *A Yankee Drummer* for English."

"*Yankee Drummer.* I don't think I know that one."

"It's about this kid in the Civil War. He's a drummer boy and practically everybody he knows gets killed."

"Sounds cheery."

Laura appeared in the doorway with three plates, one in each hand and one balanced on her forearm. The plate she set in front of Sonny had a pile of rice on it about a foot high, more than Laura and Paul had combined. Sonny raised his eyebrows.

"A lot of chickens died for this."

"Happy to do so, I'm sure," Laura said cheerfully, sitting down opposite him. Then she looked up expectantly. It seemed to Paul that someone should say a prayer or make a toast, but no one said anything. Finally his mother said, "Well, let's eat."

Sonny took a bite. "Fantastic."

"It's good, Mom."

"It is good," she said. "It's not half bad, is it?"

"Not even a quarter bad," Sonny said.

"Not even a dime," Paul added.

Silence fell again. The only sound was the tines of forks pinging against the china, and Paul felt things—things past and future, good things, possibilities—slipping away with each hushed moment. He had to do something, say something. Outside, one of the Labs started barking.

"How're the dogs?" Sonny asked, at the same moment Laura said: "When did you get back?"

They both excused themselves. You go, no, you go, no, you go, no . . .

"Wednesday," he said. "Wednesday night, I guess. It was late. I took a cab from Harrisburg."

"That must have been expensive."

"Well," he said. "Like I said, it was late."

"How's work?"

He wiped his mouth carefully. "Oh, I'm not really working. I mean, I've done some things around the station, but I'm not on the clock or anything, haven't been out on any calls." He paused. "It's warm," he said.

Laura moved to get up. "Too warm? I can open a window."

"No, no, no." He held up his hand. "Here in town, I mean. Outside. It's fine in here. Feels . . . fine." He turned to Paul. "Somebody told me you were in a fight at school. That true?"

"Not really," Paul said. "It was just me and Carson and Joe. But I busted my lip on the bulletin board."

"Is that right?"

"Yeah, and . . ." Paul stole a glance at his mother. "And Ian fixed it up for me."

"Ian did?" Sonny smiled wistfully, as if remembering a funny story about someone who had died badly. "You've seen him? Is he all right?"

"I'm not sure," Paul said. "I kinda don't think so."

Sonny looked down at his food. After a moment he closed his eyes. He sat that way for thirty seconds, perfectly still. Perhaps, Paul thought, he was wishing himself to sleep, back into his dreams.

"Honey?" Laura said.

He opened his eyes, looked at her. "I'm sorry I didn't call," he said. "When I got in."

Laura shook her head, bit the inside of her lip. "You're here now. That's the important thing."

Sonny set down his fork. He looked at Paul for a long time, then turned to Laura.

"He tell you what happened?"

Laura put her hands in her lap. "He told me you were very sad," she said simply. "And I said, well, maybe if he comes home and re-members what it's like to have us around, maybe he won't be so sad anymore."

"In that basement," he said, swallowing hard, "I lost it. I totally flipped out. My dad, you know, and everything . . . it all came down on me."

"It's all right," she said.

"I was down there thinking I was gonna die. I was thinking—"

"Stop, Sonny. You don't have to tell me."

"I *want* to tell you," he said, making fists on the table. "Sometimes, honey, I just want to tell you things. I want to tell you how scary it is, how—"

"Paul," Laura said. "Why don't you excuse yourself?"

"No," Sonny said firmly. "I want him here. I want to tell him too." He turned to Paul. "I'm sorry about how it was—how I was—out there. You deserve a lot better than that. I'm sorry I failed you."

"You didn't fail me," Paul said quickly. A lie, of course, but a neces-sary one: he couldn't stand to see his father so broken. His father had been through enough; he didn't need any more weight added to his burden.

"See?" Laura said. "You didn't fail him. He's fine."

Sonny ignored her, reached over and laid his hand firmly on top of Paul's. "Look at me," he said.

Paul stared at his plate of rice. He could not raise his eyes to meet his father's. It was almost physical, this desire to avert his eyes, as if someone had dared him to stare into the sun.

"Okay, then listen to me. Are you listening?"

"Yeah," Paul said, a lump in his throat.

"I failed you. It's okay, I know I did. And I know that you know. So you don't have to pretend just to make me feel better. Pretending doesn't make me feel better anymore. Because I *know.*"

Paul looked at his father's hand covering his own. "I know you were scared," he whispered.

"I was," Sonny said. "And I know you were too. And I'm sorry."

"Then everybody's all right," Laura said, picking up her fork. "We're all all right now."

Paul glanced at her warily. She was smiling brightly, hopefully, and he felt pity for her, sitting there innocently at the end of the table, hanging on with her fingertips to the vestiges of some old, fruitless life.

"Mom," he said. "Everybody's not all right. That's kinda the point."

Her face turned suddenly stony. "Fine," she said, her voice clipped. "You two want to wallow in all this a little while longer? You two want to be scared together? That's fine. I'll be waiting for you when the little drama has run its course."

She stood and picked up her plate.

"Would you listen to yourself?" Sonny said loudly. "Do you hear what's coming out of your mouth? I know what you want, Laura. You want the three of us to just sit here pretending everything's fine, pretending we can go back to the way it was. Well I don't want to go back to the way it was. Everything's changed, everything's—"

"Why?" she demanded. The plate tilted in her hand and clumps of rice tumbled to the table. "Because you screwed up? Fine, Sonny, you screwed up. And guess what? The world has not come to an end. The world really does not care that you screwed up."

"I care," he said. "And I think Paul cares. And because of that I think *you* should care too."

"I don't understand what you're saying. Do you *want* me to think less of you?" She held her plate at the edge of the table and began scooping the fallen rice onto it with the side of her hand. "Do you *want* me to call you a coward and a liar? Would that make you feel better?"

"I don't want to feel better," Sonny said wearily. "I just want to stop pretending."

"All right," she said. "I give you permission to stop pretending. Right now, just stop. We all know what happened, Sonny, so now it's over."

"It's not over. You can't just say it's over and have it be over."

"Why not?" she asked, carefully picking up the remaining grains of rice with her fingernails and flicking them onto the plate. "That's what people do all the time. Every minute of every day, all over the world, people say it's over and that's the only reason why things are ever over—because people say they are."

"Don't you understand?" he asked. "I don't want to go back to the way things were because the way things were was part of the pretending. I feel like I've been pretending my whole life, pretending to be something I'm not."

She walked out of the room. Her dish clattered in the sink; a rush of water followed, then the grind of the garbage disposal. Paul bit his lip, stared at his plate. Starting over meant too many things, too much work. It wasn't just the reality of what you were that had to be refigured, but the pretending too. To really start over, you have to give up both worlds: the world you have, and the world you wish for. Both were equally useless in the wake of a new life.

A moment later Laura appeared in the doorway, a towel twisted in her hands. "And so what are you, Sonny?" she asked quietly. "What are you now, exactly, that's so different than what you were before?"

He was silent for a moment. "I don't know," he finally said. "But I don't guess I'm much of a hero."

"Well," Laura said, "who is?"

The night was cold. February, it appeared, was recovering its senses. His father, carless, had walked the mile back to the station house after dinner and Paul had joined him. They'd walked in heavy silence, chancing only occasional small talk. Now, returning home, Paul passed the abandoned lot beside the Hess Station and saw a circle of boys sitting on discarded cartons at the edge of the woods. They had a small fire going—a few sticks, some crackling paper bags—but the faces around the flames were too obscured by darkness to identify. He thought he could make out the frame of Leo, the towering guy from the mall, hunched over a cigarette. Then a figure rose from one of the cartons and limped away from the circle, bent to the ground to gather some twigs. Paul stopped on the sidewalk under a dull streetlight, watched Ian across the wide, gaping field. The other boys were laughing about something; a beer can cracked open; a car horn honked from a few blocks away. Ian looked up and Paul caught his eye and smiled, though he suspected his smile would be lost in the distance and dark. He knew too that it would be foolish to wave, childish, but he wanted to do something, make some gesture of acknowledgment, of kinship. Before he could think of one, Ian turned away and limped back to the fire, tossed his twigs into the dying flames.

Monday was gray. Clouds hovered in the valley. The air smelled of snow, of returning winter, and the thought of sitting in a dim classroom on a dim Monday was almost more than Paul could stand. He was thinking of his father, living at Station #1, where he had lived as a boy. He wondered if Phil was right, if that place was really home to him, more home than their house would ever be. He trudged toward school, his backpack unnaturally heavy on his shoulders. A block away, he changed his mind, turned toward downtown on a whim, headed for the station house.

He found Sonny inside the garage, sitting in the driver's seat of Engine 14, checking all the equipment on the dashboard. He knew this was something his father did every morning, first thing. Most of fire fighting, he had told Paul many times, was preparation; the one time you slacked off on equipment checks was the time whatever you'd neglected to check would malfunction.

Paul climbed up into the truck and sat down beside his father in the cab. Sonny looked surprised but happy to see him.

"What're you doing here? Aren't you supposed to be in school?"

"No school today. Conferences or something."

Sonny looked worried. "Parent conferences?"

"Nah," Paul said. "Just some teacher thing."

"Huh," he said, either convinced or lacking the energy to call Paul on the lie. He looked tired, drawn. Had he slept? Was anyone sleeping?

"Well, okay then." He scribbled something down on the chart on his clipboard.

"Are you gonna come home ever?" Paul asked.

"Sure," he said, continuing to write.

"But really," Paul said. "Are you really going to?"

Sonny sat back in the seat of the cab, laid the clipboard on his lap, sighed. "Your mother and I . . . I guess we've got some work to do."

"She's scared too," Paul said.

"She tell you that?"

"Almost."

Sonny smiled weakly. Above them, from the kitchen, came the rattling of pots and pans. Someone would be frying bacon soon, cracking eggs into a skillet, buttering toast.

"Do you *want* to come home?" Paul asked.

"Almost," Sonny said. He glanced quickly at Paul and then looked out the windshield into the street. "I'm thinking you can't think very much of me. After everything that's happened."

"That's not true," Paul protested. "I—"

"You know," he interrupted. "My old man, no matter what, I always knew he'd do the right thing."

"He wasn't such a great dad."

Sonny thought about this. "Maybe not," he said finally. "But he was a great man, Paul. I wish you'd a known him. Just walk around this town and everybody over the age of forty'll tell you the same thing: a great man. A legend in his own time. And my time. And someday your time too."

"I don't care," Paul said. "I don't see what that has to do with me."

Sonny chewed on the eraser of his pencil, bit a piece off and spat it out the door. "I never had trouble looking at him, quarterback, I can tell you that. I looked at him every chance I got."

"So?"

"So I don't want to walk around the house feeling like you can't look at me. I don't think I can live like that. I think I'd rather never see you again than always be thinking you can't look at me."

Paul felt tears sting his eyes. Ashamed and enraged, he hopped out of the truck. Never see him again? Fine, he thought. If that was the way his father wanted it, then that was the way he was going to have it. He hurried out of the station house. A chilly rain had begun to fall. He wanted to walk away from his father, walk forever, but suddenly his legs grew weak and the weight of the rain drove him to his knees onto the pavement of the driveway. This driveway, this was the very spot his mother had pulled up thirteen years before, left her car idling in the street, ran to meet his father as he leapt off the roof of the engine and into her arms. They were soaking wet, both of them. The hose whipped and spun and they didn't care because they were together, already planning their home and their dogs and their cars and maybe even Paul, in that instant, seeing even Paul in each other's eyes. It must have been a wonderful moment, perfect even, the life they had laid out so carefully now snatched back from the abyss, never—so they thought— to escape them again.

Sonny sat down on the drive beside him.

"Hey, quarterback?"

He didn't dare look at him. "What?"

"I was just thinking about what I said about my dad, about how I wished you'd known him." He paused, cleared his throat. "Funny thing is, I think what I really wish is that he'd known *you.*"

Paul blinked the rain from his eyelashes. "How come?"

" 'Cause you're the best thing I ever did."

Paul tried to scoff, but it came out barely a squeak. "Right," he said.

"Listen," Sonny said. "Try to understand this. You're great, kiddo. It's me I'm not so sure about. I kinda feel like I'm starting from scratch. I feel like I gotta earn everything all over again. I feel like . . . like I gotta earn *you* all over again."

"Dad," Paul said.

"Yeah?"

He sat back on his heels. "We did have school today."

Sonny looked at him curiously. The rain was pouring now, drenching them both, flattening their hair and weighing their clothes. "Oh yeah?"

"Yeah," Paul said, meeting his eyes. "But I didn't want to go. I wanted to come here and hang out with you."

Sonny was silent. He drew his knees into his chest and hugged them tightly. Across the street, old Mr. Dewey came to the window of Dewey Drugs, looked out at the downpour and shook his head. The postman, shrouded in a blue slicker, trundled his bag down the puddled sidewalk. A scrawny white cat scurried across the street and into the basement window of the barbershop. Soon, the rain would end and the sun would burn away the clouds. Soon, Sonny Tucker would return to the house on Willow Lane. Soon, Paul Tucker would pass by the Hess Station with a group of his friends and would not turn his head toward the pack who hovered at the edge of the dark woods, would not look for the face of a hero among them. Soon, the Tuckers and the Casey firemen would gather before the television and listen to the voices that had once belonged to them. But now, for the morning, Paul and his father would remain in the drive of the station house, drying themselves naturally in the coming sun like dogs, like leaves, like heavy wings of birds and cowered blades of grass. And then, as humbled blades, they would rediscover their ability to stand.